This book is dedicated to

CHARLIE KAUS

because you'll always be my first fan.

DISCLAIMER

SELZNICK'S SPOTLIGHT

A NOVEL OF 1939 HOLLYWOOD

MARTIN TURNBULL

ROTHESAY
PRESS

1

Los Angeles, California
March 1939

Late-morning light splintered through the plate-glass facade of Schwab's Pharmacy, turning suspended dust into floating gold. Amelia Hartley kicked the cupboard beneath the lunch counter, not caring if her heel left a dent in the worn wood. The sharp pain in her foot was almost welcome—at least it was a distraction she could feel, along with the maddening itch in her throat.

An innocent target had to bear the brunt of her frustration, and the cupboard was hidden from her regulars: Randy, a plump gag writer from Hal Roach Studios who couldn't get enough malted milkshakes, and an RKO backdrop painter called Cobb. They sat perched on their usual stools, their shadows stretching across the floor like sundials.

Randy's eyes crinkled with amusement over the rim of his chocolate malted. "It's killing you, isn't it?"

She mustered a pinched don't-get-me-started smile. It was all she could do. And forget about talking over the honking horns and squealing brakes of the Sunset Boulevard traffic.

Stupid laryngitis. How was she supposed to sass customers when they ordered the same old stinky liverwurst sandwich? Or pretend to serve them Postum instead of the frosted root beer they'd asked for? Everyone knew the cheeky waitress with the bold copper-red hair would treat them to a good time if they were lucky enough to be seated in her section. It was as much her trademark as the starched tan uniform and sensible shoes.

And today, of all days, too.

For months now, a regular had been coming in three times a week, reliable as the Santa Fe Super Chief. Dark blue suits, white shirts, neckties with birds or flowers. Sociable and courteous, if somewhat distant. Good tipper. The quiet type with attentive eyes. Always watching. Always alert. Taking in nuance, details, gestures, unguarded moments, and jotting them all down in the open notepad he kept by his coffee cup.

For all his vigilance, Amelia doubted he'd noticed her watching him. But she had. Oh yes, she most certainly had—especially after she'd learned that he was second-in-charge of casting at Paramount. And that made him the sort of person she should be laying the charm on—extra thick, but not too thick. Casting guys knew all the tricks of the trade in the arsenal of ambitious hopefuls trying to finagle their way past the studio guards and inside the gates.

She needed a sure-fire opening line—one he hadn't heard before. The boom would fall later, but first came rapport without setting off alarm bells. For days she'd wracked her brains until she had devised the perfect hook.

"Say, mister," she'd drawl, casual as a porch swing in August, "that fountain pen of yours—it's a Waterman, right? The same model that Zanuck uses?" Then she'd adjust her paper waitress cap. "I saw it in a photo spread in *Variety* last week, and I thought to myself, 'Hey, I know someone who's got one of those.'"

Today was one of his regular-as-clockwork days, and any minute now, he'd walk through those doors for his noontime lunch. And damn it all to blazes, she couldn't make a peep. Or could she? Did laryngitis clear up as quickly and mysteriously as it appeared?

Amelia opened her mouth to force out a sound—any sound, a croak, a wheeze, even a gurgle, would give her hope—but the dreaded silence remained.

She tucked her pencil behind her ear as the crowd swelled, the air thickening with the scents of fresh-brewed coffee and hot mustard, Lucky Strikes and Old Spice, seasoned with generous splashes of exasperation. After four months, she could serve this place pie-eyed with one foot in a three-wheeled roller skate, dodging the elbows of typists on their afternoon breaks and flat-broke actors nursing nickel cups of joe. But even if Mr. Paramount Casting didn't show today, how could she work the lunchtime rush without a voice? Impossible. She wouldn't even have come in if they hadn't been two waitresses down and obliged to pull Betsy-Ann from retail.

The ceiling fans spun lazy circles, stirring the air as Amelia scribbled on a paper napkin. *This no talking business is killing me!* She held it up for Randy and Cobb to read and was flashing her best Pepsodent smile—the one she'd practised in front of her mirror at home for Mr. Paramount Casting's benefit—when Leon Schwab came to her defense. His bow tie was slightly askew, as usual, and his round spectacles glinted in the overhead lights.

"Now, boys, we're all well aware she's a chatterbox, but be nice. There's no predicting what she might slip into your eats. But, of course, that's a practice this fine-dining establishment would *never* condone." He tossed off a broad stage-wink at the three of them before heading for the pharmacy counter, where a chorus line of amber bottles waited to be filled.

One of the cooks called through the service window, his voice carrying over the clatter of pots and pans, to announce that Randy's shrimp salad and Cobb's banana split were ready. The kitchen's heat rolled out in waves, carrying with it the mingled aromas of grilled onions and toasting bread.

Randy's right, she thought, dodging Betsy-Ann at the dairy cabinet. Being voiceless during the midday rush was torture. The daily routine of serving coffee and sandwiches without a snappy comeback felt like dancing without music.

She had, however, discovered an upside.

Being forced to keep her trap shut had meant listening more, observing more—not unlike Mr. Paramount, now that she thought about it. Had Cobb always possessed that slight stutter? When did Randy stop wearing his wedding band? And how hadn't she noticed that no one over forty ordered the Schwab's Zombie, and nobody under forty chose Ry-Krisp over a sweet roll? It dawned on her now: This place was like a movie set, with its own cast of characters and daily dramas playing out between coffee refills and sandwich orders.

She gave Schwab's a brief survey. No Paramount yet, but he couldn't be far away. That was a man who found comfort in a routine.

Gosh, what she wouldn't give to regain her voice, but now she wondered what else she'd been missing all this time. And like every girl in Hollywood with a bright smile, a scrap of pizzazz, harboring hopes to make it as an actress, she ought to keep that in mind. Listen to people instead of standing around waiting for their lips to stop moving.

Balancing Randy's shrimp salad and Cobb's banana split, she pondered whether getting into the picture business was as bird-brained as she suspected. The morning trade papers were full of stories about *Gone with the Wind* and *The Wizard of Oz,* but for every Vivien Leigh or Judy Garland, how many girls went home with nothing but worn-out dreams and a one-way ticket back to Kentucky? What was that expression her father liked to quote? "Many are called, but few are chosen."

By the time she'd set down the plates—the shrimp salad glistening with mayonnaise, the banana split a masterpiece of chocolate, vanilla, and strawberry ice cream crowned with whipped cream—she had decided that if she was going to pursue a movie career, she needed to up her game. Though she enjoyed being a Schwab's waitress, it was hardly the lifetime career she had in mind. Enough waiting for all the Mr. Paramounts in town to wander in. And that agent who'd said he might represent her. Farley Winchester hadn't shown his puss around here of late. That shiny nickel in her pocket, she decided, was destined for the payphone. And soon.

The bell above the front door cut through the hurly-burly with a cheerful jingle.

"SERVICE PLEASE!"

Amelia's roommate, Polly Maddox, had been laid up since breaking her leg in a tumble on top of a particularly nasty studio boss who nobody in filmdom liked, so the incident had become legend up and down the Hollywood grapevine. After weeks of devouring every book, magazine, and newspaper in their apartment, Polly was keen to report for work back at the Selznick studios. She propped her crutches against the counter, took the offered hand of their mutual pal, Luddie, and hoisted herself onto the stool.

Amelia's grin spread wide before she even spun around and raised her eyebrows.

David Selznick's favorite Girl Friday smiled with relief. "Only four more weeks till this cast comes off—assuming I don't tangle with any of Scarlett's hoop skirts."

With Selznick's sweeping epic still in production, Amelia knew Polly's boss, Marcella, was counting the days, too. Polly was the only girl who could keep pace with the producer's rapid-fire dictation, and whose fingers flew over the typewriter keys quicker than a concert pianist at the Hollywood Bowl.

Polly smoothed her skirt over her knees, careful of the bulky cast underneath. "I wanted a Schwab's lunch before I flung myself into the maelstrom."

Trust her to use words like "maelstrom" in everyday conversation. Would her vocabulary rub off on Amelia one of these days? Probably not. Amelia mouthed the words, "Chili con carne and club number five?" The familiar order fit into their routine as seamlessly as the morning paper and evening radio shows.

"Aw, jeez." Polly winced. "Still no voice, huh?"

Over Polly's shoulder, Amelia monitored Mr. Paramount Casting's path through the retail shelves. *Yep, right on time. I shouldn't have doubted him.* Now that Polly and Luddie were here, she had only two open seats. *Please take one of them. Please.* This wasn't the day to lay her opening line on him, but was there a way to turn this pesky laryngitis to her advantage? Scribble a quip, perhaps? *I'm not giving you the silent treatment. I've got laryngitis, so it's all sign language today!*

Amelia shook her head at Polly and showed Luddie that she had already written down his standard order: number four club sandwich, Vermont maple jumbo soda, and Black Beauty chocolate ice cream. She winked at him. Luddie was as much a fixture at Schwab's as the chrome-edged counter and the shelves of patent medicines.

It was at this same lunch counter that Amelia and Polly had first caught sight of him keeping company with one of his clients who had been, as they nearly always were, older than him, richer than him, and keenly in dire need of his charms—even if it meant having to pay for them. But Ludlow Sinclair always ensured the wives of prominent Hollywood heavy hitters got their money's worth by lavishing them with wit, flattery, and sinuous dance moves.

"I may have mastered Mah Jong and the tango," he said, adjusting his monogrammed cufflinks, "but how you remember everybody's favorites is a marvel of the modern age."

Amelia acknowledged his compliment with a quick salute and had headed for the kitchen to put in their orders when the tinkle of cutlery against crockery and bantering of late-morning chatter dimmed perceptibly, as though someone had lowered the volume on *Lux Radio Theatre*.

Polly and Luddie had already swiveled their stools. Sunset's traffic roared in with the entrance of a woman who stood ramrod straight, her waist cinched by a black belt tight enough to throttle her innards. The pale blue cashmere sweater was pure Bullock's Wilshire; Amelia would've bet her last twenty bucks she'd chosen it to showcase her impressive bosom. Her skin glowed with whipped-cream radiance direct from the movie magazines, cotton-candy pink lips, and a halo of blonde spun-sugar curls tumbling to her shoulders.

"Who is *that*?" Polly's whisper carried over the muted buzz of conversation.

Amelia wished she had a buck for every time she had to tell people Lana Turner wasn't discovered here. But at least this girl was a cut above the typical Pocatello High School cheerleaders she had to deal with. She watched the dish lower her curvaceous behind onto the free stool in Amelia's section. And wouldn't you know it? Right next to Mr. Paramount Casting.

Mr. Schwab let out a low, low whistle. "She used to work here. Back then, her hair was dark chestnut, and she wore it much shorter."

"And her bust?" Luddie asked, his immaculate eyebrows rising toward his hairline.

"Yeah." Schwab tugged at his bow tie as if it had grown too tight. "It was always an eyeful."

Amelia thought of her own first weeks on the job. Good lord, the wandering eyes! She had no idea. But it hadn't taken her long to learn how to balance plates while deflecting compliments and pickup lines without endangering a decent tip after she'd served coffee and apple pie. It was a skill, and a handy one at that.

"Now she's positioned them even more prominently." Schwab was still glued to the vision that had captured everyone within a hundred-foot radius. "But her face. Something's awry there."

"Her nose." His head cashier, Ida, had crept up beside them, her voice carrying the authority of someone who tracked Hollywood gossip like other people studied horse races. "I read about it in *Photoplay*—it's called plastic surgery. Doctors can fix a star's schnoz now: Shrink it, straighten it, and presto—a pleasant mug becomes gorgeous."

The girl lifted the arms of her sunglasses between her fingertips and drew them from her face with rehearsed theatricality.

Mr. Schwab shuffled farther down the counter, his shoes squeaking against the linoleum. "It *is* you!"

"In a manner of speaking." She slid her sunglasses onto the counter with a soft click. "It's Matilda now. Matilda Charles."

Whoever this would-be Jean Harlow was, she hadn't invented the man-eater routine, but oh brother, she sure knew how to play it to the hilt. She calculated every gesture and measured each pause with Swiss-watch precision.

"Is this purely a social call," Mr. Schwab asked, "or have you returned?"

Matilda took her time laying a languid elbow on the counter. "I really don't know."

She had that mid-Atlantic accent actresses favored because it made them sound more sophisticated, but Amelia wasn't buying it. Matilda had over-enunciated every syllable with the crisp delivery of a Kaufman-and-Hart leading lady, but underneath it all, the act rang false as a tin nickel.

"Paint me purple and call me a Packard." Ida's fingers drummed against the countertop. "Six months ago, she was plain old Tillie."

This was Tillie? Amelia had snagged her job at Schwab's after a waitress had abruptly left town, spinning yarns about some ailing-but-unnamed sick aunt. Her departure had been Amelia's ticket in, but get a load of that platinum hair, that manufactured figure, that brassy swagger. Talk about Hollywood hokum, served with a side of baloney.

Mr. Schwab was heading for the kitchen when Ida stopped him with a touch on his sleeve. "Taking her back?"

"She was our most popular waitress, but let's not race ahead of ourselves. She hasn't asked for her job."

"Yet," Ida finished for him.

Amelia's heart sank. Technically, her job was temporary until Tillie returned. It hadn't occurred to her the prodigal waitress might resurface once her fictional aunt had "recovered." Popular or not, since when was Mr. Schwab under any obligation to hold a job open for someone who had abandoned him with no notice?

A steady stream of customers kept Schwab's lunch counter stools spinning—a coveted post for any waitress in town. Those all-day-every-day nickel and dime tips added up fast. Tillie-call-me-Matilda would be a fool to turn her back on this lucrative opportunity. And while her hair, her ample bosom, and her nose might be fake, Amelia could tell the girl was one tough tomato.

God! What a time to lose my voice! Amelia scribbled on her order pad: *I suppose you have a last hired-first-fired policy?*

Mr. Schwab patted her hand, his palm warm and reassuring against her suddenly cold fingers. "Anyone with the courage to be themselves can find a home here."

That's a non-yes if ever I've heard one.

Still, it wasn't a no. Or even a non-no. Meanwhile, Amelia had an order for chili con carne and number four club sandwich to put in. She nodded her agreement and threaded her way to the kitchen window, where the cook's spatula kept time with the endless rhythm of another busy day at Schwab's.

2

Amelia wiped smudges from Schwab's glass countertop, marveling at how she'd gone from scooping hot caramel sundaes to selling hair brushes in the retail section—a career shift so abrupt she was surprised she hadn't suffered whiplash.

When Matilda had returned the next day to claim her old job, Mr. Schwab asked Amelia to relinquish her order pad, adding, "That means no more customers complaining about lukewarm coffee!" But without the constant flow of tips, the move to retail wasn't the benevolent sidestep he'd attempted to paint.

Matilda slipped right back into her role: Everyone's Favorite Waitress. But her laugh came too loudly, her winks too frequently, and that industrial-strength brassiere strained its limits whenever she dipped toward a customer. At least that was how it looked from where Amelia stood arranging Tangee lipsticks.

Smart cookie, though. Why pound the Hollywood pavement when every director in town would land at Schwab's sooner or later?

Then came the surprise: Matilda sauntering over to Amelia's counter during the ten o'clock dead zone between breakfast and lunch, and toying with hair pins. "I understand my coming back meant Mr. S. had to bump you down to retail. Sorry 'bout that."

Not the most heartfelt apology Amelia had ever received, but she had gone out of her way to make it. Amelia shrugged. Her voice was back now. What a shame she had to waste it sounding noble and gracious. "You were here first, so fair's fair."

"Say"—Matilda deposited the packet of pins into the wicker basket—"I hear you've got an agent."

Ah, so that's *the game. You think I have an agent and you want mine. Well, damn you and your flawless peaches-and-cream skin.*

But did Amelia have one? Though an agent named Farley Winchester had offered to represent her, she hadn't seen him in a month. His card still lay nestled in her purse, and with tips now a memory, maybe Matilda's fishing expedition was the kick in the butt she needed.

"I don't know if he's taking on new clients," she hedged.

"Whenever you see him next, could you ask him?"

Oh my, we are pushy, aren't we? "Uh-huh."

* * *

Three phone calls to Farley's office had only resulted in busy signals. A half-hour lunch break to sprint six blocks down Sunset, talk to Farley, and get back to work was a tough deadline, but not impossible. Amelia had dashed outside, hatless, gloveless, and bagless, and had made it to Winchester's building in seven minutes.

A florist's shop filled the foyer and stairwell with sweetly botanical aromas that reached the second story. When Amelia opened the door stenciled *WINCHESTER TALENT AGENCY*, she found the only stick of furniture in the place was a telephone sitting on the bare floor, its receiver abandoned beside it.

She ran the tip of her shoe along the wood. Hmmm, no dust. What did it matter if she'd missed him by a day or a month? She wandered to the window that looked across Sunset and breathed in the jasmine and musk wafting up from below. Oh well, that little dream didn't last long, did it?

The office door squeaked and Matilda stepped into the room.

Good lord. Pushy was one thing. Brassy she could deal with. But wasn't this awfully presumptuous?

"When I saw you making a bunch of calls in one of the booths and then hurrying out, I played a hunch."

Amelia didn't buy it. The girl's too-perfect diction set off alarm bells—every word polished, each syllable carefully placed. Sure, bettering oneself was the Hollywood way, but a Schwab's waitress who clipped her words like Katharine Hepburn stretched credulity.

But what did it matter now? No Farley, no agent, no nothing.

"You gals looking to rent this office?" A balding gent with cigar ash clinging to his necktie appraised the two young women. "You're here for that human pond scum who masqueraded as a talent agent." He walked to the wall on the right and plugged two bullet holes with his fat fingers. "The father of a client accidentally-on-purpose missed after he learned Farley insisted that to get his daughter an audition, she'd have to—" He broke off to scratch the back of his neck. "You can fill in the rest."

"Don't suppose he left a forwarding address?" Amelia asked.

"You want some advice from someone who's seen it all? Skip all this malarky and go find a regular job."

"We're waitresses at Schwab's," Matilda told him.

"Fine, honorable work. Be thankful for it."

* * *

Amelia and Matilda hit the sidewalk and headed back to Schwab's, their footsteps heavy and plodding. "I might be a naïve dope," Amelia said, "but I wouldn't have thought Farley Winchester was that kind of agent."

"Maybe *they're* all pond scum and *we're* all dopes."

Amelia found it refreshing to see the girl let a glimmer of candor seep between the cracks of her forced laugh, overworked winks, and poke-out-an-eye bust. She had even dropped the elocution-school mid-Atlantic accent. "Farley Fly-By-Night isn't the only game in town, but at least his office smelled nice."

"Yardley's English Lavender brilliantine."

"Is that what it was?"

Matilda paused to check the seam in her stockings. "The guy who got me pregnant—he wore it, too."

Her frank admission was a sock in the puss. *We've given up pretending to stick with the ailing aunt whopper, have we?*

"I always rather liked it. Thought it was suave. What a green little hopeful I used to be. He told me, 'I can get you seen by all the bigwigs, but first . . .'"

"Just like Farley." Amelia stole a side-glance at this alluring creature whom she had taken to be an expert at playing the Hollywood chess game. "How long did it take for you to figure that guy out?"

"Couple of months. Nothing beats getting knocked up to bring a girl to her senses. The thing is, I didn't expect him to marry me. I come from a big family. Old-fashioned, conservative, close-knit. They'd never forgive me, so I was on my own. I only wanted someone to see me through my confinement."

Amelia would never have guessed the painful past she hid behind her golden curls and immaculate makeup. "You had the baby all by your lonesome?"

They walked the last block in silence before Matilda spoke again. "There's a convent hospital for unwed mothers in some middle-of-nowhere burg called Beaumont."

"Was it an easy birth?"

"The whole experience was awful, so I rewarded myself with a complete overhaul, et voilà!"

They had stopped at the rear door that opened into the alleyway. "Please don't tell anyone," Matilda said. "Mr. Schwab is such a gentleman; I'd hate to disappoint him."

The girl's slate-green eyes, full of steely determination, met Amelia's stare without flinching. Life had crushed her through the wringer, so was it any wonder she'd transformed herself to leave her past behind? And wasn't LA the capital city of reinvention?

Amelia crossed her heart. "Your secret's safe with me."

* * *

Polly poured the last of the cocktail mix into their glasses. "A convent in—where did you say?"

It had been a long day; one Gibson wouldn't be enough. "Beaumont." Amelia had puzzled over Matilda's confession all afternoon. They had formed a bond over their shared disappointment in Farley Fly-by-Night, but why would she spill such secrets to a stranger?

Listening to Polly's studio drama proved a welcome distraction. Mr. Selznick had fired *Gone with the Wind's* original director George Cukor, and had put the production on ice until Victor Fleming wrapped *The Wizard of Oz.*

Polly lowered her glass. "But back to Farley, with him out of the picture, where to next?"

Amelia flopped onto their sofa. "What if they're all terrible letches and you can't win no matter who you turn to?"

"They're not, and you can. If it's any consolation, Mr. Selznick has yet to mention *Pretty Pennies* in any of his interminable memos."

Pretty Pennies was a silent movie David O. Selznick's father had made in the nineteen-teens, and which Selznick had decided to remake. For a while now, Amelia had pegged her hopes on getting into the movies by trying out for the lead. If not the lead, then any role to get her foot in the door. But now it sounded as though *Pretty Pennies* was dead in the water. What a doggone shame.

Amelia jabbed a toothpick at the onion in her glass, weighing her luck. Okay, so the possibility of getting an agent was off the table, and the role she'd set her sights on had evaporated. But she had her job at Schwab's and her swell boyfriend, Benji. That counted for plenty. For now.

"I was going to give you this as soon as you got home, but you looked so wrung out I decided a snort would do more good."

Polly handed over an envelope of thick, marbled paper, its surfaces dappled with shallow ridges, and Amelia's name and address composed with a calligraphy pen. Someone had embellished the "A" with curling flourishes.

Amelia pulled out an invitation printed on stiff cardboard edged in gilt, and read the inscribed message. Her eyebrows rose. "You know my sister, Faith, the art history major from Wellesley? Turns out, she's now a published author."

"On top of dealing with her colicky baby?"

"Apparently Chester isn't colicky all day, every day because she's written some high-falutin' book called *Echoes of Elegance: How the Enduring Legacy of Renaissance, Baroque, and Rococo Shaped Modern Art in the 20th Century*."

It had been hard enough to grow up in the shadow of a sister who got straight A's throughout high school before earning her degree and then her master's in art history from the best women's college outside the Ivy League, followed by marrying her teenage sweetheart, and popping out a baby in short order. And now Faith had published a goddamn book.

Guilt pricked at Amelia's conscience. Faith had had a difficult birth and Chester had been more of a handful than his parents had bargained for. And yet she had made the most of her time in between crying spells and afternoon naps. She deserved better than petty-minded jealousy.

"It's very"—she picked up the invitation again—"impressive."

"However, you're feeling . . ."

Amelia knew only two people in this world with whom she could truthfully finish that sentence, and one of them was lounging on the sofa with her. "Somewhat on the invisible side."

Polly left Amelia's painful assessment hang for a moment, then reached over to straighten Amelia's collar. "Remember that day I got off the boat at Avalon?"

"And we eyeballed each other thinking, 'She could be my cousin.'"

"I stood there on the pier and thought 'Gosh, get a load of this girl. Her hair is brighter, her skin is clearer, her smile is wider, and her eyes are sparklier. What I wouldn't give to be half the live-wire she is.'" Polly laid a light finger on Amelia's wrist. "You're as invisible as a streetcar on fire"

Amelia took a moment to consider Polly's point, swishing the invitation like a fan. "The publisher is throwing a book launch party at Victor Hugo."

"How very swanky of him."

"Strictly a best-behavior affair."

"No pie fights, then?"

"Not even a squirt of seltzer."

Polly feigned a yawn. "Sounds terribly dull. Glad I'm not invited."

"Oh, but you are." Amelia put her forefinger against the paper and ringed the two words following her name: "and guest."

3

Amelia's first inkling that she had underestimated just how swanky Faith's book launch was going to be when she encountered a willowy blonde poured into copper-gold crêpe inside Victor Hugo's front arches. The socialite brushed at the turquoise feathers lining her collarbone as she traded champagne toasts with a well-heeled swell in a midnight-blue tux accented by black faille lapels and bow tie. Clearly, Amelia's off-the-rack dark purple georgette was going to challenge nobody in the fashion stakes.

Usually, she didn't give a hoot for social etiquette around arriving unaccompanied or adhering to strict dress codes. Though Victor Hugo typically drew the hold-out-your-pinkie crowd—Hollywood royalty, oil money, and the social register—she had reckoned on tonight's book launch attracting a different set: tweedy professors, bespectacled librarians, and artsy types with paint-stained fingernails. Polly had offered Amelia her new starburst brooch of opals set in silver. "No, thanks," Amelia had told her. "I don't want to come across too fancy-pants. This is Faith's big night. Not mine." What an oopsie. Compared to this spiffy cluster of modish eggheads, Amelia felt like the bumpkin cousin only invited to clean up afterwards.

She caught sight of her mother's frantic wave through the crowd and plunged into the animated throng. "Get a load of this turnout!"

"Where's Polly?" Lois asked.

"Her leg hasn't mended enough to stand for hours, so she bowed out."

Amelia's father, Judd, looked around the room. "And Benji?"

"On location shooting *Island of Lost Men.*"

"Couldn't that handsome Luddie chap escort you?"

"Irene Selznick nabbed him first." Amelia was surprised that a woman from the film world would be invited to an arty book launch, but assumed Irene's presence would add gravitas to the evening—perhaps enough to rate a mention in the columns the next day. "Have you spotted them?"

"Not yet, but look at your sister—she's radiant!"

The guests parted, revealing Faith in floor-length emerald chiffon that probably cost more than a month's wages at Schwab's. Every time she moved, her floaty sleeves couldn't decide if they were wings or curtains. A diamond necklace glistened around her throat in the light of the pearlescent glass tiles that covered the ceiling. Hovering around her perimeter, a photographer snapped her picture, his shutter clicking like a telegraph operator.

"Looks like a princess, doesn't she?"

The pride in her father's eyes yanked Amelia back to her first day as a freshman at Fairfax High, when everyone assumed they had another swimming sensation like Faith on their hands. Then Amelia had crashed into the pool, a sack of doorknobs in a swimsuit, and that was that.

"HI, AMELIA!" two cheeky voices called in unison.

She greeted her unruly twin brothers, Samuel and Sebastian, then raised her leery eyebrows at her mother, who reminded them, "We don't want anything to spoil this evening for Faith, do we, boys?"

Across the room, Amelia spotted Luddie's familiar face. Drowning in this gumbo of society snoots and academic aesthetes, she latched onto it like a lifeline. She excused herself as fast as propriety would allow.

"Faith is looking positively regal." Luddie flared his eyes. *And you look like you could do with a double whiskey.* He produced a glass from behind his back.

"What are you?" She seized it with both hands. "A magician?"

Irene Selznick appeared. Amelia had only exchanged pleasantries with the wife of Polly's boss, but she envied the woman's air of unruffled poise. "I think of our Mr. Sinclair as more of a gifted mind-reader."

After exchanging observations of what a grand success this party had proved to be, their conversation revolved—as most Hollywood conversations did, these days—around *Gone with the Wind.* Irene talked about how her home life had "settled down into mere hardship" now that George Cukor's replacement, Victor Fleming, had taken over the directing reins.

"How does Vivien Leigh feel about her new captain?" Luddie asked.

Irene's cool eyes glazed over. "Victor didn't exactly endear himself when he nicknamed her 'Fiddle-de-dee.' She misses George terribly, but in the face of Victor's disdain, she doesn't hesitate to speak her mind. Bravo to her, I say. Victor is very much a man's man. Standing up to him takes fortitude."

What an interesting life this woman led. Ordinarily, Amelia wouldn't have to fight against the tendrils of envy now coiling around her chest, but she now spent her days selling Tootsie Rolls until she wanted to pluck out her eyeballs. But not forever, she told herself.

"Meanwhile, David and Mr. Hitchcock have reached a deal," Irene continued, "and so now David is back to wavering on whether or not to proceed with *Pretty Pennies.*"

Amelia downed a mouthful of Kentucky's finest fire. "It's still in play?"

"That Swedish actress David has signed is en route to LA. He's been wondering if she'd be right for the lead after she's finished filming *Intermezzo.*"

Amelia put on her best that-figures expression, though hope somersaulted in her chest. With any luck, she wouldn't be selling Tootsie Rolls for much longer.

"Ladies and gentlemen, it's time for the dreaded speeches." A bespectacled man stepped onto a small platform. "I promise brevity."

Amelia hung back, letting the crowd press past.

If Selznick was importing Scandinavian talent, he'd squeeze more than one picture out of her. But if she wasn't right for the role, that meant it was up for grabs. And who better than this little redhead in georgette?

Amelia's mind drifted to her see-sawing over Matilda. That girl was so deft at adapting her act. For some, she played the dewy-eyed starlet. Others got Mae West with a coffee pot. While others still were treated to her giggling chorus girl act, batting her eyes at every moldy joke. The worst part? Customers ate it up like free soup at Clifton's Cafeteria. In a way, Amelia raised her hat to Matilda's knack for matching the customer with the persona. But who was the real Matilda Charles? Might it not be wiser to keep her at arm's length?

The other night, watching Benji pack for *Lost Men*, she'd confessed jealousy over Faith. "You ain't so terrible," he had assured her. "My kid brother's the youngest brain surgeon in the tri-state area, and here's me, who couldn't stick with college long enough to learn the difference between granite and grapefruit. Geology—what in tarnation was I thinking?"

They had laughed about how they had been dating for four months, and yet had only now gotten around to sharing their deepest secrets. And then Benji had gone one better.

"A couple of years ago, I went home to New Jersey for Christmas. My brother and I stayed up late, getting blotto on whiskey, and out it spilled. He doesn't enjoy what he does, but feels trapped by the life he has created. And *that* was when I stopped feeling like the runner-up sibling."

What a great guy that Benji was. All these weeks away filming on location were a drag, but as she'd told Polly, she wanted an interesting fellow with an interesting job, so she had no complaints.

As the Random House executive asked the crowd to "toast our girl of the moment," Amelia realized she hadn't seen Samuel and Sebastian in a while—rarely a good sign. She heard Samuel's distinct, machine-gun giggle coming from a windowless storage area down the back of the room. The twins sat cross-legged on the floor, gazing up at a woman who lounged in a brocaded chair, a long, thin cigarette poised between her fingers.

"You heard me," she told the boys. "The blood of their enemies!"

Amelia stepped inside. "The blood of who?"

"This lady!" Sebastian cried out. "She's been telling us about Indians."

"And how they decorate their teepees after battle!" Samuel's eyes were wide with a ghoulish fascination.

The woman rose from her chair. "Or so I've heard." She extended her hand. "Hello, I'm Zara Willowick."

It was a heck of a name, matched only by a penetrating shrewdness that filled her broad, tanned face.

"Amelia Hartley." Zara Willowick shook hands like a man: firm, assured. "And these two tiny terrors are my brothers, Samuel and Sebastian."

"They boys and I were talking about Indians."

"They weren't bothering you?"

"Not at all." Zara waited until the twins had run headlong into the main room. "I could see they were getting a little antsy with the speeches, so I knew I could distract them with butchery and carnage."

"You can't go wrong with butchery or carnage. By the way, blood and teepees—is that true?"

"Mostly they used red ochre or crushed iron oxide, but blood makes for a better story." She let out a throaty laugh. "Don't tell my bosses I'm inventing stories like that!"

Benji had mentioned to Amelia how Faith's book had been the

talk of Hollywood's art directors. "You work at one of the studios?"

"Nope. Chief curator of art at the Museum of History, Science, and Art. Say, you must be Faith Burke's sister." Amelia nodded silently. "My goodness. What a towering addition to the field of art appreciation. Such a source of pride for your family."

Towering? Faith's book was as remarkable as all that? "Yes, naturally."

They stared across the chattering crowd. Faith stood dead center of the room, greeting well-wishers like a European princess pressing the flesh on a good-will tour.

"I need to find my date," Zara said, "but may I offer you a piece of advice that someone dispensed to me many moons ago?"

Amelia pulled her attention away from Princess Faith. "By all means."

Zara's keen eyes stared at Amelia, unblinking and unsparing. "The best cure for jealousy is to get off your backside."

"I don't have a very good poker face, do I?"

Zara glanced sidelong at Faith. "It's only bad if you're playing poker. You know what else is regrettable?"

"I dread to ask."

"Failure to live up to one's potential." She left Amelia with a smile and launched herself into the crowd.

The attack left Amelia wondering if she'd stumbled into a prize fight. She reached for the nearest chair, needing its solid presence.

On the other hand, though . . .

Failure to live up to one's potential. I'll still be thinking about that one when I'm falling asleep tonight.

* * *

"Who was that striking woman you were talking with?" Irene Selznick asked when Amelia found them in the throng.

"A curator at the Museum of History, Science, and Art."

"Did you catch her name?"

"Zara Willowick."

"I feel like I ought to know her." Irene tapped her chin with a fingertip. "I mean to say, how many Zara Willowicks can there possibly be wandering around?"

"Sorry to interrupt." The Random House editor patted the microphone. "I've been handed an early review from tomorrow's *L.A. Times*. May I read you a couple of quotes?" His audience was now several cocktails in, so he could have offered to recite the LA City Directory and everyone would have cheered.

Praise like "ground-breaking" and "astonishing" and "innovative" rang across Victor Hugo's, but Amelia barely heard them. Louder, wiser words filled her ears instead.

Cure.

Jealousy.

Make your way in the world.

4

Amelia peered through the windshield of Polly's new Studebaker. "It's bigger than I remember." The white Selznick manse gleamed in the spring sunshine. "Have you figured out why she's invited us?"

Polly withdrew her key from the ignition. "Nope."

At the front door, a polite seven-year-old in a starched plaid shirt—worlds away from Amelia's tornado twins—led them to a sunlit living room. Baby-pink cabbage roses bloomed across every surface: drapes, sofa, and the runner stretching down a mahogany dining table built for sixteen.

Irene swept into the room, apologizing for not being available when they arrived. "When your dressmaker has a nervous breakdown over your Navy Ball gown, you can't say 'Call you later, Jeanette.'" A sliver of a smile cracked open her lips. "Follow me."

They followed Irene to a private screening room, where Amelia and Polly sank into their seats. Irene's fingers played across the projector's controls, and the screen bloomed to life, credits rippling in sharp relief.

Lewis Selznick's

Equitable Pictures
Presents
PRETTY PENNIES
Directed by Sibyl Langley

"You haven't seen this already?" Polly asked Irene.

"A couple of times." She took her seat next to them. "And again this morning."

"So why—"

"You'll see."

* * *

After all the trouble Polly had taken to track down this early silent movie, Amelia was grateful to finally be seeing it for herself.

The actors had all the grace of wind-up tin toys, and the plot wandered around like a lost tourist. Yet the spirit in it sang, especially the relationship between Juniper and her grandmother. "I sure wish Mom had seen this," Amelia said as *THE END* glowed its farewell. "Her best pal—"

"Hold on!" Irene cut in. "Wait for it. Wait for it."

The closing credits appeared one by one until the fifth and final title shimmered into place.

Cinematography - Zara Willowick

"The woman I met at Faith's book launch?" Amelia asked. "She was the cinematographer?"

"It took me eons to figure out why her name sounded familiar."

"If she ran the camera on *Pretty Pennies,*" Polly said, "then she was the one with the—*candles*." She meant the ones her father had dropped on Catalina that last night of shooting, sparking the inferno that had consumed half of Avalon, a burden that had haunted Elroy Maddox for the rest of his days. "I wonder if Sibyl Langley knows her cinematographer is still in LA."

"Sibyl is finishing up sets for *The Women* and is about to start on Lubitsch's *Ninotchka*," Irene said. "I ran into Viv Lubitsch at Missy Stanwyck's barbeque. She said Ernst is looking forward to working with Garbo."

The thought of running across Mrs. Ernst Lubitsch at a barbeque thrown by Barbara Stanwyck and talking about Garbo boggled Amelia's mind. "Sounds fun."

"I have a confession." Irene let her hands drop into her lap. "I'm dreadfully overwhelmed by the punishing stresses that *Gone with the Wind* is bearing down on David. Until this blasted picture is in the can, I've had to adopt a 'for the duration' mentality."

"Like in a war?" Polly asked.

"David living at the studio is like having a husband missing in action. Even though Victor Fleming's in the director chair now, the end of filming is months away. Then the editing phase. After that, test screening. Then the premieres—plural—and they won't be till December. And it's only April!" Irene threw up her hands. "I've got eight more months of this."

A helpless look of insecurity washed over the woman's immaculate veneer of efficiency, control, and unerring good taste. Amelia felt her envy recede. So she was only human, after all.

"Running a household and looking after two little boys isn't enough to keep me satisfied or stimulated. I need more." Irene crossed her arms over her chest. "David's already juggling *Wind*, *Intermezzo*, and *Rebecca*. He doesn't need a fourth project. However, I've decided that *I* need *Pretty Pennies* because if my life amounts to nothing more than planning menus and supervising bath-time, I shall descend into lunacy."

Polly leaned slightly forward, her voice dropping to a confidential whisper. "None of us want you to end up in the loony bin."

A fourth movie stretched Mr. Selznick's executive secretarial team to their limits, keeping them toiling from dawn till well past sunset. Yet Polly counted the boss's wife among her friends—someone she felt compelled to support however possible. She walked a precarious tightrope, but the prospect of *Pretty Pennies* returning to production spelled good fortune for Amelia.

Irene landed elbows onto knees. "Even if David passes on it, I need to feel like I'm contributing. Know what I mean?"

Oh boy, do I ever, Amelia wanted to say. After a mere three weeks at Schwab's retail counter, she longed to scream "I'M SO BORED!" across the store. The job was barely even a stop-gap measure. Zara's words rang in her head again: *The best cure for jealousy is to get off your backside.* Amelia was ready—but could she swim in Irene Selznick's deep waters, complete with her family pedigree, her movie-producer husband, her sixteen-chair dining suite?

Maybe she could; maybe she couldn't. But wouldn't it be fun trying?

"I know exactly what you mean," she told Irene. "What can I do to help?"

5

Given that David Selznick's uncle Phil owned the It Café near Hollywood and Vine, Amelia wasn't surprised when Irene chose it for what she and Polly knew would be a tearful *Pretty Pennies* reunion.

"Have either of you girls been here before?" Lois asked as they stood at the maître d's podium. The café's wall of glass bricks lent the foyer a soft, flattering glow. Or was Amelia's mother glowing with anticipation? Twenty-five years was a long separation from people she had once shared an intense experience with. Amelia would have asked Lois about it had she not been so distracted by some shocking and disappointing news about Faith that Lois had shared with them on the drive over.

Though praised at first, Faith's book had provoked a storm of hostility from fusty college art professors and amateur historians who rallied together, hurling accusations of plagiarism and unoriginality. Consequently, Faith had cloistered herself at home, ignoring phone calls and doorbells. A touch melodramatic, Amelia thought, until Polly had reminded her it was Faith's first real setback. Amelia had swallowed her retort about how making it to twenty-six before tasting defeat put her sister ahead of most. But that wisdom could wait until the sting faded.

Despite their different paths, she longed to reach out to Faith, tell her that one man's opinion carried less weight than an empty powder puff.

The maître d' led them to a corner table, away from the hubbub of the lunch rush.

Irene dropped a compact into her clutch purse and stood as they approached. "Thank you for agreeing to meet fifteen minutes early."

"I assume you've got a stratagem to win over Sibyl and Zara?" Lois said as they took their seats.

"Nothing as formal as that—but yes."

"Sibyl sold the rights to your husband," Amelia said. "I'm not sure you need to win them over."

"Because men would say, 'I own the project. Get out.'" Irene toyed with an unlit cigarette. "I prefer cooperation to conquest. Less 'winning them over,' more 'winning their blessing.' I'll need every arrow in my quiver to convince David about *Pretty Pennies*. The original had an all-female crew. Twenty-five years later, it's much less likely."

"The more allies in our corner, the better?" Amelia asked.

Irene adjusted the orchid on her shoulder. "If we're to be huddled together in a corner, I'd prefer it be women."

Was that what Faith needed? For Amelia to march over there and call through the window, "Who cares what some nasty *Time* magazine critic says?"

"Lois! Is that you?"

Zara Willowick harpooned her voice over the restaurant chatter as she rounded tables with outstretched arms. Sibyl Langley followed in her wake, a beaming smile softening an otherwise serious face.

Lois leaped up. "It's been so long!"

"How did we let so much time go by?"

After a quick round of introductions, drinks were ordered and cigarettes lit. The memories quickly flowed.

"Were you on the pier when that awful child had to dive in the water for thirty-three takes?"

"Did you know that woman who played the grandmother used to dance with Lola Montez?"

"I stole one of the pennies from the bullying scene and had it made into a pendant."

Irene let the chatter gush until they were digging into their appetizers. "Ladies," she said, with an arresting tone, "I must confess to an ulterior motive."

"Does this concern your husband's rumored remake?" Sibyl asked.

Irene set down her salad fork. "I'm convinced it would make a marvelous picture, but David needs cajoling. And so, I've gathered you to tell you that pursuing the project would carry a lot of weight if it were to receive your blessing."

Amelia expected Sibyl and Zara to clap their hands like kindergarteners, so when they sat quite still, their initial exuberance dimming, she looked at Polly. *Uh-oh.*

An uncomfortable moment dragged by.

"I must confess," Irene said, "I'd anticipated a conspicuously more enthusiastic response."

"Making that picture was the most golden time of my life," Zara said.

Sibyl added, "Mine, too."

"So of course we'd love to see a remake."

"However?"

Zara hunched her shoulders over in an uneasy shrug. "I'm not sure it's a good idea to awaken sleeping dogs."

"What sleeping dogs?"

Amelia caught the knowing look passing between Sibyl and Zara. "They're referring to the fire."

"What fire?"

Irene listened as the tale of the final day of filming *Pretty Pennies* spilled out of Polly.

"Good God." Irene realigned her silver cutlery with quick, precise movements. "That's one hell of a sleeping dog."

"We've never spoken about it," Lois said. "The last thing we want is to draw attention to it—or to us."

"It's the reason I've never gone back to Catalina," Zara said.

"Me, either," Sibyl said. "It was a horrendous black mark to leave behind. Yes, technically, it was Elroy's fault for starting it, but we all played our part. And then we snuck away like the guilty yellow-bellies we were. I'd give my eye teeth to go back and make better, more responsible decisions."

"To be honest"—Lois gulped her Sidecar—"it's a relief to admit it out loud."

"Ditto," Sibyl said.

Zara clinked both their glasses. "I'll ditto your ditto."

"But all that happened twenty-five years ago," Irene persisted. "How likely do you think a *Pretty Pennies* remake would push any of this back into the spotlight?"

"Not a lot happens on Catalina," Polly said. "A motion picture would set the village grapevine buzzing. What if people connect the dots? And what if those dots led to ruining my plan to resurrect Mad Ox bourbon so that I can pay back the money my father owed Philip Wrigley?"

Mad Ox had been Polly's father's brand of bourbon, which Polly had been hoping to resurrect. When Elroy Maddox started the distillery during Prohibition, the head of Columbia studios, the fearsome Harry Cohn, had been his financial backer. Until recently, Polly had known none of this—including Cohn's stake in its ownership. If Polly was going to put Mad Ox bourbon back into operation—and she needed to if she were ever going to pay back the money her father had embezzled from the Santa Catalina Island Company—she could only do it once she had shed herself of Cohn's interference.

This was the first Amelia had heard of Polly's reservations. Though understandable, they struck an unexpected and painful blow to her cherished dreams of playing Juniper. Her heart sank as the reality settled in. Irene could still spearhead *Pretty Pennies*, but their paths grew steeper and more daunting without the original team's blessing. The thought of moving forward without Polly's support left a hollow feeling in Amelia's chest that she couldn't quite shake.

Time to change the subject.

"What about the girl who played Juniper? Does anyone know what happened to her?"

"Bernice," Lois said. "When we were at school, her last name was Hoag. But then she got married to a traveling candy salesman whose surname I can't recall."

"What was she like?" Amelia asked.

Lois's face took on a dreamy, faraway glow. "A swan who glided through life like an Egyptian queen floating down the Nile. High class, without being stuck-up. But it was deceptive because she was also a hoot and could be ever so naughty."

"I felt her screen name, Isadora, suited her more than Bernice," Sibyl said.

"Me too," Zara agreed. "What about her husband?"

"Nice enough." Lois sighed. "But she deserved better than a traveling candy salesman. I always saw her as one of those women who run couture salons in chic department stores."

"Gosh," Irene murmured. "The PR value of having Bernice at the opening . . . Wouldn't that be wonderful?"

I see what you're doing, Amelia thought. Planting a picture in everyone's mind of being at a Hollywood premiere. "How would you go about tracking her down?"

"David and Myron have a private eye they sometimes use."

Of course they do. Don't men like them always have a private eye handy? "Aren't those guys expensive?"

"I could hide it in my household budget—up to a point." She scowled. "Between us girls, ever since David started *Wind,* his gambling has become almost manic. One might imagine creating *Gone with the Wind* was risky enough!" Her laugh had thorns in it. "Still, as long as he doesn't lose the house in some marathon poker game, I can fudge the numbers." She drained her Manhattan. "Now, who's for seconds?"

* * *

Amelia and Polly exited the café and headed south down Vine. "Did that go well?" Amelia asked. "I'm not sure."

"I have my own selfish reasons why I'm reluctant to shine a spotlight on *Pretty Pennies*," Polly said, "but I'd say yes, that went as well as any of us could have expected. Why? You think it didn't?"

Amelia spun around to face her. "I've got my hopes set on playing Juniper so much that I can't see straight, think straight, or walk straight."

"You really want this, don't you?"

"More than anything I've ever wanted before. I want it so much that I'm even surprising myself."

"For what it's worth, I think you'd make a great Juniper."

"Thanks, Pol. That makes two of us. Now all we have to do is convince the rest of Hollywood."

"Nope. Just David Selznick. Fortunately, you've got someone working on the inside." Polly winked at her as she handed over her ticket to the 25 Cents All Day parking lot attendant. "Honestly, though, if anyone can get *Pretty Pennies* made, it's Irene."

"So what you're saying is: It'll be the women who get it done?"

"What? We should leave it to the men?" Polly rolled her eyes as the attendant returned with her Studebaker and wedged it between them.

Oh, that Smarty-Pants Maddox, Amelia She's good. *Very* good. No wonder she was David O. Selznick's favorite Girl Friday.

6

The Art Deco tower of the Four Star Theatre cast an angular shadow across Wilshire Boulevard as the late afternoon sun prepared to drop from sight.

"So, Benji," Luddie said. "No more out-of-town reshoots for *Beau Geste*?"

Benji squeezed Amelia's hand. "If I had to climb one more sand dune, I'd have gone plumb loco."

Having him back in LA was bliss—his touch, his kisses, those sweet nothings murmured at dawn and dusk. And then there were his fluffy pancakes. Amelia couldn't fathom how they melted in her mouth like that. She had her suspicions about Steven, his roommate from Fox's Hair and Makeup department, being the true culinary genius, but some mysteries were better left unsolved.

"You wouldn't be the only one to go plumb loco, señor," she told him.

"I heard Bill Wellman warn Archie and Ted there might be retakes—"

"WHAT?"

"—but only on soundstages."

The theater's "Now Playing" poster blazed *WUTHERING HEIGHTS* in thick red letters beneath Merle Oberon's heroine and

Laurence Olivier's menacing glare, rendered in murky green. Above them, the tagline swooned: *I am torn by desire and tortured by hate!*

Polly let out an uncharacteristically mocking laugh. "Rumor around the studio is that Leigh and Olivier go at it constantly."

Amelia and Benji swapped a knowing look. *They ain't the only ones.* Who knew when his next location assignment would be? Best they make hay while they could. A couple of nights back, Polly had asked her, feigning nonchalance behind a copy of *McCall's*, "You guys are using protection, aren't you?" Amelia had assured her that she had no intention of landing in Matilda's predicament.

Benji had an endless supply of condoms whose source was as mysterious as his fluffy pancakes. He'd only said he "had a guy," but in a tone that broadcast they'd reached the end of that discussion, which was fine by Amelia. "Those thingies" were embarrassing enough without discussing where they came from. What a relief that buying them was a man's job.

Amelia turned from the poster in time to spot a couple in dark glasses. The woman had bound her dark brown hair in a scarf of navy blue with an interlocking pattern of green autumn leaves. Amelia elbowed Polly. They watched them walk inside. "I don't believe it."

Benji asked, "What'd we miss?"

Polly cupped her hands and peered through the glass door. "It *is*."

"Which means that's *him*?" Amelia asked.

Luddie spun so fast his fedora nearly slipped off. "Vivien Leigh and Laurence Olivier came here to see *Wuthering Heights*?"

By the time the foursome had bought their tickets, Leigh and Olivier had disappeared from the foyer.

"Shall we?" Benji asked.

"Not until we powder our noses."

Fresh-cut gardenias perfumed the ladies' room. "I don't get it,"

Amelia said, touching up her lipstick at the basin. "Didn't they go to the premiere?"

Polly joined her, though her lips were already an enviable natural red that matched her freckles—features she hated but Amelia coveted. It gave her face such an interesting character. "Vivien only gets one day off a week. You'd think she'd spend it lounging in bed." Their eyes met in the mirror. "Doing whatever." A knowing laugh passed between them, but they cut themselves off when Vivien Leigh emerged from the far stall, minus her dark glasses.

"Trust me, ladies, I would much rather be in bed." It wasn't until she had joined them at the third basin that she recognized Polly, who, along with Amelia, was busying herself with lipstick and trying not to blush. "You're one of Mr. Selznick's secretaries. We all wonder how you maintain your sanity with all those memos flying hither and yon like a plague of frantic locusts."

"It's astounding what you can get used to," Polly replied.

Vivien adjusted her headscarf, tucking away a loose strand. "On the night of the premiere, Larry developed a horrific, splitting headache, so we had to slip out the back. Poor darling never even knew if his performance was any good."

The incandescence this woman exuded set her apart from anyone else Amelia had encountered. And if she was this exquisite in a public bathroom without professional makeup or flattering lighting, what was she going to look like up there on the big screen? "So here you are, seeing the movie with a regular audience."

"Now that Madrid has fallen to the Fascists and Roosevelt recognizes the Franco government, the Spanish Civil War is over at last, but we can't help feeling it's one step closer to a wider European conflict. We had to get out of the house and escape the gloom and doom. So instead, we go see a gloom-and-doom romance!" She tossed off a wry laugh.

"How's it going on *Wind*?" Polly asked.

"How indeed." Vivien pressed her hands on top of her head. "Olivia and I miss George's patient guidance dreadfully."

"But *The Women* is far more his cup of tea," Polly said.

Vivien agreed, then added with a polite giggle, "I don't envy him manhandling those monstrous egos."

"And Victor Fleming?" Amelia asked.

"His distinctly masculine style is . . ." Vivien let the thought drift. "Mr. Selznick made him director, so it's stiff upper lip time and bloody well get on with it for the duration."

"Irene Selznick uses the same expression."

Vivien winked at Polly. "Who do you think I got it from?" She reached into her crocodile-skin purse and pulled out a cigarette. "Irene visited the set yesterday. I was grateful for the distraction. She was the one who brought up—what's the name of that remake Mr. Selznick is doing?"

"*Pretty Pennies*."

"Irene assumed I knew all about it, but *Wind* is so all-consuming that I barely know what day it is. But as it happens, I had heard of *Pretty Pennies*. One day last week they released me at a humane hour and I had the energy to venture out. We're still anonymous enough to roam around unnoticed."

"Where did you go?"

"A new place on Sunset Boulevard. Café Gala. This gorgeous glamour girl approached us. Moves like a dancer. She introduced herself as an actress named Rita—hmmm. Heywood, is it?"

"Hayworth?" Polly suggested.

"Possibly. She wanted to tell me how much she admired me for taking on Scarlett. At some point, Rita mentioned that Harry Cohn had told her of his planned remake."

"*His* remake?" Amelia cried out. "Cohn's?"

"That's the impression Rita gave me. I asked her what she was working on, and she talked about how Cohn is on the lookout for projects that will suit her in the build-up to make her a star, and *Pretty Pennies* was perfect. She made it sound as though it's all but a done deal."

Polly's mouth had trapdoored open in shock. "Mr. Selznick hasn't brought up *Pretty Pennies* in weeks."

Much as Amelia longed to press Vivien for more, the actress

was visibly eager to join her waiting paramour. They waited a discreet minute after she left, then returned to the foyer and told the boys about their encounter.

"In that case, Polly," Luddie said, "isn't it time you followed up on Cohn selling his share in Mad Ox?"

"I was giving him until I was out of my cast to do the right thing."

"Harry Cohn? Do the right thing?" Benji asked. "What a novelty."

"You're right. Getting Mad Ox going again depends on it. But I'm not sure how to go about it."

"Ask one of my roommates," Benji said. "He works at Columbia."

"Isn't that the finance guy we visited?" Luddie asked. "No love lost there, as I recall."

"Noah *hates* his boss. Says Cohn is a son-of-a-bitch negotiator who disregards facts that don't suit him. He can tell you what to expect."

"And don't forget," Amelia said, "his wife, Rose, will be on your side."

Polly absently flicked her ticket across her fingernails. "True."

The lights in the foyer dimmed to half. "Come on," Amelia told the others. "If we can be discreet, maybe we can sit behind Scarlett and Heathcliff." She herded the other three into the auditorium, but wondered how much of this movie she'd remember when all she could think about was how Cohn was buying *Pretty Pennies* for his favorite new ingenue.

7

More than a week later, Irene Selznick was still fuming about the direction *Pretty Pennies* had taken now that Harry Cohn was in the mix. She swung so hard onto Washington Boulevard that Amelia had to grab the passenger armrest.

"I keep waiting for David to mention it over morning coffee. 'Oh, and by the bye, I've been talking to the man I hate most in this world about ditching *Pretty Pennies* onto Columbia.' But no. I'm still waiting."

From the way Polly described her perfectionist boss, Amelia doubted Irene's chances. "Any luck?"

"Most days I feel like Mrs. Sisyphus. Wouldn't you think it might be a worthwhile topic of conversation? I am, let's not forget, the daughter of Louis B. Mayer. Hardly a naif when it comes to these matters."

Volcanic since she'd arrived at Amelia and Polly's apartment building near Robertson Boulevard, Irene had nearly trampled the yellow hibiscus out front. With all her connections to Hollywood's most prominent wives, Amelia was flattered that Irene was unburdening her frustrations on her, but she had to wonder if Mrs. Zanuck and Mrs. DeMille would be able to lend sympathetic ears.

Amelia also knew she ought to choose her words more carefully than she might with Benji, Polly, or Luddie.

"Why don't you kick off the conversation yourself?"

Irene let out a taut yip of a laugh. "It's a delicate dance. If I bring up work-related matters, he throws 'Don't tell me what to do' in my face. And that's why I think it's very smart of us to ask George." The colossal *METRO-GOLDWYN-MAYER* crowning Stages Six, Seven, and Eight rose over Washington Boulevard. "Even though David fired him from the highest-profile picture of the year."

They passed a half-dozen grasshopper oil pumps, dipping like giant crows feeding on a carcass. "Polly spoke to him on the day the news went out and said he didn't seem all that upset."

"Here's my theory," Irene said, smiling for the first time. "He was professionally embarrassed, but privately relieved because if *Wind* turns out to be an unmitigated disaster, it won't have his name on it." She steered into the MGM driveway and wound down her window. "Hiya, Kenny. How's tricks?"

The guy had the unlikely name of Ken Hollywood, which everybody agreed was the most delicious name for a movie studio security guard. He assured her that he was doing fine and did she need any help? She asked him which soundstages Mr. Cukor was filming *The Women* on. Ken directed her to Stage Twelve and raised the barrier.

They walked into the soundstage as an assistant director's voice rang out. "Breaking for lunch. Be back here at one-fifteen, please." Irene and Amelia stood aside as crewmembers exited the beauty parlor set. But it was like no beauty parlor Amelia had ever seen.

The sweeping Art Deco staircase unfurled like an alabaster ribbon against the stark geometry of the black-and-white room. To the right, a six-foot ceramic hand held an enormous glass ball, though for what purpose Amelia couldn't begin to guess. Above them, a mezzanine floated like the deck of an ocean liner against a painted sky dotted with clouds that would never rain.

"GEORGE!" Irene wriggled her fingers so that the huge diamond in her engagement ring twinkled. He dismissed his continuity girl and took Irene's offered hands. "Are you still available for a chat? I don't want to be a bother."

He rolled his eyes in mock disdain. "Says my boss's daughter."

After Irene had introduced Amelia, he led them to a set of four matching club chairs upholstered in dove-gray velvet. Irene wasted no words summarizing her dilemma. When she had finished, George's face fell into a wary frown.

Uh-oh. Amelia glanced at Irene, who had already clenched her jaw.

"Juggling *Wind, Rebecca,* and *Intermezzo* is a herculean task," George said. "If David adds a fourth and it drives him into a nervous breakdown, everyone will be asking, 'Who's responsible?'"

Amelia could see why Irene had sought out Cukor. He radiated the air of a wise and kindly uncle. If the circumstances were different, she'd ask him how to escape from behind the retail counter at Schwab's. And whether she should trust Matilda.

Doubt crept into Irene's eyes, dulling her usual canny expression.

"Look," Cukor said, "I'm not saying the idea is misguided, but the timing isn't ideal."

Irene drew in a sharp breath: *Whether the timing is good for my husband isn't the sole consideration here.* Polly had told Amelia once that she "admired Irene Selznick because she was so gosh-darned unflummoxable." But obviously she had her limits.

"Let's take timing out of the equation," Amelia said. "What might we say to nudge Mr. Selznick to a yes?"

He rubbed the back of his neck while taking a surreptitious peek at his watch. "You'd need to do David's job for him."

"Where would we start?" A trace of Irene's innate self-confidence had resurfaced in her question.

"All movies begin with the screenplay. And all screenplays begin with a treatment—but detailed and polished. And preferably a budget. Approximate is fine, but he needs to see what resources he'd be throwing at it."

"Finding a screenwriter is no problem," Irene said, "but budgeting? I wouldn't know where to start."

"Yes, you do," George told her. "Myron."

"Mr. Selznick's brother?" Amelia asked. "Isn't he a talent agent?"

"Agents need to know all aspects of filmmaking—especially the money side. And he's as passionate as David about resurrecting Papa Selznick's name." He swung to his feet. "Now, if there's nothing else—"

"One quick thing," Amelia said as she and Irene rose to join him. "I encountered Vivien Leigh recently, and she talked about how Rita Hayworth had told her Harry Cohn is campaigning for the rights to *Pretty Pennies*."

"You don't say!" he exclaimed with genuine surprise.

"Or loaning out Rita to Selznick. I don't suppose you've heard anything about that?"

"No, but I've been tied up with *The Women*, so I'm not the person to ask."

"David wouldn't cast an actress in a loan-out from Cohn, would he?" Irene asked. "He can't stand the bastard!"

George laughed a slow, good-natured chuckle. "David would extract great pleasure from telling Cohn no, or negotiating him down to a bargain-basement price so low that it'll infuriate Cohn. Either way, David wins. My suggestion is to include Rita's name in your pitch as a potential lead, and deal with casting later."

"So what you're saying is capture David's attention and get his creative juices flowing."

"Now you're cooking with gas."

The May sunshine warmed Amelia's face as they left the soundstage. "He was as encouraging as he could be, don't you think?"

Irene sidestepped a rolling camera dolly. "The commissary does a tasty Colorado Brook Trout Almondine. My treat."

They rounded a corner and entered the bustling hall. The din of chatter faded as the crowd parted like it was the Red Sea and Irene was Moses. The movie people Amelia dealt with at Schwab's were second- and third-rung employees, hopefuls, and has-beens. Was this what it was like to be the daughter of the boss of all bosses?

A vacant table magically materialized, and they placed their order with a waiter.

"Yes, he was, wasn't he?" Irene was replying to a question Amelia had posed so long ago it took her a moment to catch on. "Jim Taggert runs the writers' department. We could—" She shook her head. "No, no. I'd feel like we were coercing someone too scared to say no to Mayer's daughter."

"I have an idea," Amelia said. "Polly told me that when Mr. Selznick ran *Pretty Pennies* in the studio projection room, Virginia Van Somebody was there."

"Van Upp? From Paramount?"

"She was there on the QT and very enthusiastic about the remake."

"Excellent!" Irene tapped a gloved fingertip on the tabletop. "Let's see now. Who do I know at Paramount?"

"My boyfriend is an art director there. Recently finished work on *Beau Geste*."

Irene smiled as she tugged at her gloves. "Aren't you a treasure trove of surprises?"

Amelia couldn't shake off the vision of those MGM employees parting like Irene was the empress of all she surveyed. Irene Mayer Selznick, whose life experiences dwarfed Amelia's own, came across as someone who was difficult to impress. Yet somehow, Amelia had done just that.

She peeled off her own gloves. "This part you can leave to me."

8

"Now, remember, Virginia Van Upp is kind of a big deal around here."

Amelia loved it when Benji took her hand—especially when he did it spontaneously. "Is this you telling me not to be nervous?"

A crinkle of concern puckered his brow. "I only meant that if she's not at her desk, ask someone because she's often on set."

Polly had already covered this as Amelia had been unfurling hair rollers earlier that morning. "She's shrewd and articulate. Speaks her mind straight out. No dilly, no dally. The point in your favor is that you're female. That makes you a pair of rare birds."

Straight ahead of Amelia and Benji, a two-story, white-washed building bore the sign *WRITING DEPARTMENT*. He gripped her by the shoulders. "Go get 'em, Tiger." *Pretty Pennies* was perched on the shifting sands of David Selznick's whims, but if Virginia was as savvy as Polly made her out to be, she'd know an opportunity when she saw one.

"Thanks, Fletch." She sensed he got a kick out of her nickname for him, mostly because it rhymed with 'letch,' which was how he was in bed. In a fun, enthusiastic way, though. Not that she had anyone to compare to, but he sure got sweatier than anyone she'd seen in the movies. "Mucho appreciato, amigo."

. . .

The machine-gun staccato of typewriters choked the room like the thick bluish pall of smoke dense enough to blur the detailing in the pressed-metal ceiling. A platoon of wooden desks stood in three rows at the center. Offices, each barely large enough to hold a desk and a chair, rimmed the periphery. Amelia was halfway around the room before a fifty-ish woman with the unvarnished nails and wan complexion of a typing-pool veteran stopped her.

"Looking for someone?"

"Miss Van Upp," Amelia said. "I was hoping—"

"*Cat and the Canary*. Visiting Paulette Goddard on account of missing out on Scarlett. Of course, I'd be inconsolable, too, if I'd pinned my hopes on Clark Gable and got stuck with Bob Hope."

Amelia found Virginia in the middle of a living room set. The twenty-foot walls were a little on the dingy side, wallpaper curled and tattered in spots. The rug filling most of the floor was ragged at the edges. Her prey was chatting with Paulette Goddard and Gale Sondergaard, both of them coated in thick layers of cinema makeup.

"Regret is a waste of time, effort, and emotion," Gale reproached Paulette. "Do I regret turning down the Wicked Witch of the West? No, ma'am." She circled a finger around her face. "Regular movie makeup is onerous enough, but to endure all that ugly-witch greasepaint? Ugh."

Amelia saw her chance. "To say nothing of Margaret Hamilton's bad luck."

Gale fixed her with a look of stern confusion. "How so?"

"She got badly burned last week by faulty special effects."

"No! Poor darling."

"They won't be able to film her for weeks." Amelia turned to Paulette. "And I bumped into Vivien Leigh at the Four Star on Wilshire not too long ago. She's miserable now that George is out, and is counting the days until production is over."

"Excuse me, but have we met?" Virginia asked.

Amelia stepped onto the threadbare carpet. "No, but I'm a good friend of Polly Maddox, Mr. Selznick's Girl Friday." Virginia's eyebrows arched in recognition. "I was hoping we might have a moment to chat."

Paulette and Gale agreed their makeup needed retouching before filming resumed and hurried away. Virginia led Amelia to a threadbare sofa against the far wall as the crew prepared for the next shot. "How can I help you?"

From Polly's and Benji's descriptions, Amelia had been expecting a man-eater, all sharp elbows and a take-no-prisoners poise. But in person, she was more like the older sister a girl could turn to for advice about boys and hair and earrings. "It's about Mr. Selznick's *Pretty Pennies* remake."

"I assumed it was dead in the water."

"Not yet. Mrs. Selznick and I are working on it."

"*Irene* is?"

"She's very enthusiastic and wants to coax it forward. And so I'm here to ask you if you'd be prepared to work on a treatment—"

Virginia leaped from the sofa. "Edith Head is designing a dress for me." She rushed toward the elephant-door exit, maintaining a vigorous pace as she squinted sideways at Amelia, irritation corroding her face. "You cannot waltz in talking about a job with a rival studio."

Inwardly, Amelia groaned, and thought back to the previous evening when Polly and Benji had insisted Amelia practice her pitch in front of them.

"More enthusiasm!"

"Less begging!"

"Replace 'We were wondering if you might' with 'We immediately thought of you.'"

It had been a tough slog, but Amelia had been happy with her the finely tuned speech. Now that she had blown it all to smithereens, every word had flown from her mind.

"I was at that screening in secret," Virginia muttered. "Thank God none of the crew heard you."

They veered left up Avenue P. Ahead of them, past Stages One and Two, a prominent plaque read *MISS EDITH HEAD, COSTUMING*. Amelia had one minute, two at most. "If I'd known, I'm sure George Cukor would have recommended—"

Virginia paused. "What's George got to do with it?"

"Irene and I sought him out for advice."

"Did you, now?" The exasperation in her voice waned.

George Cukor hadn't brought her up at all. That had been Amelia's idea. But Amelia couldn't risk this formidable woman scoffing at her. "Mr. Cukor said all pictures start with a treatment."

"He's right, of course."

"You've already seen *Pretty Pennies*, so we immediately thought of you."

"Who's the 'we' in this scenario?"

"Irene and I."

"And David's on board with me writing the treatment?"

Amelia swallowed. Best to level with someone this astute. And as Zara Willowick had so keenly observed, Amelia had a defective poker face. "Mr. Selznick's enthusiasm has faded somewhat since the screening—but not about the project itself. It's just that he currently has more pressing issues."

"Like getting *Gone with the Wind* in the can?"

"Indeed, yes. But Irene is very committed. Between you and me, she's bored with the housewife-and-mother routine."

"Of course she is," Virginia said. "Irene's far too clever to be stuck with wiping little boys' faces and ordering the gardener around. She craves mental stimulation and a creative outlet."

Virginia stopped out front of Edith Head's office. "I've been thinking about *Pretty Pennies* since that screening," she admitted with a smirk. "I have a ton of ideas."

"Did you write them down?"

"When you're a writer, you jot everything down."

White-knuckled, Amelia clutched her purse, careful to hide her nerves. "How soon could you type up a treatment?"

"As long as my husband doesn't disturb me in the evenings, I can't imagine it'd take me two weeks. I have it half-written in my head."

"Two weeks would be terrific."

"Shall I send it to you at Selznick International?"

Leapin' lizards, she thinks I work there. "To Irene."

"The Summit Drive address?"

Amelia nodded. "I don't want you to keep Edith Head waiting, so I'll leave you to it."

Virginia held up a hand to halt her. "Don't go. I'd like a second opinion on this gown."

Who in their right mind would pass up a chance to meet Hollywood's most famous dress designer? Then again, who in their right mind would critique a dress in front of Hollywood's most famous dress designer? Virginia set off up the short flight of stairs, and Amelia followed her.

"We didn't talk about paying you," Amelia called up.

"That won't be necessary."

Amelia landed on the top step. "You'll do this for free?"

"My Paramount contract prevents me from accepting payment of any sort, so my treatment will be gratis, However, I do insist on a guarantee that I'll be hired to write the screenplay. If everything pans out, I'll let my lawyer deal with the Paramount lawyer who can deal with the Selznick lawyer."

"Sounds fair."

"But I won't do anything until David gives the picture a definite go-ahead." She landed a hand on the doorknob. "Do we have a deal?"

Did they? Was Amelia allowed to make deals? She had no idea, but this was no time to chicken out. "We do."

"Fine. Now, let's go see about this frock."

Edith Head's office was a study in whites and creams—all the better, Amelia supposed, to showcase the vibrant concoctions she dreamed up for Paramount's leading ladies. A hand-drawn sketch dominated the vestibule wall: a woman in a textured gown, her waist impossibly narrow. Amelia read the inscription.

Claudette Colbert – "Zaza"
Dir: George Cukor – 1939

"Your timing is impeccable." Though Edith Head stood no taller than a schoolgirl, she invaded the room like Sherman taking Atlanta, her knitted suit a perfect match to her office's neutral palette. "My seamstress finished your gown an hour ago." She waved them into a larger room with an expansive desk lacquered black as her hair, littered with sketches, pencils, scripts and swatches of material.

To the right, a floor-length gown of cayenne-red silk hung in soft drapes from a dressmaker's mannequin. Virginia clapped her hands together. "Oh, Edith!"

"You like?"

Virginia slid a wave of silk through her fingers. "Quit fishing for compliments."

"Dealing with quixotic movie queens is an occupational hazard," Edith said. "However, I have yet to acquire the skill of anticipating my clients' reactions. Your thoughts, Miss Hartley?"

"The color alone," Amelia gushed. "You'll be turning heads wherever you wear it," she told Virginia.

"Thank goodness the hostess of this year's Mayfair Ball didn't decree all women must wear white like Carole Lombard did a couple of years ago." Head raked her gaze over Amelia. "If Virginia doesn't care for it, perhaps you do. You're the same size. In fact, with your red hair . . ."

Amelia's pulse Lindy-hopped at the thought of wearing such a sumptuous gown.

"Don't even *think* about it!" Virginia pointed out a second gown farther into the corner, away from the light. "You're welcome to that, though."

Mid-calf length and made of dark brown bombazine, it was much boxier than Virginia's. Amelia doubted it would flatter anyone. Yeech. No thanks. Amelia would rather show up in a burlap sack. "It's a moot point," she told the two women. "I can't see myself scoring an invite."

"What a kind way to say, 'That dress is a fright,'" Edith said with a laugh. "And on you it would be, but Dorothy has a different body type, so you're safe." She broke off when an assistant walked in with a pile of sketches that needed her signature.

"Is she talking about Dorothy Lamour?" Amelia asked Virginia, sotto voce.

"Good grief, no. Dorothy Arzner, the only woman director working at her level. Probably because she's rather mannish, if you catch my meaning."

Did that mean the woman was a dyke? A pair of Amelia's regulars at Schwab's lunch counter fitted the same description. She had been shy around them until their acerbic wit had won her over. A woman director—and one with Dorothy Arzner's reputation? Perhaps she was exactly what *Pretty Pennies* needed. "What is Dorothy working on now?"

"Nothing since *The Bride Wore Red* at MGM, and that must have been two years ago."

"How might we contact her?"

"Not sure." Virginia ran her fingers along the black velvet bodice. "Edith would know. Keep in mind, though, Dorothy is hard to impress. If she agrees to meet with you, make sure Irene's there."

"I can guarantee it."

Virginia traced one last longing glance over Edith's creation. "You've got that I-have-an-idea gleam in your eye, but remember: This business runs on men's rules. An all-female picture is about as rare as an honest used car salesman. Don't get your hopes up, is all I'm saying."

"But the original *Pretty Pennies* was made by women."

Virginia fluttered a dismissive hand. "In the early days, women were far more prevalent—that is, until the men caught on that flickers could make decent money and shunted us aside."

"I was thinking how the all-female angle might make a great angle to use in promotion, like the all-female cast of *The Women*."

Virginia strummed her fingertips against her cheek. "It's worth a shot."

"So you'll talk to Miss Head about Dorothy Arzner?"

"Absolutely." The fingers continued to strum. "You've now got me wondering where the director and star of the original are now."

"The director's name is Sibyl Langley; she's at MGM."

"You don't say!"

"Bernice Hoag is unaccounted for. Irene contacted the private eye she knew of, but all she had was Bernice's maiden name, which wasn't enough to go on."

"Quelle dommage." Virginia snapped out of her daydream. "You didn't tell me how you got involved in all this." The bright California sun through the window suddenly felt like a spotlight, hot and exposing. They were minutes from goodbye, minutes from Amelia being able to dodge the admission that she was only a waitress. And not even that now. "What is it you do, exactly?"

Oh boy, here we go. "I work at Schwab's."

"I see." The screenwriter's eyes dimmed.

Now finished with her assistant, Edith turned back to Amelia and Virginia. "Time to try it on?"

Virginia said she was sure it fitted her so could someone box it up for her instead. Edith wouldn't hear of it and ordered her into the fitting room, leaving Amelia free to escape.

She flew down the steps and along Avenue P. When she had driven into the Paramount lot a couple of hours ago, she'd been so full of hope and excitement. But now?

I work at Schwab's.

She felt like a party balloon whose helium had leaked out in one long hiss.

9

"I still can't believe it," Amelia said as neon signs glowed to life amid the dimming dusk. Polly and Luddie flanked her, their shadows stretching across the Sunset Strip sidewalk.

"I'm surprised you're surprised," Luddie said. "Virginia's on board—thanks to you."

The expression on Virginia's face—*Oh, so you're not one of us?*—still made Amelia cringe. "That look in her eye when I told her I'm a lowly peon at Schwab's."

"Didn't she ask Edith to call Dorothy? And didn't Dorothy agree to meet us at Club Bali?"

"She agreed to meet with Irene Selznick. We're merely background extras."

Luddie's Bronx cheer sent heads whipping around at the Sunset News magazine stand. "None of this would have happened had you failed to captivate the not-easily-charmed Virginia Van Upp. And now we're meeting Dorothy Arzner at Club Bali, which is a huge win."

"'Huge'?" Polly asked.

"Think of it as encountering Dorothy Arzner on her home turf."

A bamboo-framed doorway announced *BALI* in electric green neon. Inside, past the concrete ramp and hostess in her pink-and-lilac muumuu, the hexagonal room was a shrine to bamboo—chairs, window frames, vases. Even the bar wore the tropical motif. Amelia, however, saw no sign of Irene. They would have arrived together, but she had called to say she was having "a monumental babysitter crisis" and had suggested they all rendezvous there.

The greeter offered, "Perhaps a drink until she arrives?"

They skirted the showroom's perimeter to the bar where the Polynesian bartender suggested their signature drink: the Balinese Breeze, concocted with two types of rum, three fruit juices, and a dash of grenadine.

Luddie ordered three, then asked Amelia for the latest news of the storm swirling around her sister.

Poor Faith. She'd penned her book for New England art history majors, but it had sparked an uproar after the *Boston Globe*'s scathing review split the field into fierce critics and fiercer defenders. Now her publisher wanted a strategic apology in a prestigious journal. "Apologize for what?" Faith had demanded. "Writing from *my* knowledge, *my* research, *my* perspective?" She had refused to draft any apology, but Amelia wondered how long Faith could hold out. A few years ago, she might have enjoyed watching Miss Perfection stumble on her perpetual tightrope of confidence. Now, she felt only sympathy for someone forced to weather a controversy she didn't deserve.

As Amelia outlined the horns of Faith's dilemma, she noticed how the club's patrons had sorted themselves like a deck of cards—kings with kings, queens with queens. "Say, Luddie, what kind of place is this?"

"Ever heard of Bruz Fletcher?"

"I don't think so."

"Back in Prohibition, female impersonators became all the rage. 'The Pansy Craze,' they called it. He didn't cross-dress, or anything, but it's where he got his start. And he's is still going strong here."

"So Dorothy Arzner choosing this place—"

"—didn't surprise me." Luddie's eyes lit up when he spied a couple of women at the entrance. "Well, well—here's our director, wearing the pants as usual."

He nodded toward a stocky woman in a tailored suit, dark hair cropped, no handbag. Her companion, a delicate blonde in a wide-brimmed hat, clung to her arm. They placed a drink order with a waiter and made straight for a reserved table.

Amelia craned her neck toward the entrance. "I sure wish Irene would get here."

"It's not like her to be late." Luddie lit up an Old Gold cigarette as he zeroed in on Arzner's table. "Bruz goes on in forty-five minutes."

"What if she doesn't get here in time?

"We'll have to approach Dorothy ourselves," Polly said.

"Virginia insisted Irene be here." Amelia reminded her.

"I'm positive those two will stay for the show."

"We still have time."

Polly plucked the Old Gold from between Luddie's fingers. "Why do you keep gawking at them?"

"Dorothy's little tootsie. The way she's tilted her hat, I can't see her face properly. I can't help feeling she—" He gasped softly and wheeled away from the room.

Amelia had never seen Luddie startled—or even mildly surprised. "What's wrong?"

Luddie half-turned from the bar but kept his back to Arzner's table. "If her parents knew, they'd be horrified."

"The blonde with the curls?"

"Her name's Eliza. She's the daughter of our new sponsor."

"For *Dick Tracy*?"

"The negotiations have been a high-stake chess game. Her father is a rock-ribbed conservative who thinks Hollywood is Sodom and Gomorrah with palm trees and a carousel on the pier. But the money he's offering!" Luddie let out a whistle. "If he discovered anyone from the show in a place like this, the whole deal would go kablooey. I'd lose a job I love, but even worse, I could be responsible for everyone else losing theirs, too."

"How did you come to meet the daughter?" Polly asked.

"The sponsor brought his family in from Pittsburgh. My first escort client—the wife of NBC Red's West Coast head—suggested I play tour guide. One fancy dinner at Perino's, and Mr. Richardson starts seeing LA's charms. Next thing I know, I'm at the Biltmore while Mrs. Richardson tries her hand at matchmaking with Goldilocks over there."

"And now," Amelia murmured, "Goldilocks is sitting with a masculine woman in a queer bar."

The bartender landed their trio of cocktails in front of them. Luddie was the first to tip a generous swig into his mouth. "Negotiations are coming down to the wire and dear ol' Dad is playing for keeps, so I toed the line. By the time dessert arrived, the atmosphere had grown awkward because it had dawned on me a little too late that Mrs. Richardson was planning June weddings in her head."

"*Too* charming, were we?" Polly teased.

"Suddenly I'm faced with fixing a situation that wasn't my doing—not intentionally, at any rate—but I had to fix it for *Dick Tracy*'s sake."

"And did you?"

"I made a crack about the Kansas City Monarchs baseball team, which I assumed was fine because by then I already knew he was a Kansas State Wildcats fan. But apparently you can only do that if you're from Kansas."

"And if you're not?"

"They close ranks."

"How did the evening end?"

"Tense." Luddie took a belt of his Balinese Breeze and thumped its bamboo cup on the counter, nearly spilling the rest of his cocktail. "We should go."

"Why?" Polly said. "Eliza's got as much at stake as you do."

Luddie stared at her as though this obvious fact hadn't occurred to him. How very unlike the guy who was usually two steps ahead of everyone else. "All I could see was four months of hard-fought negotiations falling apart at the last minute."

"You should brace yourself," Polly stage-whispered over her Balinese Breeze. "She's en route to the ladies' room in three . . . two . . . one."

Without her straw boater, Eliza Richardson's allure was obvious. Glittering eyes, dewy skin, and a bright debutante smile—until she spotted him. "LUDLOW!" Her hands flew up in defense as she glanced frantically back at her table. Finding Dorothy absorbed elsewhere, she faced him once more. "I never thought—anyone I knew—I'm here with—" Her composure crumbled like a paper fan as she hurried toward him. "Please, please, *please* don't tell my father!"

"You could blab on me as much as I could blab on you."

A couple of seconds ticked by as the girl digested Luddie's meaning. "OH!" She smoothed her silk collar with trembling fingers. "I must—I am—excuse me."

She rushed away, ignored the ladies' room, and headed for a side door.

Amelia said, "We should make sure she's okay." She and Polly each took a gulp of their Breezes—delicious, but boy howdy, they were strong—and followed. The side door opened into the alleyway running along the northern side of the club. A lone light bulb cast a yellow halo on the asphalt. They found Eliza leaning a shoulder against the wooden fence halfway down.

"We thought we'd check up on you," Amelia said.

Eliza's limp tissue had streaked her runny mascara into sooty smudges. "You must think me quite the alarmist."

Polly pulled a fresh tissue from her purse and handed it to her. "This place must be somewhat different from Pittsburgh."

"No fooling! South Pacific drinks, bamboo tables, waitresses with flower leis? There's nothing like it back home."

But that wasn't what Polly had meant by "this place."

"The woman you came in with," Amelia said. "You know who she is, right?"

"Dorothy? Oh, yes. Big-time movie director."

From what Amelia could see in the shadowy night, Eliza looked a little bit like Polly had that first day on the Catalina pier: a wide-eyed girl with little experience of the outside world, whose innocence was more charming than she knew. The smell of burning grease from the open kitchen window above their heads filled the lane. Amelia coaxed Eliza and Polly away before they all reeked of it. "Did you know her from Pittsburgh?"

Eliza laughed. "There's nobody like Dorothy in Steel City. Mother was down with one of her sick headaches, so she gave me ten bucks for lunch and a movie. But I didn't go because I got a new camera last Christmas. A new Canon Junior. I'm a real shutterbug, you see, but I was out of film. The hotel clerk recommended a camera store on Hollywood Boulevard. The customer ahead of me noticed my camera, and we got chatting."

"Dorothy?"

"Oh, brother, what that woman doesn't know about cameras. After that, we went for coffee to talk all things photography. But of course, we soon moved on to other matters, if you know what I mean. You're in this joint, so I assume you do."

Amelia breathed easier, knowing she wouldn't have to spell out the obvious. "Hit it off, did you?"

"Uh-huh, but not in *that* way. She lives with a woman named Marion. But she has been taking me out to . . . *interesting* places where I'm more likely to meet someone appropriate—because God knows I can't do it in Pittsburgh."

"Temped to move out here?" Polly asked.

"And how! Mother and Father don't know it yet, but I want to restart my life from scratch." Wiped clean of her errant mascara, she now looked even younger in a fresh-out-of-high-school sort of way. "You two a—y'know—um—a couple?"

"Gloriosky, no!" Polly burst out. "Just roommates."

"We're here to meet Dorothy to discuss a film project."

"Oh! It's you guys? Which one's the studio boss's daughter?"

"That's Irene Selznick," Polly said, "but she hasn't shown up. We're not sure how best to proceed because we want to impress Dorothy."

"Let me tell you the score—just between us?" Eliza dropped her voice to a whisper, though nobody was around. "She's desperate to work again, but knows she's at the mercy of all the men in Hollywood. Then Mrs. Selznick's name came up, and that's a whole different ballgame."

Tonight was supposed to be *The Irene Selznick Show*. But she was nearly an hour late. If they didn't approach Dorothy Arzner now, she might not agree to a second meeting.

Amelia hoped she'd find Luddie chatting to Irene, but he was still alone and ordering another Balinese Breeze when they made it back to the bar. "You'll have to make the pitch yourself," he told her.

Dorothy was now sitting with her arms barricading her chest.

Amelia surrendered to the inevitable. "I am, aren't I?"

"Want us to tag along?" Polly asked.

"Three of us descending on a table for two might scare her away." Amelia downed the rest of her bamboo highball. "Order me another. I'm going in."

"Hello, Miss Arzner, my name is Amelia Hartley."

"Was Irene ever going to be here?" Dorothy's voice was icy as the Swiss Alps.

"Absolutely. I'm a little worried that she hasn't shown up."

"Talk fast, Miss Hartley. The show starts in ten."

Eliza scooped up her champagne cocktail and headed back to the bar. "I'll leave you two professionals to talk business."

Amelia took her seat before Dorothy could object. The rum in her hastily downed Balinese Breeze had struck midway to Dorothy's table, making the room swim but crystallizing her thoughts. By the time she had introduced herself, she knew how to play this scene. "I'm sure you read in the trades that David Selznick plans to film a remake of his father's first picture."

"I did."

"Making *Gone with the Wind* has consumed him, so Irene is taking the lead in the pre-production process."

Dorothy unfolded her arms. "Go on."

"Were you aware *Pretty Pennies* was made by an all-female crew?"

"Women? All of them?" Dorothy was now modulating her responses with an even-footed tone, her initial brusqueness fading away.

Amelia laid her hands on the table, fingers splayed open. "Director, screenwriter, cinematographer, star. Irene and I think it's what made the original such a special picture."

Dorothy's dark eyes skittered around the room, rarely landing on a face, a table, a lamp, a potted plant for more than a second or two.

She's listening. She's liking what she's hearing. She's tempted. "It can't have been easy being a woman director in a field teeming with men. You must have had your fair share of frustrations with them. What I'm offering—what *we're* offering—is a vastly improved experience with you at the helm."

Dorothy's interest continued to skip from the stage curtains to a waitress's tray to a miniature palm tree sprouting from a weathered wooden tub.

"Miss Arzner, we can't imagine making the film without you."

If that doesn't clinch it, nothing will. Should I ask her to call Irene? Or for Irene to call her? This woman looks like the plain-talking type who appreciates someone who shoots from the hip. I should—

"LADIES AND GENTLEMEN!" A voice boomed over loudspeakers. The lights around the club dimmed to a murky glimmer. "Let's hear it for the star of tonight's presentation, Mister Bruz Fletcher!"

A tuxedoed gent with a perennially boyish face and a warm smile stepped through the parting curtains. The opening chords to an old Helen Morgan song filled the club. Bruz leaned into the microphone and sang the opening line to "More Than You Know." Amelia drank in every liquid note until she felt a tap on her wrist.

"Send Eliza back to me."

10

Benji parked his new Hupmobile—a deep robin's-egg blue that glowed in the late afternoon light—at the curb outside 1000 North Crescent Drive in Beverly Hills. He addressed the two girls in the back seat. "Twenty-five hundred is peanuts to a guy like this."

"Irene told me her husband and Harry Cohn have one trait in common: gamblers addicted to taking risks. It's why they both teeter on the precipice of bankruptcy. *Gone with the Wind* and *Mr. Smith Goes to Washington* flopping at the box office could end them both financially."

"Peanuts or no peanuts," Amelia told Polly, "it's the highest Dad'll go to buy Cohn out of Mad Ox and get the distillery going again. You can't agree to anything more than that.

"And I won't."

Amelia wished her father were here to persuade Cohn to accept the cut-price offer, but he was launching a new tequila on the East Coast. She couldn't let Polly face a titan like Harry Cohn alone. Following him to the top of a rickety set was one thing, but this was business. "Not a penny more."

"I won't have to," Polly reassured her. "We have Bioff and Browne up our Sears and Roebuck sleeves."

Willie Bioff and George Browne had muscled their way from the East Coast into the studio unions, collecting monthly bribes from executives who found payoffs cheaper than union wages. What these executives didn't know—but their wives did—was that Columbia's chief wasn't paying a cent. Polly touched Amelia's forest-green cuff. "Sale rack or not, you're picture perfect."

"Thanks, cuz."

Amelia and Polly shared no blood, but a powerful sisterhood had sparked between them that day on the Catalina pier. Amelia now saw that her fleeting involvement with the two-bit gangster who'd brought her there had been the wrong turn that had led to the right friend.

Benji narrowed his eyes in a wince. "Are you *sure* you don't want me there?"

His burly presence might discourage Cohn from trying anything inappropriate, but they refused to send Cohn a message that they needed a man to close their deal.

Amelia inched forward and kissed Benji. "Knowing you're ready to charge in like gangbusters is all the reassurance we need." She smooched him again, and they stepped out of the car, checked each other's teeth for lipstick, then headed toward Cohn's arched front door.

"Nice limp you got there," Amelia said, nudging her pal with the brass-hinged briefcase Irene had loaned her.

Now free of her leg cast, Polly no longer lurched around like the bride of Frankenstein. Nor did she need her walking cane, but Rose Cohn had suggested bringing it. "Those big toes Harry broke when he fell off the *Lost Horizon* set haven't healed properly, so the doctor had to re-break them!" She had giggled mischievously. "Polly should bring a cane to remind him he's not the only one who got hurt that day."

"Right on time; he'll appreciate that," Rose said as the doorbell's echo faded across the marble-tiled foyer. She led them into a cream-walled rotunda where a single narrow table held a three-foot vase crying out for long-stemmed flowers. "He's in a foul mood, so I slipped a mild sedative into his whiskey. I suggested he sit at the dining table and then I hid the canes. The fool hasn't realized he's stuck there."

She led them through a parlor so pristine that Amelia doubted it had ever been used and slid open a pair of mahogany pocket doors. Cohn remained seated. His eyeballs, too still to be reading, lingered on a script in front of him. Save the performance, buddy-boy, Amelia wanted to say. Ain't nobody in this room is fooled. She and Polly and Rose stood like dime-store mannequins, waiting out his little power play until he deigned to look up.

"Ah, the Dolly sisters make their entrance." He took stock of Polly's cane. "You're out of your cast."

"Still hobbling around, though."

Cohn grunted like a dog spotting a better bone—a temporary retreat in a longer game—and waved his hands at the two dining chairs opposite him, giving Amelia a cursory glance.

"It's a little warm today," Rose said, "so I've made some fresh lemonade and sugar cookies." She gestured toward the sideboard. "Or would you prefer stiffer refreshments?"

"Quit fussing and leave us be."

"I will *not*." Rose's affable society-hostess voice had hardened like the marble in her foyer. "We agreed, Harry, that you would include me in your life more."

As Cohn drained his whiskey, she filled three highball glasses with lemonade from the crystal pitcher. As she brought them to the table, Cohn turned to Amelia. "Who's this?" he snapped to no one in particular.

"I'm Amelia Hartley, here on behalf of City of Angels Distillery, who is buying Mad Ox." She paused, letting his predictable sneer surface. She locked her hands into a single fist and landed her elbows on the table top. "I'm sure your time is valuable."

"It is."

"So is ours," Amelia bit back. She got a grunt in response, but nothing more, so she pushed forward. "We're prepared to offer you twenty-five hundred for your stake in Mad Ox."

Cohn mimicked her aggressive posture. "That's not an offer; it's an insult."

"We're not here to haggle."

His mouth soured into a curve that drooped at the ends. "In that case, you've wasted your time. And mine."

Amelia had hoped Harry Cohn might act decently and accept the offer. After all, Polly had saved him from worse injuries in that fall, though she'd broken her own leg doing it. Letting her regain control of her father's distillery would be the perfect way to repay his debt. She saw now what a foolish fantasy that had been.

"You should reconsider, Mr. Cohn," Amelia said, with the measured delivery she had rehearsed in front of her vanity mirror.

"Rose, show these two birdbrains outta my house."

Rose stared at Amelia. *You know what to do.*

"You'll take the offer, Mr. Cohn."

"I will, huh? Why's that?"

"Because you're not paying off Bioff and Browne like your counterparts are." Cohn's eyes narrowed, but he stayed silent. "When your fellow moguls find out . . ." Amelia let the sentence trail off, channeling her inner Barbara Stanwyck—scrappy, street-smart, with a touch of wise guy. The doubt playing across Cohn's puss told Amelia that her poker face might not be so crappy after all.

He shot his wife a hateful stare. "Did you know about this?"

"All us wives do."

"Including Irene Selznick," Polly said, "whose husband I work for."

Amelia was glad that she'd turned down Benji's offer to accompany them, but wasn't it a comfort to know he sat outside on the driveway? "If you don't accept my offer, we're going home and making phone calls."

"I've seen a million four-flushing bullshit hands played, but this one takes the ever-lovin' cake." Cohn shook his head slowly. "You hare-brained harpies come in here with your cheap clothes and your Woolworth's perfume and think you have what it takes to hold Harry Cohn's feet to the fire? I'll burn you two so bad you'll wish you'd never heard of Hollywood. GET! OUT! NOW!" He pounded the dining table to punctuate each syllable.

"No, Harry," Rose said. "They're not leaving yet."

"And that means you, too."

Amelia slapped her briefcase against the tabletop. She withdrew the agreement Judd's lawyer had drawn up. An expensive fountain pen made of enameled jade lay near Cohn's elbow. Amelia reached over and laid it on top of the contract. "Twenty-five hundred bucks for everyone's silence is getting off cheap."

Cohn stared at the pen.

One second. Five seconds. Ten seconds.

Cohn picked it up as though it were as delicate as a hummingbird egg.

Under the table, Amelia bumped her knee against Polly's.

He rotated it in his fingers, three full revolutions, until he made a sound at the base of his throat, a cross between a bark and a snarl. Gripping the pen like it was a dagger, he hurled it across the room. It missed Rose's lemonade pitcher by inches, and bounced off the wall before landing onto the Persian rug.

"I will *not* be chiseled by a couple of no-account shiksas. You can all go screw yourselves." He jabbed a finger at his wife—"Same goes for you"—then spun back to Amelia. "Tell Irene Selznick and Virginia Zanuck and Margaret Mayer, and whoever else you've lured into your witches' coven, that they can screw themselves, too." He took a beat, long enough to inhale. "Have you goddamn geniuses thought about how their husbands will react when they learn nobody told *them* about Bioff and Browne?"

Amelia gripped the armrests. She hadn't considered that. None of them had. Did she want to unleash hell in Hollywood? Especially with the mob involved? She'd watched Polly play too close to that flame to risk getting burned.

Polly had gone as pale as Amelia felt.

The bastard had called their bluff.

Cohn sprawled back in his chair. "I didn't think so."

Amelia wasn't ready to give in. Not yet. She had to fill the silence. *Keep talking*.

"Rita Hayworth."

Cohn stiffened. "What about her?"

"You want her for the *Pretty Pennies* remake?"

"What the Christ-almighty hell does that have to do with Mad Ox? Or you, for that matter?"

Amelia wavered, willing herself not to blink. What was she going to do? Tell him she worked at Schwab's and risk the same face she'd gotten from Virginia Van Upp?

"Amelia is part of the team developing *Pretty Pennies* as a viable project," Polly said.

Cohn frowned as he looked Amelia up and down. "You are?"

"Yes, along with Irene Selznick."

"Dave's wife? Works? At the studio?"

Two days after missing the Club Bali meeting, Irene had confessed that her "monumental babysitting crisis" was fiction. The truth had been a scream-to-the-rafters clash with Selznick, whose gambling losses were mounting much faster than his wins. Once the storm had passed, Irene was relieved to hear Dorothy had proved so amenable.

"Bull! Shit!" Cohn blustered. "Dave mentioned nothing about his wife being involved." He sucked a morsel of food from between his teeth. "As if the Memo Magnate would delegate one of his movies to anyone, let alone to his *wife*."

Rose tightened a hand around her glass of lemonade, the knuckles of each finger straining against the skin. "Do you remember that Labor Day cookout we went to last year at Howard Hawks's beach house?"

"What of it?"

"On the drive home, you told me about a conversation you had enjoyed with some woman you'd sat next to. You commented on how savvy she was. How sharp, how insightful. Quote—especially for a woman—unquote. Do you remember?"

"What if I do?"

"The woman who impressed you so deeply was Irene Selznick." Rose watched her husband's shoulders sag the tiniest bit. "I suggest you don't make the same mistake as your counterparts—dismissing someone because of their sex."

When Rose had come to Amelia and Polly's apartment, she had

been in the company of the other "Mrs. Moguls," so Amelia hadn't been able to take the woman's full measure. She could see now that Rose Cohn was not to be trifled with.

The solemn ticking of a far-off grandfather clock penetrated the silence of the dining room as Cohn stewed. Rose picked up Amelia's Bakelite pen and laid it on the table in front of her husband as Amelia slid her father's contract toward him. He fingered his collar, tugging at it as though the silk were steel wool. His swagger wavered for a heartbeat before the mask slipped back into place. "My counter-offer is five grand."

"I was quite clear, Mr. Cohn," Amelia said. "The offer is a non-negotiable twenty-five—"

"It would have been ten grand, but credit where credit is due. Threatening me with Bioff and Browne took chutzpah."

Pop's last words to Amelia had been, "Twenty-five hundred, absolute maximum."

Dammit! We were so close!

"Fine," Polly said. "Five thousand."

Had she taken leave of her senses? Where the hell would she get the extra two and a half grand? But they had to present a united front, so Amelia bit down on her lip. Hard.

Cohn pushed the contract away. "Send me a cashier's check and an updated contract, and I'll sign it straight away."

Amelia and Polly pushed out a civil "Thank you," then got to their feet and left the dining room with their elbows touching. They said nothing until they had returned to the curb.

"POL!" Amelia exploded. "Have you lost your ever-lovin' mind?"

A furious blush in Polly's cheeks had blotted out half her freckles. "I couldn't let him get the upper hand."

"Where are you going to scare up that kind of money?"

Polly slapped her hands to her sides, tears varnishing her eyes. Amelia slung an arm around her shoulders. "We'll figure it out. But for now, I think we've earned ourselves a drink."

"A double?"

"Doubles are for amateurs. We've made a deal with Harry you-know-what Cohn. Let's start with a triple and see where the evening takes us."

11

Sheets of yellow legal paper tiled the Selznick dining table. Irene clasped her hands. "I worry that we've overlooked an obvious element."

Amelia landed a hand on the sheet lying on the far left. "Script treatment, check."

True to her word, Virginia Van Upp had sent Irene a detailed outline, together with a note: "After I'd meshed together all my notes, the story poured out of me like I'm Miss Niagara Falls 1939!"

Amelia moved to the right. "Director, check." And then right again. "Possible star, check." She would have preferred her own name on that sheet of paper, but she was no competition for a glamorous up-and-comer.

"Did you really negotiate Cohn's exit from Mad Ox?" Irene asked.

Amelia nodded. "Polly was there, too." Earlier this morning, Polly had been poring over the want ads in the *Hollywood Citizen-News* for a second job, though Amelia wasn't sure when she'd have the time or energy for it. Mr. Selznick kept her busy six long days a week. "And Mrs. Cohn."

"Rose helped?"

"She reminded him how impressed he'd been when he'd met you at some beach party."

"The cookout at the Howard Hawkses." Irene straightened up. "Most men wait for you to stop talking so they can return to their favorite subject—themselves. I was surprised to find he wasn't so self-absorbed. Not that day, at any rate."

Amelia moved to the next sheet. "Courtesy of our Miss Maddox, a catalog of pretty vistas that might make for interesting locations." She touched the fifth sheet. "And a rough budget."

"Very rough. Emphasis on 'very.'"

"Was Myron much help?"

"He might've been had I caught him sober. Alas . . ." Irene made the tippling gesture with her hand.

Amelia picked up the sheaf of six pages filled with numbers and columns. Benji's roommate Noah, the accountant at Columbia, might have fathomed their meaning, but it was all cryptic mumbo jumbo to her. "You figured all this out yourself?"

"Holy smokes, no. That's the handiwork of Mrs. Darryl Zanuck. Evidently, she plays a more productive role in her husband's life than I ever would have guessed." Irene studied the papers in Amelia's hand a touch mournfully.

Amelia returned the budget to its place in the arrangement. "That's what we're trying to do here, isn't it? Get you more involved?"

Her despondency dissipated in two blinks. "I should open with the strongest card. What's your take, director or budget?"

"I suspect Dorothy's name will get his attention."

Irene studied the papers some more. "He doesn't love surprises."

"Perhaps a martini might grease the wheels. Heavy on the gin."

"He's more of a gimlet boy, but I like your thinking."

"IRENE!" Selznick's voice boomed from the front porch. "WHERE ARE YOU?"

"Eleven-thirty in the morning?" Irene twisted her wedding ring around her finger. She beckoned Amelia to follow her when Mr. Selznick barreled into the living room. "Jesus *Christ*! It's a *disaster*!"

His hurled briefcase bounced off the nearest chair and thumped onto the rug.

"What is, dear?" Irene had dropped her voice half an octave and spoke her words with measured calm.

He yanked at his necktie. "I had to get away and clear my—" He squinted at Amelia from behind his glasses. "Have we met?"

"This is Amelia Hartley," Irene said.

"You need privacy." Amelia headed for the door, cutting a wide path around him. "I can come back another time."

"No." The word flew out of Irene like a stray bullet. "Amelia is invaluable in a crisis."

No one calmed troubled waters like the self-possessed Irene Mayer Selznick, so Amelia didn't take her compliment lightly. Both Selznicks were staring at her now. *Say something!* "Three heads are better than two when facing calamity," Amelia said.

"Not in this case." He swung open the dining room door and herded his wife inside.

Amelia knew she shouldn't eavesdrop, but his "Not in this case" statement was too intriguing. She pressed her ear to the crack in the pocket doors.

"You won't believe what she's done," Selznick blustered. "I need her to be in tip-top form every time she steps in front of my cameras."

"We're talking about Vivien?"

"She's gotten herself knocked up."

Amelia clamped her hands over her mouth to smother involuntary noises. What was it Polly had said the night they went to see *Wuthering Heights*? Leigh and Olivier go at it constantly. Too bad Olivier didn't have access to Benji's endless supply of rubber thingies.

After a sobering pause, Irene asked, "On a scale of one to ten, how sure are we?"

"She's three weeks overdue and has—to cite her own words—'a special, certain feeling.'"

"These things happen, David."

"I know. *I know.*" Bitter frustration choked his voice. "But her? Now?"

"There are remedies. Do you want me to call Dr. A.?"

A silence fell over them until Selznick croaked out, "He's still around?"

"On Mulholland Drive, not far from Errol." She indulged in a light giggle. "Ironically."

"I want her to see him *today*. She's in my car—"

"You left her out on the driveway?" Irene's aplomb vanished.

"This disaster needs to be taken care of immed—"

"Honestly, David. Sometimes you can be an utter jackass!"

Amelia stepped away a split second before Irene wedged her face through the gap between the doors. "Heard all that?"

"You weren't exactly whispering," Amelia said.

"Would you please go outside and sit with Vivien? The poor creature must be in a dreadful state." She lowered her voice to a whisper. "Try to get more information than"—she canted her head to the room behind her—"Mr. Fly off the Handle."

Vivien Leigh was nearing the end of her cigarette in the rear of David Selznick's black Chrysler Imperial. "Let me guess. David is screaming bloody murder. Irene is talking him off the ledge, and has sent you to hold my hand." Vivien gestured to the empty seat next to her.

Aromas of leather and musty aftershave wrestled with perfumed cigarette smoke. Amelia cracked open a window as Vivien ground her cigarette into submission. The actress was paler than she'd been the night at the Four Star. And thinner, too. Was no one watching how Selznick's million-dollar gamble was wilting like a hothouse flower?

"I've caused an awful lot of trouble, haven't I?"

"I've heard you're also doing marvelous work. Proving naysayers like Louella and Hedda wrong is no mean feat."

"Heard from whom?" Vivien's deep blue eyes glinted with a desperate mix of hope and resignation.

"My roommate, Polly, works in Mr. Selznick's office. She—"

"Why, you're the lass I met in the ladies' room at that cinema on Wilshire."

"I'm flattered you remember."

"And your roommate, the girl with the freckles. Remind me of your names."

"She's Polly; I'm Amelia."

"I'm so very glad to hear somebody thinks I'm doing a good job. Mr. Fleming only talks to you if he feels you've ruined the scene. And by 'talks' I mean yells like you're a witless beast of burden."

"He's no George Cukor, then?"

"You ain't juss whistlin' Dixie, honey chile." She had dropped into her Scarlett accent, but only fleetingly. "Did I use that expression correctly?"

"You did." Amelia faced her more squarely. "Are you sure about your condition?"

Vivien played with the hem of her simple cotton dress, which bore a faded poppy pattern. "I'm not the most regular person when it comes to my 'visitor,' but I'm overdue—*and* I've been nauseous for the past seven mornings."

Oh my God! She really is pregnant! "I see."

"I was counting on him knowing an appropriate physician."

"That's more Irene's department."

She sighed a delicate sigh. "It always falls to the woman."

"Irene's the one you want in your corner. She's the most capable person I've ever met."

A warmth kindled in Amelia's chest as she lingered over the thought: Irene Selznick had sought *her* help with *Pretty Pennies*. Though the two of them had very little in common, somehow they were discovering how similar they were. At least, that's how Amelia felt. Maybe one of these days, she'd bring it up to Irene. But not while the most important actress in Hollywood was facing a career-breaking crisis.

Vivien patted down the hem she'd been futzing with. "So, under Mrs. Selznick's charge, I shalln't be shunted off to some back-alley butcher? A relief, I must say." She gave a cynical little giggle. "If only Victor Fleming were so easy to be rid of."

"That bad, huh?"

"This role requires—demands, really—an ungodly effort. The accent, the costumes, the dialogue. And then *this*." She prodded herself in the stomach.

"Have you told Mr. Olivier?"

"Heavens, no. He's in New York rehearsing *No Time for Comedy* opposite Katharine Cornell, so I wouldn't dream of distracting him."

Amelia couldn't imagine how acute a crisis would need to be before this slender, wan creature with the ethereal glow would place a person-to-person call. Maybe it did always fall to the woman, after all.

Irene strode out of the house with take-charge determination. She climbed behind the wheel of the Chrysler and tossed her purse, hat, and gloves onto the passenger seat. "Holding up?" she said, turning to the two women in the back.

Vivien nodded. "Thank you for sending this sweet angel to keep me preoccupied." She reached for a gold cigarette case with the letters V and L etched into an intricate monogram.

Irene reached back and placed her hand on Vivien's. "In a couple of hours, all this'll be over."

Vivien looked out the window. "What lovely delphiniums. The nuns used to grow them at the Convent of the Sacred Heart in Roehampton. God forbid they'd allow any of us ragamuffin ducklings to help care for them."

"Want me to come along?" Amelia asked.

Irene shook her head. "He's out back in the kitchen right now, fixing himself a peanut butter sandwich. I need you to go back inside and pack up all those papers, fast as you can. I'd hate for him to see them prematurely."

Amelia wished Vivien the best of luck, then climbed out of the car and hurried as quietly as she could through the house and into the dining room. But David was already there, towering over their checkerboard of legal notepaper, one hand holding a sandwich, the other perched on a hip. "What's all this?"

A jolt of panic the size of a grizzly bear slugged Amelia in the chest. Nothing, she wanted to scream. You must have a million more important things to do.

Their pitch hinged on Dorothy Arzner. Everything else was still wishful thinking in fancy dress. Amelia began to corral the pages into a messy pile. "Oh, Mr. Selznick, your time is far too valuable to fritter away on a game of 'What If?'"

He picked up Virginia's outline. "Start talking."

Polly had once described her boss as "a gentle giant with an occasionally explosive temper, who was otherwise the bark-worse-than-bite type." She had failed to mention what an intimidating presence he possessed. He dwarfed her like Moby Dick to her Captain Ahab—not even Captain Ahab. More like the cabin boy. She remembered Irene's vote of confidence. You've dealt with tough customers like this behind the lunch counter, she told herself. Though she could think of none of his stature, she could name a few who came close.

"Last month, Irene had a few of us over to run *Pretty Pennies*."

"Why?"

"Quite by chance, I met the picture's cinematographer. After everything I've heard about it, I was glad for an opportunity to see it. And afterwards, Irene said how overwhelmed she is by the stresses *Wind* is putting on you, and that for the sake of her sanity, she's adopted a 'for the duration' mentality."

Selznick drew back. "Her actual words?"

"Yes, sir."

"What else did she say?"

"She talked about how running a household wasn't enough. She is, after all, Louis B. Mayer's daughter."

Taking a huge bite out of the sandwich, Selznick pulled out a chair and sat down, gesturing for Amelia to do the same.

She sank into the chair opposite him. "Irene needs more than motherhood," she said, emboldened now. "Celluloid runs through her veins. You've got your hands full juggling three pictures, so we thought we'd do the legwork." She laid out the pages, one by one. "Dorothy Arzner will direct. Your brother and Irene have run the numbers, Miss Van Upp has written a treatment, and Polly's offering her house as Juniper's home."

Selznick ran a skillful eye over the layout. "Yes, but why this picture? Why now? Why Irene?"

Amelia had expected him to drill her on questions about the cost of lighting on location, sourcing costumes, what happens in the picture's climax. She could handle "what" questions, but these were "whys."

"The logistics of filmmaking," he said, crossing one leg over the other. "Financing, cameras, fixing dialogue, composing the score—they're obstacles to be overcome with patience and perseverance. But it takes perception and insight to address the bigger picture. So tell me, Miss Hartley: Why?"

The answer came to Amelia as though displayed on a billboard. She ticked off his successes: "*Wind, Rebecca, Anna Karenina, Star is Born*—what do they have in common? Women who command the screen. Sure, you've got your *Zenda* and your *Copperfield*, but it's your female characters who leave marks on souls. And Juniper is one of them." She spread her hands like she was envisioning a movie poster. "You know who else is a strong female lead?"

Amelia had meant for her question to be rhetorical, but Selznick replied, "I assume you're about to tell me."

"Your wife!" Amelia almost added, "*you big dummy*," but caught herself before she had single-handedly sunk the whole enterprise. "She is the most self-assured, self-contained, self-composed woman I've ever met. Plus, she's already done most of the spadework."

He stared at her, mute and motionless. She felt she had put forward the best case she could for someone who hadn't ever pitched a baseball, much less a movie. Dorothy Arzner was one thing, but this was a Hollywood titan, for crying out loud.

The seconds ticked by.

What was this, a staring contest? Amelia stared back.

Selznick drew in a sudden lungful of air. "All this came from Irene?"

"Yes, sir."

"Because she feels stifled." He deflated in his chair, motionless as a depressed sloth. "But principal photography on *Wind* will end in only a couple of months."

"Sure, but then there's editing, scoring, test audiences, premieres. As far as your wife is concerned, 'for the duration' means clear through to the end of the year, which may as well be nineteen *forty*-nine."

Selznick kept his eyes glued to the Persian rug. "My work has distracted me."

Amelia counted to five, then, "May I ask if you're inclined to give this project the go-ahead?"

"I need a reason to put a fourth movie into pre-production. However, I can't imagine what it might be."

Amelia selected the sheet with the word *CASTING* written across the top in Irene's pristine handwriting. "How do you feel about trying to get Rita Hayworth from Columbia?"

"I've had my eye on her for some time. I think she has potential. But then I found out how that miserable putz, Harry Cohn, is pressuring the Motion Picture Association to deny my request for special dispensation to allow me to use the word 'damn' in Rhett's famous exit line."

"Why? What's it to him?"

"Because he loves to mess with people for his own joyless pleasure. As far as Rita is concerned, he would make me pay through both nostrils."

"You could drive down her price with the right bargaining chip."

"For instance?"

She shouldn't have brought it up. It wasn't her place to blab such sensitive information. What was she thinking?

Irene. That's what she was thinking. And how desperate Irene was to have control over some facet of her life. Selznick's eyes were like steel rivets. There was no going back.

"The Bioff and Browne payoffs."

"What about them?"

"Are you forking over wads of cash, too?"

"That's confidential, Miss Hartley."

"Did you know Cohn isn't paying his fair share?"

"WHAT?"

"Not one thin dime."

"Son of a *bitch*!" He slapped a meaty hand onto the table. "Are the other studio heads aware?"

"Last I heard they were all in the dark."

A sly smile snuck its way onto his mouth. "That's a mighty handy nugget of information. But how could you know?"

"To tell you would be to break an all-female circle of trust."

"The wives are in on it."

"But haven't told their husbands."

A distant glaze settled over his eyes as the cogs of his mogul-mind stirred into motion. "I'll make Cohn see the free publicity *Pretty Pennies* will get for his budding star was worth way more than a few extra bucks in loan-out fees." He crammed the last of the sandwich into his mouth. "Allow me to walk you out."

They got to their feet. As he led her toward the entrance foyer, he said, "Your pitch was very good. Most persuasive."

"Thank you, sir. I have to confess though, it was completely off the cuff."

"All the more impressive. Tell me, what do you do for a living?"

Oh God, that question again. "I work at Schwab's."

"Near the Garden of Allah?" His response held no contempt or disappointment. "A lively job like that must keep you on your toes. Stamina, good with people, think quickly, juggle any number of orders. Tell me, Miss Hartley, what's your dog in this fight?"

"Pardon?"

"*Pretty Pennies.* Why do you care so much?"

Because I want to star in it sounded appallingly self-serving. "I have a personal connection with the film."

"How so?"

"The girl who played the original Juniper was best friends with my mother."

"Is that right?" He ran his thumb along the length of his dark orange silk necktie. "Might you be interested in the stand-in job?"

Where had that question come from? They were on the driveway now, standing next to Amelia's second-hand Ford. "Why me?"

"A stand-in needs stamina, can take direction, be flexible, ready to pivot at a moment's notice. There's more to it than merely standing around. The pay's pretty good, too." Amelia could only gape at him, open-mouthed, like a clown head in a circus fun fair. "Keep it in mind, at any rate. But for now, I've got a thousand phone calls to make. Good day." His shoes crunched on the gravel as he disappeared inside.

Amelia dropped behind her steering wheel.

Did David Selznick offer me a job? In the movies?

12

A few days later, Amelia was still no clearer about the maybe-maybe-not job offer. All she knew from Polly was that Selznick had not said, hinted, or dictated anything about *Pennies*. "And trust me," Polly said, squeezing her arm as they strolled up Vine Street, "that man can't sneeze without dictating a five-page memo."

Luddie hooked her other arm. "You would take the stand-in job, though, wouldn't you?"

"If he gave the go-ahead, and if he cast Rita, and if Cohn loaned her out—it's a lot of ifs, but yes, you bet I'd jump in feet first."

"Speaking of jobs"—Polly reached around Amelia and landed a gentle punch to Luddie's shoulder—"what a great job you do."

"I second that!" Amelia chimed in. What a revelation it had been to watch him crafting sound effects on the *Dick Tracy* stage, reaching for coconut shells, wire brushes, glass jars, and cap pistols while rarely lifting his eyes from the script.

"Thank you, ladies." Luddie bowed his head in appreciation. "I'm glad you came. A shame Benji couldn't, though."

"He's juggling *Million Dollar Legs* and prepping *Remember the Night*. I don't get to see him as much as I want."

Amelia was still smarting a little from Benji's reaction to the news. Or more to the point, his indifference. Neither enthusiastic nor negative, his response had been an oddly lukewarm, "That could be exciting."

"You really know what you're doing, don't you?" she said to Luddie.

"Our director, Mr. Grayson, seems to think so." He fiddled with his signet ring, as if suddenly noticing it needed polishing. "After tonight's show, he told me my boss is contemplating retirement."

"And if he does?"

"He talked about my being instrumental in our successful negotiations with Eliza's father."

"So an upside came out of that awkward situation?"

"I'd prefer to get promoted for my excellent work, but hey, a promotion is a promotion."

"We should go for a celebratory drink at the Brown Derby," Polly said. "And I mean a Sidecar, not a chocolate milk at their coffee shop."

"It's only a possibility—for the time being." They stopped at Selma Street and waited for the light to turn green. Ahead of them, the cream neon sign for the Brown Derby glowed in the night. "But getting back to this stand-in job. You'd take it, even though it would mean giving up your regular Schwab's paycheck for a project lasting a couple of months?"

"Sure, I would. These breaks don't come along every day. And if perchance"—the light changed and they stepped off the curb—"Miss Hayworth should stumble off a cliff or get stampeded by a herd of buffalo, there I'll be, ready, willing, and able to take the lead."

But Luddie didn't laugh the way Amelia expected him to. They arrived at the Satyr Book Shop, where he wanted to pick up a copy of Daphne du Maurier's *Rebecca* "to see what all the fuss is about." He rapped his ring against the window. At the center of the display, Faith's *Echoes of Elegance* sat perched on a glass brick. Behind it hung a three-foot reproduction of the cover, and above the poster, a handwritten sign: *THIS CONTROVERSIAL TOME IS*

FLYING OFF OUR SHELVES! "I've been thinking about Benji's indifferent response to your news."

Luddie always had a well-considered perspective on situations, but Amelia couldn't see what Faith's book had to do with Benji's apathy. "I'm all ears."

"I read an article in the *Examiner* about how those art history walking encyclopedias have been questioning her work, and how they're all men, all of them twice her age, none of them published."

"It came out the day before she finally let me see her."

"How was she?"

"All fired up. A gang of female art history teachers from liberal-arts colleges have banded together, giving lectures and publishing articles about the role of women in academia and their contributions to society, so she was brimming over with piss and vinegar."

"What about her husband, Gideon? How did he look?"

"Like a deer caught in headlights who couldn't tell me when he'd last had a decent night's sleep."

"Uh-huh." Luddie shifted from the window as the streetlights came on, chasing away the shadows of dusk. "Most men," he said, parceling out his words like cards in a high-stakes game, "aren't comfortable if their women outshine them."

"You think that's what's going on with Benji?"

"I don't know him very well," Luddie conceded, "but—"

"He's not like that." Amelia knew how snappish she'd sounded, and was immediately sorry she'd cut Luddie off. He was usually right about these things, but no, no, no. Not this time. Not Benji.

"Lookit," Luddie said, "I only wanted to point out that his reaction to this exciting stand-in news was underwhelming, and so there's probably a reason for it."

Deep down—deep, deep down—Amelia sensed she'd need to wrestle with Luddie's observations later, but an evening stroll up Vine Street wasn't the time or place. "Come on," she said, "let's go in and get your *Rebecca*."

The scent of thick paper and dusty cardboard filled the still air.

A few customers browsed here and there. The front-desk clerk directed them to the aisle marked *Fiction – Crime and Gothic.*

The eight copies of *Rebecca* were easy enough to locate. Polly plucked *The Postman Always Rings Twice* off the shelf and leafed through the pages, not taking in any of the text. "I've been thinking about your Mrs. Moguls."

"You have?" Luddie asked. "Why?"

"Maybe I should marry up."

"Polly Maddox!" Amelia thwacked her with a copy of *The Rains Came.* "Where on earth did that come from?"

"Got any other ideas where I'm going to find the twenty-five hundred I need to pay off Harry Cohn?"

Amelia eased *Postman* away from Polly's face. "Being around Irene Selznick has taught me that luxury is all window dressing. Okay, so her gowns are made to measure and she drives a shiny LaSalle, but is she happy? Satisfied? Fulfilled? If she were, she wouldn't be pushing so hard on *Pretty Pennies.* So enough with that marrying-up hogwash."

"Your dad told me Desmond Radcliffe has agreed to move to Catalina and take over Mad Ox, so this is now all very real. Two and a half grand." Polly fell against the oak shelving. "What was I thinking?"

"You were desperate to restore your father's name and keep his legacy alive," Luddie said.

"But it doesn't solve—"

"I hadn't finished." The words hung there, uncommonly sharp from this master of the art of conversation. But then that smooth and knowing smile of his appeared. "I might be able to help."

"You have twenty-five hundred dollars?"

"Of course not."

"But you know someone who does?"

"Conceivably."

"Who?"

"Let's call her a benefactress."

Amelia poked his tummy. "One of your deep-pocketed Mrs. Moguls who wouldn't miss the scratch?"

"Let me be clear," he told Polly. "It wouldn't be a gift. You'll have to repay it. But no interest and no deadline. Probably."

Polly threw her arms around Luddie. "It sounds too good to be true!"

"And also, no promises, so let's hold off on the thank-yous. However, trust me when I say she'll want no acknowledgment, no big thank-you. Not even a bunch of flowers. Okay?"

She released him from her embrace. "Yes, yes, a hundred times, yes!"

He joggled *Rebecca* in his hand. "I'm going to pay for this and skip the cocktail. Someday, I'll remember how much broadcast night takes out of me."

Amelia and Polly told him they might stick around and browse some more. They watched him until he had paid for his book and melted into the twilight along Vine Street.

"A *benefactress*?"

"Who has benefactresses?"

"If anybody would, it's Mister Ludlow Sinclair, Esquire."

"But which Mrs. Mogul?"

"Not Irene. She's always talking about the gobs of cash Mr. Selznick gambles away in his poker games."

"Outside Hollywood?"

"The Chandlers?"

"Huntingtons?"

"Dohenys?"

"Hancocks?"

Polly tucked *Postman* under her arm. "We need to respect his reasons for keeping her identity a secret—even though we're dying to know."

Amelia told Polly to go make her purchase. Watching Polly count out her change, she was happy that Polly had stumbled on a solution—albeit temporary—to her unwanted obligation. Her thoughts drifted to Luddie's comments. He might have a benefactress or two up his sleeve, but she was sure he was way off target when it came to Benji's tepid response. Gideon, yes. But Benji? No way, no how, and that was the end of any discussion.

13

Amelia opened her bank book.

Eighteen dollars and seventy-two cents.

She made deposits and withdrawals at least once a week. How could she not have noticed she was worth less than twenty bucks? Unable to stomach the pitiful sum any longer, she tucked the book into her skirt pocket.

The approaching lunch hour stirred memories of golden times: coffee splashing into cups, her voice rising above the clatter to corral kitchen boys, plates whisking away, sticky remnants of ice cream. Cheeky comebacks used to zip across the counter as the hours flew by, filling her pockets with nickels and dimes, and the occasional quarter.

How did she not realize she'd been pocketing her paycheck and living on her tips? What kind of dummy was she?

If only one of the waitresses would quit, marry, retire, anything so that she could dive back into that glorious tumult instead of decomposing behind the retail counter like a dead duck.

Amelia cast around. Starting Sunday, Mr. Schwab was taking a week's vacation. Perhaps if she could have a word with him before he left. But say what? "Please fire one of my co-workers so that I can have her job?"

A pair of women in their early forties loitered at the makeup shelves. Neither read labels nor sampled perfumes, but kept stealing glances at Amelia. Their clothes, a tasteful blend of unremarkable browns, dull yellows and dark burgundies, marked them as comfortably middle class. Not the shoplifting sort, and not Hollywood wealthy. Amelia decided they were executing some type of ruse.

"Ladies!" She raised her voice enough to be heard over the growing ruckus of the lunchtime rush. "Looking for anything in particular?"

"As a matter of fact." The one who reached Amelia's counter first had flat hair that hung like starched drapes to her shoulders. It was the hairdo of busy working women with neither time nor inclination to futz around with complicated coifs. "We're here looking for *you*!"

Well now, this was an unexpected twist—and welcome to a girl feeling more and more anonymous, stuck selling peppermint Lifesavers and making change for the payphones. "Me?"

"You're Amelia Hartley, aren't you?"

"I am, but how—"

"Thelma Perry." The woman extended her hand for Amelia to shake. "I'm in the casting department of Selznick International. And this"—she gestured toward her colleague — "is Gertie Livermore."

Were they here about that stand-in job?

"How can I help you?"

"Well, you see, Amelia—may I call you Amelia?"

If you're from Casting, you can call me Buttercup Snodgrass. "Of course."

"Yesterday morning, my boss, Fred Schuessler, and I were meeting with Mr. Selznick about *Intermezzo* and *Rebecca*, and he started talking about a project I had assumed he'd abandoned."

Did this mean *Pretty Pennies* was going ahead? "The one set on Catalina?"

"Yes. He has approached Harry Cohn about getting Rita

Hayworth for the lead. The sticking point came down to Mr. Selznick insisting Rita do a screen test."

"Did they manage to unstick it?"

"Rita Hayworth is coming in later this week."

Amelia laid her hands on the cool glass countertop. It was one thing for David Selznick to mention a job in his living room; it was another to be talking to someone from Casting. "She is?"

"My counterpart at Columbia told me Rita is terribly nervous about it because she's keen to ace the screen test, which is where you come in."

A tangle of excitement lodged in Amelia's throat. "I do?"

"Mr. Selznick feels that seeing as how you and Rita are about the same age and you're both redheads, having you there would help calm her nerves. You'd be feeding her lines, giving her someone to play off."

The woman hadn't mentioned Irene or Polly. Had Mr. Selznick plowed ahead on *Pretty Pennies* without telling either of them? Was he even aware that his Girl Friday was roommates with Amelia? "When would this screen test take place?"

"On Thursday. Rita will arrive between eleven and noon, so we'll need you there at ten."

"How come so early?"

"We want you to be in a room full of redheads when she walks in."

This tactic didn't sound like Selznick's style. "To intimidate her?"

"As an incentive to ensure Rita is on her game."

Because sitting next door are twenty girls hoping she screws up. This business about the look-alikes sounded cold-hearted.

"We'd pay you for your time," Thelma said. "Twenty-five dollars for what should be around two hours' work."

Balking at calculated intimidation was one thing, but this was a chance to more than double her meager funds. Amelia could almost feel her bank book throb in her pocket.

* * *

Polly didn't ask Amelia if she was nervous until they reached the line of cars along Washington Boulevard waiting to enter the studio.

"Nah," Amelia said. "At best, the camera will catch my shoulder or ear. Nothing to be nervous about."

Benji's subdued response hadn't brightened when she'd told him about Thelma and Gertie's visit to Schwab's, but she wasn't about to let his inertia get her down. Not when someone from a real-life studio casting department had asked her to come in for a screen test. Who cared that it wasn't hers? The mere possibility of being in a major motion picture had set her nerves tingling.

"It's a good thing you're unruffled," Polly continued, "because you'll be here on a day when I suspect tensions will be high."

"Why? Who else is visiting? Roosevelt?"

As they approached the security gate, Polly described the day's ambitious shoot: Scarlett O'Hara at the Atlanta railway station surrounded by fallen Confederate soldiers. The scene would culminate in a sweeping crane shot, rising ninety feet to reveal hundreds of extras mixed with every store mannequin the props guys could gather from fifty miles around.

"I'm still astounded they're going to all that trouble for one scene," Amelia said.

"It'll be the one everybody from Louella Parsons to room-service waiters will talk about." Polly traced the crease deepening between her brows, a new souvenir from months of slaving over her Remington. "Should we live so long."

They stopped first at Polly's office to double-check the travel arrangements for Mr. Selznick's East Coast agent, who was traveling all the way to Sweden to chaperone the actress Selznick had cast in *Intermezzo*. With Polly preoccupied, Amelia smiled at a pale-skinned secretary with a Gibson Girl hairdo: an upswept, voluminous pompadour with a single sausage curl resting on one shoulder. "You're Hazel, right?"

"I am. And you must be Amelia." She retrieved a sheet of

paper from her out-tray. "You should read this before you head over to Casting."

Another of Selznick's interminable memos? Ugh. But the Gibson Girl's sly delivery sparked Amelia's curiosity. It started as Polly had described—until the fourth paragraph. In the event that Selznick approved Miss Hayworth's screen test and struck a deal with Cohn, he would pay her stand-in a weekly salary of—Amelia's hand landed on Hazel's desk with a thump, the memo still gripped between her fingers. "Kind of high, isn't it?"

Hazel nodded. "More than what Vivien Leigh's stand-in is getting."

Seventy-five dollars a week was more than three times what she earned at Schwab's. If the shoot lasted six weeks, that meant four months' salary. It could well prove to be her lucky break—*and* it would hoist her out of her financial hole.

She wasn't sure what Selznick expected her to do for seventy-five clams, but as long as it wasn't illegal or immoral, she'd be happy to oblige.

* * *

Polly walked Amelia down the corridor decorated with posters of Selznick's productions all the way back to an early Paramount picture, *Street of Chance*, which sounded like every street in Hollywood. "Was that a memo Hazel showed you while I was on the phone?"

When Amelia told her about the stupefying salary, Polly halted in front of *King Kong*. "Per week?" She stood lost in thought for a moment, her eyes tracing the outline of the Empire State building. "He must have his reasons."

"Would Irene know?"

"Yes, but not today." Polly set off for the double doors that led outside. "She blew up at Mr. Selznick when I told her about Thelma and Gertie paying you a visit."

"Is that why I haven't heard from her?" Amelia had telephoned soon after Thelma and Gertie had left, but Irene hadn't returned her call. Or the next one. Or the one after that.

"She asked me to apologize for her rudeness," Polly assured her. "She's mad at Mr. Selznick for leaving her out of the loop. His excuse was being all caught up in filming the big railway station scene, but she thinks his gambling was the real culprit."

They stepped out into sunshine dappled by a young oak.

"Haven't they made up yet?" Amelia asked.

"He's moving ahead with the picture, but only if he can find the right actress."

"Hence Rita Hayworth?"

"I have my doubts." Polly glanced over her shoulder at the closed office doors. "I suspect the test is mostly about stringing Harry Cohn along, thinking that he's going to get a big, fat loan-out fee." Amelia fought against the disappointment pressing down on her. All of this was little more than a game? "Irene hates Cohn as much as the rest of us, so the idea tickled her no end. And *that's* when they made up."

They landed on the front steps of Casting. "I truly wanted this stand-in job." Amelia's words tumbled out like a confession.

Polly stared at her, wide-eyed at the impact of her behind-the-scenes disclosure. "Mr. Selznick and Cohn will tear into each other like they're the Hatfields and the McCoys until they come to terms. And when everything's back on track, you'll get it."

"And not because of that eye-watering paycheck."

"You want to be a part of something." Polly placed her palms on Amelia's shoulders. "A moment you can look back on and say, 'I was there.'"

"See? You get it."

"I do."

"I'm not convinced Benji does."

"He'll come around." Polly withdrew her hands. "Come on, it's nearly ten. But remember: I want to hear everything at dinner tonight."

. . .

Amelia stepped into a large waiting room with wooden benches along each wall and down the center. Twenty-nine girls sat in silence, each with hair that caught the light like a sunset spectrum—rich auburn, deep burgundy, fiery copper. Usually the only redhead in any room, Amelia felt her breath catch at finding herself adrift in this crimson sea.

If the goal was to galvanize Rita Hayworth into doing her best, six girls could have done the job. Thirty was out-and-out bullying.

It also meant that she was no shoo-in. Any one of these girls could do what she was about to do.

A girl with a Louise Brooks bob shifted over. From a distance, her hair had gleamed chestnut red, but up close, Amelia detected the telltale harshness of henna. Not bad, but as a natural redhead, she knew it wasn't right for the girl. Amelia sat down. "Thanks for making room."

"We couldn't have you standing around like a scarecrow," the henna rinse said.

Although the hair color didn't suit her, the bob did. Brushing the tip of her earlobes, it framed this girl's enviably sharp jawline. And oh my, look at that skin. Not a blemish in sight. Even in a town filled with pretty faces, this girl was a standout. She was also familiar. Very familiar. Ah, yes. Of course.

"Della, isn't it?"

The Louise Brooks bob bounced as she jerked back in surprise. "Have we met?"

Amelia hadn't seen the girl who Harry Cohn had wanted to put in a family way since that afternoon three months ago when she, Polly, Luddie and all the Mrs. Moguls had ambushed Cohn at the Beverly Hills Hotel.

She was about to answer when Rita Hayworth glided through the doors. Dark cherry curls cascaded past her shoulders, matching her nails, shoes, belt, and handbag. Her dark orange organza skirt swirled at her knees, ready for a dance number to break out at any moment.

Sweet Jesus, Amelia thought, Juniper is a small-town girl. Who dressed Rita like she was here to sink her hands into the cement outside Grauman's Chinese?

Rita stopped two steps into the room, her face bleak with horror. I know how you feel, Amelia wanted to tell her. I hadn't expected any competition, either.

"Miss Hayworth!" Thelma stood in a doorway recessed into the opposite wall. "And right on time!"

Amelia waited until after Thelma had closed the door before she turned back to Della. "I was with Rose Cohn the day you approached her at the Beverly Hills Hotel."

Della's shoulders curved inward, like she was trying to make herself smaller. "I wish I could forget it ever happened."

"I thought you were gutsy."

She turned her head enough to see Amelia out of the corner of her eye. "I didn't come across like some hard-bitten tramp out for revenge?"

"More like a girl who'd had her fill of being pushed around."

"Thank you for saying that."

"How did you come to be here?" Amelia asked.

"A pal of mine sleeps with one of the RKO casting guys, so she gets all the inside job tips. When she couldn't make it, I used her name at the gate." Della surveyed the room. "This cattle call sure is one for the books."

Amelia whispered, "It's not real."

"What's all this, then?" Della circled the air with a raised finger. "Pure theater?"

"That girl who came through just now? She's a rising star at Columbia. Harry Cohn has nothing lined up for her, so he's looking to make a bundle on a loan-out."

"Well, of all the crummy stunts." She pulled a rumpled handkerchief from her purse and used it to blot the corners of her eyes. "I haven't worked in a while. My funds are running low."

"Mine too," Amelia said. "My bank balance is in the black, but hanging on by its fingernails." It felt cruel to admit that her situation would soon be twenty-five smackers further from the red.

"This was my last-ditch effort to . . ." Della brushed the air with dispirited fingers. "I guess it's back to slinging hash again."

A week ago, Amelia would have given anything to be standing behind the lunch counter. "Could be worse."

"It's like admitting defeat."

"I'm a hash-slinger, myself."

Remorse colored Della's face. "I'm sorry. I didn't mean—"

"It's time I moved on, too. But as far as waitress jobs are concerned, there are worse places than Schwab's Pharmacy."

"On Sunset? Gosh, that must be fun."

"The more you rib the customers, the bigger the tip you get. I used to have this one regular, Joseph. He sometimes tipped me a whole buck—"

"Amelia?" Thelma was wading through the pool of redheads.

She feigned a jolt of surprise and shot to her feet. "Here!"

She bid a hasty goodbye to Della and trotted after Thelma, who led her into a sun-bright room twice the size of the waiting area. Crew swarmed around cameras, chairs, and mirrors. A backdrop dominated the far wall: a cloud-dappled sky, storm-dark rocks, and a few slivers of light on surging whitecaps. "Thanks for coming in."

Amelia jacked a thumb behind her. "Did it work?"

"What's that?"

"Collecting a gaggle of redheads to spur Rita to do her best."

Thelma pinched the bridge of her nose. "I thought we'd get maybe half a dozen. Who knew we employed so many redheads?"

"You don't. Word got out. They think it's a genuine cattle call."

"Dang it! I'll have to go out there and—" Her hand slashed the air in frustration. "I hate lying to people like that." With a quick turn, she called, "Rita, darling, are you ready?"

"I'm not positive that 'ready' is the right term." The Rita Hayworth who emerged from behind a three-part changing screen was not the same Rita Hayworth who had sashayed through the front door.

No makeup.

No false eyelashes.

No lipstick.

No heels.

A plain white smock covered her organza, and someone had tossed her coif as though she'd battled a windstorm.

All the de-emphasizing in the world couldn't hide the radiance of her smile, however. "I could've stayed in bed two extra hours this morning."

Amelia found herself staring. Stripped of her razzmatazz, Rita was the image of Amelia's mother at that age, when Lois and her Hollywood High friend Bernice had filmed the original *Pretty Pennies*.

Thelma introduced Rita and Amelia to Selznick's head of casting, Fred Schuessler, who told them with neither explanation nor apology that they wouldn't be working off a script today. "I want you to improvise the scene."

Amelia nodded as she took a half-step back. *At least Rita's been in a few movies. I'm greener than a lima bean.* "You don't want us to prattle on about nothing, do you?"

"Lord have mercy, no. Rita, you're Juniper, a young woman from a sheltered background who loves her grandmother. Amelia, you're the grandmother who is deathly ill, but wants Juniper to explore life beyond the island. Juniper knows Granny's right, but refuses to leave."

He positioned Rita fifteen feet in front of a motion picture camera with the painted seascape at her back. He then guided Amelia to a stripe of white chalk drawn on the floor and told her to stand with the tips of her shoes touching the line.

Four blinding lights snapped on without warning. As Amelia shielded her eyes, she thought of Polly's story about the girl who'd tested for Scarlett but had ended up reading opposite Hattie McDaniel before her dress caught fire. Amelia might not ignite into flames, but plenty of other disasters lurked in wait.

"And action!"

He hadn't told them whose line opened the scene. Amelia blurted out the first word that came into her head. "Juniper!"

Rita stared back, lips parted, eyes wild with fear, not a peep coming out of her. Well, whaddaya know—Harry Cohn's prized starlet was terrified, too. The revelation shook Amelia straight. Rita was the star here, and Rita needed her.

"There's nothing for you here. And what's more, they're making great strides with a cure. Why, any day now, I expect that doctor to come striding in, crying out 'Eureka!'"

Fire sparked in Rita's eyes. "No, Grandma! I'm not leaving the most precious person in the world alone." *Good God, is she tearing up?* "I don't care if Dr. Schuessler himself climbs through that window with his miracle pills." *Dropping the casting director's name—well played.* "My place is right here, by your side, until you're well."

Stripping Rita of her artifice had left her without crutches. Neither her beauty, nor her body, nor a romantic musical score swelling in the background, nor captivating close-ups remained to support her. Schuessler had forced her to act—possibly for the very first time.

"Don't be like your sister, Faith." Amelia pitched her voice low, like a carnival fortune-teller. "All them plans she had. All them dreams. She didn't have the guts to break free, and look at her now. A downtrodden drudge like one of those zombies you see in horror movies."

Rita threw back her head, releasing a wail that split the difference between distress signal and jubilant roar. She followed it with a fervent monologue about seizing life's fruits while honoring her kin, every word charged with passion and doubt, determination and loyalty.

But Amelia's thoughts drifted to her sister, Faith, whose name had popped into her head out of nowhere. Between the two of them, who was the one trapped on a self-made island? Who risked becoming a Schwab's zombie weighed down with unrealized dreams? All those redheads waited outside, but *she* stood here, toes against the chalk line, under the spotlight, with Selznick's casting director watching.

"And cut."

Hold up. It was over? *Already*?

"Thank you, ladies."

Twenty-nine pairs of eyes looked up expectantly when Amelia and Rita exited, then dropped away when Thelma told them, "That'll be all for today." Della pushed a scrap of paper into Amelia's hand. "My boarding house telephone number in case an opening comes up at Schwab's."

Rita waited until the last of them had filed from the room. "I don't want to jinx us, but I think we did okay."

"Better than okay," Amelia told her.

"I'm so relieved to hear it. Now that *Only Angels Have Wings* has finished shooting, I'd love the opportunity to work at the Selznick studios. It'd be a dream come true."

"Especially working for a female director," Amelia said.

"Female?"

"Dorothy Arzner is set to direct."

Rita's eyes widened. "I want the role even more now!"

"Ladies," Thelma joined them. "Mr. Schuessler and I are pleased you scraped all that gunk off your face, Miss Hayworth. It gave the real you a chance to shine. Of course, Mr. Selznick has to view the screen test, then he and Mr. Cohn will have to reach an agreement." After telling Rita she was free to go, Thelma waited for the door to close before turning to Amelia. "Same goes for you, Miss Hartley. You weren't on camera, but you gave it your all. We were both impressed."

"Thank you!" The thrill of the past half-hour was fading now, leaving Amelia wearier than she had counted on. "It was fascinating to have a front-row seat when someone lights up."

Thelma smiled the wry smile of a woman who'd seen a hundred nobodies become somebodies. "If Rita gets the role, we would love for you to be her stand-in, as well as her body double for diving and swimming scenes."

Amelia gripped the back of the chair behind her. "You would?" She hated how her voice cracked on the second word. How horrifyingly unprofessional!

"Your contract would run for the length of the shoot, and the pay is seventy-five per week."

Hearing the figure out loud gave her pause. As everybody in this town knew, every lunch demanded its price. "That salary is surprisingly generous."

Thelma responded with a neutral "Mmmm."

"Will I be expected to do . . . anything else?"

The shock that rolled across Thelma's face surprised Amelia. As a woman who worked in Casting at a significant Hollywood studio, Thelma might not have used the casting couch, but she must have had to turn a blind eye. "No, my sweet girl. Mr. Selznick is a gentleman producer."

Amelia wasn't so sure about that. Though clumsy as a hippo on a picket fence, Selznick had made a pass at Polly on her first day—albeit tepid. "I'm relieved to hear it."

"Now, on to other matters. Naturally, we'll prepare a contract and send it to your agent."

Amelia gouged her fingernails into her palms until they left half-moons. *They think I've got an agent, like I'm Bette Davis or Norma Shearer.* "I don't have one."

"Yes, you do," Thelma responded breezily. "Myron Selznick."

A cold jolt shot through Amelia's chest, freezing her in place while her thoughts scattered like startled birds. David Selznick's brother was Hollywood's most powerful talent agent, who counted some of Hollywood's biggest names among his clients: Vivien Leigh, Lawrence Olivier, not to mention Hepburn, Lombard, and Cukor.

"Are you sure?"

"Mr. Selznick's secretary, Marcella, told me that Mr. Selznick prevailed on his brother to take you on."

"Makes me wonder how hard he had to prevail."

"Myron is a big fan of the idea of remaking his father's first picture, so when David Selznick offers you a contract for seventy-five a week, you ask Myron, 'Where do I sign?' One more thing before you go. Not afraid of open water, are you?"

"Not in the least."

Warmth crept into Thelma's welcoming smile. "You know your way out?"

The disappointed redheads had dispersed, leaving Amelia alone with her thoughts as she strolled through the studio. Mr. Schwab might prefer not to lose her, but surely he'd delight in this news. This was exactly the adventure she craved. Not as permanent as Schwab's, perhaps, but anything beat slowly dying behind that retail counter.

But what was that question about being afraid of open water? She was a native who'd grown up on Santa Monica beach. What was there to be afraid of?

14

A week and a half later, Amelia was back on the Selznick lot. In the shade of the studio's administration building, she looked across Ince Boulevard at the oil pumps behind a club called The 90-90. "Do you think they'll be impressed?"

"With what? Our behind-the-scenes tour?" Polly rubbed her fingers on one of the mint bushes Mr. Selznick had asked the studio greensman to plant for celebratory mint juleps when *Gone with the Wind* opened. "Or your stand-in job?"

"Either."

"Do you need them to be?"

"No, but it'd be nice."

"Do you feel like you're in competition with Faith?"

"I never used to."

Polly held the sprig of fresh mint under Amelia's nose for her to smell. "Maybe don't bring up the stand-in job. After all, you haven't signed the contract yet."

Nor had Polly typed any memos about Rita Hayworth or Harry Cohn. Projects collapsed daily in Hollywood. By next week, *Pretty Pennies* might end up a stiff in the morgue, another toe-tagged Tinseltown casualty.

Where were all those mirrors the studios scattered about for stars? Amelia needed to check her lipstick and powder her face. The suit she'd borrowed from Polly hugged her curves, but the suit's baby-pink hue better suited her friend's fairer complexion.

She caught sight of a familiar figure hurrying toward them from the parking lot where her father's maroon Buick should be pulling in any minute now. Luddie's glossy black hair with its meticulous side part was hard to mistake. They stepped to the edge of the patio. "What on God's green earth are you doing here?"

"I was knocking at your apartment when one of your neighbors told me you were both at the studio."

"What's happened?" Amelia asked.

"Tomorrow morning, I'm taking Leo McCarey's wife to a Rotary International dinner dance at the Arrowhead Springs Hotel and won't be back till Wednesday, so I thought I'd bring you this." Luddie laid a cashier's check on his palms and bowed like a samurai. "From my benefactress."

Polly squeezed her eyes shut. "Six months of worrying and fretting. You'd think I'd be aware of how much all this has been weighing on me."

Amelia and Luddie enveloped her in a three-pal huddle. "The important thing is," he whispered, "you'll soon be done with Cohn. Free and clear. Forever."

Amelia added, "Desmond will move to Catalina and start setting everything up."

"The sooner Mad Ox can get back in business—"

"—the sooner you reimburse my benefactress—"

"—by nineteen sixty-five. Or nineteen eighty-three at the absolute latest."

Amelia's joke cracked Polly's fragile shell. "If I'm still paying off this debt when I'm seventy, drop me into that school of sharks off Starlight Beach."

"Is this a private pow-wow, or can anyone join in?" Amelia's father stood at the head of the path, her mother beside him.

Amelia broke away from Polly and Luddie. "Just a little celebration."

Faith and her husband, Gideon, brought up the rear without baby Chester in tow, nor—Amelia breathed a furtive sigh of relief —Samuel and Sebastian to wreak havoc.

"Celebrating what?" Judd asked.

When Polly told him that she had all her Mad Ox money together, his eyebrows arched and his head tilted. Amelia knew how to read that look: *Pop is delighted.* "That's cause for dual celebrations," he said.

"Dual?" Amelia asked.

Faith raised her hand. "My book is getting a second printing."

"And three times bigger," Gideon added, though not with the oomph Amelia expected.

"Exciting." Or was it? Her sister's usual rosy complexion had taken on a bloodless pallor, as though she hadn't slept since Chester's arrival. "Last I heard, you were dealing with a backlash from—what paper was it?"

"Stupid, snooty, supercilious *Boston Globe*. Since then, detractors and defenders have been slugging it out in letters to the editor all over the country."

"Faith is being feted as a public speaker at women's clubs and auxiliaries, museums and universities."

"Including yours?" Amelia asked Gideon.

He was an English and French literature professor at UCLA. Well-respected in his field, but strictly hidebound, stiff-necked, and too high-falutin' for Amelia's tastes. She had learned to avoid bringing up any of his "Supreme Seven": Shakespeare, Voltaire, Molière, Proust, Joyce, Fitzgerald, and Kafka. "The dean of the Fine Arts department is currently drafting an invitation."

Amelia would have thought the guy would be beaming at his wife's success, but he had delivered this news with the same lethargy he'd displayed when he'd spoken about Faith's second printing. And was that an irritated eye roll from Faith when she thought nobody was looking? Amelia cast a quick glance at Luddie, who shot back the briefest eyebrow-raise. *Like I said: Most men aren't comfortable if their woman outshines them.*

Whatever was going on, a behind-the-scenes studio tour

should provide a welcome distraction. Amelia brightened, clapping her hands. "Let's begin with Scarlett and Rhett's mansion."

* * *

Blood-red carpet swept up twenty-five imposing steps, flanked by gilt candelabras standing guard at top and bottom. The hand-carved banister curved to the second-floor landing, where a towering stained-glass window bathed everything in colored light.

Earlier that morning Polly had suggested they start the tour here because it was arguably the most sumptuous set in the movie. "This six-hundred-pound chandelier took three weeks to create."

Judd looked preoccupied.

Faith looked unenthusiastic.

Gideon looked bored.

"Yes," Luddie said, "but how many cleaning women does it take to dust the thing?"

Lois smiled. It wasn't much, but it kindled a flicker of hope in Amelia. "I do like that." Lois ran her hand across the ivy-green flocked wallpaper with a floral design arranged in diamond formation.

"The art department designed it especially for this set."

Gideon pouted. "A tad gaudy, isn't it?"

Judd grunted. "It's how I imagine the insides of brothels."

"In the eighteen-sixties, perhaps." Amelia's remark met with more silence. Oh, brother. Tough crowd.

"Is this the staircase where Scarlett falls down?" Lois asked. "I hope they teach that Vivien Leigh girl how to take a spill. Imagine if she broke her neck!"

"Hey, Polly," Judd said, "now that we've got the Mad Ox funds, how about you and me get together and hash out all the details?"

"Sure. And yes, Lois, this is where Scarlett takes her fateful fall."

Amelia guided them toward the exit. If such opulence conjured only thoughts of brothels, perhaps they'd appreciate a more relatable setting.

They lined up along the southern boundary of the slab.

"It's concrete," Gideon said.

"Yes, but smooth as glass," Amelia said.

"Okay, so it's level concrete. What am I missing?"

"Have you read the book?" Amelia wanted to kick herself for asking such an absurd question.

"*Gone with the Wind* is lowbrow pablum for the masses."

Amelia swung around to her mother and sister. "There's a scene when Scarlett wanders out of a railway station and into a field of dead and dying soldiers."

"Extras," Faith corrected her.

Amelia narrowed her focus on Lois. "They needed to reach ninety feet, but pull back on silky smooth ground so that the camera didn't wobble. It took a team of engineers to build this."

"Sounds like a lot of work," was all Lois could say.

"Hey, Gideon," Polly said, "you teach F. Scott Fitzgerald, don't you?" Amelia twisted toward her. *What did I warn you about bringing up the Supreme Seven?* "Mr. Selznick employed him as a screenwriter." Gideon blinked three times in rapid succession. He didn't need to know that Fitzgerald's stint on *Wind* had lasted two weeks and none of his efforts was likely to end up on the screen. "If the movie contains some Fitzgerald flourishes, maybe it won't be all dreck?"

"Perhaps not."

Amelia seized on this tiny concession like a *Lusitania* passenger clutching at driftwood, grateful for Polly's caution not to bring up the stand-in job prematurely. It was a good thing she wasn't depending on this tour to impress her family, but gee willikers, had it been too much to expect a little more enthusiasm than this?

However, one glimmer of hope remained: Tara.

Amelia turned from the ramp and set off due west with her

little entourage until they were skirting the edge of a disordered cluster of scaffolds rising from a shallow pit.

"What's this going to be?" Lois asked.

"Manderley," Polly said. "Maxim de Winter's estate in *Rebecca*."

"'Last night, I dreamt I went to Manderley again.'" Gideon had dropped his voice half an octave. God, what a ham. "One of the better opening lines to a popular novel." Somehow, he'd made the word 'popular' sound like a substitute for 'smutty.'

"Did you know it's an example of iambic hexameter?"

Everyone stared at Luddie. *Iambic hexawhat?*

Gideon mouthed the line again. "By jingo, you're right. I shall bring that up with my students."

Amelia couldn't guess what an iambic hexameter was, but somehow Luddie had achieved the near-impossible: winning over Gideon.

Past nascent Manderley stood Tara, three hundred feet away, its four columns blazing in the sun. *If this doesn't perk them up, nothing will.* "From Manderley to Tara!"

"This is how I pictured it," Lois said breathlessly.

"Me too," Faith said.

"You read *Gone with the Wind*?" Gideon sounded like he'd swallowed a mouthful of vinegar.

"I'm in that damned house with a howling, colicky baby," Faith shot back. "Sometimes I need a break from ear-splitting screams and Renaissance Florentine friezes of the late fourteen hundreds."

Two huge arc lights switched on, bathing Tara's front porch in a bright, warm glow.

"The filming schedule said *near* Tara," Polly murmured. "Not *at*."

I can't even show them Tara? Amelia wanted to tear a fistful of hair out by its roots.

"Where there's lights, there's filming." Polly's whispering held a thoughtful note. "And where there's filming, there's Vivien."

A frisson of excitement zig-zagged across Amelia's chest. "What are our chances?"

"She might be glad for the distraction in between takes. And remember, you had that pleasant interaction with her the day of the pregnancy scare."

To everybody's relief, Irene's doctor had declared Vivien wasn't in the family way. To be doubly sure, he'd taken a urine sample and told her to pray for the rabbit. Fortunately—especially for the rabbit—her monthly had arrived the following day.

This new and improved plan put a spring in Amelia's step as she set off again. "Tara grows more impressive the closer you get to it."

"I thought it'd look—I dunno." Faith snorted. "Prettier?"

Amelia remembered it draped in lush vines and flowers, its fresh paint job blindingly white, roof tiles gleaming in the California sun. All fake, yes, but enchanting. Now the paint peeled from every column, the vines had withered to brown kindling, and half the windows gaped empty or broken.

"How come it looks so derelict?" Judd asked.

"They must have moved on to the post-war scenes," Polly explained, "after Scarlett returns to Tara to find the plantation"—she gestured toward the set—"in ruins."

"I don't care what shape it's in," Lois proclaimed. "To see Tara in any condition is a thrill. And it's how I imagined it to look after the war."

Off to the right, Vivien paced a dusty patch of ground. Her raggedy dress, a faded paisley with frayed, puffy sleeves, fell to her mud-caked ankles in tatters. Her hair hung in loose shreds, as though she hadn't seen a brush in weeks. Hardly the flirty Southern belle Amelia had been hoping for.

But it was still Vivien Leigh.

As Amelia drew closer, she could hear the actress going over lines about God being her witness and going hungry.

She paced back and forth, emphasizing different words with each successive pass. God. Witness. Never. She gripped a turnip in her hand and lifted it to accentuate each alternative. Hungry. Lie. Steal. Kill.

Sitting in the Selznicks' driveway, the actress had been a fragile butterfly, exhausted and overwhelmed. But this Vivien, turnip clenched in hand, her face steely with determination, blazed like wildfire.

Amelia only had to take half a dozen more steps and Vivien would see her, but her feet remained mired in the dirt. I oughtn't interrupt her when she's working so hard. She'd have every right to brain me with her turnip, and I wouldn't blame her.

Lois was the only one talking as they trudged back to the parking lot. "Naturally, meeting Vivien Leigh herself would have been delightful, but she was obviously preoccupied with her upcoming scene. I wouldn't forgive myself if I had ruined her concentration before a big scene. So, thank you, dear. This has been marvelous."

Polly's "Do you need them to be impressed?" still weighed heavily. Anyone with half a brain knew that Amelia Hartley was nobody's idea of a shrinking violet, but had Polly hit on a blind spot Amelia hadn't ever considered? She'd have to think about that some other time. She glanced over her shoulder. Judd was trailing behind. Faith and Gideon lagged even further back, trading barbed whispers.

"Hey, Lois, before I forget." Polly turned around. "I was speaking with Irene Selznick earlier this morning. She paid a private eye to track down your old pal, Bernice."

Lois stepped forward. "And?"

"He traced her as far as Chicago a number of years ago, but I'm afraid the trail went cold."

Lois attempted a tremulous smile. "Please thank Mrs. Selznick for her efforts."

If only Irene's PI had come through with the goods. What a glorious extra-innings grand slam it could have been.

Amelia waved as the Buick exited the lot, but it was a waste of time. Nobody was waving back.

"Are they usually that dead?" Luddie asked. Amelia laughed. He wasn't wrong. All four of them had been drearier than a June-gloom day in Santa Monica. "And do your sister and her husband usually snap at each other like alley cats?"

Polly slung a loose arm around Amelia's shoulders. "Maybe Perfect Faith isn't so perfect, after all."

"What time do you get off work?" Luddie asked Polly.

They were now standing in the double doors that led into the executive building. She checked her watch. "If I can get away before Mr. Selznick returns from shooting, maybe fifteen minutes."

"How about a drive up along Mulholland?"

Mulholland Drive was a twisting road along the spine of the Hollywood Hills. "I dunno, Luddie," Amelia replied. "It's been a tough afternoon and Mulholland is miles away."

"Yes, true, but"—he held up a hear-me-out finger—"sometimes we need to look down on this town instead of letting it look down on us."

Amelia mulled over his proposal and found no flaw in his logic. "You're right. As usual. Lead on, Macduff."

15

With Benji so busy working on two pictures at once, Amelia hadn't minded taking the evening shift. Did she love watching Matilda and the others raking in those dinner-time tips? No siree, but the retail section kept her occupied, but not so run off her feet that she'd stagger home dead on her feet.

Now that *Million Dollar Legs* was in the can, and *Remember the Night* deep in pre-production, Benji had some spare time. Not much, and more would have been better, but if the best he could manage was a flying visit at work, she'd take it.

They hadn't seen each other since before her experience in Rita Hayworth's screen test. Their snatched moments on the telephone were never near enough time to tell him about that.

He barreled through the door hatless, in shirtsleeves, and with the tie she'd bought him for his birthday askew. "A taxi on Gower collided with a truck that was carrying five hundred pullets. And real squawkers, they were."

"You stopped to help the farmer round up his chickens, didn't you?"

"You've never seen anyone so grateful." He plucked a Bavarian chocolate bar out of a box on the counter and waved it in her face. "How did your family's visit go? Did you wow them?"

He listened attentively and sympathetically as Amelia took him through the grind of steering her family from Scarlett's staircase to a raggedy Vivien Leigh.

"If I'd known it was going to be such a bust, I would've tried harder to get off work that day." They smiled at each other, knowing he couldn't have done any such thing.

He stepped aside to let a customer buy two sets of hair rollers. The woman was a regular, and Amelia would have taken the time to chat, but today she rang up the purchase and sent her on her way. "But the worst part was that with all their griping and grousing, I couldn't get a word in edgewise to tell them about how it went last week at Selznick's screen test for Rita Hayworth."

"Oh my God, honey—I never asked you about it, did I?"

At least he was owning up to it. "No, you didn't."

He wrinkled his face into a sad-puppy pout. "You must think I'm the worst."

"Not the absolute worst," she told him. "But definitely top ten."

His remorse was palpable and that was all she needed to see. She described everything, from the roomful of redheads, to Rita stripping away her glamour-girl trappings, to the two of them having to invent a scene on the spot, to how they had both managed to impress Selznick's casting department.

"Have they offered you the stand-in job?" he asked.

"It depends on Rita. First, she has to accept the lead."

"And you'll take it?"

"It's a terrific break, so of course I will. Why wouldn't I?" He shrugged. *Please don't be one of those men Luddie warned me about.* "Are you saying you don't want me to?" Amelia had tried to whisper, but it had come out more of a hiss. A pair of reproachful spinster types scrutinized her from the magazine stand.

"I didn't say that."

"What *do* you say, then? You must have some thoughts on the matter. I want to hear them."

"What? Here?"

"And now."

He stared at her for more seconds than she would have liked as he appeared to sort through his options. "The moment I saw you at Kreiss's, I knew you weren't like those Hollywood dreamers. You're the real McCoy. Sensible. Normal. Not like—" He jerked his head toward Matilda, serving sundaes to sailors in crisp uniforms.

Amelia fought against the tremors in her chest. If she'd known he was going to come out with a statement like that, she'd have held her tongue. Schwab's retail counter was no place for their first-ever fight. Not that there was a good place to have one of those. And she'd do anything to avoid it. That is to say, *almost* anything. She was nobody's doormat, and she wasn't about to start now. "It's a stand-in job. I won't be facing any cameras."

"But you wanted to be. You said yourself that you planned on trying out for the lead."

"It'd be a dream come true. What's wrong with that?"

"Nothing."

That deadpan face he was presenting her with was more of an effort than he was prepared to let on, but the trembling edges of his lips gave him away. "Yeah, well, your mouth says 'nothing,' but your eyes say 'everything.' If you can't be honest with me—"

"I never figured you as the shallow type."

That word, that horrible word—*shallow*. She'd rather he had cursed at her than deliver such a quiet judgment. "What a horrible thing to say."

"You said you wanted me to be honest."

"Well, I—I—" It was hard to argue against his logic. Still and all, there was such a thing as delicacy. And tact. And restraint. "It's a good thing you're not in the diplomatic corps," she told him, and held her breath to see where her joke landed.

It missed its mark by a wide margin. He stuffed the rest of the chocolate bar into his mouth and chewed it with solemn intensity.

"Come on," she said, more placatingly now, "you know how this works. The job only happens assuming Rita's cast *and* assuming Thelma sticks to her word. And even then, I'll be off-screen, not playing to the gallery like—" Amelia aimed a discreet finger toward Matilda.

"You're making it sound like I'm not being supportive."

If this is you being supportive, she wanted to say, *then you need to work on your boyfriend skills, mister*. The spinsters were now browsing cold creams at the end of the counter. "You need to leave," she said lowering her voice, "before you get me into trouble."

"*Into* trouble?" he spat back. "I want you to succeed, but I've seen what can happen." The empty wrapper disappeared inside his clenched fist. "If anything, I'm trying to keep you *out* of trouble."

"You've got a funny way of showing it."

He narrowed his eyes and went to respond, but when he heard one of the spinsters theatrically clear her throat, he stomped past the colored pencils and ink pots, and onto Sunset.

Through forced smiles, Amelia rang up the old biddies' purchases, then snatched up the cleaning cloth for the glass counter. If that was how he felt, then good riddance. She attacked the stubborn mess of fingerprints with extra elbow grease.

The nerve of the guy.

Rub, rub, rub.

I'm trying to keep you out of trouble. Who does he think he is? Captain Savior? I'm not some fragile hothouse orchid fresh off the Greyhound from Boise. I know a thing or two.

Rub, rub, rub.

Maybe even three.

The cleaning cloth snagged a Hudnut's Gemey display. One of the bottles teetered to the edge where it fell, shattering on the floor. *Damnation!* She ducked out from behind the counter to sweep up the mess. She was nudging the pieces of glass into a dustpan when Mr. Schwab appeared.

"Oops-a-daisy?"

The bottle had shattered into a few neat pieces, easy enough to gather. But the perfume lingered—a floral cloud that transported her to Bullocks downtown and her first whiff of Chanel No. 5. "It's like the Gemey we sell at Schwab's," she had quipped to Polly, "except ours isn't five dollars a drop."

Amelia rose to her feet. "That scent is overwhelming. I ought to mop the floor."

"No need," he said. "Toilet water dissipates fast. In the meantime, it'll serve as a tantalizing advertisement."

Amelia felt like she should offer to pay for the damage, but one-dollar-ten was a lot for someone with a woefully meager bank account.

"That young fella was your boyfriend, I take it?"

"Yes, sir. Benji's not normally like that, but I shared some news with him that I thought was exciting and he didn't see it that way."

"Share your news with me, then. I'll be excited instead."

Amelia wished it were that easy, but it meant telling him about the stand-in job, and that would mean quitting.

He must have seen the hesitation in her eyes. "Naturally, you don't have to, my dear."

She knew she shouldn't, not until a firm offer had arrived, but Leon Schwab was upright and decent in every way, so he deserved honesty. When she had finished summarizing the events of the past few weeks, he beamed. "Amelia! How thrilling. Naturally, this job is yours until Selznick needs you, but I have to say, it'll be hard to replace you."

The memory of Della's face surfaced in Amelia's mind—desperate yet clinging to hope. "I might have a replacement," she said tentatively.

"You'd be saving me an awful lot of trouble." The Gemey scent had now pervaded the surrounding air. In an hour or two, it might encourage sales, but for now, it was more likely to induce the woozies. "How about I man the counter for ten minutes while you catch your breath out back?"

Even after breaking merchandise and telling him that she was planning to leave, he still encouraged her to take a break. A girl couldn't hope for a better boss.

She thanked him and scooted through the storage room and out into the alley, where the warm June night air gusted past her.

The sweet smell of peaches clung to the wooden slats of Riverside Valencia Orchards crates stacked against the wall.

Her family's indifference she could take. But Benji's? That ached like a bruise she feared would never heal.

An empty tomato soup can lay discarded on the pockmarked concrete. She kicked it hard, watching it ricochet off the alley's brick wall. Not that she'd ever done anything special to make a fuss over. Not yet, anyway. But to be chosen for a David O. Selznick production—*that* was special. Even if Benji was blasé about her prospects.

The soup can rolled into the shallow trench that snaked down the middle of the alley. Where were Polly and Luddie when she needed them? They'd know what to say to bolster her spirits.

"Hiya." Matilda already had a lit cigarette in hand. "Everything okay?"

"You saw what happened?"

"Saw it, heard it, smelled it clear across the store." She offered her pack of Parliaments.

Amelia debated accepting a cigarette from a girl she wasn't sure she trusted. But if ever she needed a calming cigarette, it was now. She withdrew one from the pack and sandwiched it between her lips.

Matilda lit a match from an Ontra Cafeteria matchbook. "You were at that Selznick cattle call for redheads, weren't you?"

Amelia drew the smoke into her lungs. "Where'd you hear that?"

"Every redhead in Hollywood's been buzzing about it. It almost made me regret dyeing my red hair blonde until I heard how all those girls were only props for some Harry Cohn ingenue. Same old baloney, huh? What do they care? Didn't waste *their* time or get *their* hopes dashed."

"Yes, but how did you know *I* was there?"

"I got talking to a customer at the prescriptions counter. Real pretty, she was. The flapper type."

"Today?"

"Yeah, just now."

"With bobbed hair?"

"Uh-huh." Matilda drew on her cigarette. "Had a henna rinse. Decent job, but fading. I could tell she'd come for a fresh box." If Della had dropped by, why no hello? Then again, Amelia had been tangling with Benji before the Gemey disaster. "She mentioned you getting picked from the crowd. Said it was rigged, but didn't know why. What was it all for, anyway?"

"A movie David Selznick plans to make."

"*Pretty Pennies*?"

Amelia felt her shoulders surrender. This Parliament was doing the trick. "I got called in to give Cohn's girl someone to work off. I guess I did okay because they offered to make me the stand-in if it goes ahead."

"You going to take it?"

"Sure."

"Even though it's not in front of the camera?"

Amelia pictured Vivien Leigh, dressed in tatters, hair disheveled, drilling that single line over and over. Watching Vivien work had stirred a yearning deep in Amelia's soul.

"In front, no, but I'll be on a movie set and part of the production."

Matilda's eyes flashed with dismay. "Settling for second banana? Don't sell yourself short. I wouldn't. And if your fellow can't handle it, I'd cut him loose, too." She shrugged. "Some folks might swoon over a stand-in job, but it pales compared to the starring role, if you ask me." She killed her cigarette butt under her heel and headed back inside.

Amelia should have returned to her counter by now, but she lingered as long as she dared.

Damn you, Matilda Charles. Planting seeds of doubt. Or maybe I should thank you for reminding me that Rita hasn't been cast yet. Nobody has. And that means the role is still up for grabs.

Either way, it wasn't fair for Amelia to let Mr. Schwab suffer any longer at the retail counter. She snuffed out her Parliament on the peach crate. A girl didn't get far in this town by leaving her boss high and dry.

16

The Hartley house stood silent when Amelia unhooked the front gate. Why were Cookie and Jewel not already howling loud enough to split the San Andreas Fault? She reached the porch without a single bark, bay, or bellow. "I'm coming in."

Dumping her hat and bag on the Victorian fainting couch in the foyer, she walked into the living room, where her mother sat at the dining table in front of a jumble of boxes and photo albums scattered from one end to the other. "Where are Death and Destruction?"

Lois ignored her. "Isn't the Boy Scouts a marvelous organization?" She lifted a thick album from a battered cardboard box and dropped it in front of her.

Amelia joined her. "Have Samuel and Sebastian taken the hounds of the Baskervilles on a camping trip?"

"It's Pets and Animals Day. Your father drove them to some horse farm in the Burbank foothills. It gives us time to sift through these boxes together."

Lois wasn't even playing the radio; silence in this house was a rare flower that bloomed only once a decade. What a slice of heaven not to have to share her mother with perfect Faith, persnickety Gideon, colicky Chester, rambunctious dogs, and rowdy twins.

Amelia ran her finger around the corner of a photo on the bottom left of a dark-haired little girl wearing a bow almost the size of her head. "Aunt Pamela?"

Lois's sister had died of polio years before Amelia had been born. "Such a sweet little thing." She indulged in a momentary reminiscence. "I'm so glad you agreed to help me go through all this old junk to see what we can find of Bernice."

"It's not junk, Mom. It's your life."

Lois pulled back a sheet of translucent crêpe paper to reveal four photos of a middle-schooler, her hair divided into two tight braids. "I feel as though I ought to make it up to you for that day when you took us around the studio."

Make it up to me? Amelia tried to catch her mother's eye, but Lois remained absorbed by the album. "How so?"

"I'm afraid you were the indirect casualty of a dreadful argument Faith and Gideon had on the drive over."

Amelia fought to keep her voice steady. "What have those two got to fight over?"

"Gideon makes out like he's happy for Faith's success. Says all the right things. But he didn't expect *Echoes of Elegance* would have one tenth its impact. She's got speaking engagements booked clear through to the end of the year. And now this second printing."

Damn you, Ludlow Sinclair! You were right that night on Vine Street. And if you were right about Gideon, are you right about Benji, too? Their fight at work was three days ago, but she hadn't heard from him, so it felt like only three hours. "Gideon's jealous?"

"Ooooh yes."

"And all because *From the Pen of Proust* failed to set the world on fire."

A while ago, Gideon's sole topic of conversation had been an annotated collection of Proust's letters he'd worked on for eons. The publishing house reported selling ninety-one copies, unaware that Gideon had purchased forty of them. At Thanksgiving, he'd declared that academic significance outweighed commercial success, which was, Amelia thanked heaven, the last she'd heard of it.

That awful afternoon at the studio hadn't been her fault, after all? Amelia felt like she'd lost twenty pounds in one glorious instant.

"And now Faith has eclipsed him." Amelia pulled out another album. A couple of sepia-toned high-schoolers in matching sailor-girl outfits beamed at her. The smiling teens shared a cousinly resemblance, just as Amelia and Polly did.

"That's us a few weeks before graduation. Those two imps had no idea what the coming summer would bring."

Wistfulness crept into Lois's voice as she studied the photo. Her mother had always been the look-ahead type: "You can't change the past, but you can change the present before it becomes a future you don't want." This melancholic Lois was a version Amelia had never seen and couldn't quite fathom. Maybe this wasn't the time to bring up her maybe-maybe-not stand-in job.

As they pored over albums and scrapbooks, Lois recounted stories new to Amelia. Like riding all the way to Venice Beach on their Christmas bicycles. Or the afternoon they had knocked on the door of L. Frank Baum, the author of *The Wizard of Oz,* not thinking for a moment he'd invite them in for tea and Lorna Doones.

"Why haven't I heard about these adventures before?" Amelia asked.

"Different life, different time." Lois leafed through pages of clipped school newspaper articles, graduation notices, and photos of people in Halloween costumes. The backdrops in the photos changed to seashores, piers, sailing boats, and crab pots. "That was the first day of shooting. We were up over in Hamilton Cove, where they land the seaplanes these days. Look at Bernice with all her white makeup. I told her, 'You're the ghost of Christmas Never.' And here's one Polly's father took with his Kodak Brownie. They had been filming in high winds, hence the disheveled hair. Oh, and that building behind them? That's the Rose Hotel where the—" Lois's voice faltered.

"Fire started?"

"We don't need to go into that."

The fire that ended up burning down a third of Avalon had been the darkest burden of everyone involved: Lois and Judd, Bernice, Polly's father, Sibyl, Zara. That was a lot of people to hang onto an awful secret, but somehow, they'd kept it all these years. Amelia wished she could probe deeper, but her mother's face was locked down tighter than a submarine.

"Bernice and Mack!" A slightly blurry couple stood by a frosted-glass door. "Their wedding day at City Hall." The bride was in a dark, two-piece ensemble with a string of pearls around her neck and twinkling earrings. The husband was in a nondescript suit, holding Bernice's hand.

"Anything on the back?" Amelia asked.

Lois extracted the photo from its adhesive corners and flipped it over. "Nope. Darn it." She returned it to its page and reached for a scrapbook. "This," she said, opening it, "is from the premiere. Gosh, what a night that was. Lewis Selznick rented the Hollywood Theatre. Bernice and I wore our graduation gowns." She lingered over a snap of two couples, girls in white, men in tuxedos. "Polly's father hadn't met Flora, and Bernice hadn't found her husband yet, so this is Bernice with Elroy and me with your father."

How jarring to see one's parents untrammeled by life's obstacles, not much older than Amelia was now. In twenty-five years, would she be riffling through photos, marveling at how she'd once looked? Glad that she had taken the stand-in job or disappointed that she hadn't?

Lois landed a fingernail on a man in his thirties wearing pince-nez and a starched collar. Beside him stood two boys. "That's Lewis Selznick."

"And these kids are Myron and David?"

The younger Selznick had inherited a face as round and pale as his father's. Nothing about the impish boy with his tongue poking out hinted at the Hollywood titan he would become.

"Bern's postcards!" Lois raised a hefty pile of picture postcards from a Lifebuoy soap box, bound with a disintegrating rubber band. "Her husband was a traveling salesman for a candy company. He drove up and down the West Coast. He was gone more often than he was at home, so Bernice joined him. I rarely saw her after that, so she'd send me these from every stop."

"What does the first one say?" Amelia asked.

Lois read out loud, "'Dear Lulu, We're in Eureka. Mack drives like a demon, but he makes me laugh. We eat out a lot because I haven't told him yet that I can't cook!'" Lois deposited the card on the table. "I'll never understand how a girl who made her own clothes was such a terrible cook." She flicked through a few more postcards: Portland, Spokane, Reno, Tucson, Billings. "After a while, they became more and more sporadic until they stopped arriving altogether."

"Where's the last one from?"

The bottom postcard was of the Civic Opera House in Chicago, dated 1928: "'First time to Chicago and boy, do I love it. This place feels like a proper city, with proper skyscrapers, proper stores, proper everything. Psssst! Don't tell Mack but I'd happily live here.'"

"Maybe they did," Amelia said.

"Mack loved the open road." Lois retrieved newspaper clippings yellowed with age, stopping at a 1917 *Film Daily* piece. It announced MacKinley Burroughs as Delish-Delite Candy's western head of sales, highlighting his prediction that theater concession stands would rival box office profits. "Yes, of course. That was it: MacKinley Burroughs." Lois pushed up her reading glasses. "How could I have forgotten a hell of a name like that?"

Amelia thought he sounded more like one of Gideon's stuffy college professors. "Selling candy *inside* theaters? He just wanted to see his name in print, if you ask me."

"All these mementos." Lois's eyes glistened in the late-morning light slanting through the window. "I was so careless with our friendship. Bern and I were thick as thieves, and I let her slip away."

"She got married. You got married. Kids, homes, pets. Life goes on, Mom."

The words had barely left Amelia's lips when dread settled in her chest. What a void Polly would leave behind if she ever up and married some traveling salesman.

"I didn't care much for Mack. He was one of those fast-talking, promise-everything bamboozlers. I couldn't understand why she'd settle for a guy like that." The tears were flowing now. Lois pulled out a handkerchief and mopped as best she could. "Their marriage lasted a lot longer than I predicted. I should've given him the benefit of the doubt."

"Let's concentrate on the positive," Amelia said. "I'm guessing there are less than three MacKinley Burroughs in the country. *And* we know they were in Chicago ten years ago."

"Not much to go on."

"Plus, the name of the company he worked for."

"That's true."

Amelia turned and grabbed the pad next to the telephone on the sideboard behind her. She laid it on the table and jotted down some notes. "Bernice's maiden name?"

"Hoag."

"Birthday?"

"August fourth, eighteen ninety-five."

Amelia picked up the phone. "I'm calling Irene so that she can give all this to her private eye."

Lois dabbed her damp handkerchief to her face. "Do you think it's enough?"

"It's more than what we had an hour ago."

The Selznicks' maid answered their telephone and put Irene on the line. "Thank heavens you've called!"

"I've got some information about Bernice."

"Who?" Irene snapped the word like a whip.

"Have I called at a bad time?"

"As a matter of fact, your timing couldn't be better. I spoke with Polly earlier and asked her to get here after work. Can you come too? I'd so appreciate it. Shall we say six o'clock? I have someone I want you to meet. Thanks so much."

The line went dead, leaving Amelia's questions hanging in the air.

17

Amelia and Polly sat on the chintz sofa as they waited for Irene to finish reading to her sons.

"You still haven't told your mother about being Rita Hayworth's stand-in?" Polly asked.

"It wasn't the right time. Mom got all teary over losing touch with Bernice. But she did tell me Desmond has already moved to Catalina and ordered the new distillery equipment."

"It's amazing how quickly things happen once the check clears." Polly straightened Amelia's collar with sisterly mischief. "Maybe we can get Irene's private eye to track down Luddie's secret benefactress. I know we shouldn't, but this mystery is driving me a little batty."

Irene strode into the room and dropped into the club chair, her face flushed with elation. "I hope you like martinis." She started pouring from a crystal pitcher. Neither Amelia nor Polly cared for them, but it felt rude to say no. She handed Amelia and Polly their glasses and lifted her own. "Ladies, we have our lead actress."

Amelia lowered her glass to her knee to steady her hand and looked for signs that Polly already knew of this scoop, but saw only stunned surprise on her roommate's face. "Rita?"

"David informed me over dinner—if you can call grilled cheese sandwiches and beer at ten p.m. 'dinner.' He told me he could only picture the unvarnished, natural version of Rita in the role, so if Cohn backed out, he would nix the whole damn thing."

"He's been talking to Cohn this whole time?"

"Polly, dear, you look as shocked as I felt. I had no idea, either."

"Even though they hate each other?" Amelia asked.

Irene's eyes popped with derision. "Men like my husband, my father, and Harry Cohn rarely make the mistake of mixing personal animosity with advantageous business arrangements."

Polly flinched as she fortified herself with a slug of her martini. "Which they've reached?"

"Verbally, yes."

"Harry Cohn knows how to drive a hard bargain," Polly said. "I wonder how Mr. Selznick sweetened the pot."

Irene refilled her glass. "Bioff and Browne."

Amelia sucked in air, holding it tight. She'd told no one about blabbing Cohn's secret. She had only succumbed because Selznick cornered her into that impromptu pitch. Was this where it came back to haunt her? "Cohn being the only mogul *not* paying mob bribes was bound to leak eventually."

"It was the bargaining chip David needed." Irene raised her glass. "Here's to tattletales."

Relieved, Amelia finished her cocktail with a final gulp. These martinis weren't so bad when you got right down to it. She poured herself another. "No wonder you got us over here to celebrate."

"Nothing is certain until the contracts are signed. And even then, there's an escape clause. Usually around vaguely worded clauses cloaking iffy morals. But David tells me Rita is a sweet girl."

It had been a week and a half since Matilda had made that second-banana comment. Amelia hated how it still stung and resented the girl for wedging that burr under her saddle. But everything had changed now that the lead had been cast.

"Now," Irene said, decisively, "about the costumes—"

"Before we've seen the script?"

"Virginia's been sending me pages as she goes. She's well along already."

The dizzying pace of this progress left Amelia a little breathless. Regardless, if this was how it felt to work on a film, she couldn't wait to be a part of it. "You were saying about costumes?"

"This story is about ordinary people who wear everyday clothing. We can rent everything from Western Costumes. As for sets, it all takes place on Catalina. I told Virginia to write most of the scenes out of doors. The one exception will be the grandmother's house. Instead of building a set, it'll be quicker, cheaper, and easier to rent a house."

"You mean my father's?"

"I didn't want to presume, but yes, Polly. That'd be very helpful."

Polly was being helpful, but Amelia knew her real motivation: Renting the place to both Desmond *and* Selznick would help her pay off her debt that little bit faster. Polly might come across like a buttoned-down bookworm, but only buffoons underestimated her.

Polly peered past Amelia. "Who do we have here?"

A freshly scrubbed young woman Amelia's age hovered in the living room doorway. Her muslin blouse with embroidered daisies, navy skirt, and clasped hands matched her tentative smile. "Am I interrupting?" She spoke with a European accent Amelia couldn't pin down.

Irene sprang to her feet. "I bet that shower helped scour away all those days on the train." She wrapped a maternal arm around the girl and guided her to a spare club chair. "I want you to meet my friends, Amelia Hartley and Polly Maddox. Girls, this is Ingrid Bergman."

Ah, so this was the Swedish actress Selznick had hired to star in his *Intermezzo* remake.

Polly jumped up too. "I helped with the travel arrangements for you and Miss Brown. How was the *Queen Mary*?"

"Lovely, but the train! In Sweden, if you ride three hours, you are in another country. In America?" She rolled her arctic blue eyes. "I said it to Kay, 'We sit on this train for so long we must be in Peru.'"

"Are you excited about your first Hollywood movie?"

The Swede's face lit up. "Yes!" The smile dimmed. "But no. My English is okay, but not good enough for American films."

She pronounced it "fillums" with unspoiled charm. My goodness, Amelia thought, if Selznick's cameraman can capture her candid babe-in-the-woods quality, this girl would beguile the pants off every moviegoer from here to Maine.

"Now, girls," Irene said, addressing Amelia and Polly, "I have a huge favor. I was supposed to show Ingrid the sights on her first night in Hollywood, but my oldest son stepped on a rusty nail yesterday. The doctor was concerned it could give him lockjaw, so he gave Jeffrey one of those new vaccines this morning. The kid gets so clingy when he's ill that I can't enjoy myself while he's fretting. Would you two take Ingrid out instead?"

"Sure thing," they told Irene, then turned to Ingrid. "How about a restaurant in the shape of a hat?"

"Do they have ice cream sundaes? We don't have them at home and I've always wanted to try one."

"In that case," Amelia sprang to her feet, encouraging Ingrid to do the same, "we've got a lot of introductions to make."

* * *

The Swede drank in Wilshire Boulevard with unconcealed delight. "My people at home, they will not believe me when they hear I ate my dinner in a giant hat!"

Seeing it through Ingrid's eyes, the Brown Derby did seem rather silly. But no sillier than the Sphinx Realty office on Fairfax Avenue, or the Ben-Hur coffee shop on Washington Boulevard with a giant coffee pot perched on its roof.

After they'd been shown to a booth, the waitress handed them menus. Ingrid drew in a sharp breath. "So much choices! At home, we mostly choose the smorgasbord."

"The Poached Finnan Haddie is good," Polly said.

"I want a dinner of ice cream sundaes, please." She noticed the hesitancy between Amelia and Polly. "They are not good?"

"They're excellent," Amelia assured her. "But aren't you about to start filming?"

"Yes. Is this bad?"

"We're used to Hollywood actresses who starve themselves."

Ingrid frowned. "Why?"

"To make their waistline as small as possible."

"Why?"

Amelia and Polly locked eyes. *She's got a point*. The waitress didn't question Ingrid's order of a hot fudge banana split sundae alongside Polly's Spaghetti Derby and Amelia's corned beef hash.

"Tell me," Ingrid said after their waitress had departed, "what is a pretty pennies?"

"Pretty penny is an expression," Polly explained. "It means 'expensive.' Such as 'My new hat cost me a pretty penny.' Did you hear us talking with Irene?" Ingrid nodded. "*Pretty Pennies* is the name of a movie that it looks like Mr. Selznick will make."

"But Mrs. Selznick said the fillum will be cheap."

"Cheap by Mr. Selznick's standards." Polly nudged Amelia. "What if Irene cut the budget to the bone to get him to say yes? It's possible the stand-in job is gone."

A jagged disappointment sank its teeth into Amelia's stomach. "How small might the budget be?"

"*Wind* ate up most of his capital, and what's left is going to *Intermezzo* and *Rebecca*. *Pretty Pennies* is probably an interim money-maker because he can do it fast and cheap." Polly unfolded her napkin thoughtfully. "Even though he wants his legacy to be classy pictures."

With Selznick and Cohn's deal on Rita, that stand-in job had almost been hers. How cruel it felt to lose it now. "So this isn't his kind of film?"

"Strictly speaking, no. Which is why"—Polly measured her words—"it could become a Columbia release."

Amelia fell back in her seat, landing against the dark brown leather upholstery with a dull thud. "I shouldn't have told Mr. Schwab about this."

"I wondered if you were being a tad premature."

"I thought it was a dead cert. I was trying to do the right thing by a decent boss on the day I broke that bottle of Gemey and stunk up the joint."

"Please," Ingrid said, "what is Gemey?"

"Gemey is a Hudnut eau de toilette." Seeing Ingrid's baffled look, she explained, "It's a type of perfume. I sell it at the drugstore where I work. A job I believed I'd be quitting soon."

"To work on *Pretty Pennies*?" Polly said.

"Yes, but if—" Amelia threw herself forward in her seat like a runner at the starting line. "What makes you think he's planning to offload it to Columbia?"

"The other day, Hazel and I were talking about how the end of filming on *Wind* is coming up. Mr. Selznick is still waging war with the Hays Office on Rhett's last line. They want it to be 'Frankly, my dear, I don't care.'"

Ingrid gave a derisive snort. "I am hardly speaking English and I can see that version is boring."

"Exactly. That's why Selznick's in there swinging his bat. Hazel's been typing the flurry of letters to the Hays Office. She told me they mention how 'a well-known film executive of significant influence' is pressuring the Motion Picture Association to deny his application for special dispensation to use 'damn.' Selznick's begging them to ignore these 'outside influences unconnected with this project.'"

"Trust Cohn to screw with Selznick because he hates him."

"This town is strewn with people who have done more for less reason." Amelia could hear the jigsaw pieces snapping into place. "Would Selznick offer Cohn *Pretty Pennies* in exchange for Cohn backing off?"

"Could be."

"Over one stupid word?"

"The most important word in the whole *damn* movie." Polly snickered.

"I dunno, Pol. It feels like thin ice to base an entire theory on."

"It would be if that were all, but Marcella has been putting through calls to him from someone named Norma."

"Shearer?"

"Kassell—Cohn's secretary."

Only now, with the opportunity slipping away, did she realize how deeply she had wanted it. She should have been more suspicious when it had come together so quickly.

"Fact is," Polly insisted, "if *Pretty Pennies* is done on the cheap, it's more of a Columbia type of picture. Even more tempting if Cohn offers Mr. Selznick an attractive price to buy the property outright."

"Because it's all about available moolah."

"Assuming Irene is right about Mr. Selznick's gambling . . ." Polly seesawed her hand. "The question is: Will Dorothy Arzner be okay working at Columbia?"

"This Harry Cohn you talk about," Ingrid said, her substantial brows knitted together in the concentration it took a Hollywood rookie to keep up. "Who is he?"

"He runs Columbia."

"Isn't Columbia one of the big Hollywood studios?"

"It's farther down the totem pole."

"What is this, the totem pole?"

"Think of the studios sitting on a ladder in order of importance. Columbia would be on the bottom rung."

"Ah! *Rangordning*. Everywhere, people are not very different. Who is Rita?"

"You know how Mr. Selznick is pushing your career?" Polly said. "Harry Cohn is pushing hers the same way."

"And you will be her stand-in?" Ingrid asked Amelia.

"Possibly."

"That is exciting, yes?" The girl's angelic, open-hearted charm dimmed a notch or two. "In Sweden, we get the American movie magazines. They are how I practice English many times. I have learned that every year, thousands of girls, they come to Hollywood with the hopes and the dreams."

"Yes, and very few of them make it past the security gate."

"But look where you are starting! Girls like you and me, we are —what is the expression? In front of the group?"

Polly faced Amelia, unblinking. *She means 'ahead of the pack.' For the love of Mike, have we become such jaded Hollywood movieland cynics that it takes this girl from halfway around the world to remind us that we're already inside the gate?*

18

Lois locked her car door and looked south along Formosa Avenue. "They don't have ice cream sundaes in Sweden?"

"Apparently not."

"And she ate *two*?"

Several days later, Amelia still couldn't believe it. "I'm telling you, she was like Rhett Butler: 'Frankly, my dear, I don't give a damn.'"

"I didn't think girls like her existed in Hollywood."

The sight of Ingrid demolishing hot fudge sundaes for dinner, untouched by Hollywood's usual restraints, had lifted Amelia's spirits. Even now, she still felt buoyed with hope. Ingrid had made a very good point. Anything could happen if you were already inside a movie studio.

They passed the newly opened Formosa Café—a clever little place fashioned from an old railway carriage—and arrived at a square box of an office, twelve feet wide, on the south end of the diner. In the window a painted sign read:

DUDLEY HARTMAN AGENCY

Confidential Investigations
Privacy Guaranteed

"His name is Hartman?" Lois asked. "And ours is Hartley. That's a good omen, don't you think?"

Coincidence, sure, but omen? No, Amelia didn't think so. But what was the harm if her mother did?

The door was ajar. *So much for privacy guaranteed.* To their immediate right, a mountain of cardboard boxes crammed a wooden desk with towers of packing crates stacked next to it. The heady smell of fresh paint radiated throughout the place.

"Anybody home?"

A man's voice responded, "That's the last of them. Drop the boxes wherever you can."

"We're not the moving men."

A round face, wide as a Nebraskan plain and sunny as a Florida beach, peered out from behind the packing crates. "Sorry about that, folks. We're still in the process of moving in." Nothing about him suggested the brooding loner from a James M. Cain novel Amelia had imagined. "Mrs. Irene Selznick recommended you."

"Pleased to hear it." He waved them through to the back half of the office, where he had almost finished setting up his desk. "As long as you don't mind a smidgen of pandemonium." He pulled out a pad of blank paper and a sharpened pencil from a chipped coffee mug. "How can I help?"

Amelia wasn't convinced that any serious private eye worth his weight in cheap bourbon would use the word "smidgen," but someone as savvy as Irene Mayer Selznick wouldn't trust her business to a nitwit. As clearly and logically as she could, Amelia laid out the filming of *Pretty Pennies*, how Lois and Bernice had lost touch after Bernice's marriage to Mack, and how their trail had run cold in Chicago.

"Give it to us straight, Mr. Hartman," Lois said. "Is this enough information to track Bernice down?"

When he responded, "I suspect so, yes," Amelia would have felt encouraged had reluctance not weighted every word.

"I'm waiting for your *however*," she said.

A brief, fleeting smile. "There are any number of reasons Bernice, with or without her husband, might no longer be in Chicago—including the distinct possibility they never settled down there. On a more positive note, however, had she married a John Smith or a Michael Jones, we'd be dead in the water."

"MacKinley Burroughs is such an unusual name," Lois said.

"It's our ace in the hole." He set his pencil on his ink blotter. "However"—Amelia braced herself—"in my experience, people who vanish have their reasons. Tracking them can stir up a hornet's nest that's better left sealed. So I'll ask you now: Are you *sure* you want me to track down your long-lost friend?"

* * *

Silence had followed them from Hartman's office to their booth at the Formosa Café, broken only by ordering old fashioneds.

"What a question," Lois muttered. "I'm sick with regret that I lost track of her, and am determined to find her again because if there's one thing I know for sure, it's that Bern would love for us to be reunited. If this guy fails, I'll hire someone else."

"A lot can happen in ten years, Mom."

"I can't imagine under what circumstances she wouldn't want to hear from me." Lois's voice had taken on a stern, don't-fight-me-on-this tone. She picked up the menu the hostess had left behind. "Let's see what kind of food they serve here." She ran her eyes down the page. "This is a Chinese restaurant?"

"Formosa is an island off the coast of China; you were expecting tamales?" Lois was shaking her head with minuscule twitches. Amelia could see now how deeply she'd underestimated what finding her childhood bosom buddy meant. "How about we go with chop suey?"

Lois's mouth melted into a smile. "Chop suey invariably reminds me of the Chinese pirate ship on Catalina when we shot *Pretty Pennies.*"

"The *Ning Po?*"

"That's when me and Bern first tasted it. My parents steered clear of foreign food. Bern's, too. We didn't care, though. We congratulated ourselves on being adventurous." Her smile softened with nostalgia. "Sometimes I wonder if my memories have been filtered through rose-colored glasses."

"Even that final night when Polly's father ended up burning down half the town?" It was the first time Amelia had confronted Lois with a direct question about her hand in the Avalon fire. She expected her mother to change the subject, and wasn't surprised when Lois did.

"And to think, David Selznick is going to remake our movie. Gosh, how exciting it'd be to watch them film it. That's partly why I'm so keen to find Bernice. Going back to Catalina will be like reliving our youth."

"We'll see," Amelia said.

"Why do you say it like that?"

Amelia was about to quote Hartman's warning about people who vanish having their reasons when a single word shot out of Lois like a harpoon.

"GALE!"

Amelia jolted. "What gale?"

"Bernice and Mack have the same middle name. Gale was her grandmother's maiden name, and his was a family name that gets handed down to each generation. I'm sure a detail like that could be a helpful breadcrumb." Lois slipped out of the booth. "I'm going to run back to tell Mr. Hartman."

She passed their waitress as she dashed the length of the railway carriage. "What happened?" the waitress asked. "Did she lose her purse?"

Amelia sighed. *No, but I've lost the moment.* "We'd like two orders of chop suey and another round of old fashioneds."

With so many questions hovering over this movie, her mother's interference might have been a blessing. She sat in the booth, listening to ice cubes settling in water glasses and the soft click of chopsticks. Did the people who disappeared never realize they were taking pieces of others with them?

19

Despite Mr. Schwab's assurances, a faint whiff of Gemey eau to toilette still clung to the air. Amelia had finished ringing up a large order of toothbrushes when she sensed Schwab's head cashier by her side.

"I have a customer on the phone," Ida said. "Said her hair curlers would be delivered by noon. It's now twelve-fifteen and no sign of the delivery boy, so now she's all hot under the collar."

Amelia had taken no telephone orders this morning. "But I—"

"Mentioned you by name."

Dealing with irate customers was nobody's idea of fun, but agreeing with them helped to short-circuit frustration. She picked up the phone at the end of the counter. "Hello. I believe we have a problem that needs fixing."

The throaty giggle down the line could only have come from one person. "I know Mr. Schwab has a 'no personal calls at work' policy, but I have urgent news."

"Condensed version, please, ma'am."

"Three minutes ago, I was at the teletype sending out Mr. Selznick's press release announcing that he is putting *Pretty Pennies* into production, starring Columbia up-and-comer Rita Hayworth."

"It's happening?"

"Yep."

"And not at Columbia?"

"Nope."

"Somebody called somebody's bluff?"

"And I quote." Polly cleared her throat. "'To be directed by Dorothy Arzner from a script by Virginia Van Upp on special loan from Paramount, the film will be the first major Hollywood motion picture to be shot wholly on Santa Catalina Island, twenty-six miles off the coast of Los Angeles.'"

Amelia tightened her grip on the receiver. "What happens now?"

"Hazel just finished preparing all the contracts."

"Are you telling me that somewhere out there is a Selznick contract with my name on it?"

"It's already en route to Myron."

The past four months had felt like one long mental game.

If Irene convinced . . .

If David decided . . .

If Harry agreed . . .

If Rita proved . . .

If Thelma remembered . . .

Now that the moment had arrived, Amelia found herself trembling, feet glued to the floorboards. "Where are Myron's offices?

"Wilshire, corner of Roxbury, but you have to sign the contract *today*. If we don't have it back here by noon tomorrow, the offer is rescinded."

The word 'rescinded' sucked the air from Amelia's lungs. "What's the rush?"

"They plan to start shooting in two months. It's a scheduling issue, squeezing it in between *Intermezzo* and *Rebecca*. Virginia has almost finished the script; there are no sets to be built or fancy costumes. The only role that hasn't been cast is the male love interest, but Fred and Thelma are already auditioning actors."

"I have an early shift tomorrow," Amelia said, as much to

herself as to Polly. "I start at seven a.m., so that only leaves this afternoon."

"When do you finish up today?"

"Five-thirty."

"The office closes at six. Can you get down there in time?"

Schwab's had another pharmacy half a block away from Myron's office. Amelia knew exactly where it was. "I'll have to."

Amelia thanked her roommate and hung up. Hmmmm . . . taking Sunset to Roxbury, then south to Wilshire would be easiest, but Crescent Heights to Santa Monica Boulevard, then south on Doheny to Wilshire would be quicker.

"Get it sorted out?"

The sound of Ida's voice startled Amelia—she hadn't seen her standing close by. "Wrong Schwab's. They thought they were talking to the one on Roxbury."

"Even though she asked for you by name?"

Caught red-handed, Amelia couldn't think of a convincing response, so she merely shrugged.

Ida raised a skeptical eyebrow. "How's your friend Polly Maddox doing these days?"

Mr. Schwab had filched Ida from the Ship Café in Venice. Fashioned after a Spanish galleon, it had been a prime speakeasy during Prohibition. So Amelia should have known better than to try putting anything over on this dame.

"I have a good chance to work on a new Selznick picture."

"How good?"

"I have to get to Wilshire and Roxbury by six to sign the contract."

"You finish at five-thirty, don't you, hon?"

"As long as there are no car accidents, broken signals, traffic snarls—"

"What if you left at five-fifteen and I clocked your time card at five-thirty?"

With so many staff members coming and going on revolving shifts, Ida had always been a rigid Army drill sergeant about punching in and punching out. Bending the rules by even so much as fifteen minutes was unprecedented.

"You'd do that for me?"

"Listen, sweetie." Ida rested an elbow on Amelia's counter like she had all the time in the world, which she didn't. "In my job, you learn to take stock of people real fast. For instance, that one?" She jacked a thumb toward Matilda. "Never took to her. And her burly-Q fan-dancer malarky, even less. But you, my blazing gorgeous redhead, when I look across the store, it's like you're standing under your own personal spotlight."

The compliment caught in Amelia's chest like a hook. She pressed her palms flat against her skirt, steadying herself. Why was the most uplifting compliment anyone had ever paid her coming from a work colleague?

"Now, now, don't get all mushy on me." Ida gave Amelia's wrist an encouraging squeeze. "I've been meaning to say so from the moment you got banished to Siberia." A customer clutching a handful of headache powder packets approached. "Give me a quiet sign when you're about to scram and leave everything else to your Aunt Ida."

* * *

The brakes on Amelia's old Ford squeaked as she headed down the steep Doheny Drive incline. Twenty-nine minutes to go.

Standing under your own personal spotlight. Gadzooks. Not even honey-tongued Ludlow Sinclair knew how to make a compliment like that work. Not unless he was angling for an extra boudoir tip near the close of an evening. But from the lips of seen-it-all Ida with her no-nonsense hair bun coiled like a rattlesnake, a word of approval meant so much more.

Benji's efforts in the sweet nothings department hadn't been too shabby since they'd smoothed over their recent spat, but she doubted he could pull off such flowery flattery, either.

Their first conversation had been a little stilted, a tad mechanical, and she would've preferred it hadn't been over the telephone, but at least he'd called. And it had led to a spontaneous beach picnic, which in turn had led to necking in the back row of the Egyptian Theatre as *Five Came Back* unfolded on the screen.

Amelia turned west onto Wilshire. *How can you be satisfied with playing second banana?* Amelia still disagreed with Matilda about putting up with leftovers when a main course was up for grabs. But Rita was getting the main course. And anyway, everyone knew heated-up leftovers tasted better the next day, so how bad could they be?

You don't have to decide, she told herself. She had fifteen blocks and twenty minutes left on the clock. The decision is in your hands until the moment you sign. Or don't.

* * *

Myron Selznick's secretary had the telephone to her ear when Amelia entered. She cupped her hand over the receiver. "On hold with the *Citizen-News*. What do you need?" When Amelia told her, she plucked a contract from one of her four correspondence trays, added it to a stack, and pushed the bundle across her desk. "The standard rigmarole."

For fifteen blocks, Amelia had fretted over battling through impenetrable legalese. What a relief to find two scant pages stating that she'd be the lead actress's stand-in for the duration of filming, however long that might be.

There it was! In writing! Okay, so maybe she wasn't the only girl in Hollywood offered a contract this week. She probably wasn't the only one today. But this one was *her* contract. Seventy-five a week felt like a mouthful of French champagne.

Still on her call, the secretary tapped a pen on the three blank lines at the bottom of the page. "Print your name, then sign your autograph and today's date."

The gold nib was an inch from the surface of the paper when a name caught her eye: Matilda Charles.

Why was Matilda's name on Amelia's contract?

She returned to the first page and took the time to read the heading that she had skipped.

Contract between
Myron Selznick & Company
and
Matilda Charles
June 22, 1939

Even worse, Matilda had already signed it.

"Jesus, Harvey!" The secretary's voice bordered on hysteria. "I could've given birth to twins by now. I want you to read me what you've got, slowly and verbatim, because we can't go through this again." She bent over her dictation pad and ran a pencil along each line.

Amelia peeked at the contract underneath hers. It was with RKO for someone whose name wasn't familiar. The one under that was a real estate lease for a storefront in Culver City. But then she read the third one.

Contract between
Selznick International Pictures
and
Amelia Hartley
June 22, 1939

Selznick International held Amelia's contract and Myron Selznick held Matilda's, but both contracts used the same template.

Except . . .

Identical pencil strokes marked the top of the page—"#1" on Amelia's, "#2" on Matilda's.

So much for Miss Never Be Second Banana.

The secretary dropped the telephone into its cradle. "Sorry about that, dearie."

"One question," Amelia said. "Is it usual to put a stand-in under contract for a single picture?"

"David Selznick is keen to get *Pretty Pennies* on its legs, so he wants everybody locked down and ready to go." She tapped Matilda's contract with the end of her pencil. "What *is* unusual, however, is a backup. But that's the Selznick boys for you. Always have a backup plan."

20

On the drive to work the following morning, Amelia see-sawed with fluctuating emotions.

On the upside was Benji. She'd driven from Selznick's offices to his house, where he'd been nursing his second post-work, pre-dinner whiskey. She had breathed easier when she'd seen he was two drinks in. He was such a mushy cuddle-bear when he'd had a few. She didn't want to risk another quarrel now that she'd gone and signed a legal contract.

When she showed him her copy of the contract, hoping for hoorays and congratulations, he had admitted that while disappointed, he wasn't shocked. But his stoic acceptance hadn't lasted long and soon they were enjoying a vigorous tumble between the sheets. Maybe, Amelia mused as she steered north onto Crescent Heights Boulevard, that was how galoots like him said, "Good for you, buckaroo."

However, on the downside of the see-saw sat Matilda.

Will you be content with a second-banana role?

What a double-dealing, double-crossing, back-stabbing snake in the grass.

Why had Amelia been so surprised? Showbiz swarmed with

people like her. You're surprised, she told herself, because you didn't think it would happen *to you*.

* * *

Amelia spent the morning selling rubbing alcohol to nurses and Bayer Aspirin to dipsomaniacs until she glimpsed Matilda pantomiming smoking a cigarette to one of the waitresses and slinking out the back.

Amelia charged into the alley after her. "You've got some nerve."

Matilda drew long and hard on her Parliament. "Is that a bad thing?"

"Your whole speech about not wanting to play second banana."

"What of it?"

"It was a load of stinky old baloney."

Matilda spat a shred of tobacco from the side of her mouth—or pretended to for effect. "How'd you find out?"

"Myron Selznick's secretary gave me the wrong contract to sign. Imagine my surprise when I found *your* autograph on the dotted line. YOU'RE A DIRTY SCHEMING ROTTEN LITTLE LIAR!" Amelia hadn't intended to yell. If Mr. Schwab should overhear, it would make *her* look bad, not Matilda.

"Listen," Matilda insisted, "I meant what I said, honest. But my neighbor at Fox—just a bit player, but she knows things—she opened my eyes about getting in. Then I heard you'd landed Myron Selznick, and, well . . ." Matilda made a circle in the air with her cigarette. "So later, when my brother's neighbor paid me twenty bucks to play his girlfriend for a business dinner at Perino's—a chance to hobnob with real money? You bet I jumped."

"Is that where you met Myron?"

Matilda nodded. "Bold as brass, I walked up and talked to him. Easy to do with men like that. When I mentioned *Pretty Pennies*, he could see I knew what I was talking about. If it's any comfort, I practically had to beg him to take me on."

Outside of Polly, Luddie, and Benji, Amelia drew a blank on discussing Myron with anyone. Especially not at work.

Unless . . .

What about that conversation with Mr. Schwab the day she broke the perfume bottle? Had she mentioned Myron's name then? She'd been so rattled by Benji that anything could've spilled out.

Was Matilda telling her the God's honest truth? Amelia couldn't be sure. And anyway, she had to get back to selling aspirin.

"You'd better watch it," she said, pulling on the door that led back inside. "You're about to burn your fingers. On the cigarette, I mean."

* * *

"And I'd never have known if some distracted secretary hadn't handed me the wrong contract."

"On such happenstance, life turns." Luddie tossed a Scotchmallow into his mouth. "What does Benji say about all this?"

The audience from the previous session at the Fox Wilshire Theatre was streaming onto the sidewalk, so Amelia, Polly, and Luddie lingered at the edge of its rainbow-patterned terrazzo.

"He didn't leap over the moon about it, but he didn't put his foot down or anything."

"He knows better than to try that with you," Polly said.

Amelia stole a Scotchmallow and bit down. That caramel. So buttery. That chocolate. So smooth. Was it too late to run back to See's Candies and get her own box? "Anyhow, it's a moot point. I've signed the contract and he's now back at work on *Beau Geste*."

"Isn't that movie coming out in a few weeks?"

"William Wellman is still fiddling with it, and will be until the day before the official release, so Benji'll be busy eighteen hours a day. Or at least that's what he said over the phone. You don't think he's punishing me, do you?"

"For taking the stand-in job?" Polly filched a Scotchmallow too. "I wouldn't have guessed he was that petty."

"Me, either." Amelia eyed the "Now Playing" poster. "Mind you, I'd never have pictured Henry Fonda as Abraham Lincoln, so don't ask me."

A sly smile had wriggled onto Luddie's face. "Benji's roommate might know." He lifted his chin at a rake-thin guy in shirtsleeves. "That's him, isn't it?" he asked Polly. "The guy we saw on New Year's Day when Harry Cohn nearly caught us on his lot."

Polly led them through the thinning crowds to where he was standing alone, hands jammed into his pockets.

"Noah, right?" Polly said. "Remember us? Polly Maddox and Ludlow Sinclair."

His prominent Adam's apple jiggled as it pressed against his bow tie. "What a pleasant surprise."

Amelia stepped out from behind them. "Hi, Noah."

"Gosh!" The guy's crooked teeth didn't hamper his smile. "It seems like ages since the household sat down for a marathon Sunday breakfast."

That first morning at Benji's, Amelia had emerged from his bedroom to find two of his housemates had also brought girls home. She'd felt decadently bohemian, drinking black coffee and wolfing sweet rolls while they had discussed Churchill, Sartre, and Bugsy Siegel.

"Where's Benji?" he asked. "Oh, right. *Beau Geste* reshoots? Every crewmember, down to the Saharan sand guy, is counting the hours until that blasted movie is in the can."

Relieved that Benji had been telling her the truth, Amelia asked, "Coming in or going out?"

"Coming in. May I join you?"

If Amelia hadn't been looking him straight in the eye, she'd have missed the flicker of interest he sent Polly's way. *My, my.*

The line for tickets stretched almost as far as the door.

"Congratulations on getting the stand-in job on Selznick's new picture," Noah said.

"Benji told you?"

"It's all he talks about." Noah sighed as they inched forward. "And all I can think is 'Here we go again.'"

"Again?"

"A repeat of his last girlf—" His wallet slipped through his fingers and landed on the terrazzo. As he stooped to pick it up, Amelia caught Polly's eye. *What am I supposed to say to that?*

"Don't stop now." Polly coaxed him with a docile smile that lingered longer than it needed to. "How is Amelia like Benji's last girlfriend?"

Benji had never mentioned past girlfriends; she had always assumed that, like her, he had no old flames to talk about. Noah watched her, waiting. She made a rolling gesture with her hand.

"He's not happy about your stand-in job."

"Kinda odd, isn't it, for someone who works in a studio?"

"He's around actresses and he considers them all to be self-centered egomaniacs, so he fears you'll go down the same path."

The line shuffled forward again. "But Amelia will be a stand-in," Polly said. "Not on screen."

"Yes, but he sees it as the top of a very slippery slope."

"What's so slippery about standing under hot lights for hours?"

"She had no intention of going into the movies, either." Noah dropped his ever-so-slightly reedy voice down half an octave. "But then a Twentieth Century-Fox scout offered her a contract that paid her four times what she was earning at her dental receptionist job. Darryl Zanuck's libidinous peepers zeroed in on her straight away."

"Uh-oh," Luddie muttered.

"And pretty soon she became one of his regular four o'clock girls."

"Benji didn't know?"

"She landed a featured role in a Shirley Temple picture and got bumped to a hundred a week. We thought she was on her way, but the drinking got worse. Benji threw her a surprise birthday party to cheer her up. Instead, everything came out that night, real ugly. She disappeared a few days later. Sent him a Dear John letter with no return address. Never heard from her again."

They reached the box office window. If Benji wasn't pushing a deadline, Amelia might have skipped *Young Mr. Lincoln* and run straight to Paramount. I'm made of sterner stuff, she'd tell him. You should have trusted me with your history so I could allay all your silly fears. I'm not that other girl. "Explains a lot," she said. "Wish I'd known."

Luddie swung away from the window, four tickets in hand, eyebrows sky high. "What would it change? Are you saying you wouldn't have taken the job?"

"Oh, please. You ought to know me better than that by now."

"I also know a lot of girls who'd do more for less reason."

Off the top of her head, Amelia could think of several herself. "I'm not one of them. But if I'd known what was going on backstage, I might have approached the subject with a little more consideration."

Luddie handed out the tickets as they ambled toward the auditorium doors. "Because God forbid he should come right out and tell you."

He delivered his assertion with a little more force than Amelia was used to. Not that he was wrong, but, she reminded herself, the important thing was to keep this nugget about his history in mind the next time she saw him. "The point is, I know now, and I have time to think about how to talk about it with him.

"You should hold off until after *Beau Geste* has wrapped," Noah said. "The studio's breathing down their necks. He needs to focus one hundred percent on his job." He wagged a bony finger in her face. "Benji *cannot* know I've spilled the beans about the old girlfriend. I only did it because I think you two make a very agreeable couple."

It sounded like Benji would be imprisoned in *Beau Geste* until its release date, more than a week away. Meanwhile, Noah was making goo-goo eyes at Polly, and unless Amelia was wildly mistaken, Polly wasn't hating his moonstruck glances.

The theater had started to fill up, but they found a quartet of ideal seats. Working in tandem, Amelia and Luddie discreetly maneuvered Polly and Noah into sitting together. Polly surveyed the rows around them to ensure nobody was within eavesdropping distance.

"I don't suppose there's any Columbia scuttlebutt you can share about *Pretty Pennies*?"

"My charming boss got his nose out of joint over how much Selznick screwed him on Rita's loan-out fee. His opening offer was two grand per week. Selznick countered with a firm one thousand seventy-five. First, final, and only offer."

"One thousand and seventy-five dollars?" Luddie said. "A remarkably odd figure."

"That's what I thought."

Polly turned to Amelia. "One thousand—*and seventy-five*. That explains why Mr. Selznick is forking out so much for your stand-in job: He's not the one paying."

"Care to explain?" Noah asked.

"Don't worry," Amelia said, smooth as a soda fountain counter. "Polly will lay it all out for you later." She ignored her roommate's *Quit it!* knee nudge. "Tell me, is Cohn getting nervous about how well *Mr. Smith Goes to Washington* will fare at the box office?"

"Very. That's what the Hayworth loan-out was about. Hedging his financial bets in case *Mr. Smith* lays an egg. He wants to piggyback on Selznick's refined taste—of which he has zero. But Rita is beyond thrilled."

"Good parts don't come along too often."

"Yes, that, as well as the fact that filming on Catalina will take her outside Cohn's grip. And also"—he lowered his voice when a couple of housewives took seats in the row behind them—"her marriage isn't going too great. Her husband is twice her age and feels entitled to help himself to her money. Wild horses couldn't stop her from getting on that Catalina steamer."

A year ago, Amelia hadn't heard of Rita Hayworth. But now rarely a day went by that she didn't get mentioned by Louella, Hedda, Sheilah, or Kathryn. When the right time came, she would make Benji see she was nothing like that rotten cow who'd screwed him over. But for now, she wanted to know more about this girl who had changed the course of her life. "I only met Rita briefly during the screen test. What's she like?"

"She was a nice, regular girl whose only aim was pleasing her father. I'm not convinced she even planned on having a career. Now that it's taking off, I think she feels like she's standing on quicksand." He thought for a moment, then added, "She needs a friend in her corner."

"I could be that friend."

"She'd love that," Noah said. "I'll find a way to pass along that message and see if we can get the two of you together before filming starts."

"Yes, do." Amelia kept her eyes on Polly. "Getting together can be so much fun."

21

Amelia knocked on the doorjamb of the executive suite before she saw Polly was on the phone. "I can wait outside," she told Marcella.

"Waiting outside is for messenger boys and obnoxious reporters." Marcella waved her in. "Polly's talking to Hitchcock's secretary. Now that we've built Manderley, they want to change the exterior like it's a sandcastle."

Amelia took the seat at Marcella's desk. "Is Rita here yet?"

"No, but Irene is." She dropped to a stage whisper. "Rearranging his office."

A few nights ago, Polly had come home from work with the news that Rita Hayworth would pose for publicity shots while signing her contract with David O. Selznick on her first visit to the studio.

Never mind that Rita's contract was with Cohn or that her initial visit had been the day of her screen test. All that mattered was the daily newspapers and trades having photographs to accompany news of Rita Hayworth's loan-out.

Amelia had asked Polly about being there. Not for the photo, but because of what Noah had said about Rita needing a friend. When Polly had mentioned her upcoming visit, Amelia went to

Irene, who approached her husband, who had responded, "All the better to put Rita at ease."

Polly dropped her telephone into its cradle and gave Amelia a quick smile by way of greeting. "I've talked them out of changing the shape of the windows and the angle of the roof," she told Marcella. "If we can add a few more chimneys and darken the front door to appear heavier, Mr. Hitchcock will be appeased."

Marcella shot Amelia a deadpan smile. "Like anybody's going to know or care if Manderley has ten chimneys or twelve."

"Morning, ladies!" A chipper fellow with a Mickey Rooney go-get-'em vigor charged into the room, a bulky camera slung around his neck. "I assume that ravishing dish sashaying in this direction is why I've been summoned?"

"Hush now!" Marcella scolded. "The dish is a bit nervous, so ixnay on your usual party trick of coming on strong." She emerged from behind her desk. "Miss Hayworth! Welcome! I'll pop my head in to alert Mr. Selznick you've arrived."

Rita's artfully curled hair swept her shoulder pads; her makeup was understated, her pale-yellow suit flattering. She extended her hand to Amelia. "I feel like such a fink for not thanking you properly. I doubt I'd be here if I hadn't had you to play off." Her eyes twinkled when Polly mentioned Amelia would be her stand-in. "I haven't had one before!"

Marcella appeared at Selznick's office door and whisked Rita inside.

"It's not fair!" Hazel used the corner of a manila folder to brush away a lock of hair. "The nerve of her being even more attractive in person."

Polly tsk-tsked. "Thank heavens *I'm* not the one who'll be standing on the set being compared to her, every single hour of every single day." She taunted Amelia with deadpan eyes. "Can you imagine?"

"For seventy-five bucks a week, I'll stand on my head and dance the hoochie-coochie," Amelia replied. "For a hundred, I'd do it in my unmentionables." She held back a joke about prancing around stark-naked for two hundred, unsure if Hazel, with her yesteryear sensibilities, would appreciate the humor.

Mr. Selznick strode out of his office. "I need to get over to the mansion set and have a stern word with Clark."

Last weekend, a tractor had nearly crushed Gable while he'd been clearing stumps on his Encino ranch. An injury would have cost Selznick the only man audiences would accept as Rhett Butler —and *Wind* might have sunk without a trace.

As Selznick disappeared into the corridor, Irene appeared arm-in-arm with Rita. "How about some lunch? One eats well here when one is with the boss's wife."

Irene was too distracted by winking at Amelia to notice the twinge of hesitation on Rita's face. But Amelia caught it and knew what the girl wanted. "Maybe we could swing by one of the *Wind* sets and give Rita a great dinner-party story."

Unlike the day Amelia's family had visited, tension crackled through Stage Eleven as crewmembers rushed the wide staircase, intent on their tasks. "Are movie sets always so tense?" she asked Irene.

"We're here on a stressful day. After Scarlett and Rhett have a fight, she nose-dives down the stairs."

Horror crinkled Rita's otherwise flawless face. "Vivien does all her own nosedives?"

"Heavens, no!" Irene said. "It's Miss Warp's job to take those chances."

Amelia asked, "You call her Miss Warp?" It sounded a tad formal for someone called on to execute such unladylike feats.

"It reminds everyone she takes risks so that the star doesn't have to." Irene's comment reminded Amelia of Thelma's question: *You're not afraid of open water, are you?* "Vivien's not terribly happy. My husband has rethought the ending of the picture. She's had to cancel her New York trip to see Larry, so naturally she's livid, and now she has to play an emotional scene, which pleases Mr. Fleming. He prefers when an actress brings real turmoil to the performance. Look!"

She directed their attention to the staircase where Gable and Leigh stood waiting, Gable in a heavy blue wool suit, and Leigh in a brocaded orange robe with black fur trim over her ruffled nightgown. When those Klieg lights switched on, they'd be sweltering.

A tall man whose graying hair lent an air of imposing authority stood at the head of the stairs with Gable and Leigh, giving them last-minute instructions about what he wanted in the scene where Scarlett told Rhett she was pregnant and Rhett leeringly asked who the father was. Fleming got what he was after in two takes. While the crew fiddled with the enormous Technicolor camera perched at the top of the staircase, Vivien shrugged off her elaborate robe and handed it to a woman in a wig that resembled Scarlett's disheveled hair.

Irene took Rita by the hand to say hello to Vivien. Amelia elected to observe Vivien's stand-in. She crept closer to secure a clearer view.

"Now, Miss Warp," Fleming said, "raise those fists above your head and try to beat them down on Clark. He'll block with his left arm. Your momentum carries you forward. Plant your hands on that second step, tuck your head and flip over. Roll once more, then fling yourself toward the bottom. One final flip when you hit those last steps." He addressed Gable. "Freeze in horror before you throw your hat aside. Take a few steps, but stumble because you're in shock. Don't get up fast, though. Still be near the top of the stairs when she rolls onto the rug."

Gable and Miss Warp stepped into place in front of the camera. A moment later, the overhead banks switched on, pouring ungodly torrents of glare and stifling heat onto the set. Amelia shielded her eyes. How were they supposed to see anything? She squinted as Miss Warp hurled herself down the steps and sprawled on the carpeting like a discarded rag doll.

Amelia was still recoiling at the clunk of bone hitting steps when Fleming yelled, "CUT!" from behind the camera. "But in the next take—"

Next take? She had to do it again?

"—widen your legs as you somersault down. That way, we can see Scarlett's skirts flare."

Miss Warp nodded, straightening her costume as she remounted the steps.

Gable and Miss Warp took their places a second time and waited until Fleming called out "ACTION!"

And then a third time. "Fling your arms out."

A fourth. "Don't fall so smoothly. You're a Southern belle, not a Hollywood stuntwoman."

A fifth. "Roll twice onto the rug; otherwise, it won't match the insert."

Each time Miss Warp scaled the stairs to her starting position, she took longer and moved less gracefully. Had Fleming not been looking at Gable when he announced one more take "for insurance," he'd have seen relief sweep across her face.

And Amelia's, too. What if that had been her up there in the heavy robe? Would anyone expect her to take such daunting chances? Had she been so naïve as to think her job on *Pretty Pennies* was simply to stand around?

"You should see that gal on a horse," Irene said by Amelia's side. "She gives those Gower Gulch cowboys a gallop for their money."

Oh, sweet Jesus. What if Virginia includes a scene with a stampeding horse?

They strolled into the warmth of the early summer. "Thank heavens for you," Rita said. "It's bad enough I'll have to dive into the ocean for loose change. I'm not that great in the water."

"No need to fret," Irene reassured her. "Amelia's being paid well for her troubles." The women angled up the short pathway leading up to the commissary. Amelia lagged behind. Was that why the job paid so well? Because of the stunt-work danger money?

Although it was not yet noon, the dining hall was already buzzing with contract players and craftspeople seated at tables for four and six, wolfing down soups, salads, and sandwiches. As

Amelia, Irene, and Rita passed by, the people at each table paused their lively chatter to stare—not at the boss's wife, this time, but at the inescapably gorgeous Rita. If she noticed the attention, she gave no outward signs but instead glided in Irene's wake like a paper boat.

Irene led them to a quiet corner at the far end of the commissary and flagged a passing waiter. "Jean-Claude, *mon cheri,* I'll have the French Lamb Chops with Bearnaise sauce, and Risotto Milanese on the side." She turned to Amelia. "And you?"

Still flummoxed by being punched in the guts over what her stand-in job truly entailed, Amelia told the waiter that she'd have the same. Rita ordered a Cobb Salad, "but light on the blue cheese and green onions."

Amelia should have guessed she wouldn't order anything that came smothered in Bearnaise sauce. What a difference from Ingrid Bergman devouring two ice cream sundaes in a row.

Oh, Benji, Amelia thought. Is that why you're reluctant for me to go down this slippery slope? Because you've witnessed actresses gulping down black coffee and nibbling on plain salads to fit into suffocating corsets before performing on sweltering sets?

"Yoo-hoo!" Irene snapped her fingers in front of Amelia's nose. "Are you with us?"

"Sorry." Amelia shook her napkin—*Linen? How fancy.* "What did I miss?"

Rita smiled, sweet as one of the cookies she probably never ate. "I'm thrilled at the chance to do a picture like this, and I wanted you to be aware that I know about the intrinsic part you've played in making this project happen."

Amelia narrowed her eyes at Irene, who shook her head. "Don't look at me."

"Noah Briggs," Rita said, "who I suspect is forced to do the bookkeeping equivalent of fancy footwork."

"He's not alone in that department," Irene put in.

Amelia wondered if she was referring to herself and how she had to manage a household budget based on her husband's wretched luck at card games. "Noah told me he'd try to get a message to you."

"And he did. He also told me about what you've been doing behind the scenes, and I wanted to thank you."

"You're very welcome." Helping Irene to nudge *Pretty Pennies* toward the screen had evolved so naturally that Amelia had given no thought to how an outsider might see it. Her only intention had been to get a more interesting career underway. A blush crept onto her cheeks; it was time to change the subject.

"I don't suppose Noah mentioned my roommate?"

"Cute redhead with freckles?"

"Our Polly?" Irene asked. "What's she got to do with this?"

Rita winked at Amelia. "No question the boy is smitten. How does your roomie feel?"

Amelia suspected it had taken Polly longer to get over the disappointment of Gil than she wanted to admit. And while Noah was a bit too bookwormy for Amelia's tastes, he struck her as a good match for Pol. "I wouldn't say she's been sitting by the phone, but I did hear her calling the operator to check that the line was working."

"Should we encourage things along?" Irene asked.

"Yes," Amelia said. "We absolutely should."

22

Amelia unwound the last of her hair curlers. "I still haven't decided," she called out to Polly. "The pale pink with white piping, or the dark emerald with black stitching?"

"Green with black." The electric iron whooshed as Polly stood it upright. "And yes, you can borrow my black blouse because I'm appropriating your crocodile-skin shoulder bag."

Amelia had left the curlers in too long; she looked like Fox's backup plan for when Shirley Temple grew up. "Did you ever think this day would arrive?" she asked, attacking her scalp with a hairbrush.

"It seems like only yesterday that *Wind* started shooting. Suddenly here we are five months later—"

"Five months is 'suddenly' in nobody's book."

"It feels like one long memo that I can stop typing today at noon and then we'll all head on in."

"Thanks again for the invite."

"I already told you. It was Irene's doing."

Amelia had barely heard anything after Polly had announced two nights ago that she could take Amelia to the *Gone with the Wind* wrap party. Just being included was thrilling, and she was determined to absorb every detail, from Vivien Leigh's nail polish to Olivia de Havilland's brooch.

"You should've seen Ida's face when I told her," Amelia said. "Can you believe she's read that book *seventeen* times?"

The telephone shrieked behind Polly. "There's going to be cake. A huge one. Maybe we can steal Ida a piece."

Amelia called out, "DON'T THINK IDA HASN'T ALREADY ASKED FOR A SLICE!" Her curls were finally relaxing. Perhaps she should wear it up? It wouldn't hurt to come across a bit more sophisticated.

Polly appeared in the bathroom mirror, worry creasing her brow. "Mr. Schwab's on the line."

"Did he—oh no. Please. Not today." Amelia couldn't ignore the sinking feeling dropping into the pit of her stomach. "Tell him I've left already."

"He heard you screaming about cake."

Damn Mr. Schwab, damn the cake, and damn me and my big mouth.

* * *

On any other day, Amelia would have been pleased as all get-out to be serving up fried-egg sandwiches and grape juice cobbler once more. And on any other day, she might have said, "No can do." But Mr. Schwab was two waitresses short and had always been a decent boss whose policy was "Nobody wants a waitress who looks like she's about to upchuck into their mushroom soup." She had assured him, "I'll be there in a jiffy," then rushed out, telling Polly, "I'm too nice for my own good."

She hadn't given much thought to Matilda being one of the waitresses who had called in sick until her favorite customer, Joseph, a Warner Bros. security guard, plunked his behind on a stool. "What's the latest over at Warners?" she asked him.

"Fireworks!" He wiggled his fingers like a minstrel dancer. "Bette Davis, Errol Flynn, and Michael Curtiz are locked in a three-way hate triangle on *The Private Lives of Elizabeth and Essex*. Don't be surprised if you read Kathryn Massey in *The Hollywood Reporter* telling you how one of them's been pushed out a window."

Their conversation meandered through a tapestry of subjects: rumors that *Wunderkind* Orson Welles was arriving in Hollywood soon, the recently opened New York World's Fair, and what might happen to Spain now that it was at peace and Europe was lumbering toward all-out war.

When Amelia mentioned the *Gone with the Wind* wrap party, Joseph smirked. "Only one Schwab's waitress could go, and you drew the short straw?" That was when she learned one of Joseph's pinochle buddies, a security guard at Selznick International, who drooled into his Schwab's shrimp salad over Matilda, had arranged for her to be on the lot today.

When the first opportunity arose, Amelia coaxed Ida to cover for her and snuck into a phone booth. Polly didn't answer her phone, but Hazel did.

"She's running an errand for Mr. Selznick. Can I help?"

"Has she mentioned a girl I work with named Matilda?" Amelia asked.

"The gal who came back from her . . . *ahem* . . . nine-month sabbatical, all blonde and bouncy?"

"I don't suppose you've seen anyone answering to that description around there today?"

Hazel registered no surprise when Amelia ran through what Joseph had told her. "My dad runs the Follies Theatre on Main Street in downtown, so I can spot that type from a hundred paces. I'll tell Polly you called. Don't worry, we'll keep an eye out for Matilda."

Back at the counter, she asked Joseph, "Ever been to the Follies Theatre?"

Joseph possessed the rough-and-ready face of a saloon brawler, so Amelia wasn't prepared for the carmine blush that suffused his face. He stirred his coffee even though he took it black. "I may have."

She wiped imaginary crumbs from the counter near his plate. "Whatcha not telling me, Joseph, ol' pal?"

"A nice girl like you shouldn't know about such joints."

"Why not?"

"The Follies is a notorious burlesque house."

* * *

Through the mid-morning coffee-and-donuts rush, Amelia didn't have time to mull over the revolving carousel of reasons Matilda might have for finagling her way onto the Selznick lot. Had she tried her luck with Mr. Schuessler, the casting director? Nah, that wasn't right. Polly had assured her that Fred was a stand-up guy, impervious to the charms of girls like Matilda. Had she pushed her heaving bosom into Selznick's face? He had, after all, propositioned Polly on her very first day.

As the huge clock above the entrance ticked toward noon, Ida slipped in alongside Amelia. "I took a message from your roommate," she said in a low voice. "Matilda at SIP. Defend your territory."

Amelia arranged a double order of donuts into a pyramid for a couple of firemen and slid the plate across. "Dammit."

"Is SIP short for Selznick International Pictures? Is that where she is right now?"

"'Fraid so."

"New look, new name, same ambition."

Amelia had witnessed that hard-edged flintiness too, but had written it off as a determination to not let life kick her in the teeth a second time. It was a quality Amelia had admired—but not anymore.

"I'll call one of the afternoon shift girls to come in early," Ida said in her ear. "I can invent an excuse to tell Mr. S."

"Thank you, but no." Amelia looked around and saw Mr. Schwab at the pharmacy counter. "He doesn't deserve to be lied to."

"And *that*, my dear girl"—Ida patted her maternally on the back—"is why he's going to say, 'Go do what you need to do and leave me to deal with Matilda.'"

* * *

Hazel led Amelia onto Stage Five, where a crowd had gathered around Aunt Pittypat's house. Polly stood by a staircase to nowhere, her attention locked on a cluster of crew to the right. Amelia threaded through the throng until Polly was close enough to grip her arm. "You made it!"

"I have territory to defend." They faced the flock of rubberneckers. "Who are those guys?"

"Mr. Selznick asked me to keep tabs on Vivien."

"Is she okay?"

"She finished the opening scene this morning in Walter's new costume, then ran from the porch to her dressing room and changed into"—the admirers loosened to reveal Vivien Leigh in an unadorned navy-blue suit—"that."

"Why so dowdy?"

"She wore it for her *Rebecca* screen test. Now that Olivier's locked in as Maxim, she's desperate to play opposite him."

"So she went from playing sixteen-year-old Scarlett O'Hara complaining about how the talk of war was spoiling all the fun to the whimpering second Mrs. de Winter? And now the wrap party? Talk about stamina."

"I give her an hour after the cake is served. Hazel thinks she won't last twenty minutes, but that's not enough time to shake everyone's hands before she flees home to sleep for a week."

"Speaking of Hazel, did you know her dad runs a burlesque house?"

"*What?*"

Amelia was glad to see her pal was still shockable. "The Follies on Main Street."

Polly surveyed the swelling crowd. "Look, there's Irene." Mrs. Selznick stood at the elephant door in a crisp cream linen suit, looking around for a familiar face. "Let's see if she knows."

Irene brightened as they approached. "Can you believe we've reached the marathon finishing line?" When Amelia shared the snippet about Hazel, Irene's eyes widened. "Well, well. Our very own Gibson Girl isn't so demure, after all. I love it when people surprise me." She tapped her clutch to her chin. "Should we pry more details from her?"

A buzz swept the onlookers as Marcella wheeled a giant cake on an oversized brass cocktail cart toward Selznick's group—Vivien Leigh, Victor Fleming, and the newly wedded Clark Gable and Carole Lombard, fresh from their Arizona nuptials. Marcella wasn't yet halfway to the VIPs when a full-throated wag sang, "Glory, glory, hallelujah! Glory, glory, hallelujah! Glory, glory, hallelujah! The picture's done at last!"

The crowd applauded as Marcella positioned the cake in front of Mr. Selznick and lit the blue tapers planted at each corner. Pale yellow frosting on top read:

GONE WITH THE WIND
January 26 to June 27
152 days of giving a damn.
THANK YOU EVERYONE!

Irene giggled to herself. "The dedication was my idea. A subtle 'screw you' to those bluenoses at the Breen Office. David roared with laughter when I suggested it." She studied her husband with an unvarnished mix of tenderness and nostalgia. "I can't remember the last time he laughed like that. It warmed my heart to know I can still pull it off."

"If you'll indulge me," Mr. Selznick boomed over the hubbub. "Long-winded as I may sometimes get—"

"Sometimes?" Irene lobbed back at him.

He took her jibe on the chin like a good sport. "This project has tested our endurance. I demanded much from you, and no one disappointed. Hal Kern and I have been assembling the footage, and I assure you our collective effort has created a triumph. When you see the final version, you'll be as proud as I am to have brought *Gone with the Wind* to the screen."

After the eruption of applause died down, he plunged a wide knife between *WITH* and *THE*.

Hazel inserted herself between Polly and Amelia. "Mrs. Selznick, I suspect that was the shortest speech your husband has ever given."

"I suggested as much over breakfast this morning, but I'd assumed it fell on deaf ears." Irene rounded the four of them into a huddle. "Let's talk about you."

"What about me?" Hazel asked.

"You tight-lipped clam," Polly chided. "All these months and not one mention about your father running a burlesque house?"

"There's not much to tell." She twisted her charm bracelet with studied indifference. "Mother was a headlining stripper in her prime. Had an act with a trained parakeet that removed her clothes—'Dance of the Seventeen Veils.' She came to LA to play the Follies. Dad was just another theater manager to her, but he fell hard."

"And pursued her?"

"Mom had no shortage of suitors, so whatever tactic he used, it must've worked. And that was before he saw she has a head for numbers."

Amelia marveled at the difference between this girl's family life and hers. She didn't know whether to be jealous or thankful. "She keeps the books?"

"Yes, but who knows for how long? Mayor La Guardia's cracking down on burlesque in New York. Once they close there, the rest will topple like domin—" She broke off, catching sight of a Harlow blonde in the crowd. "Is that who you meant?"

Amelia had grown used to Matilda's brash side-sassing customers, flirting like a cigarette girl on commission. But this was the other Matilda, the one who had followed her to Farley's office and talked about Catholic convents and unwed mothers. Arms folded, she lingered on the fringe, speaking with nobody.

"That girl?" Irene asked, a tad scornfully. "I've seen her with Thelma from Casting a few times at the Retake Room down near MGM. Every now and then I take David there after work for some married-people one-on-one time."

"Matilda's been chumming up with Thelma?" Polly glanced at Amelia. *The plot thickens.*

Irene's two-fingered whistle pierced the air, halting Thelma en route to the cake. "Our stand-in has a question for you."

"About Matilda Charles," Amelia added.

Thelma changed course. "Yes?"

"I'm curious to know what she's been jockeying for at the Retake Room."

Thelma's face was a blank page. "Jockeying?"

Hazel tsked. "Dames like that butter you up, then they lower the boom."

"I thought so, too—at first. But then we discovered we have interests in common."

"Such as?" Polly asked.

"Pinochle. My husband and I play it socially. You wouldn't think it to look at her, but she's a first-rate player."

Pinochle—that's what Joseph from Warner Bros. played with the Selznick security guard. A coincidence? Amelia doubted it.

"And then there's Charles Dickens," Thelma continued. "That girl has devoured everything he wrote—even *Barnaby Rudge*, and nobody reads that one."

"You sit there talking about card games and old books?" Amelia asked.

"As well as her prowess in the pool. She was her high school's swimming and diving champion. And she can hold her breath under water for over two minutes. Quite a feat, isn't it? I can't imagine holding mine for thirty seconds."

Somebody called Thelma's name, and she flitted away, quickly swallowed by the crowd.

"Two minutes. Impressive," Irene said. "Rita Hayworth is a nice gal and all, but she won't be jumping off any cliffs. You can do all that, right?" she asked Amelia.

Amelia managed a spirited "Yuh-huh!" Even though the closest she'd come to real diving was a running jump off the Malibu pontoon. And she certainly, definitely, absolutely couldn't hold her breath for anywhere near two minutes.

Did all this mean Matilda was far better suited to the stand-in job than she was?

Hazel was right. Sweet-talkers like Matilda butter you up first, then they lower the boom. *And she's lowering it right down on my head.*

* * *

While they savored the chocolate cake and Irene mused about life after *Wind's* principal photography, Amelia's thoughts returned to Thelma's question at the redhead cattle call: "You're not afraid of open water, are you?"

Amelia had assumed Thelma had meant jumping off a boat in the protected waters of Avalon Bay. But had she been talking about out in the middle of the Pacific? Where jellyfish drifted? Whales lurked? Sharks prowled?

Somewhere on the soundstage's periphery, a piano struck up "Happy Days Are Here Again" and the throng joined in. As voices proclaimed their cares and troubles gone, Amelia fretted about the dangerous stunts that might be expected of her.

Jump off cliffs?

Or from the crow's nest of a sailing ship?

Would she have to dive into Avalon Bay and pick up pennies off the seabed?

How long would it take to reach the bottom and return to the surface?

Around her, people swigged beer and guzzled champagne as they sang a song of cheer again. The excitement and anticipation of attending this party leaked away as dread swooped down on her like a flock of plunging pelicans. She couldn't even muster the energy to confront Matilda as she had planned—although she probably should have. But if she caused a scene at an otherwise cheerful party, it might reflect badly on Polly. Better, she decided, to keep mum until she had deciphered this contradictory girl. She jostled a path through the revelers until she saw a red exit sign.

An unfamiliar scent of smoke caught her off guard. To her left, the girl of the hour sat perched on a rickety bench, her cigarette's orange glow suspended between delicate fingers.

"Had enough of the revelry?" Amelia asked.

"'Fraid so." Vivien Leigh offered Amelia a cigarette from a long, gold pack with a fancy logo.

Amelia withdrew one and lit it with a match from the Cock 'n Bull, a mock British pub on the Sunset Strip. "Sorry to intrude on your privacy."

"There's no such thing as privacy on a movie set."

Amelia drew on the cigarette. The taste was smokier than any American cigarette she had tried. Smoother, too. No wonder Vivien preferred—she read the packet's label—Benson & Hedges. "I heard your little situation resolved itself. I bet that was a relief."

"'Relief' barely covers it. Especially as Larry and I aren't even married." A surprisingly girlish titter slipped out of her. "Not to each other, anyway."

That day in Selznick's car, Vivien had looked as diaphanous as gossamer. One moderately stiff wind and she'd be blown halfway to Catalina. But she came across more grounded now. Fatigue crinkled the edges of her eyes and jittered her restless fingertips. But at the same time, a blanket of contentment enveloped her.

"I admire the way you've taken on such a quintessentially American role," Amelia said. "It took guts."

Vivien crushed her cigarette stub with the heel of her shoe and lit another. "I felt I knew what the screen version of Scarlett O'Hara needed. Fortunately, Mr. Cukor and Mr. Selznick agreed."

"Now that it's over, were you right? Or were you fooling yourself?" Amelia asked the question lightly, but secretly, she was asking for herself.

Vivien gave a joyful laugh. "I'll admit the accent was difficult to master. And running around in those wretched hoop skirts took some getting used to. But no, I don't think I was fooling myself. I understood way back in my youth, growing up in Bangalore and Saint Malo, Biarritz and San Remo, it's a matter of having confidence in oneself. Without it, you have nothing. But with it, you can get everything you want."

23

Amelia kicked and kicked and kicked until she felt the edge of the pool. She lifted her head out of the water. "How'd I do?"

Irene looked up from her wristwatch. "A new personal best."

Slicing a couple of seconds off the time it took Amelia to swim two lengths of the Selznick swimming pool was encouraging, but her goal was still out of reach. Then again, she was lucky to have access to a private pool at all.

After Amelia had confessed that she was only a fair swimmer and unskilled at deep diving, Irene could have appointed Matilda as her replacement. But instead, Irene had said, "In that case, we'd better get you up to snuff. Our house. Sunday morning. Eleven a.m. I'll show you everything Johnny Weissmuller taught me."

Irene deposited her watch on the patio table. "Next up, dead man's float. Do you know about the trick with the hips?" She was slipping off her silk Siamese sun robe when the maid appeared at the patio's French doors.

"Mrs. Selznick, a Mr. Hartman is on the line."

"Dudley Hartman?"

"Didn't say, ma'am. Shall I inquire?"

Irene had hired the private eye to plunge down the Bernice

Hoag rabbit hole, but Amelia figured the odds he'd track her down were stacked against him. "You think he's got news?"

"I can't imagine how he could possibly have tracked down Bernice." Irene marched toward the house. "If he has, I'll eat my hat. And I've got several that'll do the job nicely. Meanwhile, skip the floating hips. Get back to doing laps."

Amelia clambered out of the pool, took a deep breath, and dove back into the cool, clear water. True, Santa Monica Beach might have been the smarter place to practice, but what was a more fitting place to start boosting her confidence than Irene's pool, with Johnny Weissmuller's second-hand instruction?

She was completing her fifth lap when Irene's strident voice sang out, "He wants to drop by to share what he's learned."

"Which implies he's got news worth sharing."

"He'll be here in around forty-five minutes, but you need to shave off at least ten seconds before I'll let you go home."

* * *

Amelia and Irene skipped doing their makeup and fixing their hair ahead of Hartman's arrival. A man who dealt with Hollywood's slimy skunks and dirty dogs would hardly flinch at seeing them without mascara.

"Good morning, ladies. Sorry for the short notice, but I have a last-minute meeting at the Beverly Hills Hotel. Shall we get down to business?"

They had been seated around the dining table for only a few seconds when he launched into his findings.

"First up, Amelia, tell your mother the 'Gale' piece of the puzzle made all the difference." He flipped open a folder he had brought with him. "Okay, so, MacKinley Burroughs left Delish-Delite Candy in nineteen-nineteen and bought the Cicero Bijou, a movie house west of downtown Chicago. Mack died in early twenty-nine. Later that year, the IRS presented Bernice with a huge bill."

"In other words," Irene said, "Mack was a tax evader."

"That's why the Bijou changed hands by year's end. I couldn't find the sale price, but I tracked down what a similar theater went for nearby. If Bernice got roughly the same for the Bijou, after the IRS took their share, she'd have had a little left over, but not much."

This was already more than Amelia and Lois had expected. And if that was the sum total of his detective work, he could have shared that with Irene over the phone. "What else?"

"I assumed Bernice went out and got a job. I scoured census records, telephone directories, tax audits, obituaries, classified ads—"

"What did you find?" Irene asked.

"It got very convoluted. I won't bore you with all the ins and outs, but let me ask you this: Ever heard of someone called Dora Gibbs?"

The name rang no bells with Amelia. When Irene mused that Lois knew Bernice better than anyone, Amelia went to the telephone and got her mother on the line. But, no, 'Dora Gibbs' didn't sound familiar. Back at the dining table, Amelia asked Hartman how that name had come up.

"It's from a moving company that transported a houseful of furniture from Cicero early in thirty-five."

"Moving company?" Irene asked. "Goodness gracious, Mr. Hartman, talk about no stone left unturned."

"A stretch, I know, but in the private eye business, you develop a hunch for these little coincidences. Movers are most often booked and paid for by the husbands. A woman's name usually means a widow."

The living room telephone rang. "Speaking of hunches," Irene said, rising from her chair, "women's intuition tells me that's your mom calling back."

A waiting silence fell between Amelia and Hartman until Irene called out, "It's Lois! Come listen to this!" When all three were gathered around the receiver, Irene told Lois to repeat what she'd said.

"I know it's a shot in the dark, but I wanted to point out that when Bernice made *Pretty Pennies*, her screen name was *Isadora* Gibbs. It's not the same, but gosh, it's close!"

They thanked Lois and rang off, then went back to the dining room table.

Amelia could picture the *Pretty Pennies* poster that adorned the corridor leading to Mr. Selznick's offices. Beneath the four-inch title were two-inch words: *Starring Isadora Gibbs*.

Hartman admitted he was getting the tingles.

"That's good, right?" Amelia asked. When he didn't respond straight away, she squirmed in her seat. "Or is it?"

"Depends."

"On?"

"This Dora Gibbs I came across, the one who moved from Cicero?"

"Yes?"

"She moved to Palm Springs."

"For pity's sake, man," Irene spluttered, "spit it out."

Hartman flattened his palms on the mahogany tabletop. "She runs the Sapphire Moon."

"NO!" The word bolted from Irene Selznick with none of her usual restraint.

"What's the Sapphire Moon?" Amelia asked.

"A bordello. Way past the outskirts. Caters to moneyed gents from LA and San Francisco. Hollywood stars, movie execs, oilmen and aviation hotshots—pretty much anyone with a thick wallet. The Sapphire Moon is elegant, exclusive, and ex-pen-sive."

"You're saying Bernice Hoag, a.k.a. Bernice Burroughs a.k.a. Isadora Gibbs a.k.a. Dora Gibbs, is a"—Amelia was still catching up with the sharp right turn this conversation had taken—"a *madam*?"

"So it seems," Irene said.

"I'm sorry, Mr. Hartman," Amelia said, "I don't mean to rain on your tingling parade, but this is rather far-fetched. The Bernice my mother described hardly sounded like the type."

"How many madams have you met?" Coming from anyone else, the question might have been malicious. But from Irene, it was merely a reminder they had wandered into territory in which she had no experience.

"That's fair," Amelia admitted, "but I still think your theory is, if not far-fetched, then . . . near-fetched."

"I thought so, too," Hartman agreed, "so I kept digging."

"And what buried bones did you find?"

"I discovered that Cicero also had a house of ill repute called the Opal Moon. And guess what—it shared a back alley with the Bijou."

"To recap," Irene said, "Mack and Bernice own the Bijou, which backs onto a brothel called the Opal Moon. A few years later, a woman with a name very similar to Bernice's screen name moves to Palm Springs, where she runs the *Sapphire* Moon." She whistled, long and low. "That's a lot to take in."

Hartman nodded. "In my line of work, we refer to that as 'one coincidence too many.'"

Amelia couldn't wait to run back to the telephone. On second thought, though, perhaps this was news best delivered in person. "I'm going to have to tread carefully when I share all this with my mother."

Hartman closed his folder. "Remember, this is a *theory*—until proven otherwise."

"How do you propose we do that?"

"Isn't it obvious?" Irene mimed an imaginary steering wheel. "Road trip to Palm Springs!"

"And what? Press our faces against the window like we're a couple of lecherous oilmen?"

"Got any better ideas?"

"I—I—" No, Amelia had to admit, she didn't. "What do you think?" she asked Hartman.

He fixed her with an earnest eye. "I'll bet my fee that if you go to Palm Springs and knock on the door of the Sapphire Moon, you'll find your mother's long-lost friend."

24

Amelia steered onto Highland Avenue; ahead of them, the pink of early dusk silhouetted the Hollywood Hills. "I'm getting jumpy."

"What have *you* got to be nervous about?" Polly asked. "I only said yes because this is a double date."

"Wasn't it obvious at *Young Mr. Lincoln* that Noah's sweet on you?"

"He's the first guy who's caught my fancy since Gil. But he works for Harry Cohn." Polly slapped her mended leg. "And you remember how *that* worked out."

"He *hates* Cohn. Isn't that a point in his favor?"

"What are the chances this is all Cohn's doing?" Polly asked. "And he's sent Noah to pitch woo?"

"To learn what?"

"Now that Mad Ox is up and running again, I keep worrying that Cohn'll come along and pull it all out from under me."

"Paging Paranoid Pol-Pol," Amelia quipped.

Polly craned her neck, searching for an open parking space. "Of all places for a nice guy like Noah to work at."

"Dontcha adore Cupid's sense of irony?" Amelia ignored Polly's snort. "Lookit, Benji and I will be there to run interference if anything goes haywire. And if it blows up in your face, we can beat a hasty retreat over there." She tapped her windshield at the Currie's ice cream parlor on the corner of Sunset. "My treat."

"Deal. But why are *you* jumpy?"

They were almost at Hollywood Boulevard before Amelia could muster the courage to voice her fear out loud. "I have a feeling Benji's going to dump me."

"Because you got the *Pretty Pennies* job?"

"Yes. No. Maybe?"

"I thought you said he was okay when you went around to tell him you'd signed the contract."

"He was."

"So what's the problem?"

"He was also drunk."

"Didn't the two of you have a nice bedtime tango later that night?"

"We did."

"Again, what's the problem here?"

Saying all this out loud sounded as silly as Amelia suspected it might, which was why she hadn't aired her misgivings before now. But because of *Beau Geste*'s marathon reshoots, she was about to see Benji for the first time since that night, and her anxiety, no matter how ill-founded, had been eating at her on the whole drive over.

"Never mind," she sighed.

"You can 'never mind' your parents; you can 'never mind' your sister; you can 'never mind' your boss, but you can't 'never mind' me." Polly prodded Amelia's shoulder with a sharp finger. "Out. With. It."

"When did you become Miss Bossy Boots?"

"And when did you become Miss Wishy-Washy?"

God help me, Amelia thought. That's how I sound. It's how I am—or might be if I don't watch myself. "He's been so busy with *Beau Geste* that I haven't seen him since then. We've had a few phone calls, but they're brief, and he's always distant and preoccupied."

"With the ex-girlfriend, I imagine."

"I keep wishing he'd bring her up."

"Not that I have a wealth of experience, but from what I can see, guys aren't very good at that sort of thing."

An extravaganza of neon greeted them as they turned onto Hollywood Boulevard. Amelia calculated she had half a dozen side streets she could use as an escape hatch before Sardi's shimmered into view.

"In other words, you're advising me to bring it up myself."

"But you can't do that, not without incriminating Noah."

"What's my alternative?"

"Quit expecting he'll voluntarily tell you about the girl." Polly laughed, hollow and self-deprecating. "Listen to me giving out romance advice. We both remember how the Gil situation turned out."

Relieved at the opportunity to change the subject, Amelia asked, "Do you miss him?"

"Heavens, no! He was the wrong guy living in the wrong city. Noah, on the other hand . . ." The rest of her thought evaporated in the honking horns of rush hour traffic.

* * *

Benji waved at them from a booth near the back, away from the shrill after-office-hours drinkers packed three deep at the bar. Amelia slid in next to Benji, while Polly sat beside Noah, who wore a midnight-blue silk bow tie with tiny gold stars, matching a jacket so tasteful that it would have been at home in Luddie's closet. Benji also looked spiffy in a pale apricot seersucker suit Amelia hadn't seen before. It was ideal for summer evenings, with a crisp rakishness that suggested he, too, had made an effort.

As they debated over Sardi's sugar-cured ham steak versus Trout Meuniere, Amelia noticed how Benji's fingers toyed with the matchbook, gripped his cigarette five different ways, stroked the stem of his martini glass, touched his collar, his cufflinks, the seam of their white linen table cloth. Noah's hands rested on the table, motionless, but his eyes were as fidgety as Benji's fingers: from water glass, to Polly, to the overflowing bar, to the front windows, back to Polly, then over to the oil painting of the Chrysler building.

Amelia settled deeper into the leather upholstery. *If that don't beat all. These two chumps are as nervous as we are.*

Noah's nerves made sense—it was his first date with Polly. But Benji? Their last face-to-face encounter had been so heated, so maddening. She hoped the care he'd taken to make himself presentable for this dinner was his way of making amends for his recent behavior, and not a sign that he'd chosen to end things in a public place.

Just shows you don't know someone till the pinch comes. If he's planning to cut me loose, let's have it over with.

She waited until after the waiter had delivered a tray of old fashioneds. "I've been in training."

"For what?" Noah asked.

"It occurred to me that my stand-in job on *Pretty Pennies* might entail open-water swimming, deep diving, jumping off cliffs. Johnny Weissmuller taught Irene how to swim, so she's been passing along his tips in her pool. I can now complete a lap in under thirty-two seconds."

"Congrats!" Noah exclaimed.

Amelia would rather have heard it from Benji. "By the time filming starts, I'll be a regular mermaid."

"Will you be jumping off actual cliffs?"

"Virginia's been sending over pages from her latest draft," Polly said. "From what Marcella has said, no cliffs so far, but she's talked about having to send someone over to Catalina to scout for locations."

"She has?" This was news to Amelia. "Meaning you?"

Polly shimmied her shoulders as though she didn't care one way or the other. The boys may have been fooled, but Amelia knew it was a telltale sign that her true feelings were the opposite of what she was about to say. "I guess I'm the obvious choice. If I get the green light, I was thinking you could go with me."

"I'd love to!"

Amelia sensed Benji stiffen beside her. The moment had come to have it out. She turned to him. "Hey, if you've got a beef over my *Pretty Pennies* job, open your trap and let's hear it."

"Okay, then." He took his time flicking cigarette ash into the triangular glass ashtray at the center of their table. "Initially, I was against the idea of you signing on because I had a terrible experience with—with someone who started out the way you did."

"One of Zanuck's four o'clock girls?" Dammit. *DAMMIT!* Amelia wanted to kick herself in the butt.

The muscles in Benji's jaw tightened "You know about her? Who told you?"

"I have regular customers from every studio," Amelia said quickly, jumping in before Benji could take a swing at the guilty party next to him. "Come to think of it, I probably know more people in the movie business than you do."

Polly laid a light, placating hand on Amelia's forearm. "You said 'initially.'" She pitched her tactful tone at Benji exactly right. "But now you're not?"

"I've had time to think about it."

Amelia wanted to wrap her arms around his neck. Would it ruin the moment, though?

"If you go location scouting on Catalina, it'll prove you can do more than stand in front of a camera and look pretty. There's so much more to you than that. I hate to see you wasting time."

"Hold your cotton-pickin' horses!" Polly thumped her empty glass onto the table. Amelia had only taken a couple of sips—how had Polly finished hers so quickly? "You see how hard those so-called pretty actresses work. I didn't realize the effort required to emote for the cameras until I watched Vivien Leigh film her scenes. The sheer concentration is exhausting."

Amelia tried to catch Polly's eye. *What are you doing? Don't spoil it now that he's come around.* But Polly was too fixated on Benji to notice.

"You missed my point, Polly."

Amelia cringed at the rising rancor in his voice.

"Your point was that Amelia is a girl with many talents."

Benji nodded. "And her job won't be to emote for the cameras, but to stand under hot lights and who knows what other arduous conditions, probably for hours, and for a thankless job. And while she can do all that standing on her head, I believe her talents can be more gainfully employed. That's all I meant."

"Maybe you did, maybe not." Polly ignored Amelia's side-eye. "These eight months at Selznick have taught me plenty. Watching Dorothy, Sibyl, Irene, Marcella—they all work twice as hard to stay in the game. They're an inspiration. I love this job more than I ever believed possible and can't imagine working anywhere else. That's all *I'm* saying."

She discreetly flared her eyes at Amelia. *How'd I do?*

Ah, so it was a performance? For Noah's benefit?

"I'm glad we've got that settled." Wry bemusement had crept back into Benji's voice. And not a moment too soon. "New topic?"

"Please," Amelia said.

"I had some rare quiet time at work this past week and I've planned out the route for my West Coast adventure."

For as long as she had known Benji, he had talked wistfully of an enthralling—to him, at least—pipe dream of driving from San Ysidro at the Mexican border up the entire West Coast to Blaine, Washington, at the Canadian border. Amelia was all for having dreams—she had one or two of her own—but couldn't he have chosen one a little more practical? Lately, whenever he'd talked about it, she had tuned him out. Why listen when they both knew he was never going to quit a good job to do it? "And is it feasible?" she asked him.

"There are a few more dirt roads than I'd like, but yeah."

"I wouldn't have thought so, but that's good news. And speaking of new topics," Amelia sidestepped, "remember that private eye Mom and I went to see?"

"Don't tell me he's tracked down your mom's friend."

"Possibly."

"Sounds intriguing. Has she been up to mischief?"

"Would you call it mischief?" Amelia asked Polly.

"Depends on your moral perspective."

"What did she do," Benji said, "rob Fort Knox and give all the gold to Dust Bowl hobos?"

"She's a madam. In a brothel!"

"Holy mackerel."

"Assuming it's the right person."

"Where is this cathouse?" Noah asked.

"Palm Springs."

"Sapphire Moon?"

"Noah Anthony Briggs!" Benji clamped a hand on his shoulder. "You sly old coonhound, you."

Noah shrugged it away. "I've sent Miss Gibbs packages of cash on more than one occasion."

Benji, Amelia, and Polly chimed a long "Ahhhh."

"And I could've saved you the cost of a private dick if I'd known you were looking for her."

"The evidence Hartman gathered is circumstantial," Polly remarked. "It only checks out if Bernice has been living under an assumed name. And we won't know that for sure unless we go out there and ring the Sapphire Moon's doorbell."

"What's stopping you?" Noah asked.

"I know it sounds like titillating, scandalous fun, but Mom's convinced there's no way in the world her best friend could possibly be running a brothel."

"She'd rather not know?"

Amelia appreciated how tenderly Benji had asked. "She keeps saying, 'Drive three hours only to embarrass ourselves when we find the madam is someone else?'"

Polly skimmed the faces in the crowd in search of their waiter. "What if you and I drove to Palm Springs?"

"Without Mom?"

"In case it isn't Bernice."

"But if it is her, Mom'll be thrilled—I think." Amelia twisted her napkin ring, watching it catch the light. "And horrified. But mostly thrilled."

"Do it." Benji took Amelia's hand in his meaty paw and kissed it. Oh my, how she'd missed him doing that. She stared at Polly. *He's right*. "We should invite Irene."

Polly arched a sardonic eyebrow. "Because she has the fanciest, biggest, most comfortable car?"

"Heading out to the desert in July is one devilishly hot and long drive."

"She thought she'd be seeing more of her husband now that *Wind* has finished filming, but those thirty hours of exposed film won't carve themselves down to four by magic."

"So we're going on a road trip?"

"We are."

"And I for one"—Benji kissed Amelia's hand again—"can't wait to hear all about it."

"Me too?" Noah cast a hopeful glance in Polly's direction.

She nodded. "Yes, you too."

25

Amelia read the sign passing by Irene's LaSalle: *Thanks for visiting Ontario!* "I've been wondering," she announced, "what's the difference between brothel and bordello?"

"'Bordello' sounds classier," Polly said. "Plush velvet curtains, flocked wallpaper, every room reeking of French perfume."

"Apparently, Polly's given this question quite a bit of thought," Irene mused from behind the steering wheel. "My dear Miss Maddox, how you do surprise."

"Is that a bad thing?"

"Quite the contrary. It's why I've been pushing *Pretty Pennies* along. It wouldn't have crossed David's feverish little mind that I'd have any interest in developing a movie project. You should have seen his face when I laid out the path forward."

"Flabbergasted?" Lois asked.

"Floored?" Amelia asked.

"Flummoxed?" Polly asked.

"All of the above. And now he doesn't regard me in quite the same way."

"What did he say about our road trip?" Polly asked.

"You're assuming I told him."

Lois whistled. "My husband would have a fit if I didn't tell him."

"Yes, but your husband would be around to tell. Meanwhile, mine is editing a twenty-hour monster down to four as *Intermezzo* wraps—and he wants to edit that, too. It's insanity!"

"Jumping Jehoshaphat, when does your husband sleep?"

"The coffee-and-cigarettes diet works wonders." Irene snuck a glance at Polly in the back seat, but Amelia knew how to interpret it: *And Benzedrine. Plus whatever's in those shots that quack gives him several times a week.*

Amelia stuck her hand out of her open window in a futile effort to cool down. In the last half-hour, the fourth-of-July heat must have climbed past a hundred degrees. "You've gone AWOL?"

"The kids have their nanny, so as long as nobody dies, everything'll be fine."

"Pol told me he's also started to cast *Rebecca*," Amelia said.

Irene shifted her rearview-mirror eyeballs to Amelia. *Bless you for switching topics.* "Vivien's screen test was underwhelming, so he's now leaning toward Joan Fontaine." She switched on the radio. "It's almost time."

Amelia had heard that car manufacturers were now installing built-in radios, but this was her first. Irene was so plainspoken it was easy to forget she swam in LA's ritzier pools.

The crackling settled as an announcer described Lou Gehrig walking to the podium, where microphones awaited his speech ahead of what the papers had breathlessly announced might be the baseball star's final public appearance.

"For the past two weeks, you have been reading about a bad break," the humble player began haltingly. "Yet today I consider myself the luckiest man on the face of the earth. I have been in ballparks for seventeen years and have received nothing but kindness and encouragement from you fans." Despite his crippling disease —or perhaps because of it—his sincerity and humility bled through Irene's shiny chrome speaker. He finished to the thunderous applause of an estimated sixty thousand sports fans packed to the rafters in Yankee Stadium.

Irene lowered the volume. "Not even thirty-five yet, and struck down in the prime of life. What's that Latin saying? Carpe diem? Devil of a way to be reminded to seize the hell out of every day. Tell me, ladies, what would you do if you knew you only had a finite amount of time left to enjoy? Be honest. There ain't nobody here but us chickens."

"That's easy," Polly said with a laugh. "I keep thinking about Ingrid Bergman and her ice cream sundaes. I'd run all over town eating all the fattening foods and damn the waistline."

The other three treated her to a vigorous round of applause.

"And you, Amelia?" Irene asked.

"I'd tell people what I truthfully think of them."

"Goodness!" Lois twisted around to face the back seat. "Where did *that* come from?"

"The morning of *Wind*'s wrap party, I finally stepped back behind the lunch counter," Amelia said, "but forgot what a show you put on—the smiling, the kidding, the flattery, the cajoling. I never noticed before how some customers lord it over you, dropping crumbs and hogging space, then leave you nickels for your trouble."

She sucked in a lungful of dry desert air, surprised by the sudden relief flooding through her. Only now, unburdened, did she realize how heavily the discovery had weighed on her.

Polly prodded her with a knee. "You'd have a few choice words for Matilda, wouldn't you?"

"That snake in the grass. After I got through talking to Vivien Leigh at the *Wind* wrap party, I decided it'd be best to avoid her. The next day, she acted as if nothing had happened. But I have to work with her, and Mr. S. is big on amicable staff relations."

"We're halfway." Irene jacked a thumb as they passed a sign—*Riverside, 10 miles.*

"What about you?"

Irene didn't hesitate. "I'd leave David and pursue a producing career of my own."

Amelia bet that Irene, as the daughter of Louis B. Mayer, had seen her fair share of behind-the-scenes chicanery. "Your own movie studio?"

"Live theater," Irene replied with brisk conviction. "Dramatic plays. Preferably on Broadway, if I could swing it." When her three companions found themselves stuck for an appropriate response, she filled the silence with, "I've shocked you, haven't I?"

"I shouldn't be as surprised as I am," Lois said. "Bravo for carpe-ing your diem."

"I appreciate that, but what about you?"

"Me?" Lois released an airy laugh. "I'd be doing what I'm doing right this very second: tracking down Bernice."

A sobering silence fell over the LaSalle's interior until Amelia asked, "Deep down in your bones, do you think it's her?"

"We live in a crazy world, but honestly? No, I don't expect Bern will be answering the door."

"You could've sent a letter."

Lois turned to the girls in the back. "And pass up the opportunity to have an adventure like this?"

"That reminds me of a Ralph Waldo Emerson quote," Polly said. "'It's not the destination, it's the journey.'"

"Even when the destination is a brothel."

"*Bordello*, Mom. Keep it classy."

* * *

"Do we know where the airport is?" Amelia asked as they left Route 60 and headed into Palm Springs.

"Air*strip*," Irene corrected her. "Look for Ramon Road. The Sapphire Moon is opposite the runway, way past the end of town."

Lois ran a finger down her fold-out map. "Found it."

"Mighty convenient for fellows with their own planes," Polly mused.

"When you're a movie star," Irene said, "or oil baron craving discreet companionship, why risk dodging familiar faces on the Sunset Strip when you can fly forty-five minutes to Palm Springs and take a stroll across an empty field?"

Lois stared out at the sparse town shimmering in the heat. "Imagine what life's like for those girls."

The words came out more slowly now, as if each one carried extra weight. "Everything okay, Mom?" Amelia asked. "You sound a tad—"

"We must have been off our rockers to think Bernice was a madam," Lois burst out. "Why, the very idea. It's ludicrous."

Amelia stared at Polly. *What's happening here?* "Hey Mom, you want to go home?"

Lois hurriedly tried to fold the map, mangling it as she fought against its original creases. "We wanted Bernice for the remake's publicity. But if she turns out to be Dora Gibbs . . ." Her hands stilled on the crumpled paper.

"Not necessarily." Irene turned left onto Ramon Road. "The history of Hollywood is the history of people wallpapering over their sordid past. David's PR department could whip up a backstory for Bernice that'd make Mata Hari look like a Vestal Virgin."

Amelia rested her chin on the back of the front seats, where she could smell the citrusy upholstery shampoo. "Are you hoping Bernice is running the Sapphire Moon? Or that she isn't?"

"A little from column A, a little from column B." Lois abandoned the map and squirmed in her seat for an uncomfortably long moment. "I suppose it'd be silly to go home after we've come all this way."

Amelia dropped back onto the rear seat. "Ready for your first brothel?" she whispered to Polly.

"You're assuming it's my first."

Amelia elbowed her. "Noah's going to be aghast when he learns his new girlfriend has such a sordid past."

"What's that?" Irene demanded. "Polly has a new beau?"

"Hardly," Polly said. "We've been on one date. A double date, at that. I got tipsy and shot my mouth off in a half-baked attempt to impress him—which I didn't because he hasn't called."

"But if he does"—Amelia put little effort into suppressing a smile—"imagine how in awe of you he'll be when he learns you've visited the notorious Sapphire Moon."

* * *

The unpaved road wound through towering Mexican fan palms and elephant-eared monsteras. Matching circular rock gardens, big as wagon wheels, flanked the driveway, their crushed white quartz studded with miniature cacti.

Irene inched her car toward a patchworked building, part adobe, part Spanish Colonial, and part Mission Revival. White-washed walls, red roof tiles, arched front door. They parked next to an olive tree at the edge of an empty parking lot, but nobody got out.

Lois pressed her handbag to her chest. "Do we walk up and knock on the door like a Fuller Brush man?"

"Or," Polly asked, "do men simply waltz through like it's the Biltmore?"

"Irene?" Amelia prodded. "Is there an accepted etiquette?"

"How should I know?"

"You're the only one in this car who's heard of this joint."

"*Heard* of it, yes, but that's as close as I've come."

"Enough dithering!" Amelia threw open her car door. "Who's joining me?"

The front entrance had neither doorbell nor knocker, so Amelia pushed down on the black wrought-iron handle. It gave way, allowing Amelia to ease the thick wooden door open.

The foyer opened before them like a hexagonal jewel box. Olive-green tiles the size of dinner plates gleamed in the daylight. A single painting dominated the terracotta walls—a Rubenesque beauty on a velvet chaise, her sky-blue silk dress contouring every curve. The next room deepened into shadow, its walls papered in poinsettia-red stripes. More tasteful nudes kept the silk-draped lady company. Amelia breathed in the blessed coolness after the desert sun.

"HELLO?" she called out. "ANYBODY HOME?"

The sound of dainty footsteps heralded the approach of a

woman Lois's age, her floor-length robe of cream muslin billowing in the draft. Her face was pale as milk, her cinnamon hair pulled back into an elegant chignon. "I'm sorry, ladies, but you're too late. Our last caller left at four-thirty this morning. If you were hoping to catch your husbands *in flagrante delicto,* I can't help you."

Lois stepped forward. "Hiya, Bern," she said. "It's me."

"LULU!" Bernice squealed. "LUUU! LUUU!"

They fell into each other's arms, each woman's face buried in the neck of her long-lost pal, both hoarsely blubbering half-sentences.

"So very sorry—"

"We lost touch—"

"Nobody's to blame—"

"I've missed you so much—"

"I should've written—"

"Life got in the way—"

"How did we ever—"

"You of all people—"

"Look where I've ended up—"

"Nobody cares—"

"We've found each other—"

Only when they broke apart, dabbing at mascara-streaked cheeks and lipstick-stained collars, did Amelia first glimpse the young woman her mother had been—before the three-headed dragon of life, marriage, and children had swallowed her whole.

"Don't tell me!" Bernice's voice cracked as she studied Amelia's face. "Oh, Lulu, she could only be your daughter. You're gorgeous! What's your name, dear heart?"

"Amelia."

Bernice swooped in for a kiss to the cheek. She smelled of the Chanel No. 5 Amelia had sampled at Bullocks.

"And this," Lois continued, "is Polly Maddox."

Bernice studied Polly's face as she addressed Lois. "You know who these two remind me of?"

Lois bounced a finger between her and Bernice. "Uncanny, isn't it? And this is Mrs. Selznick."

Bernice warmly shook Irene's hand. "Myron or David?"

Her question snapped Amelia back to their surroundings. *Oh my. Was this about to get real awkward real fast?* "David," Irene replied evenly. *Phew!*

"Enough standing around like scarecrows," Bernice said briskly. "Let's all go back to my office, where I'll get Marion to make coffee and scrounge up some of her molasses cookies."

Contrasting with the dimly lit reception, Bernice's office was an airy room, painted yellow, with large doors that led to a shaded patio. In one corner, a black-and-white cat dozing in a wicker basket raised its head and opened its eyes at Amelia before curling back into a ball. "That's Charley," Bernice said, "and her blink means welcome."

"So," Bernice said as they settled on mis-matching sofas facing each other over a brass-and-glass coffee table, "why in heaven's name are you here?"

Irene said, "My husband plans to remake *Pretty Pennies*."

"Gracious! He does?"

"And we thought what a marvelous PR stunt it would be to have the original star at the opening."

"My goodness, if that isn't the most thoughtful notion!"

Amelia began to understand her mother's comparison—Bernice moved like an Egyptian queen, all swan-like poise and dignity. She shared Polly's innate serenity, a quality Amelia could never match.

"But Bern," Lois said, "I have to ask. From traveling candy salesman to Palm Springs brothel?"

"Ah, well now, that's a story. Mack tired of the road, so we bought a movie house near Chicago and were very happy running it. But then he died, which is when I learned he both owed the IRS and was in debt up to his eyeballs to a local bookie. In Chicago you *always* pay the bookie first, so I sold the theater, settled with him and worked out payments with the IRS. But it was the depth of the Depression and here was I looking for work. I found a job managing a theater downtown, but the pay wasn't enough. I needed more income."

"Is that where the Opal Moon comes in?"

"Say!" Bernice sat up like she'd been electrocuted. "How come you lot know so much?"

Lois filled her in. After hearing about Hartman's hunch, Bernice explained she had spotted men slipping through her theater's emergency exit. Across the rear alley, she discovered a brothel called the Opal Moon. "So after closing time, I marched straight to Madam Stella and told her I wouldn't stand for such goings-on."

Marion appeared with a sterling silver coffee pot and a plate piled with fresh brown molasses cookies that filled Bernice's office with the aroma of sweet caramel.

Bernice continued, "After my indignation cooled down, we found we had a lot in common: crochet and knitting, competitive poker, and we both love novels set in Tudor times."

"Oh!" Lois cried out. "You and your Tudors. I'd quite forgotten."

"I couldn't believe how well I got on with an honest-to-God brothel madam! I went back the following night, which is when Stella made me the same offer she had with the previous theater manager. Fifty a week to allow men to hoof it over to her bawdy-house via the back door."

"And you took it?"

"I had an enormous IRS debt and meager income, so, yes, you bet I did." Bernice let out a reflective sigh. "It took a while, but I paid off the IRS. And then, right after my final payment, I came down with consumption."

"Oh, Bern." Lois cradled her long-lost friend's hand in her palm. "I wish I'd known."

"Chicago is no place for a lunger, so out I came. Not only for the desert air but also because Stella's sister, Veronica, lived here."

"So, Stella ran the Opal Moon and Veronica ran the Sapphire Moon?" Amelia said.

Bernice gave Lois's hands a final squeeze and let go. "Veronica put me up, but I never did find my own place. My TB took a year to clear, but by then her chain smoking had caught up with her—

emphysema, naturally. As I got stronger, she got weaker, and I gradually took over the Moon. Then, about three years ago, the Plaza Theatre opened on Palm Canyon Drive. MGM hosted Garbo's *Camille* premiere. Ten bucks a seat and knocked the whole town on its ear."

"A big weekend for Palm Springs meant a big weekend for this place, I suppose?" Irene asked.

"And how. Open forty-eight straight hours. All hands on deck. No sheets left unwashed. By then, Veronica could no longer get out of bed. Talk about baptism by fire!"

"You must have made a small fortune," Amelia said.

"Nothing small about it, sweet pea. We were sticking cash in cookie jars, tin cans, shoe boxes. Somewhere around here there's an old Smucker's jam jar we still haven't found. But all that profit paid for improvements around the place, and I got everything shipshape. Word spread the Sapphire Moon was doing gangbuster business."

"Don't you worry about getting raided?" Lois asked.

"By whom? Palm Springs doesn't even have a police department. We're under the jurisdiction of the Riverside County Sheriff's Office, and that's a *very* wide swath of land."

"It's the same on Catalina," Polly said, "which is how Papa could get away with making Mad Ox moonshine and running an outdoor gambling joint."

Worry lines crossed Lois's brow the way they did whenever she heard a loud crash coming from the twins' bedroom. "Sounds dicey to me."

"Oh, Lulu, no need to fret. We're way out of town. Nobody pays us no never-mind. And besides, the Riverside sheriff and I are chums. But what about this private eye you hired to find me? I've never been so flattered!"

"Speaking of," Amelia said. It was, after all, the reason they'd endured driving three hours in hundred-degree heat. "Any chance you'll take part in the PR for the *Pretty Pennies* remake?"

"I could get you headlines, but"—Bernice swept her hands in a wide arc—"I doubt they're of the variety you'd savor. There is such a thing as sticking your head over the parapet unnecessarily."

"Is that your nice way of turning us down?"

"I am, yes. But seeing as how you've driven all the way out here, I insist on treating you to luncheon. The Palm Springs Racquet Club has an excellent restaurant—*and* it's where the Riverside sheriff dines whenever he's in town. If our timing is good, and if you ask him nicely, he might even let you stroke his pistol."

26

Amelia probed the red blotches on her left arm. "I should've asked our waiter at the racquet club to shift the umbrella as the sun moved. My skin still hurts."

Polly stepped to their bathroom mirror and ran lipstick along her bottom lip. She seldom fussed with makeup, but Amelia had noticed her making more of an effort since Noah had landed on the scene. "We were dunces not to bring sombreros to the desert in July." She eyed Amelia in the reflection. "I'm still of two minds."

Amelia lifted her fingertip, leaving a light pink mark. "About Bernice?"

"Yes. I'm glad Dora Gibbs turned out to be Bernice for your mother's sake—"

"But not for Irene's."

Polly reexamined her handiwork and wiped her mouth. "Are you happy with what happened?"

"I don't remember the last time my mother looked so—so—"

"Euphoric?"

Lois had floated home last week, all but hovering above the car seat, bubbling with "Bernice this" and "Bernice that" and "I'll never forget when we . . ."

Amelia pulled a bottle of sunburn-relieving linseed oil from the medicine cabinet. Maybe she could wash it off when she got to work. A frantic pounding filled the apartment. "Who knocks like that at six-fifty in the morning?"

"Is the building on fire?"

They dashed through the living room to their front door.

Irene strode in wearing a Chinese silk housecoat over her lounging pajamas; no hat, no gloves, no purse. She hoisted her *LA Times*. Its two-inch headline screamed

PALM SPRINGS BROTHEL
RANSACKED IN LAPD &
COUNTY SHERIFF RAID

The next photo showed Bernice's arrest at the Sapphire Moon—handcuffed and ringed by a dozen county sheriffs.

Irene paced in front of the fireplace. "Little alarm bells went off in my head when she was so cavalier about her business."

"Mine, too," Amelia said. "But then Bernice mentioned Palm Springs doesn't even have a police department." She reread the headline. "LAPD *and* the Riverside County sheriff?"

Irene shoved the newspaper into Amelia's hands. "Those sheriffs had to drive an hour to Palm Springs. And why were the LAPD involved?"

A thorny vine of apprehension crawled down Amelia's back. "You think it was planned?"

"This was no spur-of-the-moment raid. Brothels are golden geese for crooked cops happy to take under-the-table payoffs to ensure the doors stay open."

"Maybe Bernice's place was taking business away from her LA counterparts?" Amelia suggested.

"I doubt—oof, I need to sit down." Irene flopped onto the sofa. "Palm Springs is in the middle of nowhere."

"The Moon *is* located next to the airstr—"

Irene sliced through Polly's observation with a flick of her manicured finger. "A fox lurks in this henhouse somewhere." She tapped Bernice's photograph. "A professional took that."

"Someone tipped off the press?"

The three sat in silence to absorb the sucker-punch this report had delivered as the coffee percolator gurgled on the kitchen counter. The *L.A. Times*, *Herald-Express*, and *Hollywood Citizen-News* would have hit the Hartley porch by now.

"Here's a silver lining." Polly picked up the paper. "They're calling Bernice by her real name, so I'd say it's unlikely anybody will connect Bernice Hoag with Isadora Gibbs."

Irene's hooded eyes widened. "We only figured it out because it occurred to Lois, even though I've passed that poster outside my husband's office a thousand times."

Amelia checked the carriage clock on the mantel. Running late for work already. "It's the timing that bothers me the most." Her feet found the shoes abandoned the night before. "Bernice wasn't the slightest bit worried about the authorities, but gets arrested less than a week after our visit?"

Polly followed Amelia's example and plucked a hair ribbon from the pocket of her jacket. "You suspect *we're* responsible?"

Amelia knew what she was thinking. Last year, the two of them had inadvertently led the police to Elroy Maddox's hideout in the mountains north of Pasadena. Although they hadn't done it knowingly, Amelia suspected Polly might never forgive herself for her part in the death of her father.

"The timing is oddly coincidental, is all I'm saying."

"We must pay Mr. Hartman a visit." Irene swung to her feet and scooped up the newspaper. "What time do you finish work?"

"Four."

"Meet you out front of his office at four-thirty?"

Amelia wished she could phone her mother, but that conversation would stretch like coastal fog. Better to wait until after they'd spoken to Hartman. She picked up her handbag. "Don't go in without me."

* * *

Hartman had stored away all those ceiling-high boxes, leaving his space civilized. He gestured across his paper-strewn desk toward the guest chairs. "What day did you visit her?"

"July fourth." Amelia wished her mother could have joined them, but Lois was lost in telephone calls, navigating the rabbit warren of bureaucracy to unearth where Bernice had been locked up.

He nodded thoughtfully. "Five days later, the cops descend."

"We think the timing is strangely coincidental, too," Irene said.

Hartman leaned back in his chair. "The thing I've found about coincidences is that the stranger they are, the more suspect they become."

Amelia twisted the gloves in her lap. "What does your professional private eye intuition say about all this?"

"I got the impression you put little stock in my hunches."

"Let's say I'm a convert."

He met her admission with a quietly gratified smile. "It's like we drew attention to Bernice, leading the sheriffs straight to her."

"What's this 'we' business?" Irene asked. "Were you in my trunk?"

"If I hadn't tracked her down, Bernice might not be in lockup right now."

All Amelia's notions of private eyes came from the movies—cynical loners drowning in rye and cigarette smoke, shunning decent society. This fellow was a pleasant surprise. "Did you discuss this case with anyone?"

"Certainly not."

"So you're as stumped as we are."

"I was for a while after you called. But then I asked myself the question that's always useful: Who benefits most?"

"Any suspects?"

"There's this bureaucrat running for the office of the Chair of the Riverside County Board of Supervisors."

"Is he as dull as he sounds?" Irene asked.

"The centerpiece of his campaign is clamping down on vice and corruption, which means he'll be flogging that horse until late September."

"Vice and corruption, huh?" Amelia drawled. "Those two old chestnuts." The connection between Bernice and some provincial administrator felt flimsy at best, but it was all they had.

"He's in the afternoon edition." Hartman spun the newspaper around and tapped a picture of a man named Wyatt Greene standing on a wooden box stamped *Riverside Valencia Orchards*, his arm raised with his finger pointing to the heavens like a male Aimee Semple McPherson. With thinning hair and a pale, pinched face, he looked like he hadn't heard a decent joke since Harold Lloyd was hanging from that clock. "I'm going to dig around. See what I can come up with."

"Mr. Hartman," Irene said, softening her voice, "I could only pay your fee by fudging my household budget. I made it work, but I've stretched it to its limits."

"No, no." He brushed their protests away. "This one's on me."

"Mr. Hartman! I'm all for worthwhile charity, but—"

"I assure you, charity's got nothing to do with it."

Amelia tilted her head and squinted at him. "Another one of your hunches?"

"I'd hate to discover I had a hand in leading this firebrand to Bernice's door."

They stepped onto Formosa Avenue and wandered up the block like they had nowhere to go, passing a jasmine bush that infused the air with sweet perfume.

"Is Mr. Selznick aware you went to Palm Springs?" Amelia asked.

"Not unless the nanny blabbed."

"Did he read about the raid in this morning's paper?"

"He pulled an all-nighter. Whether he was actually editing like he said remains to be seen." Irene stopped at the corner. "Nobody warns you about marrying men like David. The whole lot of them

—Zanuck, Goldwyn, Warner, Cohn—they succeed because they're high-wire trapeze artists who perform without a net. The same nerve that builds studios also sends them chasing women, guzzling booze, and gambling sums of money so outrageous that King Solomon would faint dead away."

Amelia thought of Benji. Even if he hated the idea of this stand-in job, his many fine qualities outweighed it. "Take the good with the bad?"

"Precisely. Marriage isn't like Clifton's Cafeteria where you get to choose the dishes you like and glide past the ones you don't."

Everyone in Hollywood regarded the Selznick marriage and said to themselves, "There's a couple who has everything." It was comforting to know they didn't. Because if David and Irene Selznick didn't have it all, nobody did.

27

The police sergeant surveyed Lois with yawning indifference. "Bail's a grand."

She met the cop's unblinking stare. "I'm aware."

"Cash."

She presented him with a thick envelope like it was the cure for polio. "Do I pay you?"

"The sooner I have your money, the sooner I can release the prisoner into your custody."

The way he said "the prisoner" made Amelia wince. Such a harsh label for the elegant, welcoming woman she'd met in Palm Springs. Metal slammed against metal somewhere deeper in the building as Lois counted out fifty-dollar bills. Amelia's mother had surprised her with this one—marching right up to the Riverside County sheriff's desk and stating her business. No uniformed baboon with a badge was going to get the best of her.

She laid out the last bill. "A receipt, if you please."

He handed a slip of paper to a nearby deputy and jutted his chin toward the main entrance. "Turn right. Halfway down the block. Door marked 'Releases.'"

Outside, the prison gloom fell away as they left behind banging doors and harsh lighting. The summer sky, endless and blue, washed over them. Lois's fingers twisted her handkerchief into worried knots. "Do they feed you in jail?"

Amelia slung an arm around Lois's shoulders. "It's county lockup, not a Siberian salt mine. Bernice has been accused, not found guilty."

"But she *is* guilty!"

A fair point. "Okay, look, I know you've got it all planned, but I have to be sure. After we spring Bernice from the hoosegow, we're bringing her to back to the house?"

"That's right."

"To live with you?"

"She needs peace, and privacy, and support."

"Dad's on board with this?"

"Naturally. Remember, we all go back such a long way."

As they waited in front of the jail, Amelia watched her mother unwrap the handkerchief from around her left index finger and rewind it in the opposite direction. "Does she know you share a house with the devil's spawn?"

"Hush now. Samuel and Sebastian aren't so bad."

"That's what they said about Captain Kidd and Blackbeard."

The door swung wide. Bernice flinched at the sunlight, all traces of the poised businesswoman stripped away: limp hair, torn sleeve, French cuff in ruins. She fell into Lois's arms. "You're here. You came. You rescued me."

Lois patted her back and vowed she'd have driven to Maine to set her free.

Amelia waited until they were speeding westward on Route 60 before she asked if Bernice had had any clue a raid was imminent.

"Not one of my law enforcement chums gave me any inkling."

"I thought you didn't worry about the long arm of the law."

"It doesn't hurt to have acquaintances with influence."

"Does that mean these acquaintances of yours didn't know, or they were told to keep quiet?"

Amelia's question met with uncomfortable silence until Bernice said, "I suspect the latter," punctuating it with a bitter laugh. "I thought we were better friends than that."

"Remember our private eye?" Lois asked. "He thinks the timing of the raid is too coincidental to ignore."

"Oh, Lulu, sweetie," Bernice cried out. "Don't think for a moment that you caused this mess."

"He's looking into it without charging a fee. A matter of professional pride, he calls it."

"Be that as it may, I have more pressing problems now that my court case has been set."

"Already?" Amelia asked. "They're not messing around. When is it?"

"September nineteenth."

"The Riverside County Board of Supervisors election is September twenty-sixth. Awfully specific timing, if you ask me."

"Never mind about local politics—I can't tell you how good it is to see you."

"Don't you worry, Bern," Lois assured her. "We're in your corner all the way."

"As long as you keep your link to the Selznick studios hush-hush," Amelia said. It was Irene's sole request.

"My lips are sealed," Bernice replied, her voice weighty with fatigue. "As I sat there in my cramped, stinky cell with nothing to do but think, it occurred to me that I only saw *Pretty Pennies* once."

"At the premiere?" Lois asked.

"Yes, and that's, what, twenty-five years ago?"

"On October third."

"You even remember the date?"

"I remember everything from that time." Nostalgia shaded Lois's voice. Did they both cherish those years before marriage as their idyllic time when the wondrous possibilities of life felt boundless? They passed the turnoff to Pomona. *Where will Pol and I be in nineteen sixty-four? If we're going to be looking back through rose-colored glasses, we should make the most of it while we can.* "I think you need a fresh wind in your sails. How about I ask Polly to organize a showing?"

"Of *Pretty Pennies*?" Amelia wouldn't have picked Bernice as the squealing type. "I'd *love* it!"

"But first, lunch at the famous Schwab's Pharmacy? I recommend the corned beef sandwich."

"Hot or cold?"

"Definitely hot." Amelia floored the gas pedal. With thirty miles still to cover, she'd have to giddy-up if she were to reach Sunset Boulevard by noon.

* * *

Schwab's buzzed with its usual lunchtime energy, but today's commotion carried an extra spark. "Don't look now," Amelia told Lois and Bernice, "but Charles Laughton and Elsa Lanchester are at the counter like regular folks."

She had grown used to spotting the screen's snippy librarians, habitual drunks, and stern-faced judges. But the Laughtons moved in loftier circles, especially with Charles causing such a stir as RKO's Quasimodo.

She hurried into the break room, where she threw her hat and gloves into a locker and took her position.

"I've stocked the Westmore Brothers' new line of beauty products on the shelves," the morning-shift girl said.

Amelia watched Lois and Bernice take seats in what used to be Amelia's station. Bernice might have dominated yesterday's headlines, but here she was, another anonymous customer. What lucky timing that Laughton and Lanchester were drawing all the stares.

"Which means," Betsy-Ann continued, "older Westmore items are now twenty percent off."

What a crying shame she couldn't serve Mom and Bernice. She'd have slipped them extra fries or piled more ice cream on their banana splits. Betsy-Ann hadn't been gone thirty seconds when her first customer stepped to the counter, arms laden with Westmore foundation, cold cream, rouge, and eyeshadow. "Am I being foolish buying so much?"

Amelia was just about to answer when she spotted Matilda

approaching to take Lois and Bernice's orders. She caught the peculiar expression that crossed Matilda's face. Part shock, part surprise, part fear, part defiance. Or was she only imagining that Matilda had recognized the woman whom the *Herald-Express* was already calling "The Notorious Palm Springs Madam"?

"Yes, ma'am."

"Excuse me?"

The irritation in the customer's question roped Amelia back to her side of the store. "I'm sorry, what was your question?"

"Did you call me foolish?"

"Heavens, no!" Amelia longed to fan away the blush rising up her neck with the cardboard standee for the new Westmore line of face powders. She tilted her head toward the end of the lunch counter. "Did you see Charles Laughton and Elsa Lanchester are dining here today?"

The ruse worked. As the customer rubbernecked to get a better view, Amelia wrote up her purchases. "People who don't take advantage of sales like these, they're the foolish ones."

Flattered now, the customer wheeled around to Amelia. "Their rouge is heaven—although with your rosy complexion, I expect you have no need for it."

Even at twenty percent off, Westmore's products were beyond Amelia's budget. She stole a glance at the lunch counter. Matilda was haranguing Mr. Schwab, her lecture decidedly one-sided. Amelia totaled the purchase. "You've saved nearly six dollars today. I'd say that makes you one smart shopper."

As the woman fumbled around her handbag for her wallet, Mr. Schwab was addressing Lois and Bernice. Amelia couldn't see their faces, but they were pulling back the way people do in a horror movie.

The customer laid out a wad of one-dollar bills and a stack of coins as Amelia filled a paper bag.

Lois and Bernice slid off their stools and jammed their hats back onto their heads.

Amelia eased the package across the glass. "Wear it all in good health." She didn't dare look away until the customer had left. But by then, Lois and Bernice had already stomped through the exit and dissolved into the passers-by along Sunset.

* * *

Women had swarmed the Westmore display all afternoon. By six o'clock, Amelia was able to take her break. Mr. Schwab darted between the counter, pharmacy, and office, but she spotted her chance while fetching more foundation from storage and asked for a minute of his time.

"Be quick. I have a large delivery for Robert Benchley at the Garden of Allah."

"I noticed the commotion at Matilda's station."

"Those two women? Matilda recognized one as the madam from that Palm Springs brothel raid yesterday. Why do you ask?"

"The other one is my mother." Amelia stifled the quake in her voice—but barely. Even now, hours later, Bernice and Lois's expulsion still nettled her.

"Your mother is friends—with a madam?"

"They went to high school together. In fact, Bernice was the star of the original *Pretty Pennies*."

Amelia wanted to slap herself across the mouth. They had agreed to keep Bernice at arm's length from the remake to avoid controversy. And here she was, blabbing like the biggest chatterbox south of the North Pole.

"I can*not* have anyone so scandalous in my establishment. Now, I must get this delivery out."

He left Amelia alone in the storage room. She sagged against the produce crates, breathing in the sweet mingling of peaches and apricots, but froze when Matilda walked by. Had she heard everything?

Matilda appeared in the doorway. "Did you catch who I had to deal with earlier?"

"It's been hectic today."

"Those two old bags at my station at lunchtime." Amelia's palms tingled with the urge to slap this backstabber, but she decided to let her keep tying her own noose. "Would you believe one of them was the Notorious Palm Springs Madam?"

"And the other one?"

"Christ only knows who she was. Not bad looking in her day, but now?" Matilda's shoulders lifted with casual contempt. "Probably the cleaning lady."

"Cleaning lady?" The metal-lined storage room hurled Amelia's words back at her like angry projectiles. "Do you always risk your neck leaping to conclusions? If you're not careful, you might snap your own—" Matilda's mouth curved into a haughty smile. "You were eavesdropping."

The girl drew circles in the chilly air with a forefinger. "You know how this cave is such an echo chamber." She left before Amelia could summon a retort.

Amelia melted into the doorway's shadow. Her eyes fell on a crate labeled *RIVERSIDE VALENCIA ORCHARDS*.

She had seen that name recently.

Not here.

Somewhere else.

The answer came to her like a flashbulb going off: in the *Times*, under the photo of that horse's ass running for the Riverside County Board of Supervisors. She hurried out to where Mr. Schwab was rearranging the Westmore display.

"Why do we buy most of our produce from Riverside Valencia Orchards?"

"Because Matilda gets us an excellent price on their oranges, lemons, limes, grapefruits, and kumquats."

"How does she do that?"

"It's her family's business."

"Is that why you held her job?"

"Sure is. You take cost-saving opportunities where you find them."

"So her name is Matilda *Greene*? And Wyatt Greene is her father?"

"Brother—twenty years older, with five siblings between. Religious family, those Greenes. No rhythm method for them."

And now Matilda knew about the Notorious Palm Springs Madam's starring role in *Pretty Pennies*, and her connection to Amelia's mother.

Well, now, isn't that peachy?

28

The thick foliage blanketing Pershing Square rustled with a warm July breeze blowing across downtown. Amelia squeezed Benji's arm extra hard. "Oh boy, am I ever ready for a normal night out."

"Your life isn't all about brothels, hookers, and police raids?"

"Don't forget co-workers with murky motives," Polly added.

"When did my life become a Kay Francis melodrama?" Amelia pulled out a cigarette and waited for Benji. The flame of his lighter danced against the purple sunset. She'd been smoking a pack a day lately and promised herself to cut down. But now wasn't the time. "Just so that you know," she said to Noah, "I'm not normally the Kay Francis type."

"Just so that *you* know," he shot back in a stage whisper over the Sixth Street traffic, "I'm a Kay Francis fan."

At first, Amelia hadn't warmed to Noah. Too stiff, too play-by-the-rules. Polly wasn't as strait-laced as she'd been last summer, but she was still more Sunday morning than Saturday night. Maybe that's why she and Amelia got on so well: They balanced each other out. But now she was beginning to see how Polly and Noah were a good match.

They reached Hill Street, watching for the *GO* sign to pop out of the semaphore signal. "Where's Luddie?" Benji asked.

"Five felt like an odd number," Polly told him, "so I invited Hazel. He's picking her up."

"Speaking of Kay Francis melodramas," Amelia giggled, "I find Hazel more interesting now that I know her folks own a burlesque house."

"Which one?" Noah asked.

"The Follies."

"Over on Main? It's only a few blocks away." His eyes sparked with mischief. "Instead of the Biltmore bar for a drink afterwards, how about we go there?"

Amelia side-eyed Polly. *I'll go if you go.*

When Benji assured them they wouldn't be the only women in the audience, Amelia executed a slow, theatrical turn. "Is that right?"

"My younger brother's in the Navy. He was on shore leave a couple of years ago and wanted to check out a burlesque show."

"And?" Polly prompted.

He shrugged casually. "Let's go. You can experience one for yourself."

"Hazel never talks about it," Polly said. "I'd hate to embarrass her."

Amelia heard the words Polly didn't dare say out loud: *But I really do want to go.* "We could bring it up, casual as you please, and see how she reacts."

The Paramount Theater marquee twinkled like snowflakes, its large black letters announcing *PRIVATE PREVIEW TONITE.* Director William Wellman had arranged this special screening of *Beau Geste* to thank his cast and crew for enduring the grueling shoot. Amelia had insisted they attend. She needed to know if this picture that had consumed so much of Benji's time had been worth the sacrifice.

Waiting outside was Luddie, dressed in the expensive suit he'd bought for Myron Selznick's birthday bash. Hazel had gathered her signature nest of hair into a single braid that hung down her back, revealing a face that belonged not with the classic beauty of Lamarr or Young, but among the striking features of Hepburn and Fontaine.

"I'm so glad you could join us," Amelia told her.

"You'd be hard-pressed to find a bigger Gary Cooper fan than me. If he's here tonight, I'm liable to make a dreadful fool of myself."

Luddie cast an eye around the growing throng filling the sidewalk. "Quite a turnout."

"Mussolini and his gang of fascist thugs have banned *Beau Geste* because it portrays the British—and therefore democracy—too positively."

"Which will make the public even more keen to see the picture," Noah commented.

"People are coming in from all directions. Let's nab some decent seats."

"Hazel," Amelia said, as they were filing into the foyer, "instead of going to the Biltmore, any chance we could go visit your folks' theater?"

* * *

As they emerged onto the sidewalk afterwards, Amelia's mind was still swirling with vivid images of marauding tribesmen, desert forts, and French Foreign Legionnaires. "Paramount's got a swell hit on their hands."

"After all the overtime and weeks out of town"—Benji ran a loving finger down her cheek—"I sure hope so."

It hadn't escaped her notice that he'd been indulging in mushy romantic gestures like that more and more lately. She wanted to think that it was his attempt to make up for his sour attitude over her stand-in job—but was it? She didn't know, but she hoped these tender moments continued. "It was worth all those endless hours," she said to the group, but singled him out to ensure he knew that she appreciated the gesture. "Even though I assume it was hideously uncomfortable filming in the desert." They stopped at the Fourth Street corner; the *FOLLIES* blade sign glowed in neon a block away. Amelia nudged Hazel. "Anything we shouldn't do?"

"Yeah." Hazel laughed. "Don't embarrass me."

The theater's glamour faded at close range; paint curled from the entrance, and a web of cracks splintered the foyer window.

Hazel guided them through a gold-and-crimson foyer into the auditorium. The thousand-seat interior had weathered better than the facade. Fresh blue carpet with a rose-petal motif ran down the center aisle. A sparse crowd watched a dancer's half-hearted wiggle. Four musicians showed as much interest in their instruments as she did in her routine.

"That's Fifi Champagne," Hazel whispered. "Not much of stripper, but sews a G-string like nobody's business." She led them to a door at the right-hand end of the stage. A leggy woman on the hard-living side of forty stood in the wings, fluffing up daffodil-yellow feathers that Amelia guessed would dazzle in the lights.

Hazel didn't bother lowering her voice. "Everybody, this is Pepper Mills."

"'Cause I like to grind it," she said, giggling.

"How's your mom?"

"In better spirits since she got back from Reno."

"Sixth divorce is the charm?"

Pepper laughed the laugh of someone who'd picked up her first cigarette in elementary school. "She keeps talking about the new mechanic at her local gas station, so don't hold your breath."

They continued to the dressing room, where seven performers in various stages of dress and undress sat at their mirrors or fastened each other's snaps. Polly unleashed a yip of surprise. The guys weren't sure where to look.

"You've caught our bevy of troupers on a demure night," Hazel told the foursome. "I've been in here when nobody had a stitch on."

"When ya peel for a living," a platinum blonde said, "how

much you're showing is so far down our list of concerns, it might as well be in the basement furnace burning to ashes."

"Yeah!" a brunette with thick Wagnerian braids cracked. "Along with our dignity."

"I need to say hello to the folks." Hazel headed back out the door. "Won't be long." She swayed a warning finger at the strippers. "You have civilians in your midst."

Bargain-basement perfume thickened the air like a saccharine fog. Past a jury-rigged clothesline hung with rinsed-out stockings and brassieres, a tall, narrow vase held a thicket of peacock feathers. Amelia pointed to them. "Do they feature in somebody's act?"

"Mine." A busty girl nearing thirty leapt to her feet. She wore her flaming red hair—too bright to be natural—piled high on top of her head and had cinched herself into a corset that accentuated her tiny waist. "I pluck those feathers off, one by one. And I do it to classical music."

"Which piece?" Noah asked.

"It's from an opera called *Carmen*."

"'Habanera'?"

"OHMYGAWD!" the redhead screeched. "A fellow music afficionado! So few people are cultured these days." She stuck her hand out at an angle that suggested Noah was supposed to kiss it. "The name's Mamie Flamer." She gently stroked the back of her hair as though it were a skittish kitten. "On accounta my coif."

Noah opened his mouth to interject, but Mamie launched into an autobiography of her youth in Morgantown, West Virginia, before she'd "cleared out like my ass was on fire" to nearby Indianapolis, then Oklahoma City, followed by several more pitstops, each of them a little farther west, until "Greyhound dumped my bags, boobs, and belongings two blocks from here."

Amelia turned to the dancer on her right, a raven-haired beauty with alabaster skin. "Is she always this . . .?"

"Forthcoming?" The woman possessed an indistinguishable European accent. "We are a lively bunch, but tonight's different."

"How so?"

She toyed with a double string of black pearls hanging to her waist. "Mamie thinks she's got a shot at nabbing the lead role in some movie David Selznick says he still plans to make now that Rita Hayworth is out." She rolled her eyes as though to say, *Fat chance, sister.*

"Rita Hayworth has quit *Pretty Pennies*?" The question tumbled from Amelia.

"That can't be right," Polly said. "I work for Selznick. Where did you hear it?"

"Winchell." Mamie blinked slowly. "He told me all about it when I was getting ready for work."

"Did he say why?" Amelia asked.

She started inserting peacock feathers into tiny holes dimpling her costume. "He had a big scoop about the madam of that Palm Springs brothel, the one what got arrested. She starred in the original back in the silent days. So now there's this whole scandal about the remake. Winchell calls Harry Cohn, and o' course Cohn gets hot under the collar. He's all, 'Rita is my most promising ingenue. It's my job and my duty to protect her from anything so tawdry as a brothel!'"

Amelia addressed Polly. "All of this must have happened as we were going into *Beau Geste*."

Hazel charged into the dressing room. "My folks told me about Winchell!"

"We heard," Amelia said. "If Rita's out, does that mean the remake is kaput?"

"It might. What else did Winchell say? Any other names?" she asked Mamie.

"Yeah . . . a coupla guys called . . . um . . . I wanna say Biteoff and something . . .?"

"Bioff and Browne?"

"Could be."

"Oh, shit," Noah said. "News about Mr. C. not paying up is leaking out."

"What's the bet your Mr. C. and my Mr. S. had words?" Polly said. "Those words got heated, and it all came pouring out worse than the St. Francis Dam."

"Or . . ." Noah rubbed the edge of his jaw. "Mr. C. changed his mind about loaning his up-and-comer to a guy whose guts he hates."

"And used the scandal about Bernice as an excuse?"

"Ironic, seeing as how Mr. C. is no stranger to brothels."

"Which Mr. S. would know. And to punish him for pulling out, he's leveraged the Bioff and Browne news as payback."

Amelia slumped against a wall. All she'd wanted was a pleasant evening. No drama. No scandal. No big decisions.

No Rita probably meant no *Pretty Pennies*. And no *Pretty Pennies* meant no stand-in job. No stand-in job meant she was stuck behind the retail counter.

As wretched as she felt right now, she could think of someone who was probably even more miserable.

"Is there a phone around here?" Amelia asked Hazel.

"In my dad's office."

"It's a quarter of midnight!" Polly reminded her. "You're not calling who I suspect you're calling, are you?"

"You think Irene Selznick is asleep right now?"

29

The next day, Amelia was behind her counter. Again. Only now it felt like her escape had receded farther from her grasp. It was a slow morning, though, so she had swiped a *Hollywood Reporter* and thumbed straight to its "Window on Hollywood" column.

Last night, the maid had answered the Selznick telephone. Mr. and Mrs. Selznick had been at the Roosevelt Hotel for a Hollywood Anti-Nazi League fundraiser. And while the peacock-feathered Mamie Flamer appeared to be in possession of the facts, Amelia felt Kathryn Massey would be a far more reliable source of information. But while Massey's account matched Mamie's, she speculated how the Sapphire Moon incident might be a huge publicity gambit for all concerned.

"Selznick's Scarlett hunt was a masterstroke," Massey wrote, "crowned by his British discovery. But lightning won't strike twice. This new arrangement benefits everyone: Selznick, *Pretty Pennies*, Cohn and Columbia, even Hayworth. All except the Notorious Palm Springs Madam, who's left holding the bag while the law closes in."

Amelia stashed the *Reporter* under the counter as college students approached for bargain pens, nibs, and ink. Her mind buzzed with questions that swooped and pecked like territorial blackbirds.

A publicity stunt? If Hartman had found Bernice, other PIs could, too. Maybe their visit hadn't been pure chance. Had Selznick orchestrated the raid, knowing it would spook Cohn into pulling Rita, leaving him free to cast someone else?

But the theory soon crumbled. Could Selznick manage this without Irene's or Marcella's involvement? And orchestrating an arrest—with real jail time—to promote a picture? It wasn't his style. Ambitious, yes. Hollywood's Rasputin, no.

Where does that get me? Amelia counted out the students' change. Back at square one.

Meanwhile, Matilda served French toast to jacketless slobs, unaware that Amelia knew about her connection to the opportunist making headlines over Bernice's arrest. The *Times*, *Herald-Express*, and *Daily News* all carried her brother's statements.

Watching Matilda flirt and soft-soap gave Amelia an idea.

She bided her time until late afternoon, when she caught her chance near the stationery cabinet by the washrooms.

"I guess there goes my foot in the door," she said, shooting for an easy-come-easy-go glibness.

Matilda stopped, her eyes wide with what registered as genuine surprise. "Not-so-pretty pennies, huh?" She hooked her thumb in her apron pocket. "One minute you've got your foot in the door. The next, you're missing three toes."

"I'd even signed the contract!"

"Contracts." Matilda unleashed an over-inflated sigh. "They're only worth a damn if the picture goes forward." Her tone struck Amelia as remarkably sympathetic, considering Amelia's lost opportunity was her loss, too. "That brothel raid out in the desert. Talk about a curveball. And that means anything can happen. So" —she tapped Amelia's wrist, the same way Polly would—"don't give up on it yet."

* * *

Amelia leaned into Polly's ear. "Do you see what I see?"

A dozen people waited in the screening room foyer for Selznick's arrival. Bernice, Zara, and Sibyl hadn't let go of each other's hands since their teary reunion ten minutes before. Polly nodded. "It's very touching."

"No, not that—though, yes, it's sweet." Amelia curved her hand in a wide circle from left to right. "Irene, Hazel, Virginia, Mom, Bernice, Thelma from Casting, Dorothy Arzner, Zara Willowick, and Sibyl Langley. All women."

When Amelia had asked Polly what the odds might be that Mr. Selznick would allow a screening of *Pretty Pennies* for the woman who had derailed the project from a PR bonanza to disaster, Polly had rated her chances as fifty/fifty. When she had worked up the courage to approach Selznick, he had told Polly to organize a screening as he wanted to run it once more before he decided to go ahead—or not. And yes, he was more than happy to invite anyone she liked—including Bernice.

Amelia gestured to Irene to join her and Polly. "Do you know which way your husband's leaning?"

Irene shrugged. "He doesn't agree that *all* publicity is good publicity."

"Is it too much to dream that sentimentality wins the day?" Amelia asked.

"David can be abominably sentimental at times, so let's hope so. I'd like to think he's watching it again in case he sees a gem he can salvage."

"So it's our job to convince him?"

Irene did a double-take and shot Amelia a look. "That's right. We'll keep our eyes peeled for—"

Selznick strode into the foyer, shirtsleeves folded to his elbows and a lit Montecristo cigar jammed into his mouth. Bernice stepped forward with her hand extended. "Mr. Selznick, I sincerely wish we could've met again under more congenial circumstances."

He recoiled, a gesture of surprise tinged with irritation. Had she jumped the gun and blown it? Amelia wished they'd talked about the best strategy on the drive over, but they'd gossiped about the Hayworth business. Polly had also mentioned that Selznick and Cohn couldn't be feuding. They still played poker with the usual crowd, often at the 90-90 Club across the street from Selznick International. How these men could be at each other's throats by day then sit down at the card table come nightfall was a paradox Amelia could never understand.

Whatever his initial reaction, he masked it with a slight shrug that said *What's done is done*. Irene gripped her husband's arm—a distraction tactic—and kissed him on the cheek before introducing Zara and Sibyl, reminding him that the last time they had seen one another, Selznick been a wide-eyed boy of twelve.

He took it in his stride, but impatience darkened his face, so Irene suggested they all file in. After everyone had taken a seat, she stood up at the front of the screen. "Some of you haven't watched this picture in twenty-five years. Whatever your perspective, we're here to determine its viability. Remember: there are no wrong opinions."

In the back row, Amelia found Polly's hand. *Here goes plenty o' nothin'*.

* * *

As the film's final image—the Equitable Pictures logo—faded to black and the lights came on, silence fell over the screening room.

Even Bernice, who had quietly sobbed through pretty much the entire movie—was silent as a statue. You heard Irene, Amelia wanted to remind them, no wrong opinions! She might have opened her fat mouth had she not felt a warning nudge from Polly. *The boss always speaks first*.

"It's more outdated than I remember when we ran it six months ago." Selznick see-sawed his Montecristo between his fingers. "I suppose I was caught up in the romance of seeing my father's first picture. But I'm not so sure this story will play well to modern audiences." It was Amelia's worst fear come true. She closed her eyes. More silence. Then, "Virginia, what did *you* think?"

"I agree." Van Upp took her time turning to face Selznick. "And as long as we're laying our cards on the table, I'll admit to having misgivings ever since I began working on the script."

"Why have we not heard about these misgivings before now?" Irene's voice shook with frustration.

"I'm sorry, dear. You have every right to be upset. When Polly found those reels on Catalina, we were so enchanted we didn't consider how the story would play today. I thought I could modernize it—you know how I love a challenge. But my goodness, what an uphill battle it's been."

"Perhaps Bernice's raid is a positive thing," Dorothy said, taking care to choose her words. "Otherwise, we might not be sitting here reviewing it with fresh eyes."

Finally! Someone who doesn't want to hurl Pennies *into the trash.*

"However, now that we have," Dorothy continued, "I must confess."

Or does she?

"The story is too old-fashioned, too simplistic, too naïve. Also, the Sapphire Moon's raid has tainted the name *Pretty Pennies*. Sorry, but it has."

Bernice fluttered a hand. "No need to apologize."

"All in all, it seems like a dicier proposition than it did when I first signed on."

"Are you quitting?" Irene asked.

"Did you hear me say that?" Dorothy parried, her tone dry as gin.

As much as she hated to, Amelia agreed. Seeing *Pennies* a second time, it was impossible to overlook its dated charm and corny flaws. But she wasn't ready to let the idea go. She looked down the rows of seating and was happy to see Irene's chin set in firm determination. "For starters," Irene said, "how about changing the name?"

"To distance it from the original?" Virginia mused. "I like that. Suggestions, anyone?"

"One of the main things that struck me," Polly said, "was that back then, kids were diving for pennies. Twenty-five years later, they're not prepared to risk their necks for mere pennies. They dive for dimes and quarters and the almighty half-dollar."

Zara sat up straighter. "How about *Loose Change*?"

"Has potential," Selznick said, measuring each word with practised caution.

But Amelia had a better idea. She cleared her throat. "What about *Sea Change*?"

The group drew a single, shared breath. Yes, they all agreed, an excellent title.

Sibyl winced. "Slapping on a new label isn't enough. We'll need to change the plot."

Emboldened now, Amelia perched herself on the edge of her seat. "Change the plot to a story about the *making* of a remake."

Virginia snapped her fingers. "Now we're getting somewhere. Go on."

Go on with what? She'd played her only card, but their expectant faces galvanized her. "What if it's about a newcomer remaking a lost silent film? Keep it on Catalina, keep the diving girl from *Pretty Pennies*, but now it's also about this actress diving into stardom. A sea change in her life while she plays a character who changes while she's diving into the sea." Amelia held her breath as the group grew still, rolling her suggestion over in their minds.

Soon, the conversation ripened into a brainstorming session.

Conflict with her director.

Betrayal by her leading man.

Wild storm at sea.

Climax at a lighthouse.

Deceitful best friend.

Love story with a local lad. A sailor or fisherman, perhaps.

Polly's pen flew across the pages, taking down every suggestion.

"Ladies, I have a civil war to edit." Selznick hoisted himself to his feet. "I walked into this session ready to nix the whole thing, but I think we've found a way to turn things around. Virginia, rustle up a new outline."

She tapped her temple. "Already started."

Selznick zeroed in on Amelia. "Why is your voice so familiar?"

"I was the one who pitched you the film the day Vivien Leigh needed—"

"I remember. But specifically, your voice."

"Amelia was the scene partner in Rita Hayworth's screen test," Thelma told him.

Selznick's eyes glowed from behind his wire spectacles. "That was you?"

Was he impressed? Or put off?

He was headed for the exit. She let him go, then followed the others out into the foyer, where Irene slipped a hand around her elbow. "Do you realize what you've done?"

"What?"

"Dreamed up a new title *and* come up with a new plot. Why, my dear, you have single-handedly saved the whole movie."

30

"I like it when you do that," Benji murmured.

Amelia lifted her tongue from his earlobe. "Why do you suppose I do it for so long?" She ran a finger down his neck, through his chest hair, and to his right nipple. She didn't squeeze it —not yet—but instead circled his areola, slowly at first, then faster as his breaths shortened.

"Care to go again?" he asked.

"We rarely get the place to ourselves. Yours or mine."

"You should ask for the four p.m. shift more often."

Even with the drapes drawn against the summer sun, Amelia's bedroom was heating up. In half an hour it'd be even hotter, and in an hour she'd have to get ready for work. She nestled her nose against his chest and breathed in his Ivory soap. "We've got fifty minutes."

"In that case." He flipped Amelia over onto her back as though she weighed nothing more than a flapjack.

Her squeal of delight skewered the still afternoon air as he angled a leg over her torso, pinning her to the mattress. "A guy could get used to this."

"So could a gal." Her hand was heading south when a loud thumping on the front door punched a hole in their cocoon.

"Expecting someone?" he asked.

Whoever was knocking, their timing was atrocious. "In case you weren't available, I phoned Ronald Colman."

"At least I'm being superseded by an A-lister."

A second knock, as insistent as the first. She pressed her lips against his. The eager soul at the door would take the hint and leave the two of them alone to catch up on "lost opportunities," as Benji had called them when he'd been preoccupied with *Beau Geste*.

His tongue found hers and probed deeper. She wrapped her legs around his back and locked them against his hip bones as he—

An adamant voice followed a third knocking. "MISS HARTLEY! PLEASE ANSWER!"

Benji pulled his mouth away. "What if it's an urgent telegram?"

Amelia draped herself in Benji's discarded shirt as she approached the door. "Who is it?"

"My name is Nathan Leroux. I'm a production assistant at Selznick International."

Great name for an actor or a director, but it didn't sound the least bit familiar. Polly hadn't mentioned him, which meant the kid sat way down the pecking order. "What's this all about? I'm kind of in the middle of—I'm busy."

"Yeah, you are!" Benji called from the bedroom.

"I'm here to fetch you."

Fetch her? Who could resist such bait? She opened the door.

From what Amelia had seen, most studio lackeys were pasty-faced from living under the lights and thin as yesterday's soup. But not this Leroux fellow. No sirree. With his boxer's build, he looked like the sort who'd be the last man standing in any barroom brawl.

"Sent by who? To fetch me for what?"

"Miss Maddox."

"Is Polly okay?"

"Yes, yes. I'll explain in the car. Time is of the ess—"

"You'll explain now before the lady gets into a stranger's vehicle," said Benji, coming up behind Amelia.

A delicious shiver raced up her spine. Clearly, he wasn't about to let his girlfriend disappear with a guy who probably had, in all likelihood, little problem finding girlfriends of his own. *He's jealous!* It was a side of Benji Amelia hadn't seen before. How delightful.

"Mr. Selznick has a spare half-hour," Leroux said, speaking quickly now, "in between a *Wind* editing session and an *Intermezzo* advertising meeting."

"A half-hour for what?"

"Again, I'll explain in the car, so . . ." He gestured at Benji's shirt. "But do step on it. The available half-hour is from two-thirty to three o'clock."

Two-thirty meant Amelia had ten minutes to make herself presentable, plus ten minutes to get to the studio. If they were finished by three, that would give her an hour to get to Schwab's for her shift. It was enough time—in theory. "Okay, fine. I'll meet you in the street."

"The hell you will," Benji said. "*I'll* be driving you."

Benji's green-eyed monster now sounded a little too "me Tarzan, you Jane" for Amelia's liking. "This has come from Polly," she told him. "I'm sure it's on the up-and-up."

"We'll see you downstairs." He slammed the door.

Amelia ripped off his shirt. "You picked a fine time to play Sir Galahad." She dashed into the bedroom and chose her pale pink suit with the white piping.

"What if that guy isn't who he said he was?"

"Who do you think sent him? Al Capone?" She couldn't spare a minute to iron a blouse, but it wouldn't matter if she kept the jacket buttoned. "He mentioned Pol by name." Her white pumps were still scuffed from last night at Seven Seas, but maybe Selznick wouldn't notice. "Who the hell knows what's going on, but they've dispatched a car and driver, for Pete's sake." Her brown imitation snakeskin purse clashed with the pink, but style had to take a back seat. "But if you absolutely insist on driving, at least put on some pants."

* * *

Polly was waiting for Amelia on the brick path outside the administration building. "I told Nathan, 'Say whatever you need to say, but get her here!'" She followed Amelia's glance back to the parking lot where Benji was stewing in his car. "Benji drove you?"

The whole ride over, the temperature in the driver's seat had dropped to sub-zero; Amelia could still feel the frost. "I don't remember you mentioning a Nathan Leroux before."

"He's new." Polly set off down the path.

"When he started pounding on our door, Benji went from lovey-dovey cuddle-bunny to Frankenstein with his thumb slammed in a car door."

The closer they had got to the studio, the more Benji had retreated into himself, but Amelia held her tongue. This mysterious summons left no room in her mind for his brooding. Had Bernice thrown a new wrench into the works? Had Selznick and Irene locked horns again? When she leaned in for a goodbye kiss, Benji had pecked her cheek, his lips hard and unyielding. She'd deal with Mr. Grouchy later. For now, she worried that her lipstick was crooked. "Pol, why am I here?"

But she had left her question too late. They walked into Selznick's office where Thelma sat at the small conference table with Mr. Schuessler, the head of casting. Polly took a seat and directed Amelia to the only other free chair.

"Miss Hartley," Selznick said, "thank you for coming at such short notice."

"It's not every day a girl like me gets sent a car, a driver, and a summons." Amelia glanced at Polly, who flared her eyes so imperceptibly that only Amelia could see.

"I'll level with you," Selznick continued. "Harry pulling Rita from *Pretty Pennies* was a huge relief. She might have done a decent job, I suppose, but she's too picture-perfect. Harry and his team will turn her into a screen goddess, so she'll get along fine without us. But Miss Hartley, when you pitched *Sea Change* at the screening, turning it into a story about an actress making her debut in a silent film remake, well, my goodness!" Selznick smiled for the first time. "That's when everything fell into place."

Amelia interwove her fingers to keep them steady. "Uh-huh." If this was about *Sea Change*, why wasn't Irene here?

"The puzzle pieces eventually snapped into place with *Wind*, with *Intermezzo*, with *Rebecca*, but never with *Pretty Pennies*, which is why I vacillated over the idea. But when you made your perceptive suggestions, ideas came bubbling up like lava. I've been dictating plotting memos to Polly by the ton, haven't I, Miss Maddox?"

"It's been my observation, sir, that dictating your thoughts is how you arrive at conclusions and decisions."

"I suppose that's true, isn't it?" He pulled a cigarette—Benson & Hedges, Amelia noted, Vivien Leigh's brand—and threaded it between his fingers. "Miss Hartley, it wasn't until I learned you were the other girl in Rita's screen test that I realized that Juniper was under my nose all along. Did you know your voice records beautifully on film?"

Amelia's brain had frozen. Was Selznick paying her a compliment? "I'm sorry, but did I know what?"

"You have a crisp delivery. Natural but lively. Rather like Tallulah Bankhead crossed with Ann Sheridan."

"Goodness!" she exclaimed breathlessly. "That's heady company."

"Most crisp speakers sound fresh from elocution school," Schuessler said. "Suitable for a Vassar valedictorian." Amelia pictured Matilda, speaking carefully as though each word were a precious bead of crystal, part of her transformation from Tillie. "But not for dialogue," Schuessler continued. "During Miss Hayworth's test, your delivery caught my ear, and I thought, 'Hello? Who do we have here?'"

Thelma removed her reading glasses. "You have an appealing huskiness to your voice."

Amelia could only breathe in shallow, light breaths. This was too much. Far too much to take in. "I'm glad you think so."

"It adds depth of character," Selznick said. "Plus, you have the perfect looks for what I've had in mind since the title change."

These people should have known better than to bowl a girl over with talk of "Who do we have here?" She sought Polly's face. There were those flared eyes again.

Amelia had drifted off on countless nights to visions of stardom. Limos, furs, microphones, gowns. What girl hadn't? And sure, lightning struck now and then in real life, but far more often on the screen. Now that stardom appeared to be beckoning, Amelia took a mental step back in case the chickens she was counting weren't going to hatch. Or weren't even chickens.

"I'm still unclear on—Mr. Selznick, what are you saying?"

"I want you to come in to test for Juniper."

"A screen test?"

"I'm thinking one of the early scenes. Basic costume, minimal hair and makeup. I've learned with Miss Bergman that less is more. How does that sound?"

His proposal sounded good to Amelia. Fun, even. But wasn't this how Benji's last girl started her downhill slide? The drive to the studio had told her plenty. First snippy, then sullen until he caught himself. After that, he'd played diplomat, but his white-knuckled grip on the steering wheel had given him away.

What would his reaction be if Selznick wanted to cast her as Juniper? Would he be fine with it as long as she didn't accept? Would he seethe in silent resentment? Or would he become the yell-swear-intimidate type?

Hold on a cotton-pickin' minute, she told herself. When did you become a drippy female who makes decisions based on what some guy thinks? You've never been that kind of girl. Why in blazes would you start now?

"I only have one question," she told Selznick.

"What's that?"

"Which day should I report?"

31

When Amelia had asked Selznick about the date of her screen test, she hadn't expected him to say, "Does this same hour next week suit you?" She would have preferred sooner—less time to fret. But, as Luddie had explained over banana splits at Kreiss's Coffee Shop, "Selznick wasn't asking. It's his genteel way of saying 'Be here when I need you here,' without sounding like a European despot. Considerate bosses are rare."

But what about considerate boyfriends?

When Amelia had told Benji about Selznick offering her a screen test, he hadn't become angry. No temper tantrum. No terse words through gritted teeth. There had been signs, however. Drumming his fingernails on the steering wheel. Sucking his teeth like he had poppy seeds caught between them. Once Benji adjusted, she had told herself that day, they'd find their rhythm again. And so, when he offered to drive her to the screen test, she saw it as an olive branch.

But vapid chitchat now filled the car. Not about how she felt about today's screen test. Or what she might do if—miracle of miracles!—she wound up landing the part. And God forbid they talk about how he would feel if such a golden opportunity should happen. No, instead, she heard how the Yankees were faring since Gehrig's retirement. What it must be like to fly Pan Am's new *Dixie Clipper* straight through to Portugal. And how it wouldn't be long before the Santa Anas started up. It was better than steely silence—but not by much.

Okay, fine, Amelia thought. Stew in your juices if you insist. I don't have the wherewithal to jolly you up. And it's not my job to crowbar your emotions out of you. And even if it were, I'm not about to jump into that briar patch of hurt feelings before I embark on the opportunity that could change the course of my life.

He swung his Hupmobile into the driveway and braked at the security booth. "I'll wait for you."

Did he honestly think she couldn't see right through his light and airy facade? Still, he was trying, and that counted for a lot. Gosh, though, wouldn't all this be easier if they could just talk about that girl who did the dirty on him? "But honey," she said, careful to match his nonchalance, "I could be quite some time."

He retrieved a copy of *Drums Along the Mohawk* from the back seat. "I've got this to keep me company."

The guard checked off Amelia's name on his list and waved them through. Benji pulled into a vacant space and opened his car door. "I'll escort you as far as Casting if you li—" He froze when he noticed the pair of women walking toward them.

"Today's the day!" Irene cried out. "I hate that I wasn't here last week, but I had my hands full tending a child sick with pink-eye, a blocked commode, and a box of Bourbon roses delivered to the wrong address."

"Have you met my boyfriend?" Amelia said. "Benji, this is Irene Selznick and Ingrid Bergman."

Ingrid greeted him with a warm smile and extended her hand for him to shake. Irene, however, stiffened. "Amelia is here for her screen test," she told Ingrid.

"*The Sea Change*, yes?" Ingrid pressed her hands to her cheeks. "I miss my Baltic Sea. From Stockholm you can sail to Copenhagen, to Helsinki, to Riga. So many charming places to visit."

"Your English has improved." Amelia kept half an eye on Irene doing her level best to size up Benji with practiced indifference.

"Thank you. I have worked very hard."

"Would you share any useful tips for Amelia's screen test?" Irene said.

Ingrid touched Amelia's shoulder with sisterly warmth. "Be yourself. The camera will catch and—what's the word?—make bigger your personality."

"Enhance?" Irene suggested.

"The camera will *enhance* your personality. This is why you must be yourself. You cannot lie to the camera."

Irene seized Amelia by the shoulders. "Thank you, Benji, for seeing her to the studio, but we can't have non-essential personnel on a closed set. By all means, though, roam the backlot. All the *Wind* sets are still standing." She hustled Amelia along the path before Benji was able to say goodbye.

"What's with the bum's rush?" Amelia asked her. "You didn't give Benj—"

Irene whirled around. "Prepare yourself."

"I'm ready as I'll ever be."

"You most definitely are not."

Dormant butterflies in Amelia's stomach took wing when Irene let loose with an uncharacteristically girlish giggle. "Why is that?"

"You'll be screen-testing today opposite an actor auditioning for the male lead."

"Is that unusual?"

"My goodness. How shall I put this?"

"Look, Irene, if this is your idea of a psychological trick—"

"The actor, he—he looks like Benji."

The butterflies in Amelia's stomach subsided to an occasional flutter. "Is that all? Don't you think it'll be easier to follow Ingrid's advice if I'm with someone who reminds me of my beau?"

Irene wrapped a maternal arm around Amelia's shoulders. "We'll see."

. . .

The man in the waiting room was pacing back and forth like a restless zoo beast. "Mrs. Selznick!"

With no chair nearby to steady herself, Amelia trembled. *Oh, Irene, you should've warned me looked—like—like THIS.*

He reached them in four steps.

"Amelia Hartley," Irene said, "may I present Kendrick Moss."

He matched Benji's height and hair, but his eyes were a deeper blue, his smile broader and pearlier. He moved with the confidence of a charmer for whom doors always opened.

"This'll be my first screen test," Moss said.

Holy moly. The guy was Benji with the volume dialed to maximum—radiating presence and charisma. The perfect actor to cast in *The Benji Fletcher Story*. A tremor ran through Amelia that she hoped nobody noticed, not even hawk-eyed Irene.

"I hear it's your first, too," he continued. "Nervous?"

Any normal person would be. Getting a screen test was like winning a slot-machine jackpot in Reno. Millions dream about it, but few score one. And here was Amelia about to walk into hers. But was she *nervous*? No, she had to admit. Standing in on Rita's test hadn't rattled her, but she'd only been window dressing. Now that Selznick's camera would be aimed straight at her, shouldn't she feel at least the teeniest bit twitchy? She could only do her best and hand over the worrying to tomorrow.

Meanwhile, get a load of this panting slab of manliness. I bet the camera will adore him. "Nervous?" She tossed Moss a devil-may-care grin. "Nah."

He grinned, his twin rows of teeth white as Benji's Ivory soap.

Oh, God! Benji! If we have chemistry, and if we get cast, I'll be acting opposite this handful of manful. One glimpse of this guy and there'll be blood in the water.

* * *

Dorothy Arzner handed over a sheaf of papers.

As glad as Amelia had been to find her and Zara waiting next to the camera, maybe six pages of dialogue was why she should be nervous. "How much time do I have?"

"Fifteen minutes."

Zara's lights were all on, blazing and blinding. Amelia fanned herself. "It's a lot."

"The specific words aren't as important as how the light catches you, what the mic picks up, the way you move, gestures, mannerisms. The chemistry between you and Kendrick beats everything else combined." Dorothy shifted closer to establish a more intimate space. "The stiffer you are, the harder it'll be, so don't get flustered."

Amelia scanned the pages. Virginia had reimagined Juniper as a first-time actress opposite Dominic, also a newcomer to the movies. Their characters discussed the coins missed by kid divers, now at the bottom of Avalon Harbor.

On second reading, Amelia caught the metaphor: They were each other's treasure, but co-stars were forbidden fruit. The scene peaked with what Virginia called "a passionate clinch that lasts as long as Breen will allow—plus five seconds."

What was the Hays Code's maximum? Ten seconds? Twelve? Twenty? Amelia doubted those old-fashioned prudes in the Breen Office permitted a kiss lasting a whole minute. What was she supposed to do? Kiss the very kissable Kendrick Moss until Dorothy said, "Cut"?

Oh, my.

Dorothy asked Amelia to join them on the set—although to call it a "set" was an exaggeration. Someone had erected a large white-and-green-striped beach umbrella between a matching pair of potted miniature palm trees in front of a plain sky-blue backdrop. Moss was already waiting for her, the tips of his brogues touching a length of tape fixed to the floor.

"Zara," Dorothy called, "whenever you're ready."

A row of diffused baby-pink bulbs sprang to life. Amelia lifted her chin to Moss. He'd been attractive out in the anteroom, but in this flattering lighting he was impossibly good-looking. What a damn shame he wasn't a pompous heel.

She stepped back from the tape laid out for her.

It was going to be hard enough delivering everything required of her, but while she was also drowning in that handsomeness? What if Benji walked in and found her smooching his more attractive twin? He'd be upset, to say the very least. And she wouldn't blame him. Much as she wanted this, maybe it wasn't worth risking the resentment of the only guy she'd ever fallen for.

A list of ways she could torpedo this screen test reeled off in her head.

Try too hard.

Fumble lines.

Cut him off.

Pull distracting faces.

Dorothy would see it was all a waste of time and she'd call "cut" before Amelia and Moss went in for the clinch.

On the other hand, if Benji couldn't stand a bit of competition, maybe he wasn't half the man she took him for.

"My dear?" Dorothy had softened her voice. "We need you to position yourself on the tape."

Now Amelia could see Polly lingering behind Dorothy and Zara. To her right, Irene stood next to Sibyl with her hands clasped. Amelia hadn't noticed her when she'd stepped inside, but her presence warmed her heart. And to Polly's left—*Good God, is that Luddie?* A sheen of tears blurred Amelia's vision. He'd driven across town to show his support? And on broadcast day, too. He'd have to get his skates on to make it into the studio in time.

Look at them all. Their hopeful, expectant faces that say, "We believe in you."

Wasn't it possible that Benji might find it funny that Kendrick Moss resembled him, but was better looking? Weirder things than that happened all the time. Especially here in Weirdsville. Give your man some credit.

Amelia blew a kiss to Luddie and mouthed "Thank you." He pretended to doff a hat.

"May we proceed?" Dorothy called from beside Zara's camera.

Irene raised her eyebrows. *May we?*

Amelia steeled her innards. "Yes," she told Irene. "We certainly may."

32

"And cut." Dorothy's command shot through the impromptu set.

Amelia and Kendrick unclinched, but she needed a moment before she faced everyone.

His lips felt nothing like Benji's. They were fuller and softer, but his kisses weren't so urgent, so passionate. Of course, it had only been for the camera, so it wasn't a real smooch. But still, it was everything an intimate kiss should be: warm and lingering, with a hint of more to come.

Irene was the first person to reach her. "You did great."

Her ripple of exuberance caught Amelia off guard. "You're not just saying that to be nice?"

She tilted her head back imperiously. "I don't say anything just to be nice."

A pair of arms encircled her waist, and she smelled Luddie's rich, smoky Acqua di Parma cologne. "I second that."

She clapped her hands onto his. "You came! It means more to me than I can say."

He hugged her extra hard. "You were a revelation."

Amelia's memory was already fading. She couldn't recall how closely she'd followed the script, but that hardly mattered—everything had flowed between her and Mr. Moss as though they'd known each other for years.

"He's right," Polly said. "You looked natural up there, like you'd been acting since you were a child star."

Luddie released her, saying he had to get to NBC. He took off as Sibyl and Zara converged on her.

"Have you done this before?" Zara asked.

"Does a high school audition for *Peg o' My Heart* count?"

"Not in the least."

His lips, though. His lips! "Was our chemistry what you were looking for?"

The silence that settled over Polly, Sibyl, Zara, and Irene lingered for longer than Amelia would have liked.

"Oh, yes," Polly said at last. "All good, chemistry-wise."

What was the insider dish Polly had told her about casting pictures? *They imagine the co-stars in bed together. If they can picture it, they greenlight it.* Would that be running through the minds of Selznick's team as they watched?

"What's *your* impression of how it went?" Sibyl asked.

"Hard to say. It's such a blur now."

"In that case," Polly said, "how are you feeling?"

Buoyant was the first word that came to mind. "Like I'm filled with bubbles."

Irene cocked an eyebrow. "Moët et Chandon or Dom Perignon?"

Irene had named two French champagnes, neither of which Amelia could afford. "The most expensive one."

"Correct answer!" She slung a protective arm around Amelia's shoulder. "Let me walk you back to your car."

They passed through the doorway and Amelia glanced at the waiting room. A couple of hours ago, it had been empty. But now—Amelia quickly counted—eleven girls, all around Amelia's age, sat on the chairs lining the walls, interest mixed with hope filling their faces. Interest to see who had preceded them; hope that Amelia had been no good and Selznick was still looking for the best girl to play Juniper.

Of course I'm not the only girl they're auditioning.

Amelia pictured the look on Rita Hayworth's face when she'd walked into this same room filled with redheads. The dismay Rita must have felt now drained the color from Amelia's face.

Why wouldn't *they be looking at other ingenue types?*

What a ghastly feeling this was, spiraling from "You're so special" to "You're so easily replaceable" in less time than it took a girl to powder her nose.

I was a prize donkey's ass to think I was their only choice.

She waited until they had stepped outside. "Are all those girls getting a screen test, too?"

"Heavens, no," Irene replied. "David would never permit that expense. Only the best three."

Amelia told herself she ought to be grateful she didn't have to sit in that waiting room alongside all the others. "Now that we're alone," she began. It was hard getting out the words with all the wind knocked out of her sails. "How did I do?"

"You thought I was fibbing in there?"

"People often say things they don't mean."

Irene hooked her elbow. "You should be proud of how you handled yourself." She guided them around a camera dolly, her grip warm through Amelia's sleeve. "I'll admit I had my doubts." She slowed their pace to a dawdle. "I've seen first-hand how people change when you shove them in front of a lens."

A soft sigh escaped Amelia as she silently counted her blessings for being spared this observation before her test. "Change how?"

"Some performers turn into wooden puppets. Others loosen up, like they've had a double shot of Jack Daniels. And then there's the third, rarest category. They bloom like roses in May. It happens to Garbo. And Judy."

"Garland?"

"Uh-huh. I saw it with Vivien, too." Irene adjusted her hatpin. "Put you and Kenny into a large bowl, add a movie camera, stir in a good script, mix well, and wait for the sparks to fly. Those sparks are called screen chemistry, and it's where those bubbles come from."

The parking lot was in sight now. "Speaking of Kenny, where'd you find him?"

"He was one of the extras in the Atlanta railway station scene. I noticed him standing in line for his boxed lunch. He assumed I was with Costuming and asked me if I had any safety pins to hitch up his britches."

"You weren't aware how much he resembles my boyfriend?"

"Not a clue!"

"Except that Kenny's more handsome."

"Well," Irene said, lowering her voice to a conspiratorial tone, "now that you mention it."

"Imagine how I felt!"

They were still laughing as they stepped out from behind a scenery truck and found Benji leaning against his car. "I have a child to pick up from kindergarten," Irene said. "He howls like a banshee if I send the nanny." She hurried off in the direction of her car.

Benji ground a half-smoked cigarette into the gravel. "How'd it go?"

Amelia summoned a non-committal smile. To say it went well would sound like bragging. Benji deserved an honest answer, but one that didn't dredge up memories of his last girlfriend unraveling. She debated whether to mention the waiting room packed with competition—something she'd foolishly overlooked. He took her silence as evasiveness, sauntered to the driver's side, and slid in.

"AMELIA! HEY! AMELIA!"

Kenny Moss bounded toward her like a Saint Bernard puppy. "I didn't get to thank you properly for being such a swell scene partner! I was plenty nervous, but then Dorothy yelled 'action' and —well, I forgot to be antsy!" Amelia doubted he'd ever had an antsy moment in his blessed life. "I think that's what they call 'screen chemistry.' Whatever it was, my nerves vanished lickety-split—thanks to you."

Benji stepped back out of his Hupmobile, one foot on the

gravel, the other on the running board, as he sized Kenny up with a furious, sweeping scrutiny.

"I'd like to introduce my boyfriend, Benji Fletcher," Amelia said. "Benji, this is Kendrick Moss, who I did my screen test with."

"You weren't by yourself?"

"I assumed I would be, but when I arrived, there was Kenny, raring to go."

Amelia cringed. She should've worded that better.

Benji spat a wad of spittle onto the ground, as though he were Doc Holliday and this was the O.K. Corral.

"SAY!" Kenny slapped the hood of Benji's car. "You and me, we kinda resemble each other, don't we? Ain't that the funniest thing?" Amelia could see he was still fizzing with those champagne bubbles. "Nice to meet you, friend!" He casually saluted Benji and bounced away across the parking lot, turning around to cup his hands to his mouth. "See you on the set—fingers crossed!"

Benji sat back down behind his steering wheel and adjusted the rearview mirror four times before letting his hand fall to his lap.

This is going to be one long ride home. She slipped in beside him. He didn't turn on the ignition, but instead stared straight ahead. "That aw-shucks Boy Scout is an actor?"

"I would've preferred to know they were screen-testing both of us *before* I stepped into—"

"Trying out for the male lead, was he?"

You've got nothing to be ashamed of, she told herself. If we have a problem, it's sitting right here in the driver's seat.

"So," Benji persisted, "if you're cast and he's cast . . .?"

Don't explode. Don't attack. Don't cuss. And most of all, don't defend yourself. You've done nothing wrong. Could she short-circuit this brewing spat by telling him she was only one of a dozen girls up for the role? Yes, she could. Would it make him feel better? Yes, it would. But was it her job to defuse fears she wasn't responsible for creating in the first place? No, it wasn't.

"If we're both cast, we'd be the leads," Amelia replied evenly. "And yes, he does look like you." If anything, Kenny was too handsome, too amiable—like he wasn't aware of his own appeal. But Amelia only had eyes for Benji.

Before she could say so, he yelled, "I've heard enough!" He kicked open the door and hurled himself from the car.

Amelia stayed put. Let him cool off walking around Tara and Manderley. Twice if he needed to. And when he returned, she could soothe that fragile ego made of dandelion puffs—nope. Nope. Nope. The hell with that. She threw open her door. "HEY!"

To Benji's credit, he stopped. He did not, however, turn around. It was lunchtime now, so most employees were in the commissary.

She marched up to him. "You're being insulting right now," she snapped at him. Or rather, his back.

"How do you figure?"

She poked him between the shoulder blades, as hard as she could. "You don't think I've got the self-control to stop myself from falling at that guy's feet."

That did it. He spun around. "So you admit it. He's a looker."

"Jesus! I'd have to be blind as Helen Keller with the lights off not to notice. But that's beside the point."

He uncrossed his arms like he was escaping a straitjacket. "It's absolutely the point."

"Because he looks like you?" She ached to add *but better looking,* but that would have been a blow too low. Screaming at each other wasn't going to get them anywhere, so she softened her tone. "You have nothing to worry about. I promise. Cross my heart—"

"It's not you I'm worried about."

"I can handle Kenny. What do you think I do all day at Schwab's?"

Consternation flickered across his face. "Guys make passes at you?"

"It's what men do if they reckon they stand a chance to get to third base. Or second. Hell's bells, they'd do it to get to first."

"You never told me that."

"Since when am I required to lodge a full report of my daily activities?"

"Now you're being ridiculous."

"*Someone*'s being ridiculous around here."

"I need to know that you won't—that you're not—"

Now they were getting somewhere. Amelia stepped closer to him. A couple more steps and she'd be near enough to fold her arms around his waist—or slug him with her purse. "Go on," she urged. "Say it. Tell me what you want me to reassure you of."

"I—uh—" He dropped his arms to his sides.

"You need me to tell you that I'm not that other girl. The one that got picked up by Fox and went downhill fast. Benji, I'm not her."

"I know you're not." His rebuttal held all the strength of a wet Kleenex.

"If you did, you wouldn't be barking orders at me. Now, listen." She poked him in the sternum. Not hard, but firmly enough to get the message across. "I'm over twenty-one and free to make my own choices. If they offer me this role, I'll take it. And if Kenny's the lead, I'll be on Catalina with him making this picture." She refused to spend the *Sea Change* shoot skirting around Benji's feelings. Best to have it out now, and damn the consequences. "Love. Scenes. And. All."

She could almost see the cogs whirling in his mind. Yes, she'd been blunt with him, but they'd be better for it in the long run.

He opened his mouth, but didn't speak.

Go on. Say you're sorry. Then I'll say I'm glad we've got that out of the way. And then we'll drive to Carpenter's for hamburgers and thick shakes because they make your favorite French-fried potatoes.

His face hardened. His lips etched into a thin, pale line; his jaw jutted out, grim and determined.

"Polly can give you a lift home."

His voice was so low that she had to lean forward. "A *lift*?"

"Or catch a taxi."

"What?!"

"I can't do this, Amelia. Not again. It hurt too much the last time. I thought I could, but that Kenny guy, he's—he's too—" He couldn't bring himself to state the obvious. "And even then, maybe I could have, but then you had to go and say it out loud."

"Say what?"

He pressed his lips together as he marshaled the effort it took to reply. "'Love scenes and all.'"

"One of us has to be realistic."

"That's the thing, though. I think I'm the one being realistic."

"By focusing on the 'love' part when you should be focusing on the 'scenes' part? Scenes from a movie. It's called 'acting,' which, let me remind you, is another word for 'pretending.'"

"I work in the movies, too. And I've seen more than my fair share of love scenes spilling over after the director yells cut." He took a step backward toward his car. And then another.

When he took a third, she said, "Are you breaking up with me? Over something that hasn't happened? That I'm promising you won't—"

"She promised, too. Over and over. I told myself that I wouldn't ever be one of those fools who don't learn from their mistakes."

"And I'm not one of those fools who should tiptoe around your delicate feelings about some girl in your past. I'm in your *present*, Benji—" She reached out to grab his arm and stop him from walking away, but he wrenched himself clear and headed back to his car.

She could have chased after him. Mounted a better defense. Explained why he was wrong and she was right. Or, for the sake of expediency, she could have given in. Turned down the job if they offered it to her, kept the peace, and allowed this awful fight to fade away.

And she might have done it, too, if it hadn't been for those blasted champagne bubbles. They'd made her feel so light. So sparkling. Like anything was possible. She had more to offer the world than to be somebody's stand-in. She liked the feeling, and she wanted to savor it again. She watched Benji slam his car door and roar the Hupmobile to life.

Even if it's at the cost of the only guy I've ever truly cared for.

33

Polly steered to the curb two houses down from the Hartley house and cut the engine. "How are you feeling?"

"I can't decide if I want to lie down for a week or enter a dance marathon. On the one hand, I get cast in a movie. The lead, no less. I couldn't be more excited."

Preoccupied with fourteen-hour days editing *Wind,* Selznick had delegated to his wife the task of breaking the news of his casting Amelia as the lead in *Sea Change*. Frankly, Amelia preferred it that way. She couldn't shake loose the image of all those waiting-room competitors, and had resigned herself to the distinct probability that Selznick would go with someone else. "You were the clear choice," Irene had said, her voice shaking with elation. Privately, Amelia doubted that were true, but in the moment—that gloriously electrifying moment when Irene had said those seven exhilarating words: "We want you to play the lead!"—all her misgivings had dropped away. That is to say, all but one.

"But on the other hand?"

"Benji dumps me because he can't handle the competition."

"Kenny Moss *is* dreamy," Luddie said from the back seat in that faintly mocking tone of his.

"You're not helping, bucko."

Polly laid a light hand on Amelia's elbow. "Bucko was being ironic."

She twisted around to face him. "Care to explain?"

"Kenny isn't the competition."

"The guy's got 'heartthrob' written all over him, so if he's not the problem, what is?"

"Take a moment to think about it."

The answer was as obvious as a run in a silk stocking. "The ex-girlfriend."

"He doesn't want to go through that again, which is understandable. Equally, you can try to stab that ghost, but you'll be wasting your time."

"She's not my ghost to stab, is she?" Amelia flopped her arm along the front seat. "Where in tarnation did you learn to always know the right thing to say?"

Luddie kissed her wrist, gentle as a hummingbird. She understood him well enough to know that it was his way of avoiding her question.

"Come on." Polly collected her handbag. "We're here to celebrate your big news."

"You've got big news, too."

"Mine doesn't compare. This is *your* moment."

Amelia cast a rueful glance down the sidewalk. "And if they think it's no big deal?"

"I can't imagine a more exciting one."

"Meaning, if this doesn't impress the folks, nothing will."

Luddie opened his car door. "If your announcement fails to set a fire under their asses—which it absolutely will, but if it doesn't—we'll go to Don the Beachcomber and get drunk on Vicious Virgins."

"Can we skip the first part?" The three of them stood at the front gate as Amelia tried to shoo away the thought that Faith was the impressive person in this family. She was the little sister who banged her head against the wall while nobody noticed. "Thanks, guys."

"For what?" Polly asked.

"For jumping up and down with me like a bunch of lunatic scarecrows when I got the news."

"It's not every day Mister David O. Selznick calls to offer the lead role in one of his movies," Polly said. A warm summer breeze blew over them, carrying with it the sweet scent of the creeping night phlox bushes in the Stevens place two doors down. "I knew it the minute I saw your screen test. So did Dorothy. And Sibyl. Zara, too."

"Has everyone seen my screen test but me?"

"Selznick's policy. Not even Vivien watched hers, so quit asking."

Luddie swung the gate open and made a gentlemanly *After you* gesture with his hand. "It's show time."

Cookie and Jewel raised their usual racket at the door until Gideon tempted them outside with dinosaur-sized bones. Faith sighed with relief as they bounded away.

"You don't look too chipper," Amelia told her.

"I've been slapped with three lawsuits from art history professors from different podunk liberal-arts colleges, each contending *they* came up with the central thesis in *Echoes of Elegance*."

"In other words, there's not a chance in hell that someone like you could have pieced it together?" Luddie asked.

Faith's hastily dabbed rouge stood out like fever marks against her chalk-white cheeks. "Precisely."

"What does your lawyer say?"

"These blowhards don't have a leg to stand on, which is why we're counter-suing. God, I wish I'd never started that infernal book." Faith ran her hands through her thinning hair. "But enough of that. You said you had news to share."

"Good news, I hope," Bernice said from the sofa where her cat, Charley, sat on her lap, ears perked, eyes watchful. "We could all use some."

Amelia folded her fingers to her lips as though in prayer that her revelation wouldn't make Faith feel like she was getting kicked in the ribs. "Remember how I got the job of standing in for Rita Hayworth in the new Selznick picture?"

Lois flopped backward on the sofa next to Bernice, startling Charley for a second. "Didn't she pull out because of Bernice?"

"They don't cancel a motion picture because the lead quits," Polly said. "They cast somebody else."

"And so." Amelia slapped her hands together to generate a loud clap. She'd seen Bette Davis do it in a movie once when she wanted to command the room. Everybody jolted. "Because of Rita's departure—"

"DON'T TELL ME!" Lois screeched. "You're David O. Selznick's new leading lady!"

Anyone else hijacking her news would have stung, but her mother's face glowed with such delight, such excitement—and was that pride?—that Amelia's annoyance dissolved. "They have! I am!"

Amelia surrendered to her mother's tenacious embrace. It wasn't long before tears wet her cheeks. Soon, another embrace enveloped them. The heady menthol smell of Judd's shaving cream filled the air. "My daughter! The movie star!"

Another pair of arms joined them. "From the old Juniper to the new one!" Bernice whooped like an owl.

When they broke apart, Amelia found even Gideon had joined their group huddle—and he seldom showed interest in anyone who didn't wear an embroidered silk waistcoat and knee breeches. "This is worth celebrating," he crowed. "As Voltaire said, 'Appreciation is a wonderful thing. It makes what is excellent in others belong to us as well.'"

Everyone stared at him, unsure how to respond. This was the most animated Amelia had ever seen him. If a cryptic quote that dampened the room's cheer was the price of his enthusiasm, she was happy to pay it.

Thankfully, Luddie came to the rescue. "And as Proust said: 'Let us be grateful to the people who make us happy; they are the charming gardeners who make our souls blossom.'"

"I have the very thing to help make our souls blossom." Judd's face shone bright with glee. "Pol Roger champagne."

"It's the favorite of the British First Lord of the Admiralty," Gideon said. "They say one day Churchill might become prime minister." He and Judd disappeared into the basement.

"Benji must be very proud of you," Lois said. "Working late, is he?"

"Oh, Mom. The news on the boyfriend front isn't so great."

On the drive over, they had puzzled over the girls' awkward predicament: Polly was dating the roommate of the guy who had dumped Amelia. Leave it to Luddie to crack wise that this made them "proper adults who have to deal with messes not entirely of their own making."

Judd and Gideon reentered the living room, each holding two bottles with black-and-gold foil labels. "We've been guessing which movie star you'll be playing opposite."

Judd twisted the cork of the first bottle. "Gid bet me two bits it's Robert Taylor, but my money's on Robert Montgomery."

"It's a new guy," Amelia told them. "We'll be making our screen debuts together." The concept that she'd be making her screen debut at all was still fresh enough to send a charge through her. "His name is Kendrick Moss."

Judd handed her a coupe fizzing with champagne. "Gentleman or rake?"

"If you saw him, you'd think, 'Here comes Mister Romeo.' Funny thing is, he's the only one who doesn't notice his own charms."

Lois and Bernice returned from the kitchen with platters heaped with cheeses, crackers, pretzels, and every pickle and potato chip in the house. "Thank God you have the knack of improvising a party out of thin air," Faith said. "Left to me, you'd be eating stale saltines and a rind of gouda I bought last Christmas."

As indulgent laughter filled the room, Amelia caught Polly's eye. *Have I managed to impress them?*

Polly winked back. *No more Miss Invisible!*

"Time for a toast," Ludlow proclaimed.

"Let me! Let me!" Bernice insisted. "Back when Lois and I were on Catalina, who'd have thought we'd be celebrating a remake starring Lois's daughter?"

"Hey," Judd protested. "I helped, too."

"My apologies, your honor. Let me rephrase: Lois and Judd's lovely daughter. I'm delighted to pass the Juniper torch to you, dear, sweet Amelia. May you enjoy her as much as I did." Bernice's eyes glinted with mischief. "Though let's hope it doesn't lead to becoming a madam—a career choice that hasn't panned out quite so well."

Luddie held his coupe aloft. "Three cheers for Amelia!"

After everybody had taken their first mouthful, Faith asked, "What's your boss's take on losing you to the movies? It can't have been the first time this has happened."

"I suspect Mr. Schwab loves the idea that his waitress has been cast in a Hollywood movie. He's sick of telling people that Lana Turner was *not* discovered at Schwab's."

Luddie raised his hand. "Amelia isn't the only one with news today." He lifted his glass toward Polly.

"Nah." A blush crept across her face. "Tonight belongs to Amelia."

"Don't keep quiet on my account," said Amelia, feeling relief filter through her at the shift in attention. "I'll tell them if you won't."

"Come on, Polly," Judd urged, "you have to come clean now."

She twisted her napkin, as though trying to wring a confession from it. "Mr. Selznick has asked me if I'd like to be the official location scout for *Sea Change*."

"From Girl Friday to location scout?" Gideon said. "Sounds like a promotion."

"You better believe it." Luddie beamed, as though he were a proud parent himself.

"I don't know that he had much choice." Polly dissolved into a nervous laugh. "Irene Selznick has sold her husband on the idea of an all-female crew."

"Like *we* had!" Bernice said.

"He needed a lot of nudging, so she pointed out that George Cukor has finished directing *The Women,* whose cast is all women. She told Mr. Selznick how further elevating the concept could only be achieved by 'an innovative producer.' And he bought it!"

"When do you go?" Lois asked.

"The starting date for *Sea Change* depends on Virginia Van Upp delivering her screenplay, which won't be long. Good golly, but that woman is a fast writer." Polly turned to Amelia. "Care to join me?"

A break from this whirlwind was what Amelia needed. "My current roster gives me weekends off."

"Next week, then?"

All heads turned as Cookie and Jewel exploded into barking at the back door, as though the bougainvillea had caught fire. "Just the afternoon *Times,*" Judd explained, heading out to collect it. He reappeared with the paper unfurled. "Guess who made the front page?" He held it out toward them, displaying the headline.

GREENE ANNOUNCES MORALS CRUCADE
Vows to sweep from east to west

Judd read out loud, "'In a press conference at Riverside City Hall, Wyatt Greene, candidate for Chair of the County Board of Supervisors, announced a wide-reaching sweep of'—and these are his words—'anything and anyone whose very existence threatens the moral fabric upon which our decent citizens stand in this great state.'"

"Oh, brother," Amelia murmured. "Someone likes to lay it on thick."

"'Anyone,'" Bernice quoted, "meaning me, I suppose?"

"I think it's safe to assume he'll be bringing up your name as often as he can." Judd ran his eyes down the rest of the article.

"The usual baloney: 'won't stand for the base elements of society' . . . 'starting his crusade in the town of Blythe at the easternmost end of the county—'"

"Blythe?" Lois mocked. "There can't be more than a couple of hundred people. How many cathouses does he think he'll find?"

"'—and sweep west to Palm Springs where he'll lobby for the demolition of the now-infamous Sapphire Moon, site of the widely publicized raid.'"

"DEMOLITION?!" Bernice cried out. "Over my dead body."

Judd tapped the paper. "They can if the owner gives in to pressure like this."

"You're looking at her," Bernice retorted.

"You *own* the Sapphire Moon?" Amelia asked.

"Veronica bequeathed it to me, lock, stock, and mattresses."

"Including the land?" Luddie asked.

"Every square inch down to the last cactus. I might have a dozen charges filed against me, but that doesn't give this loudmouth the right to fire up the nearest bulldozer." When nobody answered, she added, "Does it?"

"A building can't be *un*bulldozed," Judd answered. "If this Wyatt Greene shyster drums up momentum, it might pay to take him more seriously."

"Stamping out vice and corruption is an age-old tactic," Gideon said. "Flaubert faced obscenity charges for writing *Madame Bovary* solely because Emma had an adulterous affair. It worked in the eighteen-fifties, and it'll work now."

Judd kept his eyes on the paper. "Get a load of this: '—after which he plans to work his way west until he reaches the city of Riverside. And, Mr. Greene added, "Who knows? Perhaps I shall sweep my broom of purity all the way to the fleshpots of Hollywood."'"

"For crying out loud!" Bernice muttered. "Give me half an hour. I'll take his preposterous Broom of Purity and make toothpicks out of it."

"Hey, even if we have to watch out for this blustering blowhard," Faith said, raising her glass, "let's not allow him to detract from today's celebration. Gid, honey, got any literary quotes about celebrations you can pull out of your top hat?"

"From Shakespeare's *A Midsummer Night's Dream*." He raised his near-empty coupe. "'Though she be but little, she is fierce.'"

Amelia gaped at him, thunderstruck by the only compliment he'd ever paid her. Before she could thank him, Cookie and Jewel romped in. Their boisterous arrival launched the conversation into fresh territory: *Pretty Pennies*, Catalina summers, the premier of *The Women* at Grauman's Chinese, whispers of *Gone with the Wind* opening in Atlanta.

Amelia sank onto the windowsill, fighting a sudden emptiness hollowing her chest. Where had that come from? Why wasn't she enjoying this moment quite as much as she expected to? She was thrilled, God knew. And her family's delight was as intoxicating as it was unexpected. So shouldn't she be bouncing off the walls like a kangaroo hopped up on Mr. Selznick's pep pills? I could walk down Hollywood Boulevard right this very minute and find a hundred girls who'd smother their grandmothers for the chance I've been handed. And yet here I am, trying to be excited. What the hell's wrong with me?

She felt the heat of someone staring at her.

Luddie narrowed his eyes. *Everything okay?*

She swallowed hard and smiled. The act wouldn't fool him, but it would do the job. For now.

He was about to launch himself across the room to join her, but stopped when Bernice rattled Judd's *LA Times*. "This is Wyatt Greene?" She tapped the large photo under the headline. "*This* guy?"

Lois leaned across. "He's been your most vocal opponent; how could you not have noticed what he looks like?"

"I decided the only way to hold on to my sanity was to ignore the awful things the world was saying about me, so I've made a point of avoiding everything but the funnies." She returned to Greene's picture. "He goes to the Palm Springs Racquet Club, always lunching with the same fellow. I asked my favorite waiter about them. Greene wasn't familiar, but he identified the other man as Cyrus Pattinson."

"Who's that?" Judd asked.

"His name—or, more precisely, the name of his company, Cee-Pat Construction—is on development sites around town. The Army Air Corps awarded his company the job of constructing the new Palm Springs airstrip."

"The one next to the Moon?" Lois asked.

"I saw his name for months and months on end."

"I don't suppose this Pattinson guy was a Sapphire Moon regular?" Faith asked. "Because if he was, the irony would be worthy of Mark Twain."

Bernice tapped her pinched lips. "Not in person."

"I'm no expert on brothels," Luddie said, "but don't those transactions need to be conducted in the flesh?"

Bernice took so long to respond that Amelia wondered if she'd heard him. "Remember when I told you about the weekend that MGM held the world premiere of *Camille* at the Plaza Theatre?"

"And how it helped put Palm Springs on the map because it was such a big deal?"

"Right. Legions of movie folks flocked into town. Bigshots, mid-rung front-office guys, yes-men, all the hangers-on. I'll give you three guesses who rented out the Sapphire Moon for the whole weekend."

"Wouldn't that have cost him a small fortune?" Lois asked.

"We made the equivalent of two months' income in three days. I never did figure out what he got out of it."

"Currying favor with Hollywood up-and-comers whom he could use later," Judd said. "You're sure it was this Cyrus Pattinson guy who rented the Moon?"

"I didn't know it was him at the time. After we kicked out the last straggler Monday morning, we sent our bill to the address some secretary had given us."

"And they paid?"

"In full, the next day."

"By check?"

"Heavens, no! Brothels operate in a hazy gray zone with one foot in the law and one foot outside."

"Cash?"

"A thick, fat, bulging envelope of it."

Amelia was all too familiar with the frown that crossed her father's face. He was onto something. "No evidence of any financial transactions? Nothing incriminating at all?"

"Well," Bernice cooed, with a sly smile, "I didn't say that."

34

Polly eyed Amelia with a cunning smile as she poured steaming coffee from the pot their waitress had brought to the table.

"What?" Amelia asked.

Polly dumped cream into her cup. Hotel St. Catherine's coffee was a heck of a lot stronger than Schwab's. "The last time you set foot in this hotel, you were washing bed sheets."

"I'm *still* woozy from breathing in all that ammonia."

"You're a guest now. I was wondering if it felt odd, is all."

"I'm here location scouting on a movie, which is completely different."

"A movie that you will be starring in," Polly reminded her.

"I can't think about that yet. This weekend you're calling the shots. I'm nothing more than the assistant to do your bidding."

Polly's sly smile faded to an enigmatic brood as she lifted her coffee cup. Amelia was about to apologize when Polly's eyes flew open.

"Yoo-hoo!" Irene called to them as she bypassed the restaurant's hostess. "Surprise!" She yanked off her floppy white straw sunhat, dropped an overnight bag on the floor, and collapsed into an empty chair beside them. "Is that coffee fresh?" She pilfered a spare cup from a neighboring table, then returned to take a second one. "I'm not traveling alone."

Who was this whirlwind in light, wafty cotton, sky-blue with bold gray anchors, and her hair sticking up every which way?

"Irene, what are you doing here?" Amelia said.

Polly sat upright. "Is Mr. Selznick with you?"

"God, no!" Irene waved away her concern. "He's so preoccupied that he doesn't have the faintest idea I've left the boys with their grandmother and caught the early seaplane out of Long Beach."

"What was the fight about?" The knowing look in Polly's eyes told Amelia these scenes were familiar territory.

"Quite possibly our worst ever." Irene pulled her cigarette holder from her purse and searched around for a book of matches. Seeing nothing in reach, she tapped it on the tablecloth like she was sending out Morse code. "The usual."

"How much?"

Although no one was within earshot, she leaned forward onto her elbows. "Ten thousand, nine hundred, and twenty-five."

To a girl earning thirty-five a week, an eleven-thousand-dollar debt was unthinkable. "In one sitting?" Amelia asked.

"These men and their all-nighters!" Irene barked out, forgetting her caution. "It took every ounce of restraint to stop myself from choking him to death." She slapped the tabletop. "His money is all tied up with the studio. I have some income of my own, thanks to Father, but it's in long-term investments. He wrote Sam a check—"

"Goldwyn?"

"Yes. But it'll bounce, so he told him not to cash it yet. Meanwhile, how am I supposed to pay the nanny? And the maid? Not to mention my accounts at Jurgensen's and Bullocks. If I renege on them, every Beverly Hills housewife between here and Mulholland Drive will know before cocktail hour."

"So you did the only sensible thing and ran away."

Irene's mouth drooped downward at the edges and her eyebrows curved upward into the center of her forehead. "I knew you two would understand."

"But if you didn't bring your husband, who came with you?"

"Well!" A gleam of delight shone through. "Last week, the West Coast editor of *Look* magazine called me. I met him at Faith's book party. He was there with a shutterbug."

"The one who roamed around all evening?"

"That's him. James Tate. The editor suggested a photo spread for *Sea Change*—carte blanche on content. I was mulling it over, but after Dave and I fought the Battle of the Alamo last night, I needed an escape. Poor chap—the editor, not David. I dragged him out of bed at a quarter of six. Told him if his photographer made the nine o'clock seaplane to Catalina, I'd give Mr. Tate free rein."

"Where is he?"

"On the flight over, the dreadful news from Europe came through. He spilled orange juice all over himself, so he's cleaning up."

"Europe?" Polly asked. "What's happened?"

Now lit from a matchbook their waitress had dropped off, Irene's cigarette missed the ashtray, scattering ash across the tablecloth. "Hitler and Stalin have signed a pact to divide Europe."

"So, if Germany doesn't have to worry about Russia . . ."

Polly's unfinished question hung heavy. Since *Kristallnacht* last year, the possibility of another Great War had been looming, but now it felt probable.

They sat in somber silence until a man in his thirties approached, thinning blonde hair, jacket over one arm. "Thank goodness it's August." He flapped his damp, pale brown shirt. "Should dry in no time." He took the fourth seat and accepted the coffee Irene had poured for him as she made her introductions.

He had a long, narrow face with sharp features and keen eyes. Amelia had only the vaguest recollection of him at Faith's party, which she supposed proved him good at his job.

"Ready when you are, ladies."

* * *

The Catalina Chimes Tower crowned the trail leading past Zane Grey's house. A tall gazebo of brick and white plaster, its arches opened in the four cardinal directions; its famous bells chimed every quarter-hour toward the circular Catalina Casino below.

Polly led them to the side facing the ocean, where the Pacific sparkled like a shattered mirror. Boats of all sizes swayed with the outgoing tide. "I wish Virginia had given us an outline. We're flying blind."

Irene shrugged. "Some blinder than others."

Polly and Amelia swapped looks. *We can't tackle her husband's gambling in front of this guy.*

Amelia said, "Unless we're all gypsy fortune-tellers who can read the future at the bottom of our Sanka, we are all winging it. Isn't that right, Mr. Tate?"

"True—to a degree." His eye stayed glued to his Rolleiflex. "Speaking as someone hoping to land at *Look* full time, you've got to keep your hand on the tiller if you want any proper control over your course."

Amelia kept her eyes trained on the horizon shimmering in the heat as doubts swooped down on her. She pictured standing on this spot, in makeup and costume, in front of a dozen people staring at her as she tried to ignore a giant movie camera that might be twelve inches from her face. Back at Selznick's casting department, she'd felt safe and in control. But out here? Where she would actually be filming? How had she not noticed the wind, the heat, the steep cliffside, the droning bugs, the loose gravel underfoot on her previous visits?

"Be sure to get the pier," Polly told Tate. "It's where kids dive for coins tossed from the steamships."

Even from this height, the whitecaps scattered across the choppy water were clearly visible. And if she could see them from here, how rough would that water be if she had to dive into it? One thing was for sure: It'd be nothing like the Selznicks' Beverly Hills pool.

Tate wiped his brow and patted his sparsely covered dome. "In my hurry this morning, I neglected to bring my Panama."

Polly picked up a discarded newspaper lying on the plaster fence. "*Catalina Islander* to the rescue." She pulled out the two innermost pages and started folding them. "Living at a summer resort, you get handy at fashioning hats out of whatever comes to hand." Her creation came to sharp points at the front and back, and rose to a low peak in the middle.

He took it gratefully and slipped it on his head. "I thank you. My scalp thanks you. My dermatologist definitely thanks you."

Polly didn't respond. She stared at the headline splashed across the *Islander*.

LOCAL MAN RETURNS HOME TO
MAKE DEATH-BED CONFESSION

"Someone you know?" Amelia asked.

Polly shook her head. "He left Catalina twenty-five years ago. I've met the priest a few times, though."

"What did he confess?"

"Father Raymond says he won't break confidentiality until after Mr."—Polly scanned the article—"Yates has met his maker."

"Well, my oh my, who do we have here?" cried a familiar voice.

Amelia and Polly hadn't seen the daughter of *Dick Tracy*'s new sponsor since they'd cornered Dorothy Arzner at Club Bali three months before. Gone was the sheltered schoolgirl, yearning for a bolder life. A summer's worth of California sun had bronzed her pale Pittsburgh complexion to a deep almond, bringing out the hazel-green in her eyes and accentuating her pearly-white teeth. Left to its own devices, her hair now framed her face in tight, frizzy curls ready to defy any hair brush or beauty parlor.

"Don't you pop up in the darndest places?" Amelia waved a hand over the girl's outfit. Gone, too, were the gloves, hair ribbon, fascinator cocktail hat and matching bag. This Eliza wore dungarees, work boots, and a shirt made of faded whipcord, tied at the waist, sleeves ripped off at the shoulders.

Eliza steadied herself against a rake as though she'd been struck. "So much has happened since I met you that night with Dorothy."

"Dorothy Arzner?" Irene asked.

Once introductions were made, Eliza exclaimed, "Hold the presses! You aren't here about *Sea Change*, are you?"

"You know of our little project?"

"A whole movie filmed on Catalina? It's all us locals have been talking about until"—she flicked a grubby finger at the *Islander* dangling from Polly's hand—"Mr. Confession came home."

"Back up," Amelia said. "'Us locals'? You live here now?"

"I always thought of myself as a big-city girl, but I kept hearing about this place, so I caught the steamer over. I hadn't been here but three seconds before I found myself chatting with the gardener who maintains the public grounds: the Wrigley Memorial, the cemetery, the public parks."

"All that?" Irene said. "One person?"

"Yup. Until a few weeks ago, she worked for the island's groundskeeper. But he signed up to the Navy in case war breaks out in Europe and America jumps in. So now it's all up to Ursula, with me helping her on my day off."

"Where do you work?" Polly asked.

"Jack's bicycle rentals, sales, and repairs."

"Near the amphitheater?" Amelia marveled at how this bicycle-repairing debutante had traveled Matilda's path in reverse, trading her silver spoon for bicycle grease and garden tools. Talk about a sea change.

"Ursula and I share a cute little bungalow at 200 Eucalyptus Avenue, and of course"—Eliza tugged off her work gloves, shooting Polly a sidelong glance—"you know what happened *there*."

Polly wrinkled her nose. "Remind me."

"The fire that gutted the town back in nineteen-fifteen."

Polly gave a small huff only Amelia could pick up. "What of it?"

"Ursula told me that the reason it got so out of hand was because the fire brigade was busy tending to different fire."

"Different?" Polly's voice shuddered.

"Yes. A ferocious fire started up at the other end of town. At two hundred Eucalyptus. By the time they'd put it out, a second fire had broken out."

"Second fire?" Amelia wrapped an arm around Polly's shoulders.

"The one that burned down half the town. It took volunteers so long to get there, it had spread beyond their control."

Amelia felt Polly's shoulders sink. "*Two* fires?"

Eliza flicked a finger against the *Catalina Islander* still clutched in Polly's hand. "That guy with the death-bed confession—let me tell you, everybody's got their opinion."

Polly faced Amelia. *Can you believe what we're hearing?* She pivoted back to Eliza. "Such as?"

"A crabby mother-in-law trapped inside the Rose Hotel. And how the owner had been smuggling out his valuables the week before. And how the fire on Eucalyptus started fifteen minutes *before* the one at the Rose broke out."

Polly held her breath to steady herself, but a long, pained cry tore free.

"Oh, dear!" Eliza's shoulders hunched as her face contorted. "What have I said?"

Polly rested her face on Amelia's shoulder as tears overwhelmed her.

If the dying man's confession were true—if he'd torched the Rose Hotel to do away with his mother-in-law—then Polly's father wasn't to blame. The *Pretty Pennies* cast and their damned candles had simply been in the wrong place at the wrong time. But now Irene, Eliza, and Mr. Tate stood gawking, wondering what in tarnation was happening.

"It's complicated," Amelia told them. She leaned into Polly's ear. "What do you need?" she said softly.

"I want to go see him. Or at least try."

Amelia turned back to Eliza. "This dying Yates guy—do you know where he is?"

"Hotel MacRae, but he's left strict instructions not to be disturbed."

It was the same hotel Polly and Amelia had stayed at in January with Judd and Desmond. "Does Roger still work the front desk?"

Eliza shrugged. "No idea."

"It appears our next stop will be the MacRae." Irene had adopted a take-charge voice for the benefit of, Amelia suspected, Mr. *Look* Magazine. "And after that detour, the Wrigley Memorial might be worth checking out. What do you think?"

Polly nodded, albeit slightly.

"Come on, Pol-Pol." Amelia guided her toward the road. "It's fifteen minutes back into town. Enough time to pull yourself together." When Polly didn't respond, she added, "How else are you going to clear your father's name?"

* * *

Amelia and Polly faced Room 10. Roger had been on duty. He was normally a stickler for the rules—except, evidently, when it came to Polly. "Mr. Yates said no visitors," he'd told them. A year ago, Polly would have slunk away. But that was before watching the cops gun down her father, and before falling three stories with a movie mogul. Miss Maddox was no longer wet behind the ears.

Amelia jiggled the key Polly had wangled from Roger. "Ready?"

"As I'll ever be."

The room had space for only a bed, a postage-stamp table, and a tiny closet with lone coat hanger. Its stale air was a pungent cocktail of carbolic acid, camphor, and rubbing alcohol that struggled to mask the astringent stench of decay. Amelia followed Polly inside.

"Mr. Yates?" Polly tucked her *Catalina Islander* under her arm. "Are you awake?"

The lump in the tangled bed sheets stirred. "Leave me be."

"We've come to see you. About the—fire."

"Damned padre." Yates grunted. "Promised he'd keep my confession a secret."

"I haven't spoken to Father Raymond." Polly kept her voice steady as she crept closer.

"Go away."

"I must hear it for myself."

"Get lost, I tell ya."

She sagged in defeat, the ache of disappointment like a crushing weight on her chest. "Mr. Yates, we wouldn't bother you if it wasn't so terribly important."

He peered at them through rheumy, bloodshot eyes. "I oughta call the manager."

"A couple of minutes is all we need."

He leveled them each with a once-over, blinking several times as though to clear his vision. "Where's m'pillow?"

Polly retrieved an abandoned pillow from the scuffed floorboards and inserted it behind his head. "I believe I know what you confessed to Father Raymond."

"Yeah?"

"You lit the fires that night. The one on Eucalyptus Avenue and the one that destroyed the Rose."

"What's it to you?"

"My dad was at the Rose that night. With others." She choked out the words like they were stones in her throat. Amelia took her by the hand and squeezed hard. *Keep going*. "They got into a fight. Behind the Rose. Then they staggered to bed. And then the whole town was on—"

"I saw 'em," Yates said.

Polly breathed in sharply. "Yes?"

"Movie people. They were blitzed."

"Where were you?"

"I was hiding behind the manzanitas out back, waiting for my chance to torch the joint. Getting ready to go inside. They came staggering along. Wouldn't've been twenty feet away when they started yelling and throwing candles at each other. I saw a way to pin it on someone else."

Polly swallowed. "So my father *didn't* start the fire?"

"The candles burned for a while, then sputtered out. After that, the coast was clear, so I snuck inside the hotel and—did what I did."

"Did you light the fire up on Eucalyptus to distract the fire department?" Amelia asked.

"Guilty of ev'thing, girlie. Eucalyptus. The Rose. My mother-in-law in the attic. Burned down half of Avalon. I'm a despicable, shameful heel. Been eating at my innards for decades."

Polly wrenched her hand away from Amelia's and stepped up to the bed. "My father thought *he* caused the Avalon fire. Carried the guilt with him till the day he died. The police thought he was at fault, too, and riddled him with bullets for it."

She rolled her *Catalina Islander* into a baseball bat.

Aw jeez, Amelia thought. Okay, so he's a heel, but he's got one foot in the grave. That's punishment enough. "You got what you came for," she said gently. She ran her hand down Polly's arm and worked the bludgeon free from her rigid fingers. "Sorry to disturb you," she told Yates, "and good luck with . . ." With what? Your impending death? Whatever horrible disease is devouring your soul?

She hustled Polly into the hallway's mercifully breathable air.

* * *

By the time they reached the modest hotel bar, Polly's spine had straightened and her chin had lifted, leaving Amelia to wonder how long the dam would hold.

"Any satisfaction?" Irene inquired.

"All that I needed. And sorry for the dramatics," she told Tate.

"Life takes unexpected turns we don't see coming."

The sharp edges left Polly's face. "Boy, oh boy, you can say that again."

"I'm very glad to hear you didn't come away empty-handed," Irene said. "I stopped off at our hotel in case I got any messages." She rattled a telegram in their faces. "I've been commanded to return home on the next seaplane."

Ever since Irene's appearance in the hotel coffee shop, Amelia had been hoping she could have a heart-to-heart with Irene; the sooner they could talk through her misgivings, the easier she'd feel. But now she was leaving? "Did you send a reply?"

"Absolutely! I reminded him that his irresponsibility puts him in no position to dictate. And now I'm ordering another Ramos Gin Fizz to calm me down." She raised her empty glass to catch the bartender's eye.

"I've got to say," Tate squared his shoulders, "I'd be negligent if I didn't bring Yates's revelation to my editor."

Irene was too preoccupied with her husband's demands and too full of Ramos Gin Fizz to grasp the man's implication, but it was quite clear to Amelia that this could be his ticket to a permanent job.

"There's no scoop until Mr. Yates kicks the bucket," Amelia told him. "He smelled like a morgue, but I doubt he'll be drawing his last breath between now and afternoon tea time."

"Oh!" Irene slapped the edge of their table, startling their waiter. "It's an exclusive you're after?" She shot out a hand toward Amelia. "We've got one for you right here."

No, Amelia thought. Let me keep my anonymity a little longer. I'm not ready to give it up yet—or at all. She sliced her hand across her throat. *Ixnay on the ewsnay*.

But Irene had already pulled Tate into a conspiratorial huddle. "Amelia here has been cast in the lead role of *Sea Change*."

"Is that right?" A satisfied smile played Tate's lips. "This changes the emphasis to 'Newly minted Hollywood movie star is more involved than showing up at dawn for hair and makeup.'"

"Not only that," Irene continued, "but *Sea Change* is about a young actress making her first movie starring a young actress making her first movie."

"*Ars refert vitam*," Tate said.

"Say what now?" Irene asked.

"Latin for 'art reflects life,'" Polly said, fixing Amelia with meaningful eyes. *Like it or not, you're about to become famous.*

Amelia didn't like it. Not yet. If it hadn't been for Irene's mid-morning Ramos Gin Fizzes, she might have been able to hold on to obscurity a little longer. "It's coming up to eleven o'clock and we've only visited one location. Shall we get going?"

* * *

As they rounded the final turn, honeysuckle sweetened the sea breeze gusting up from below. Straight ahead, taller and grander than the Chimes Tower, the Wrigley Memorial stood sentinel.

"You were right, Pol. This'll make a memorable background."

But Polly had slowed her pace. "I brought Papa with me." She patted a bulge in her pocket Amelia hadn't noticed.

"His ashes?"

"Half of them. I wasn't sure that I was ready to let them go until—" Her eyes strayed back toward Avalon, where Mr. Yates was stinking up Room 10. "Papa was involved in the memorial's construction after Mr. Wrigley died. It was one of his favorite spots."

"You want me to distract those two?"

"Could you?"

Amelia swallowed her frustration. She had been hoping that Polly would divert Tate while she took Irene aside. But poor old Pol had had a rough morning. And now her dad's ashes, too. "Leave it to me."

"So, Mr. Tate, what does it take to convince *Look* magazine to hire you full time?"

"If I knew the answer"—he snapped a series of photos of the

azure tiles lining the fountain at the base of the memorial—"I'd already be on staff."

"Competitive field, is it?"

"About as competitive a field as yours, Miss Hartley."

"Oh, I don't know. Unfailingly cheerful lunch-counter waitresses don't come along every day."

He aimed his camera overhead to capture the intricate mosaic that adorned the ceiling of the three arches inside the main tower. "I'm talking about the competition to get into the movies."

"Oh! That!" Amelia's laugh echoed off the ceramic walls. "I guess that'll be my job when I start filming. Until then, I work at Schwab's."

"On Sunset?"

She didn't like the way she saw his thoughts churning behind his eyes, intricate and precise as the mechanism of an antique timepiece.

"Which brother runs that one?"

"Leon, and he's a terrific boss—"

"Any chance he'd let me take photos of you behind the counter?"

Irene hovered several feet behind him, nodding her head.

"We get a lot of celebrities," she said evenly. "Mr. Schwab is very conscious of their privacy."

"They traded it away when they entered the movies."

Irene's eyes narrowed. "Sometimes all they want is to eat a club sandwich and down a root beer in quiet, y'know?"

"I guess."

Amelia hadn't expected him to be quite so willing to back down; she breathed a little easier—but not for long.

"Didn't you tell me," Irene said, "that Leon Schwab would give anything to combat the rumor that Lana Turner was discovered at Schwab's?"

"She wasn't?" Tate asked.

"Nope. It was at the Top Hat near Hollywood High."

"There's my angle!" Tate said. "You're the *real* Schwab's Pharmacy Hollywood discovery. My editor'll eat it up!"

As far as publicity went, Tate's idea was terrific, but it left Amelia fighting a nagging sense that the reins of her life were already slipping through her fingers.

Eliza's voice echoed inside the tower, rescuing Amelia from answering. "I figured I'd find you guys here." She emerged at the top step, silhouetted against the shimmering Pacific. Beside her stood a woman in dirt-smudged overalls, her brown curls untamed, her face open and honest. "This is Ursula." She gestured to her companion. "I want you to meet Amelia, Irene, and Mr. Tate. Where's Polly?"

"Needed some time to herself." Amelia turned to Ursula. "Eliza tells me that your boss decamped to the Navy, leaving you to shoulder all this on your lonesome."

"Not entirely." Ursula bumped her hip to Eliza's. "I have my trusty assistant."

She radiated an earthy wholesomeness, the kind of woman who loved to plunge her hands into rich, damp soil. A grow-anything, cook-anything, fix-anything soul whose practical wisdom would make a person wonder, "Why didn't I think of that?"

"Sounds to me like you and your trusty assistant were lucky to have found each other."

Ursula shot Amelia a loving glance, which Eliza returned in full measure. "And don't I know it."

Schwab's had shown Amelia every type: effeminate men passing for girls, mannish dykes dressed like lumberjacks, bargain-basement streetwalkers, secretaries being courted by silver-haired bosses, and aging socialites fawning over smarmy gigolos. But two regular women looking at each other like that? That was new.

"Hey," Ursula said, "did I hear right? You work at Schwab's?"

"I do."

"You must know Tillie Greene?"

"Also known as Matilda Charles?"

"Oh, yeah. I keep forgetting about her do-over."

"Sounds like you and Matilda go way back."

Ursula shoved her hands into the front pockets of her overalls;

the knuckles of her fists strained against the fabric. "My last . . . uh, *friend*—her name was Rhea. She works at the RKO ranch in Encino. In the greenery department, ironically."

Irene's penciled brows arched. "Why's that ironic?"

"Because Rhea's surname is Greene."

"Greene?" Amelia cried out. "Related to Tillie?"

"Tillie and Rhea are sisters."

One glance at Irene told Amelia they were thinking the same thing. "Did you meet their brother, Wyatt?"

"Unfortunately." Ursula rolled her big, nutmeg-brown eyes. "That man is capital-H horrible. He says and does all the right things in public, dealing with customers, at church."

"They're religious?"

"High-Church Catholic, but it's only for show. They're all about ingratiating themselves deeper into the community. They're all a bunch of fakers. Him worst of all. I broke it off with Rhea the day I realized she worships her older brother. It was at Thanksgiving. The whole family was there."

"A real big dinner, I'll bet."

"A circus, more like—but not a fun one. They all got roaring drunk before the turkey was served. After a few drinks, nobody's watching what they're saying. Everyone's drinking and cussing and smoking, so it all comes out."

"Like what, for instance?"

"Who they hate, who they tricked. Wyatt's plans to take over the county board—that was the worst of them all. I tell you, those people are down-to-the-bone awful."

Amelia had long suspected Matilda was all facade, but she hadn't yet encountered anyone confirming her suspicions—until now. "I bet Matilda was right in there slugging away, too."

Ursula shook her head slightly, as though in astonishment. "You'd think so. With the platinum-blonde hair and that bosom on display."

"Are you saying she's not as awful as the rest of her family?"

"At one point, I needed a break from the mayhem, so I snuck

into the backyard for a breather. I found Matilda having a quiet cigarette by herself."

"And?"

"That's when I learned that Matilda hates her family."

"*Hates* them?" Irene's horror mirrored Amelia's disbelief.

"She almost didn't come because last year's Thanksgiving was even worse, but at the last minute she succumbed to guilt."

"Catholic guilt?" Tate asked. "I know a thing or two about that."

Ursula nodded. "She regretted her decision two seconds after she got there."

"Because they're awful?"

"Sober, they're awful. Drunk, they're horrendous. Tillie became Matilda to escape it all. And who'd blame her? But I thank her."

"For what?"

"Showing me Rhea's true colors. As soon as I learned big brother Wyatt can do no wrong in Rhea's book, I vamoosed the hell out of there. And now I couldn't be happier."

All this time, Amelia had grouped Matilda with those ambitious would-be starlets who swanned in and out of Schwab's, all batting eyelashes and flirty pouts for one-track-minded fools that Matilda played like a Wurlitzer.

But now Amelia needed a moment to recalibrate this new version of someone she thought she'd sized up. The Matilda who'd followed her to Farley's office and admitted hiding out in a nunnery way out west in Beaumont—had that been the real Matilda all along?

This turnaround was too much to handle on her own. When would Polly finish scattering those ashes? Ursula and Eliza were staring at her, as though it were her turn to speak. Oh, God. What was the question?

Polly appeared behind them and caught the distress signal flashing across Amelia's face. She redirected her attention to Tate. "Got enough photos of this location?"

"I think so, yes."

"Where next, Miss Location Scout?" *Get me out of here.*

Polly didn't miss a beat. "We have this old amphitheater. Ruins, mostly, but not without its rustic charm suitable for an interesting backdrop."

Tate clicked his lens cover into place. "I'm all for rustic charm."

The amphitheater was where Amelia and Polly had swigged Mad Ox bourbon and decided Polly should leave Catalina and move to LA. She thought of it now as the place where they had cemented their friendship. "It oozes atmosphere," she told Tate. "You and your Rolleiflex will love it."

* * *

"You're right." Tate stood on the remnants of the Catalina Island Amphitheater. A year or two more and the planks of gnarled wood rotted around rusted nails, would collapse under his weight. In fact, Amelia wasn't sure he should be teetering on them now and hoped he wouldn't ask her to join him.

"It must have been lovely on summer evenings," Irene said. "Listening to orchestras under the stars."

Now that they were here and Tate was lining up his camera, checking for angles and suitable backgrounds, Amelia felt the jitters descend on her. With the wind blowing every which way, her hair must be a mess, and here she was without a brush. The nerve of Irene, expecting her to appear in a magazine looking like this. Those pictures were of pretty girls with flawless makeup and immaculate coifs.

As Tate jumped off the stage and hiked up the center aisle, she sidled up to Irene. "I don't think this is such a good idea."

"What? This old amphitheater reeks of ambiance."

"I'm a dreadful sight! Barely any makeup, hair a mess. Worse still . . ." She looked ruefully down at her clothes. Though comfortable and cool, her shapeless cheesecloth blouse did nothing for her figure. "I doubt your husband will want me in *Look* magazine photographed like I haven't showered all week."

"Kick off those shoes," Irene ordered.

"What?"

"No hat, no gloves, no footwear."

"Who am I, Robinson Crusoe?"

"You're a girl who doesn't need Edith Head to design her wardrobe or a Westmore to fix her face."

"Mrs. Selznick is right," Tate agreed. "Your movie will be filmed on location and in as much daylight as possible. A movie like that needs someone whose beauty matches her surroundings. And that, my dear, is you."

"The heart of David's *Intermezzo* campaign is selling Ingrid as a natural beauty," Irene put in, "who isn't reliant on three shades of lipstick and perfectly placed spotlights. It's one of the reasons why he has signed you for the lead."

It was? Natural beauty? And Amelia was hearing about this *now*?

Tate swung his camera lens away from a crowd of at least thirty people, all of them staring in their direction. "Chop-chop," he said, "before the sun moves."

Amelia kicked off her espadrilles and perched on a weather-beaten bleacher no safer than the ruined stage. She had barely been in place for more than a second or two before Tate launched into his rapid-fire commands: "Chin up. Higher. Look left. Cross legs. Right hand on knee, left on hip. Look at me. Don't look at me. Look past me."

Focusing on his instructions, she missed the crowd doubling to sixty, creeping closer until they huddled behind Tate.

If these gawkers knew the genuine celebrity was the woman in the sun hat whose husband was editing the year's biggest picture, they'd flock to her instead. Amelia wished they would. Being scrutinized by sixty pairs of eyes made her skin crawl.

Tate checked his camera. "I need to reload. Take five."

When he stepped to one side, a pair of housewives in head-scarves seized their opportunity. One of them pulled out an envelope from the gas company. "May I please have your autograph?"

"I think you must have the wrong person," Amelia said.

"You're starring in that new movie, the one David Selznick is producing."

"*Sea Change*," the other one said. "You got the part after Rita Hayworth said no."

"How do you know—"

"That lovely lass, Ursula, who keeps all the public parks and grounds so neat and trim. She helped me revive my hibiscus! As soon as she told us you were here with a magazine photographer, we had to come see for ourselves."

"You have no idea the excitement that news of this picture has brought to the island." The woman's friend wielded her utility envelope like a weapon, ready to strike, until Amelia gave in.

She had always imagined being asked for an autograph would be thrilling. Yet now, faced with the reality, she retreated. The rough rock fence loomed ten feet behind her as the women closed in, their demands for her signature more like threats than requests. They weren't asking—they were commanding, as if her autograph were their constitutional right.

"Ladies," Amelia said, "I'm sorry, but I don't have a pen with me—"

The second woman snapped open the brass clasp on her handbag. "I've got one."

The rest of the crowd surged forward. Before Amelia could draw another breath, they had surrounded her on three sides. The stone fence was now six feet away. Five feet. Four.

"Found it!" The housewife thrust her pen into the air.

A pot-bellied man with a wrinkled face called out, "I'm next!"

Somebody else cried out, "Quit shoving!"

Amelia stepped back, searching for Polly, Irene, Tate—anyone. The noon sun knifed through the shade of a maple tree, blinding her. "Hold up!" Her attempt at cheeriness came out as a bellow. "This is all so silly. We haven't even shot the first frame. I'm not a movie star—just someone who has no business signing your utility bills."

"Get a load of her," someone said. "Already thinks she's too good for autographs."

"Hollywood people," another voice said, sour with resentment. "They're so selfish."

"You've got it all wrong." Amelia raised her hand to block out the glaring sun.

A loud gasp cut the air.

"Did she try to hit you?"

"No!" Amelia cried out. Her head swam from the heat. Suddenly it was difficult to breath. "That's not it at all."

"LADIES AND GENTLEMEN!" Tate's voice echoed up the amphitheater. "If I may explain?" His arm brushed hers as he stepped beside her. "My name is James Tate, and I'm a photographer from *Look*."

"The magazine?" the first housewife asked.

"We're here to take preliminary shots and to scout locations, in and around town."

"That's right." Polly now stood to Amelia's right. "We'll be filming *Sea Change* on location, so naturally we want to make Catalina look as scenic as possible."

"Say," a voice from the crowd called, "ain't you the gal who used to work in the telegraph office?"

"That's right, Mr. Luder. It's me, Polly Maddox."

"I heard you got yourself a job at the Selznick studios."

"You heard right."

"So you watched them filming *Gone with the Wind?*" a much younger voice asked.

"I did, Johnny. And I promise you're in for a treat."

"You've seen it already?"

"Bits and pieces."

Amelia smiled to herself. Polly had seen none of the footage except a few of the screen tests for Scarlett O'Hara, so she was flat-out lying to these people. But Amelia didn't give a fig. Polly and Tate had come to her rescue, and that's all she cared about.

"What else can you tell us?" yelled someone near the back of the throng.

"Let's see . . ." Polly tapped her cheek. "The mayor of Atlanta is campaigning for *Gone with the Wind* to hold its world premiere there." She waited for the crowd's ooohhs and aaahhhs to subside. "But I'm asking you to keep that top secret."

"In fact . . ." Amelia scanned around for Irene, planning to introduce her. But Irene shook her head. *Don't tell them who I'm married to.* Inspiration struck. If Garbo's *Camille* could premiere in Palm Springs . . . "How about we talk Mr. Selznick into holding the *Sea Change* premiere here at the Avalon Theatre in the Casino building?"

The idea of a Hollywood movie opening in their isolated corner of the Pacific whipped these locals into a lather. A few people clapped. Others called out "Bravo!" Another one suggested they organize a letter-writing campaign.

"See?" the first woman said. "You *are* somebody! Or will be soon enough." She shoved her gas bill envelope at Amelia again.

The mob surged forward.

Polly yelped as she was shoved backward.

Someone prodded a pen into Amelia's hand. "SIGN!"

A hand grabbed Amelia's arm. Another voice: "You're not going no place till I get mine."

"PEOPLE!" Tate yelled. "PLEASE!"

A ripping sound, a rush of cool air, and her sleeve ripped away at the shoulder. A shove sent her reeling into the crowd, where an old man bellowed "HEY!" and pushed back. Amelia's knees buckled, and she sank beneath a roiling sea of limbs and fury.

35

Irene braked behind a horse-drawn delivery wagon clip-clopping down Fairfax Avenue. "That scratch down the side of your face looks like it's healing."

Amelia ran her finger down the four-inch welt left by an unkempt fingernail. She had been on her knees then, eyes clenched against the pressing swarm. It wasn't her only souvenir. A silver-dollar-sized bruise stained her right shoulder.

"Could have been a lot worse," Bernice chimed in from the back seat.

Thank heavens for Tate. After passing his camera to Polly, he'd plowed ahead, shoving aside the men and women as though they were nothing but hay bales. The next few minutes blurred into shouts of "Watch it!" and "Where'd she go?" The chaos of bodies and fingers and elbows drove her to the dirt. Dazed, she'd stayed down until powerful hands hauled her up.

Ahead of them, the horse and cart cleared the intersection. Irene shifted into first gear and continued east along Santa Monica Boulevard. "I still feel dreadfully guilty."

"It's not like you incited that mob to violence," Lois told her—again. This wasn't the first time they'd had this conversation. "The situation got out of hand. That's all."

The mob had rattled Amelia more than she'd admitted to anyone but Polly. She had been wrestling with her decision—should she try and get out of her contract or shouldn't she, back and forth, yes, no, yes, no—until that ugly business on Catalina had kicked her straight to "Thanks, but no thanks." If this was fame, they could keep it.

A Catalina veterinarian, whose office was close by, had patched her up, but Irene insisted Amelia see their family physician and had flown them on the late afternoon seaplane back to the mainland. It was comforting to witness the Mama-takes-charge side of Irene Selznick, and Amelia had gratefully surrendered.

Two days later, she had felt like she was ready to tackle the issue head on. But when Irene had stopped by, loaded with a Jurgensen's care basket as bountiful as the one she'd supplied after Polly had broken her leg, the time hadn't been right.

What had blindsided her was the new contract promoting her from stand-in to star that Irene had brought with her. Still only a one-picture deal, it lifted her weekly pay to a dizzying five hundred smackers for ten guaranteed weeks, plus six hundred for each week *Sea Change* ran over schedule. She might have signed it, too, had Irene insisted on getting her signature there and then. But it hadn't been hard to distract Irene and hide the contract out of sight. When Polly had later asked her why she was hesitating now that the role was hers, Amelia had replied, "A golden cage is still a cage." She found cold comfort knowing that every fresh-off-the-bus hopeful would trade her eyeteeth for such a prison.

"Do we think Mr. Hartman will have good news for us?" Amelia asked Irene and Bernice.

"He's resourceful. I'll give him that," Bernice said. "Anyone who can track me down deserves a medal."

"You're facing very serious charges, and a substantial probability of jail time," Irene warned. "Let's take it step by step." After a pause, she added, "And if the news is terrible, we can go next door to the Formosa Café for a drink to drown our disappointment."

"Or," Amelia suggested, "to celebrate our progress."

* * *

Unlike her cinematic counterparts, Hartman's new receptionist had a maternal air better suited to meetings of the local PTA. She set about making them all coffee as Amelia, Irene, and Bernice took their seats at Hartman's desk.

"As per your request," he said, steepling his fingers, "I've been digging into Cyrus Pattinson and have uncovered some interesting information."

"Interesting good or interesting bad?" Irene asked.

"It appears our Mr. Pattinson has a history of not paying his sub-contractors until more than a hundred twenty days out."

"That's late, isn't it?"

"When the industry standard is thirty, it's very tardy. But Cee-Pat Construction is by far the biggest game in town."

"Forcing everybody to play by his rules."

"Most of his creditors—lumberyards, brickmakers, excavators, painters and the like—wouldn't give me much to go on. Except for one. A doctor by the name of"—he fixed Bernice with an unflinching gaze—"Yarborough."

She yipped with surprise. "*Orlando* Yarborough? In Beaumont?"

Amelia hadn't heard of Dr. Yarborough, but Matilda's nunnery lay in Beaumont. A curious turn of events. "Who's he?"

"Doc Yar came to the Moon every other month to give the girls check-ups because you don't know what's out there and it's best to catch these things early."

"Why did you choose him?" Hartman asked.

"For starters, he was from outside Palm Springs, which dampened local gossip. But it was his expertise treating VD. He sees folks from all over—Lake Arrowhead to San Diego. As you might imagine, the Hollywood crowd values his discretion. They land on the tarmac and meet Doc Yar at the Moon. Afterwards, Mister Movie Star strolls back to his plane and heads home with nobody the wiser."

Amelia listened to Bernice's explanation in stunned silence.

And to think she'd been floating through life without a clue this sort of thing went on, but had pegged Polly as the naïve one.

"Did Pattinson ever frequent the Moon?" he asked Bernice.

"Definitely not."

"So he didn't contract syphilis there."

"The Sapphire Moon is a high-class establishment." Bernice's face had flushed a sudden flamingo pink. Evidently, this was a point of pride among madams. Amelia couldn't wait to get home and tell Pol everything. "We were not some cheap hot-sheet hotel, thank you very much. Thanks to Doc Yar, my girls were always clean."

"Hold on a sec," Irene said. "Pattinson has syphilis? You must be skilled at encouraging strangers to share information like that."

He drummed his fingers on his mahogany desk as though he were weighing pros and cons. "Dr. Yarborough is also a client of mine."

"So what can you tell us about Pattinson's case of the pox?"

"He ignored the symptoms until they were advanced. And that meant his Salvarsan treatment had to be both stringent and lengthy."

"What a fool!" Bernice shivered. "The side effects of that stuff are dreadful. Headaches. Vomiting. Liver damage. But what else should one expect if your so-called cure is made of arsenic?"

"It's better than syphilis killing you—but not much."

The secretary set down the coffee service on Hartman's blotter, silent as a church mouse.

"You'd think Pattinson would be grateful that his pox didn't kill him," Hartman said, "but he even stiffed the doctor who saved his life."

"I think I get the picture now." Bernice leaned forward. "Doc Yar approached you to dig around on Pattinson."

"He did."

"But why not use somebody closer to home?"

"I assume you ladies are familiar with Jerry Giesler?"

The name meant nothing to Amelia, but Irene erupted with,

"Who hasn't? He's defended Alexander Pantages, Buron Fitts, Busby Berkeley. Acquittal is his trademark."

"I did a whole bunch of legwork during Busby's murder trial and got quite chummy with Buzz. After wrapping *Babes in Arms*, he came knocking. Three of his chorus girls had picked up VD, and he needed someone discreet. Hollywood gossipmongers being what they are, he wanted treatment far from prying eyes."

"Pattinson infected them, too?" Bernice asked.

"It was tricker than that. Each girl caught gonorrhea from a different studio exec, so pressure came from all sides. My discreet inquiries led me to Yarborough, and he remembered me when he needed a private eye. He told me Pattinson's still fighting the infection, but won't pay up. Yarborough wouldn't stop treatment —partly because of his oath, partly because Pattinson's the type to seek revenge. But every time he asks for payment, he gets palmed off on some greasy charmer named"—he checked his notes—"Winchester."

Amelia's coffee cup clattered against its saucer. *"Farley* Winchester?"

Hartman nodded. "Heard of him?"

Suddenly, this whole sordid business had twisted into something personal. "He was the talent agent who did a disappearing act on me earlier this year."

Hartman turned to the second page of a *Herald-Express*. Under the headline *GREEN'S BROOM OF PURITY PUSHES WESTWARD,* he read aloud a subheading: "'All manner of vice and evil shall be swept away, vows campaign manager Farley Winchester.'"

"So this Winchester snake is Greene's campaign manager?" Bernice groaned. "Why am I not surprised?"

"Ladies, if working in this field has taught me one thing, it's this: There may be seven million people in California, but everything is connected to everything else; everyone to everyone else. Investigating one person is like pulling a thread on a Persian carpet."

Amelia was silent for a moment, absorbing everything she'd just heard. She needed to talk to Matilda again, for one thing.

Matilda had vanished for a four-day weekend when Amelia had returned from Catalina, robbing her of the chance to confront her about Ursula's revelation that Matilda was the black sheep of an awful family. Or did that make her the white sheep? Either way, Amelia needed to size up Matilda all over again. "Did you uncover any other skeletons during your excavation?" she asked Hartman.

"The Agua Caliente Land Management Corporation. Do you know of it, Bernice?"

"I don't think so."

"Just curious. It's a dummy corporation based in Palm Springs designed to look like every other developer who builds homes or apartments. They've never built anything, so I kept digging."

"And?"

"In the last year or so, they've acquired every square foot of land north of Ramon Road, east of Farrell Drive, and all the way to the airstrip."

Bernice's match hung unlit over her Pall Mall. "But that's where the Moon is."

"Let me rephrase that. Every square foot of that land—except the site of the Sapphire Moon. You're standing in the way of their owning all the land to the immediate west."

Bernice brushed off Hartman's statement with a dismissive tut. "Past the city limits, there's nothing but desert. They'd have to sit on that land for decades before the town grows enough to reach the airstrip. Assuming it ever does." She took a drag from her lit cigarette.

"Unless we join the war in Europe."

"What's Europe got to do with our puny little airstrip?"

Understanding hit Amelia like a spotlight. "Puny now, but what if it gets expanded into an airport?"

"For a measly three thousand people?"

Hartman explained, "When the U.S. enters the war, we'll have to train an awful lot of flyboys. They'll need to find somewhere to practice take-offs and landings. And even if we don't get sucked into that conflict, Palm Springs is becoming a popular getaway. It'll need a commercial airport, eventually."

"And when that happens," Amelia continued, "the surrounding land will skyrocket in value. Especially the Moon's pocket of scrub grass and cacti because it's the only piece of the puzzle not in their greedy little paws."

They waited until the clouds of confusion parted in Bernice's eyes. "If I get convicted, I'll have to sell the Moon."

"For a song."

"To this Agua Caliente company?"

"If they're the only outfit offering to buy it."

"Which they will be because Cee-Pat Construction is the biggest game in town."

Bernice flicked the butt of her cigarette with a manicured nail as she digested the implications of what Hartman had uncovered. "How sure are you about all this?"

"The same chicanery went on a couple of years back when LA decided it required a bigger municipal airport and purchased Mines Field."

"But do you have any proof?" Amelia insisted. "In writing?" When the private eye shook his head, the letdown struck like a snapping clapperboard.

"Prosecuting Bernice into prison is their route to covertly buying the Moon's land. Pattinson's too smart to write anything down. That's the way intimidation works."

"So what do we do?" Amelia already knew the answer before she'd finished her question. "We'll need to figure this out ourselves."

36

Amelia took off her straw mushroom hat as soon as she was seated in Irene's LaSalle. "Thanks for inviting me to tag along."

Irene turned onto Robertson Avenue and headed north toward the Hollywood Hills. "I'm glad it happened to be your day off."

Amelia suspected Irene had sweet-talked her schedule out of Polly. Not that she minded—these moments alone with Irene were precious. No crowds or cameras, no snooping eyes or family duties getting in the way.

But it was harder than Amelia had imagined for her to tell Irene that she had been putting off signing the contract. Irene could be stridently vocal when she decided to be, and Amelia dreaded the moment where she had to deliver her news. Irene's enthusiasm for the casting made it worse—her friend had staked so much on this picture that Amelia's doubts stuck in her throat.

Maybe it would be easier to give in and film the movie.

Maybe the cameras would melt away all this ridiculous dithering.

Maybe she'd find her spark again. After all, wasn't this why she'd started down this path in the first place?

And don't forget: Five hundred a week ain't nothing to sneeze at.

She toyed with the new peach ribbon she had sewn into the brim of her old hat. "Remind me who you're seeing?"

"Sonya Levien. She's a screenwriter who's having quite a year. Not only did she co-write *Drums Along the Mohawk* for Fox, but *Hunchback of Notre Dame*, too."

"Which is why we're going out to the RKO ranch?"

Irene nodded. "It'll be ten degrees hotter in Encino, so I'm glad to see you had the sense to dress coolly."

According to Ursula, the ranch was where Matilda's sister, Rhea, worked. The chance to talk to Irene alone combined with the prospect of seeing this Rhea girl for herself was a two-birds-one-stone opportunity. Not that she knew what she'd say to Rhea if the occasion presented itself. "Does Mr. Selznick have his eye on Sonya?"

"Today's fishing expedition is on behalf of my father to determine if she's open to signing with MGM. Her husband has a somewhat spotty employment record and they have four kids."

"Making her the sole breadwinner."

"Normally, Father would approach her through more legit channels, but he suspects a friendlier tactic might prove more successful."

"Woman to woman?"

"Specifically Jewish woman to Jewish woman."

"Has he ever done that before?"

"Not once, not ever." Pride tinted Irene's voice—a new tone that made Amelia wonder: Was Mayer watching from the wings as his daughter shepherded *Sea Change* to life?

Passing Chasen's on Beverly, Irene rat-a-tatted her wedding ring against the steering wheel. "Father asking me to do this—I was so flattered, I didn't care what his reasons were." The tapping continued. "A woman needs to feel useful. God only knows I wouldn't want to be a man for all Astaire's dancing shoes, but they do get to have careers."

"Do you regret getting married?" Amelia kept her voice light.

"No . . . I suppose not." The pause spoke volumes. "Though I do envy the Dorothy Arzners and Edith Heads. And Margaret Booth over at Metro—she's best editor in the business. *Merry Widow* to *Camille,* von Stroheim to Cukor, she's done it all, seen it all, cut it all. I'd love a week in her shoes. Or a month." She laughed. "Who am I kidding? I'd trade my left arm for a year. But my boys would need a substitute mommy."

The LaSalle engine growled louder as the incline up Benedict Canyon steepened en route to Mulholland Drive, which ran along the crest of the Hollywood Hills.

A substitute.

Might that be the smoothest way Amelia could exit *Sea Change*?

Those early weeks with Irene, filled with plotting and planning, had been the happiest of her life. Even as a stand-in, she was thrilled to be in the thick of it. But stepping up to being a star and living through the ugliness of that amphitheater nightmare—that's when it had soured. Smart Ingrid Bergman had fled town the moment *Intermezzo* wrapped.

Amelia ran a fingertip along the edge of the glove box as Irene chatted about how the boundless energy of two little boys could power a small town with enough energy to last all winter. But Amelia was barely listening. The more she thought about it, the more she liked this idea of providing her own substitute.

* * *

Amelia squinted at the Notre Dame facade. Two stories of arches crowned the cathedral's entrances, each peak unique, each detail carved with meticulous precision by the studio craftsmen. "I wonder if this is how the real Notre Dame looks?"

"Special effects will paint in the rest, but yes, that's how I remember it." Irene's casual reminiscence was a splash of cold water—their friendship might have been genuine, but their worlds stood oceans apart. "Perc Westmore told me it takes hours to transform Charles Laughton into Quasimodo. It's unspeakably uncomfortable, but the results are astounding."

Extras in fifteenth-century costumes milled about the forecourt—peasants in threadbare rags beside merchants sporting paisley cravats and silver buckles, women in embroidered aprons and velvet bonnets. Above, a camera perched on its scaffolding like a mechanical gargoyle while Klieg lights flooded the cathedral steps. Below, technicians huddled around their director, whose nose was buried in the script.

"That's William Dieterle," Irene said. "Laughton often wants to change his lines, which means Sonya must be nearby." She skirted the crew's circle. "There!" A dark-haired woman in polka dots held court like a queen in sateen. "It might take some fancy footwork to catch her ear," Irene murmured. "Go explore."

Amelia drew close to RKO's masterpiece of papier-mâché transformed into holy stone; every statue's fold of robe and wisp of hair had been crafted with devotion. She might never see the real Notre Dame, but this slice of Paris intoxicated her. Even the grime had been painstakingly reproduced, dark streaks suggesting centuries of smoke. The paint's fresh tang made her head swim. She backed away and turned to the costumed hordes below: jesters with bells, milk maids with buckets, blacksmiths in leather aprons.

A single face in the crowd captured Amelia's eye—a girl draped in a blue gown, stripes of gold in shimmering folds from shoulder to ankle. It must have been torture in the ninety-degree heat. The girl caught her staring and offered back a smile—warm but wary.

"Approve of my handiwork?" said a familiar voice from behind.

Amelia hadn't seen Sibyl Langley since the It Café reunion. "Handiwork?"

"I'm the Vice President in Charge of Dirt." Sibyl rapped a knuckle against the nearest saint mottled with painted-on muck.

"No longer at MGM?"

"After my contact ran out, a pal of mine told me they had an opening on *Hunchback*. They informed me I had three weeks to paint it. I retorted, 'Only if I don't sleep, don't eat, and pee into a cup.' So they gave me an assistant from the greenery department.'"

The greenery department? "I don't suppose it's Rhea?"

"No. Some big lug with height on his side. I know who you mean, though."

"Ever spoken with her?"

"Ooooh, yeeeesss." Sibyl rolled her pretty green eyes. "That gal is an unrelenting perfectionist, so it's hard to put anything over on her. And when she tells a story, she's the type to throw in ev-er-y de-tail."

"Too much?"

"Now look, I'm no prude. Broadminded as the next person—that's me. But do I need to hear all the ins and outs when the romance-gone-wrong is with another woman? And yet I got the whole blessed soap opera. Say, why are you asking about her?"

Amelia imagined romance bloomed in mysterious places, but she had trouble picturing someone as level-headed as Ursula putting up with a woman like that for any longer than a day or two. "Did Rhea talk about her sister?"

"Which one? She's got four. Plus two or three brothers."

"The one who wants to be in movies."

"Ah, the black sheep!"

"What did she say?"

"She was mid-rant about Tillie—something about having a baby, or not having it, and fleeing to some backwater town. She got awfully emotional about it, so it was difficult keeping track, except when she branded her sister the family Jezebel. I was glad I had an excuse to go paint more muck, so I skedaddled away fast as I could; otherwise, I'd still be there."

Having a baby—or not *having it?* "Where might I find her?"

Sibyl pointed past a row of ramshackle houses with crooked windows and missing roof tiles. "Western Street is on the other side. Walk to the far end, turn right, and you'll see a jungle of Boston ferns and elderberry bushes. Trust me, she's hard to miss."

* * *

Amelia lingered between a manzanita and a corn stalk, watching Rhea at a battered workbench filling a large ceramic pot with dirt, until her throat-clearing broke the spell. A black curl whipped aside as the girl looked up. Eyes darker than coffee grounds pinned her. "You lost?"

The earthy smell of rich soil mingled with the scent of a flower Amelia couldn't identify, and contrasted with the maple syrup, bacon, and cigarettes that filled Amelia's workaday world. "Not if you're Rhea."

"If you're from the front office, I'm way ahead of you." Rhea returned to her task. "The chrysanthemums for *Everything's on Ice* will be ready by next Monday, as promised. The tulips for *Two Thoroughbreds* were at their prime three weeks ago; I can't be held responsible if the stupid horse went lame."

How long would it take Irene to convince that screenwriter to consider an MGM offer? Five minutes? Four hours? Amelia wished she'd thought to ask. "I've come seeking your advice."

Rhea's eyebrow rose, more in curiosity than wariness. "Yeah?"

Amelia pictured the large bush out front of her apartment building. "Hibiscus."

"Dying?"

"Wilting."

Rhea slapped the dirt from her palms. "Tough li'l sum'bitches, but they ain't bulletproof. All they need is everything." She ticked off fingers. "Sun, water, acidic soil—no clay, mind you. Compost till kingdom come, then leave them alone."

"To put it another way, I'm doing it all wrong." Amelia injected a giggle into her response. "I thank you, and my hibiscus thanks you."

"I haven't seen you around here before." Rhea resumed potting. "Who sent you?"

Amelia mentally checked off a list of names, assessing each one for its potential to set off the girl's instincts. Unable to settle on a single name, she decided to use all three. "I'm here with Irene Selznick."

"Oh?"

"But then I bumped into Zara Willowick."

"Well connected, aren't you?"

"But the person who praised your green thumb was"—Amelia braced—"Ursula."

"Ursula?" Rhea continued to fill the pot, methodical trowelful by methodical trowelful. From this close, the girl's freckles showed dark as her eyes, scattered across her nose like buckshot. "Spoke of *me*?"

"On Catalina recently. Through a friend—"

"Got a new *friend*, has she?"

"I wouldn't jump to conclu—"

"Didn't take her long." Rhea chewed on the inside of her lower lip. Any harder and she'd draw blood. "She happy?"

"I barely know her." Amelia angled away from the hornets' nest of Rhea's intensity. She'd come hunting for Matilda's guarded secrets, not Rhea's failed romance. "We stuck to pleasantries."

"What *did* she say, then?"

Oh, Lord, sweetie, you don't want to hear that. "When it comes to plants, there's nobody smarter."

"Decent of her." A sliver of a smile emerged, softening the harsh lines of Rhea's face. Not by much, but enough for Amelia to reconsider beating a hasty exit.

"She holds no grudge over what happened." Amelia was wading blind into their history, but didn't all hearts break the same way?

"It was Thanksgiving that broke her camel's back, wasn't it?"

Amelia heard the door of opportunity creak open. "She talked more about your sister."

"Which one?"

"The black sheep."

"Tillie." She belched Matilda's name like it was the final remnant of a rancid meal. "How much did she tell you?"

"Schwab's, getting a nose job, Wyatt, the family orchard, and why she went to Beaumont."

"Even Beaumont, huh? You got the full run-down. I presume Ursula thinks Tillie should've had that bastard child of hers."

Matilda didn't have that baby? If there was no nunnery in Beaumont, then what—ohhh.

"All she said was that she was glad Tillie was in the hands of some expert of all things 'down there.' Some doc called Yarborough."

Rhea strained from the effort of swallowing her true thoughts. "What about the kid's father?"

If Amelia kept up the pretense of knowing more than she did, would she pry loose the father's name, too? "Mixed feelings about him."

"Yeah, I get it. On the one hand, he forced Tillie to terminate, though he understood full well we Greenes take our faith seriously."

The question burned in Amelia's throat—what would this somber, vehement girl's local priest say about her relationships with women? But why sink this conversation when they were getting somewhere? "And on the other hand?"

"He's calling the shots with my brother's campaign. I hate to admit it, but he's doing a heck of a good job."

Amelia wished she could hide behind the thicket of potted manzanita bushes off to the right. Farley Winchester was running Wyatt Greene's campaign. *He* had fathered Matilda's baby? Was that why she had followed Amelia to Farley's office that day?

Or . . .

Did campaign managers carry out the shots called by someone further up the chain of command? Like, for instance, Cyrus Pattinson? "So when you say the father calls the—"

"Did Ursula bring up my brother's Broom of Purity? Not that I care what she thinks." Her face took on a dreamy quality that Amelia wouldn't have thought possible ten minutes before. "Wyatt doesn't need her help to know how to pull at the public's heart strings."

"What about Matilda?"

The distracted smile fell away. "I refuse to call Tillie by that name."

"I assumed Tillie was short for Matilda."

"It is." Rhea crossed her arms. "It's also short for 'I Pretend to be Somebody I'm Not.' And I have no patience for hypocrites. As Proverbs 26:24 says, 'An enemy disguises himself with his lips, but in his heart he harbors deceit.'"

Amelia shifted her weight from one foot to the other. When the biblical quotes started flying, it was time to exit stage right.

"There you are!" cried a voice off to her right.

What a relief to see a familiar face emerge from beyond a trio of elephant palms. "Why, if it isn't Mister *Look* magazine."

"We've been searching for you."

"We?"

Trailing a step or two behind him was the dress extra in the blue gown with gold striping, whom Amelia had noticed from the Notre Dame steps. "I don't suppose a waitressing job has opened up at Schwab's like you mentioned on that phony casting call."

"Della!" Amelia slapped a palm against her forehead. "You look so different in this get-up." She went to make introductions, but Rhea had vanished—a blessed relief.

Four months had hollowed Della's cheeks and dimmed her glow. What she needed was to feast on one of Schwab's triple-deckers with all the trimmings. "Your costume's pretty, but aren't you roasting in it?"

"Like a baked potato." Della swiped at the sheen of sweat glistening across her brow. "Dress extras get paid more, so it sure has saved my bacon." She flapped the bottom of her tunic to create a breeze. "I'm at my wits' end about next month's rent." She laughed, but it came out harsh. "I doubt my landlord has an installment plan."

Ordinarily, Amelia would have jumped in feet first with some story illustrating how close she, too, had skated to the poorhouse, but thought the better of it. "How do you two know each other?"

"We don't." Tate lifted his Rolleiflex. "My editor sent me along for a photo layout on the spectacular Notre Dame set. And this charming young maiden"—he made a gentlemanly flourish with his free hand—"agreed to pose in front of the doors for me."

Della curtseyed. "Which he probably wouldn't have wanted me to do if they had dressed me in tattered rags."

"That's where you're wrong." He wriggled a finger at her. He meant it to be admonishing, but his gesture carried a flirtatious edge. "I'd still pick you out even if they threw you into a burlap sack and rolled you around in the mud."

"I don't know about that," Della said, "but out of four hundred extras, I'm flattered you picked me."

"How did I come up in conversation?" Amelia asked Tate.

"The set decorator asked me if I had permission to photograph it."

"And," Della said, "that's when I asked her where she'd sent you because the way I figure it, you owe me a job." Her giggle was a silver wind-chime. "Because I don't know how much longer I can stand to pretend it's the year fourteen ninety-two."

As she was talking, Tate's eyes bounced between Amelia and Della, comparing and contrasting.

Amelia recognized that appraisal—she'd faced it since puberty, generally from the losing side. Della had that classical beauty, while Amelia was all pluck and pep, another Priscilla Lane in a world of Dietrichs. Usually she'd envy their polish, but not today. Irene's words about needing a backup echoed too loudly. She retreated, focusing on the crimson blooms of a nearby crêpe myrtle.

"Do me a favor?" she asked Tate. "Take a few photos of Della next to that."

A voice, amplified by a megaphone, sailed over the roofs of the medieval village set. "Extras and minor cast, five minutes to places."

"I must be getting back," Della said.

"Please?" Amelia implored. "A half-dozen is all I need."

"If I knew why I was taking them, it would help me frame them better."

Amelia prodded him toward the crêpe myrtle. "Shoot now, ask questions later."

37

Polly had parked on a stretch of Wilshire with no trees to protect her car from the heat of a week-long Indian summer. Lois, Bernice, Polly, and Amelia opened their doors to an oven.

Lois sighed. "I think we can all agree that went about as well as bacon-wrapped shrimp at a bar mitzvah."

"'Of course, you must be aware,'" Amelia said, mimicking the voice of Bernice's lawyer, who looked more like an accountant at a funeral home, "'all of Palm Springs knows you've been running the Sapphire Moon, so your best course of action is to throw yourself on the mercy of the court.' What a bonehead!" She slapped the upholstery, wishing it was the bonehead's pasty face.

"That boob had already thrown in the towel," Polly said.

"*And* the shower curtain," Amelia added. "Did you see what happened when we said he should look into Wyatt Greene and his string-puller, Cyrus Pattinson?"

The attorney's clipped mustache had bristled as he worked himself up into a conniption fit. "If that's how you feel," he had said, spittle clogging the corners of his pale lips, "you can find yourself another lawyer."

"Bern's trial is in nine days!" Lois said. "What the devil are we going to do?"

Polly roared her engine to life. "We're off to see Irene."

"Unannounced?" Bernice asked.

"Pol's right," Amelia said. "She wanted us to tell her the outcome of today's meeting. If anyone can recommend a lawyer who'll show some spine, it'll be her."

* * *

Irene answered the door, her skittery eyes glazed with tears. "Oh, hello," she said, breathlessly. "Did we have plans?"

Uh-oh. We should've called ahead. "No—we—" Amelia stammered. "We've come at a bad time—"

Irene grabbed at Amelia's wrist. "I could do with the distraction." She led them into the living room, where all the LA dailies overflowed from the glass coffee table onto the rug. "I suppose you've heard about Roosevelt's proclamation?"

"We've been in a meeting with Bernice's lawyer since before eight this morning. Why? What's he said?"

"He's declared neutrality in the European war," Irene told them. "We're staying out of it, after all. That should make Lindbergh happy."

Once the hero of the nation, Charles Lindbergh had been making headlines for the past year as spokesman for the America First Committee's isolationist policies. Personally, Amelia thought he was burying his head in the sand.

"And if all that isn't enough, David called me not ten minutes ago to announce they completed editing on *Wind* late last night."

"It's done? They've finished?" Lois was all but squealing.

"No, but it does mean they're ready to preview."

"Soon?" Amelia asked.

Irene bugged out her eyes as though to say *You won't believe it.*

"Holy Moses," Polly murmured. "Tonight?"

Irene nodded. "This afternoon, David, Jock Whitney, and I will take one car; the editor and script girl will follow with all fifty film cans. We'll convoy through sixty miles in this god-awful heatwave to surprise a few hundred folks who're expecting *Beau Geste*. Dave and I are jumpy as cats! But enough of that. Tell me, what brings you here?"

Amelia looked at Polly, who returned her uneasy glance: *We can't pile our problems on top of all that.* "This is a big day in your household. We don't want to disturb—"

"That's where you're wrong!" A feverish, almost hysterical edge sliced through Irene's response. "I've arranged for the nanny to stay the night, selected my outfit, and put together a picnic supper for us to eat on the drive over. I've got nothing but this"—she motioned to the slew of newspapers—"to keep me occupied. Why? What's going on?"

"My lawyer quit!" Bernice wailed.

"But your trial. It's only—"

"Nine days away. He thinks I should throw myself on the court's mercy."

"Horse feathers. Since when is guilt a reason to hurl your client to the lions?"

"He got spooked when we brought up Greene and Pattinson."

Irene nodded slowly as she contemplated the morning's events. "Do we still think those two are pulling strings?"

"Yep and yep."

"Well, then, you need a lawyer with a sharp pair of scissors who isn't afraid to use them."

"And we were hoping you might have some suggestions?" Lois said.

"You can't swing a rabid ferret in this town without hitting a lawyer. But Bernice, my dear, you haven't much time to get your legal ducks in order. You need someone who is top-notch, tenacious as a shark, and will put up a fight until the very last second." Irene absently twirled her jade pendant on its gold chain. "It's such short notice. Plus, he's frightfully expensive."

"Who is?" Bernice asked. "And how expensive is he?"

"Never you mind." David Selznick strode through the open

French doors and fixed his wife with a shrewd eye. "There's only one person for this assignment."

"Yes, David, but even if he were available, his fee is—"

"—is no concern of Bernice's." He laid a hand on her shoulder. "The last thing you should be worrying about is how to pay Jerry Giesler."

That was the lawyer Dudley Hartman had worked for. "Isn't he the guy who defended Busby Berkeley?" Amelia asked.

Bernice pressed her hands to her chest. "What on earth did *he* do?"

Selznick was too agitated to sit down. "Plowed into a couple of cars on the Roosevelt Highway, drunk as a skunk. Two people were killed and he was charged with second degree murder. Now he's directed *Babes in Arms*, which tells you how good Jerry Giesler is."

Bernice peered up at him. "Do you think this Mr. Giesler will take my case?"

"Bernice, honey," Irene said, her voice soft as cotton candy. "One step at a time." She pierced her husband with a steely glare. *How the hell can we afford to pay the most expensive lawyer in town?* But Selznick wasn't looking at his wife.

"Giesler's pulled off bigger miracles. Failing that, you'll get a light sentence." His smile warmed with paternal confidence. "But for now, you'll have to excuse us."

Amelia stood, encouraging the others to follow her lead. "If we swear an undying oath to not disclose the location . . .?"

"Fox Theatre in Riverside," Irene whispered.

Amelia cocked an eyebrow. "How ironic."

"Why is that?"

"All our problems stem from Riverside."

Irene didn't reply, but Amelia caught a flicker in her gaze she couldn't interpret. And there was no time to ask. "Break a leg," she told the Selznicks and herded the others toward the front door.

* * *

The next morning, newspapers trumpeted how the luckiest audience in America had whooped and wept through a four-hour *Gone with the Wind*. Amelia itched to hear Irene's take, but a sick waitress had landed her back behind the lunch counter.

Ursula had warned that Rhea was the Greene sister to watch out for, but old habits died hard. Amelia studied Matilda, searching for . . . what exactly? Now that she knew the truth about the Riverside nunnery, Amelia could no longer be sure who this woman behind the platinum curls and calculated winks truly was. Matilda was running an endless audition, and she'd keep running it until some chap with pull plunked himself down in front of her. What a shame Mr. Paramount Casting hadn't shown his face around here in a while. He'd have made a perfect target.

The regulars filed in: Joseph from Warner's gate, Cobb from RKO, and that Columbia makeup guy Amelia had met through Noah at a housewarming party below the Hollywood sign. Lordy, but it felt good to be hollering orders, trading sass, pushing the bacon-tomato sandwich over the minced ham. She might not have noticed how the time had flown except that a newly familiar face slipped onto one of the lunch-counter seats.

"Mr. Tate, what a pleasant surprise."

"Mrs. Selznick told me I might find you here." His hopeful tone made it sound as though he were working up his courage to ask a favor. She placed a menu in front of him, but he didn't look at it. "Coffee. Black. Two donuts. With sugar and cinnamon, if you have them."

As she poured his cup and plated the donuts, he retrieved an envelope of photographs from his pocket. "Thought these might interest you."

The first handful were candid snapshots of her at the Catalina bell tower and Wrigley Monument, capturing her in unguarded moments of surprise, delight, and contemplation. Following them were a few he'd taken while she'd been talking to Zara in front of Notre Dame.

"These are lovely," she told Tate, "and quite flattering. But they're not 'magazine photographs' as such."

"No?" he asked, more amused than insulted. "Tell me more."

She held up a photo he'd taken as Sibyl had been telling her about Rhea. Her mouth was gaping open like a bullfrog about to gobble a passing dragonfly. "Real models only *act* surprised."

"*Look* magazine is interested in more than models posing on bridges," he said around a mouthful of donut. "Hardly anyone can relate to that."

On Catalina and at the RKO ranch, he'd come across as somewhat detached. And fair enough, too. He was chasing an assignment he'd hoped would impress his editor. But here amid the lunchtime bustle, a warm humor revealed a gentler side beneath his previously guarded exterior.

Amelia continued flipping through his photos until she found his shots of Della at RKO. "Now, *these* are magazine photos. She's posing for them."

"That girl needed little direction from me."

The last photo showed Della poised like a bird about to take flight, her blue gown's sleeves rippling from outstretched arms. Her gaze met the camera's lens with quiet grace. "This is the best one."

"For what purpose?" Tate wore the unblinking face of someone who was already a step ahead.

Amelia waited until the customer next to him, an old fellow with a withered arm—a souvenir of the Great War—slipped off his stool. "I've had second thoughts."

"About?"

"The lead in *Sea Change*."

"You don't want it?" His chin dipped in a slight nod, as if checking off a mental box. "It's a tremendous opportunity."

"For the right girl."

"But not for you."

"I'm sure most people would think I've lost my marbles."

"I'm from Topeka, Kansas." He dusted cinnamon from his lips. "My dad's a dentist. Wanted me to be one, too. I shocked everyone—family, friends, neighbors, congregation—when I told them my plans. Many of them told me how brave I was, but I knew what I was doing, so it took no courage at all. So, yeah, I get it."

"May I have these photos of Della?"

"I figured you had a plan. But don't you have a contract?"

"Having one and signing it are two different things."

His eyes flared slightly. "You're serious, aren't you?"

"I figure if I can supply my replacement . . ."

"Smart idea."

Amelia had voiced her scheme only to Polly and Luddie. His words—just two from a virtual stranger—set her heart racing with possibility. She waved the photos at him. "So that's a yes?"

"One condition."

Behind him, Kendrick Moss walked through the front door and scoured the retail counter. Failing to find Amelia there, he widened his search, straining his tailored dark gray gabardine suit. She shifted to the right, so that Tate blocked her from him. "What's your one condition?"

"Della's last name, address, and / or telephone number."

A fair exchange. Della's number was among the debris at the bottom of the purse in Amelia's locker. "I'll be back in two shakes."

She lifted a menu like a shield against Kendrick's gaze. She'd seen that look on plenty of fellows on the make: eager, hopeful, with that swagger of a sure thing. No doubt he'd caught wind of her splitting with Benji, and that made her fair game—in his mind, at least.

She reached the end of the counter and withdrew, blocking out the room behind her.

"Who are you avoiding?" Matilda stood next to the cutlery station, where waitresses loitered for a break in between customers. "Don't tell me it's that six-foot-two slab of *Photoplay* perfection?"

"Yep."

"He's the dream catch that girls knock over little old ladies to get to, yet you're creeping about like Lizzie Borden caught with an ax up her skirt."

Amelia chanced a peek, using her menu as cover. Kendrick sat at the far end now, eyes darting about. He was still too handsome for words, but the eager confidence had drained from his puss.

"What's wrong with him?" Matilda asked.

"He's not for me, is all."

The more Kendrick's self-assurance faded away, the more he looked like Benji. Pangs of regret smacked her heart. The smacks soon became slugs. Couldn't they have tried working a little harder to find common ground?

Matilda pressed a gentle shoulder to Amelia's. "Shall I ask Mr. Schwab to show Heartthrob Harry the door?"

"No, I—uh—he's . . ." Amelia studied her own reflection in the chrome coffee urn, distorted and wavering, barely recognizable. "It's just that he gave me a bit of a shock."

"We get all types coming through here, don't we?" Matilda dropped her snappy waitress persona. Not for long, but enough for Amelia to glimpse the real Tillie Greene, who hadn't waited out her pregnancy surrounded by nuns. She frowned at Amelia. "What is it?"

"There is no convent in Beaumont."

Tillie vanished as the Matilda smokescreen resurfaced. "Perhaps not in the strictest sense of the word. More like a home for wayward girls."

"Run by Dr. Yarborough?"

Matilda's lips trembled as panic churned behind her cool slate-green eyes. "How did you know?"

"I was in Avalon a couple of weeks ago and met Ursula."

"Oh!" Matilda blinked rapidly. "Wait. She knew about Yarborough?"

"No, but when I was at the RKO ranch with Irene Selznick—"

"You do get around."

"I figured it was my best chance to talk to Rhea—"

"You got some nerve snooping around my private life." Matilda planted her hands on her hips. "You've scored the lead in *Sea Change*. You won. There's no need to rub my nose in Yarborough—"

"You've got it all wrong." Amelia hadn't made up her mind about this poser, but she still didn't want her thinking she'd been snooping around her life. "Yarborough is the doctor Bernice Hoag called on with her Sapphire Moon girls."

Matilda drew back. "The madam that was in here a while back?"

"With her best friend, my mother."

"That was your *mom*?"

This wasn't the time to remind Matilda that she had referred to Lois as the brothel's janitor. "And it was Bernice who discovered Wyatt being thick as thieves with a land developer out Palm Springs way named Cyrus Pattinson." Matilda's eyes flared at the mention of the name. "By the bye, Pattinson is a patient of Dr. Yarborough."

"Why would Cyrus need to see him?"

So it's 'Cyrus,' is it? "Yarborough also treats"—Amelia lowered her voice to a whisper—"venereal diseases."

Matilda's face reddened like the cherries lining up on a slot machine, the payout coming in torrents. "Miserable son of a bitch," she murmured. "Well, well. Glad to hear it. Seeing as how he lumbered me with—" There was no need for her to finish that sentence, and they both knew it.

Ye gods, it was Cyrus Pattinson who knocked her up. Amelia's order pad slipped from limp fingers, scattering guest checks across the tiled floor. She bent down to gather them up. *Pulling one little thread is all it takes to see how everything and everyone is connected to everything and everyone else.* "Did Cyrus find Yarborough for you?"

"The only good turn he ever did me."

"Didn't he drive you to Beaumont?"

"You're assuming he'd make time for anything as inconvenient as that."

Amelia stood up. "Too busy running your brother's campaign?"

"What a pair of two-bit chiselers!" Finally, a flash of the real Tillie. "Wyatt and Cyrus deserve each other."

"AMELIAAAA!" Kendrick Moss's voice carried the length of the counter. "THERE YOU ARE!"

All heads in the room snapped toward Amelia. She waved and called back that she'd be with him in a moment.

She dawdled, taking her time selecting spoons, forks, and knives. "No love lost between you and Mr. Pattinson?"

"The way he forced me to get rid of—God, how I hate his guts with a murderous passion."

"Wait—you *wanted* to have it?"

"I hadn't decided. What got my goat was how Wyatt and Cyrus took the decision out of my hands. The only choice they gave me was which side of the car to sit on." She caught sight what Amelia hoped was a sympathetic smile, but it must have fallen short because the Matilda veneer dropped back into place like a drawbridge as she gathered up her empty sundae dishes and sailed back to her section.

38

"I'm not cross!" Irene stormed into Sak's Fifth Avenue's new store, leaving Amelia to trail behind. She swatted her white cotton skirt, its tailored fit revealing hip bones that would photograph well but worried Amelia. With the big premiere looming, Irene's husband was scarce and her meals scarcer. "Okay, maybe I'm a teensy bit mad."

"About what?" Amelia already knew, but she'd jumped on this shopping trip to break her news about Juniper. Sak's seemed safe ground. Not that she expected Irene to make a scene—she was too much of a class act—but no one lost their composure in a joint where the powder room had a lounging parlor.

"I've put *Sea Change* together with little help from him. You'd think that'd be enough to show my own husband I've got more to contribute than a gift-buying errand."

"Irene, it isn't any old gift he's asked you to pick out." Amelia gently steered Irene toward a sign—*OBJETS D'ART*. "It's his parting gift for his leading lady."

"Why not send Marcella or Polly?"

Amelia pulled a droll face. "Pol tells me the *Rebecca* and *Intermezzo* memos are coming as thick and fast as the *Wind* ones did."

They reached a shelf of Lalique vases. She picked up a tall, slender piece with a sliver of lavender running through it. She read the price tag and replaced it more gently.

"Tell me," Amelia said, "was Riverside everything you two hoped for?"

She propped a bony hip against the glass top, her eyes misting. "You should've heard the audience when Margaret Mitchell's name appeared. Lord have mercy, the roaring! The yelling! One fellow was so excited he leapt up like he was at the World Series."

"You cried, didn't you?"

"Buckets and buckets. David, too. All that work. All those sleepless nights. All the fights. The monumental risk." Irene's face flushed as she relived the memory. "When the title scrolled across the screen? Such cheering!"

"And at the end?"

"The applause was deafening. Felt like it went on for hours. I have to say, David has pulled it off magnificently. It's true to the book, it's gorgeous to watch, and Clark is everything the public expects of their Rhett Butler."

"And Vivien?"

Irene shook her head, blinking away tears of joy. "Wait till you see her. Honestly, Amelia, she's breathtaking." Irene thumped the glass countertop with her gloved hands. "Sheer perfection!"

This is it, Amelia told herself. The opening you were hoping for. She's talking about actresses being a perfect fit for their roles. "Speaking of, I need to—"

"Oh, and let me tell you about the manager of the Fox Theatre. We had about forty minutes to kill before his cue to go on stage and warn the audience that once the movie started, the doors would be locked."

"You locked everybody inside?"

"They were free to leave, but David wanted to prevent word getting out in case we were stampeded, so they weren't allowed back in. The others were giving the film a final check, so it was just Roy and me chatting in his office."

Amelia pinched her mouth into a smile. Whatever Irene was

about to tell her, couldn't it wait until she had coughed up her confession?

"I brought up Wyatt Greene. Well! You should have seen the way he turned up his nose."

"Not a fan?"

"He said Wyatt is the slyest snake and that he can't understand how his campaign has gotten as far as it has."

Okay, so maybe Amelia's confession could wait. "Did you bring up Cyrus Pattinson?"

"He said Pattinson and Greene are birds of a feather—and those birds are vultures. Roy is involved in the Riverside branch of Rotary. He said the Greene family have wormed their way into all sorts of organizations and branches of local government and committees and whatnot. He said you can't swing a dead coyote in Riverside without hitting a Greene."

Amelia drummed her fingers on the glass top. "What are the chances of Jerry Giesler getting Bernice's trial moved to Los Angeles?"

Irene scowled. "Bernice's crimes took place outside LA County."

"The further we can be from Greene and Pattinson's grasp, the better."

"If anyone can, it's Jerry."

"And while you were blubbering out there in Riverside, I learned an interesting fact about our Mr. Pattinson."

Her lips dipped at the edges in a grim pout. "I dread to ask." She listened as Amelia told her how Pattinson was the father of Matilda's baby and how he'd forced her to go see Dr. Yarborough. She cast her gaze farther down the counter. "Sometimes I wonder if girls like Eliza and Ursula have the right idea. Leave men out of the equation altogether." Irene chuckled for the first time today. "I knew you were smart, Amelia Hartley, but I'm bowled over by what you've uncovered."

Now that Amelia had impressed the hard-to-sway Irene Mayer Selznick, what better time to reveal her news? She was still drawing in a deep breath to steady her nerves when Irene's eyes flew open. "An elephant!" She hurried over to a display of animal figurines: snoozing cats, howling wolves, bunny rabbits sniffing at the air, dogs with bones. In the center stood an elephant carved in pale red sandstone, its trunk raised high over its head.

Amelia pictured the genteel, lady-like Vivien Leigh as more the Siamese-cat-in-lap type. "Are you sure?"

"A while ago, we were seated together at a dinner. She told me about her childhood. Did you know she grew up in Bangalore? I had to ask her where it was. India, as it turns out. It's where she made her first stage appearance. Little Bo Peep—you can picture it, can't you? She said elephants were as common a sight in Bangalore as turbans." Irene rotated the elephant in her palm to scrutinize every detail. "Your mind is elsewhere. What gives?"

Irene's mild delivery almost hid her deft sidestep.

"You're right." Amelia swallowed the metallic tang of dread that had been accumulating since breakfast. "I've had a change of heart."

Irene lowered the elephant back into place. "About what?"

"Playing Juniper."

"Oh?"

You two have a solid friendship, Polly had told Amelia this morning. *She'll understand.* "I've thought about this long and hard, and I—"

"No!" Irene flattened hand toward Amelia. "Don't you dare say what I think you're about to say."

"I don't want to do it—"

"Is this why you've been dragging your feet over signing the contract?"

"I'm not the right—"

"David hasn't been too distracted whittling down *Wind*'s runtime to ask for your signed contract. 'Don't worry about it,' I keep telling him. 'You've got bigger fish to fry right now.' It never occurred to me that you'd change your mind."

"But you needn't worry, I've found a—"

"Which is it? You don't want to do it or you're not right for it? Those are two different assertions. I, for one, believe you *are* right.

You cannot know how hard I campaigned to bring David around to casting you!"

"He didn't want me?"

"At first, he was thrilled with the idea and very satisfied with your screen test. We both agreed that none of those other girls even came close. Not one of them was good enough to screen test. But then he changed his mind. Because. That's. What. He. Does. One. Thousand. Times. A. Day." Irene's voice grew steadily louder as she worked herself into a temper. Heads were turning. Whispers behind hands. "Every decision gets *un*decided. Then *re*decided, but in a *different* direction. He tells everybody he is unequivocally sure—until he's not."

This shrill outburst wasn't so much about Amelia wanting to withdraw from *Sea Change*, she knew, but a final frustration that had cleaved Irene in two. "Perhaps this isn't the best place to—"

"Everything from how to burn down Atlanta to whether to have pork chops for dinner. I cannot count on anything or anyone, and I've had it up to *here*."

Her own screech made her flinch. She tsked and headed for the Wilshire Boulevard exit.

She was already halfway down the block before Amelia caught up with her. "Stop!"

Irene faced her, eyes blazing and her mouth crushed into a thin line. "Casting a lead is an involved and exhaustive process. You saw how long it took David to find his Scarlett. But once Rita fell by the wayside, we bypassed all of that."

"I thought it was because Mr. Selznick was keen to streamline this one to get it into the theaters for cash flow."

"Well, yes, that's true. But that's why we were so happy to be able to bypass it when your screen test turned out so well. We were thrilled. Everything fell into place. And now you've *changed your mind*?"

"People do change their minds," Amelia pushed back.

"Don't I know it." Irene threw her head back. "I'm married to the king of mind-changing. Just once I'd like to be able to stick with a decision. Talk about wishful thinking. Myron's as bad as his brother."

"I guess that's part of the privilege of being a male. When you're in charge, you get to call the shots."

Irene coiled for a sharp reply, then unspooled as she realized Amelia was right. "I can't argue with that."

"I was hoping we wouldn't have to argue at all."

When the light switched to green, Amelia steered Irene across Wilshire with the mob of pedestrians. She waited until they swung onto Rodeo Drive. "Truthfully, was I the best girl for the job?"

Irene nodded. "I should've let you see your screen test. You were very, *very* good. Not to mention the idea of all of us making this picture together."

"All right, but you must keep your producer hat on, which means you have to cast the best candidate for the job."

"Weeks out from filming, we have no leading lady."

"Yes, you do. Or might." Amelia pulled from her pocketbook the best of Tate's photos. "This girl would be perfect."

They ducked into the doorway of a knitting store to give Irene a chance to study them. "Isn't she the one who came up to Rose Cohn that day at the Beverly Hills Hotel?"

"Uh-huh."

"She seemed awfully unhinged that day."

"Harry Cohn wanted to pay her to have his kid. Della mustered a lot of courage to confront Rose. I've gotten to know her since then."

"What's she like?"

Amelia weighed her next words carefully. Her future teetered on whether she could make Irene see Della as Juniper. "Not the least bit unhinged. In fact, I'd say she's the most hinged girl I've met in a good, long while."

"Not being a nut case isn't the heartiest recommendation I've ever heard."

"You've got to admit, though, she does look the part." Cutting off Irene's brewing rebuff, she added, "Give her a screen test."

"I'm not sure David will want to authorize the cost when he's already found his leading lady."

"Tell your husband whatever you like about my bowing out, but remind him he could recast with the girl Harry Cohn tried to breed like a prize mare. Wouldn't that yank Cohn's tail?"

Irene laughed. "It absolutely would."

"Enough for me to avoid facing your husband's wrath?"

Irene didn't need to reply. The mischievous glow in her eyes told Amelia, "Ah, now *that* I can't promise."

39

The pharmacy clock read eleven-twenty. Amelia mopped up after two sailors on shore leave—their mess generous, their tip not so much. Forty minutes till freedom, and still no sign of Lois and Bernice. Had Giesler declined the case? What could be harder than saving Busby Berkeley from the gas chamber? Selznick had worked his magic, landing them a nine a.m. appointment. Maybe those sorts of meetings ran long?

Amelia still hadn't heard what Selznick's reaction had been to Amelia's decision not to sign the contract and her idea of casting Della in her place. She tried to convince herself that no news meant good news, but she believed it less with every passing hour.

She was starting to wonder if maybe they wouldn't show when Lois and a companion sporting a pale blue fascinator pinned to an unconvincing coal-black wig meandered through Schwab's front door. Amelia waved them toward empty stools in her section. Once handbags were tucked away, gloves peeled off, and sunglasses lifted, Lois said, "My goodness, but that man is a force of nature! Right, Bern?"

"When we brought up the possibility of getting my trial moved to LA, he tapped his nose and said, 'Leave it to me, ladies.'"

"So then we asked him about a continuance to stall the trial until after the election."

"Did he tap his nose again?"

"Nah. 'One or the other,' he said, 'not both.' So we went with what Mr. Giesler called 'a change of venue.' That way, the jury won't be made up of any Riverside residents connected to those horrible Greenes. Speaking of." Lois tilted her head toward Matilda, who was waving a drinking straw over a man in overalls as though it were a magic wand.

"I don't know what to think about her anymore," Amelia confessed. "She detests her family enough that she moved to a different county."

"Doesn't excuse trying to steal Juniper out from under you, though, does it?"

"It just makes her no different from all the other do-anything-to-get-aheads." That was another reason to not sign Selznick's contract. The five-hundred-a-week paycheck would've been handy —well, more than handy—but she had decided Benji had a good point about the slippery slope. If only he was around to tell him of her realization.

"In that case," Lois said, "steer clear. Those sorts of girls can't help themselves. Now, how about some tea?"

When Amelia returned with their pot, she heard how Giesler had grilled Bernice about the Sapphire Moon. Did anyone coerce her to work there? Blackmail her? Threaten to make life difficult for her in any way? No, Bernice had told him, nothing like that. However, his enthusiasm had escalated when Lois brought up Hartman's theory about the land grab around the Palm Springs airstrip.

"'But for now,'" Lois said, quoting Giesler, "'try to relax. Things are well in hand.' Oh sure. We'll go get a Swedish massage and everything'll be both hunky *and* dory."

By the time they'd had finished their tea, Amelia had cleaned up after her remaining customers and settled accounts with Ida. Outside, the last of the summer heat had relinquished its hold. "Shall we take a stroll?"

"Parisian Florist always has such lovely blooming crocuses this time of year."

It stood ten blocks west, on the corner of Sierra Bonita Avenue —ideal strolling distance.

"What's the latest from Mr. Selznick about you turning down Juniper?" Lois asked.

"Still in the dark. The wait is killing me."

"Aren't you and his wife chums?" Bernice asked.

Their contretemps at Sak's had ended on a good note, so Amelia had imagined Irene would tell her husband, he'd wave her away with his usual "Whatever you think best, dear," and Thelma would summon Della for her test. She should have known it wouldn't be that easy. But the cold shoulder wasn't Irene's style. Did she have horrible news she dreaded to reveal? Or was no news good news, and Amelia ought to leave well enough alone?

"Uh-oh," Lois said to Bernice in a not-so-subtle aside, "we seem to have planted spring bulbs of doubt."

"Mr. Selznick is so busy with *Wind* and *Intermezzo* and *Rebecca*," Amelia said. "Catching him at the right time can be tricky."

But Bernice wasn't buying it. "If Mrs. Selznick can't carve out five minutes with her own husband, she's got bigger problems."

As they crossed Stanley Avenue, Amelia caught sight of the neon blade sign flashing *VISTA DINER* in emerald green. She'd hadn't been there before, but Luddie often stopped there for early dinner ahead of a *Dick Tracy* broadcast.

"They have public phones at the Vista. Why don't you check out the crocus situation and I'll catch up with you there. If I disappear, assume Mister David O. Selznick is out for my hide and I've gone on the lam."

* * *

The diner smelled of the same sizzling burgers and boiled ham as Schwab's. Only one of the three waitresses appeared to be busy, though.

The phone booth door closed behind Amelia with a squeak.

She dropped a nickel into the slot and dialed. Had Irene given *no* thought to the tenterhooks—

"This is Irene Selznick." Her voice came through barely above a whisper, each syllable measured as if she were testing thin ice.

"Amelia here. You okay?"

"No," Irene replied flatly. "I feel terrible."

"Have I dragged you out of a sick bed?"

"No. More like—it's because—*oh hell!*"

A surge of disappointment washed through Amelia. "Out with it already."

"It was awful!" A sob had snuck into Irene's voice. "He came home on time for once. Hallelujah, I thought. I waited till he was halfway through his second Manhattan before I brought up your change of heart."

"Didn't take it calmly?"

"Positively livid. Stomped around like a grizzly bear with his paw in a wasp nest. He kept repeating how a contract is a contract—"

"Even though I hadn't signed it?"

"And if we can't trust that selfish, ungrateful, little—well, I won't say the word he used."

He'd insulted her with a cuss so awful Irene couldn't bring herself to say it out loud? How was she supposed to *not* take it personally? "What did you do?"

"I changed tack and started talking about Della."

"Did he listen?"

"No."

Amelia's shoulders folded inward. Mr. Selznick had been nothing but kind and gentlemanly toward her. She hated the thought of disappointing him so badly. And then there was Polly to consider. Would he look at her as being guilty by association? Would he take his frustrations out on her? Or even—God forbid—fire her?! "Thanks for trying." Maybe she should take the role after all. At least Kendrick was good-looking, so acting opposite him wouldn't be like working in the salt mines.

"Not so fast. Later—much later—I left the best of Tate's photos in his home office."

Amelia laughed. "You sure know what makes him tick, don't you?"

"He likes to think he's complex and inscrutable and one chess move ahead of everyone else."

"Tell me truthfully: Am I out of the woods?"

"You can't even see the edge of the woods from where you're standing. He's still on the warpath, tomahawks in both hands."

"What can I do to convince him?"

"Nothing. We plant seeds, we water them, and we let him come around."

"How long is that likely to take?"

A long exhale rattled over the line. "Even I can't answer that one."

Her response wasn't the comforting reassurance Amelia needed, but a businessman in a battered felt pork pie hat stood outside the booth, tapping his wristwatch.

Amelia thanked Irene and replaced the receiver. She longed to linger in the booth's quiet, but the pork pie hat was pressing his lips together. She slid past him. "All yours." How naïve to think David Selznick wouldn't care if she dropped out of his picture. This was show business. Emphasis on *business*. She knew exactly what he'd say. "Time is money, and thanks for wasting both precious commodities, young lady."

Footsteps pounded the sidewalk as she emerged onto Sunset. A tall, slim man raced past, and her breath caught—Luddie? Strange to see him bolt down the boulevard like Hedda Hopper with a scoop and a deadline. He didn't answer when she called, and she almost doubted herself until he veered south onto Vista Street. That profile was unmistakable.

Even if today was *Dick Tracy* broadcast day, the show hit the airwaves at five in the afternoon and it wasn't one o'clock yet.

That wasn't the sprint of a guy in a hurry, she decided. He was in a panic.

Her mom and Bernice would survive without her.

By the time she rounded the corner, he had reached Plummer Park, but not quite. He made a hard right a couple of houses north of Fountain. She followed until she was standing at the worn cobblestone driveway leading to a Victorian with a wraparound porch and cone-shaped turret. Paint flakes of indeterminate color clung to the decaying balustrade. A rocking chair creaked in the wind, as if pushed by long-dead residents.

This was where Luddie lived? In a shabby, dilapidated ruin? What a far cry from what she and Polly had imagined: a tasteful bachelor apartment in a swanky part of town where life was a constant round of chic cocktail parties with bons mots flying across the room like champagne corks.

It did, however, explain why Luddie never talked about his past, nor had invited the girls to his place.

She had one foot on the porch's bottom step when she heard him yell, "DAMMIT!"

She followed his voice to a carriage house that flanked the mansion, a relic of the days when Angelenos lodged their horses and buggies. Weather had worn away the paint, sheets of cardboard covered broken windows, and the shingles above the front door hung so precariously that Amelia half-expected the next storm might claim them.

"DAMMITALLTOHELL!"

The door to Luddie's cramped quarters stood open. Amelia hesitated at the threshold, peering into the gloom. It took her a moment to realize he was standing ten feet in front of her.

"Luddie?" She had said his name in the softest whisper, but startled him anyway. "I was outside the Vista Diner when you raced past me." She gambled a half-step inside. "It's just that—gee, Luddie, I thought you were in trouble."

He stared at her, his eyes twin moons, mouth open but mute, eyebrows curled upward in the effort to hold himself together.

"I feel as though my being here is making it worse. If you need an ear to bend, you know where to find us." She was back in the door frame now. "Me and Polly, I mean. We—we're—I'm sorry, Lud. I'll leave you be."

She was almost at the sidewalk when he called her name.

The Luddie who beckoned her from the door had vanquished his distraught, tongue-tied twin. "Coffee?"

Amelia ached for a stronger concoction to scrape away the rough edges of her morning, but Luddie's offer was a pretext for keeping his hands occupied and his embarrassment deflected. As he disappeared into the kitchen, gloom closed in from all sides. The bookshelf stood stuffed with volumes, a stark contrast to walls stripped of everything but peeling wallpaper. No artwork to brighten the space. No movie posters. Not even a single framed photograph. An empty ceramic vase perched on the mantel, its clean surface catching what little light filtered through the heavy drapes. A seaman's chest serving as a coffee table wore its scratches and dents like battle scars, though someone—Luddie, she supposed—had lovingly polished its brass hinges until they winked in the gloom. She saw it now—a gentleman's poverty was tidier than most.

She had a hundred questions, but let him speak first.

"You caught me in the middle of a pickle."

"A tricky pickle?" she asked. "Or merely a fickle pickle?"

The joke worked. He smiled. Not enough to split his face in half, but a good start.

"*The Women* premiered a couple of weeks ago."

"I assume you escorted someone to Grauman's?"

"Dolores del Río."

"Isn't she married to some big MGM mucky-muck?"

"Cedric Gibbons, yes, but Lubitsch was having enormous problems with *The Shop Around the Corner*."

"He worked late and Dolores was furious?"

"Furious enough to call Lubitsch's wife to bitch and moan, assuming Vivian wasn't able to go either. But she had already scrounged up someone." He brought two cups of coffee to the sofa. Frayed at the edges and stippled with unidentifiable stains, it was the lumpiest sofa Amelia had ever parked her behind on.

"Dolores was capital-M miffed, and happy that I was free at short notice. But she was still in a snit when I collected her in Santa

Monica, so I promised her I'd see that we enjoyed a memorable evening."

Luddie had served no sugar, no cream; Amelia sipped at his strong, tar-black coffee. "And you did?"

"Yes. And it was memorable, but not in the way I had in mind."

"Uh-oh! I smell a tricky pickle coming on."

Luddie flared his blue eyes. "She was decked out to the nines, including a dazzling necklace. Rubies, emeralds, diamonds. The works."

"*The Women* premiere was a big deal, I'll bet."

"Oh, yeah. MGM pulled out *all* the stops. We get inside the foyer and Dolores is greeting everyone, blowing kisses, telling them how magnificent they look. Then she slips off the necklace and presses it into my hand."

Amelia couldn't drink coffee this strong without sugar or cream to cushion the bitterness. She deposited her cup onto the seaman's chest. "Why'd she do that?"

"Lupe Vélez had swept in, fresh from divorcing Johnny Weissmuller. Dolores said to me, 'We have a love-hate relationship—mostly hate. It will be worse if I don't say hello, because Lupe will make a scene, and brother, does she know how.' So now I'm stuck with this necklace—it had to be worth five grand—smack dab in the center of this craziness. Stars everywhere. Photographers everywhere. Fans everywhere. Newsreels everywhere. It was almost overwhelming."

Outside of Irene Selznick, Luddie was the most implacable person Amelia knew, so if *he* found it overwhelming . . . Then again, she was going to have to reexamine every assumption she'd ever made about her most refined friend. She breathed a lungful of stale air. Did he never open his windows? She caught a whiff of lemon-scented Old Dutch and the heady aroma of ammonia. As drab as this place was, he certainly kept it spit-spot. "What did you do?"

"I shoved the damned thing into the inside breast pocket of my tux. After the movie finished—which really is marvelous—everybody's all whipped up into a frenzy. They're all kissing and hugging everyone they didn't kiss and hug before the show. And then Dolores wanted to congratulate Cukor, so I told her I'd wait right where I was. So I waited. And I waited. And I kept on waiting until I was the last person there."

"You lost Dolores del Río?"

"Never saw her again."

"But you still had the necklace?"

"Yep."

"What did you do?"

"What could I do? I brought it home with me and slept with it under my pillow. The next day I went to their house, but nobody was there. I couldn't leave it on the doorstep like I was a Penney's delivery man, so I called again—nothing. I phoned Gibbons at the studio—nothing. Meanwhile, I hid it away for safekeeping."

He crossed to a bookcase, its volumes arranged by spine color, and selected a volume from the blue shelf and returned to the sofa. "I put it in this."

Amelia opened *The Amateur Gentleman* by Jeffrey Farnol to find that he had cut a square hole in each page. "What a smart hiding place!"

He took back the book and ran a pensive finger down the edge. "If I were smart, I'd have left Dolores's necklace there. But there's been a spate of home robberies along this street, so I moved it somewhere I knew nobody would ever, ever, *ever* find it."

"Oh Luddie, no."

"Oh Luddie, yes." He hung his head. "Naturally, Dolores is demanding I bring back the necklace before Cedric asks where it is."

"But you can't find it."

"I've ransacked this place umpteen times! But no luck—until a few minutes ago. I was at the market next to Schwab's and suddenly I remembered."

"No wonder you were flying down the street."

"But it wasn't where I thought it was. So I'm stumped again." His brow wrinkled in despair. "How am I supposed to replace it when I live . . ." He wafted a limp hand at the room around them and fell into a morose silence. "I expect"—he kept his eyes downcast, his voice meek—"you're wondering about all this."

A wave of relief rippled through Amelia. For all his witty repartee, impeccable clothing, and expert dance-floor dips, he was human, after all. Yes, she had questions about all the whats, wheres, hows, and whys that had led him here. But that wasn't the pressing issue.

She took stock of their dismal surroundings. "You've searched all the obvious places, so now we get inventive." She tapped her foot on a scruffy rug whose pattern had long since faded. "I assume it's in a cleverer hidey-hole than your scooped-out book?"

"I'm so panicked. So frazzled that I—I—"

His voice had a brittle edge now; she took his hand in hers. "I've heard that rich women hide jewels in their shoes."

"I know several wives who do that."

"Your closet. Where is it?"

He laughed. "You mean the wardrobe so derelict that its hinges are being held together with toothpicks?"

Good grief, Luddie, we have to get you out of here.

She dismissed his protest that he'd remember hiding Dolores's necklace among his oxfords and brogues, telling him they had to start somewhere. The wardrobe stood in the corner, its once-ornate carvings now chipped and faded. When Luddie opened the door, the pungent aroma of mothballs wafted from the splintering wood.

He had arranged his shoes in three neat rows. "You take the left; I'll take the right."

They had inspected four pairs each before Luddie said, "This isn't what you pictured, is it?"

"I must admit . . ." She allowed the silence to finish itself.

"I have my priorities, and they don't—"

"You owe me no explanations."

He wriggled his fingers inside a pair of espadrilles before rocking back on his haunches. "I only spend money on what people see: clothes, shoes, watches, tiepins, grooming. Sounds shallow, doesn't it?"

"But important for your nighttime service."

He smiled weakly. "I bank as much of the rest as I can. Fact of the matter is, I—ah, I grew up in rather wretched circumstances. It was the Depression, so we weren't the only ones. But if you bent over and scraped the bottom of the barrel, that's where you would've found us."

Amelia and Polly already knew he'd grown up in a Hooverville of shanties and lean-tos that had once sprawled across an intersection south of downtown. He'd never spoken of it. Nor had they asked. But now, surveying this dreary place through his eyes, Amelia understood how after a childhood of packing-crate shelters and dirt floors, even peeling wallpaper and creaking floorboards spelled luxury.

"Must have been some tough, hardscrabble living."

"Mom and Pop had been quite successful in the twenties. But then the Depression hit the same time vaudeville died, and the wind went out of their sails and they gave up. It was bleak to watch, which is why I swore I'd never be in the same position. Not to be melodramatic, but I'd hang myself before I—" He shot to his feet. "I hung it." His eyes darted back and forth. "In a bag."

She stood up to join him. "Paper sack?"

"Velvet. Dark. Drawstring."

"A reticule?"

"Yes."

"Good idea. The velvet would protect the diamonds. Okay, so you put it in the reticule and—?"

Luddie's usual polish cracked like old stage makeup. "I can't believe I've forgotten. Of all things."

"I'd be scared witless with a responsibility like that." Amelia surveyed the shirts, jackets, and suits squashed into a space far too small to accommodate them. "From a hanger?"

A spark of hope flinted in his eyes. "Worth a shot." He wrapped his arm around a dozen suits and unhooked them from the wooden pole. "You check what's left. Every pocket. Some of those shirts will have French cuffs, so don't forget to check inside them."

They rifled through his clothes, each familiar piece perfumed with the Acqua di Parma aftershave she had come to associate with Luddie. Through all their nights on the town and impromptu parties, she'd never guessed these pristinely pressed suits came from such a derelict chifforobe.

She was about to tell Luddie that she had struck out when she spied a hessian bag. It might not have caught her notice had it not been gaping open and filled with—with—were they *rubbers*? Dozens and dozens and dozens. She pulled out a fistful and shoved them in his face. "Christ almighty, Casanova, how many of these do you need?"

He studied them for a moment, then grinned. "They're not for me. Not all of them, anyway."

She shook them at him. *Who are they for?*

"I have other customers. Men in need of . . . protection."

The jigsaw pieces snapped into place. "You're the one," she said, breathless from the shock. "Benji has never had a problem getting his hands on these things."

He lifted a nonchalant shoulder. "I'm pals with someone at the factory. It's all you need to know." They sat down side by side on the bed. It wasn't as lumpy as the sofa, but only slightly less so. He returned them to the bag and eyed her coolly. "It's how I make extra scratch on the side. When you grow up miserably poor like I did, you'll do whatever it takes to make sure you don't ever end up there again."

How long had he been hauling around this burden? His debonair worldliness made his age impossible to pin down—somewhere between twenty and forty-five, though surely closer to her and Polly's vintage. Holding shame so close to his chest had trained Luddie well: Polish your manners, read widely, stay alert, be observant, and sharpen your wit enough so that nobody asks uncomfortable questions. Even this shabby house couldn't quite dim his shine.

He switched on a lamp nestled below the window, revealing its frayed cord twisted against the baseboard. Amelia noticed a picture postcard of a wide city street, an arch stretching from one side to the other with a sign. *RENO—The Biggest Little City in the*

World was a catchy slogan for a town whose residents were mostly there to qualify for a quickie divorce.

"From Gil," he said.

"Polly's Gil? You've kept in touch?"

He studied the card impassively. "We had more in common than I ever would have guessed."

Gil and Luddie had been Hooverville neighbors, but Amelia wasn't sure she should admit to knowing that. "How's he doing?"

"Works on a dude ranch, mending fences, tending to the horses —saddle tramp stuff. The only part he doesn't like is when he's out in the desert where the temperatures nosedive after the sun goes down. He says it's a giant icebox—" He snapped his fingers. "IDIOT!"

He raced to the other side of the room where an antiquated icebox, its wooden casing worn with neglect, stood beside a tiny basin. He reached around the back. "Dammit! I can't get to it." He pointed to a drawer next to the basin. "Crochet hook."

Amelia ransacked the tangle of corks, buttons, thumb tacks, a hammer, and paper clips. "You crochet?" she asked, handing over the hook.

He lowered it behind the icebox. "I use it as a boot hook, so no wise cracks."

"If I give you the wool, will you crochet me a new winter blanket?"

"Remember back five seconds ago when I said 'no wise-cracks'?" He flattened the side of his face to the peeling wallpaper. "This hiding place is so good even I can't reach it."

Amelia surveyed the drawer's contents spread across the narrow counter. How did Luddie cook in such quarters? As she scooped up a ball of rubber bands, a Hollywood National Bank passbook fell open. She wasn't one to pry, but the balance drew her gaze.

$1,802.37

Amelia held her breath.

Luddie had a small fortune, and yet he was living in *this* horrible place?

She ran her eyes down the column of growing totals. The sole withdrawal stood out.

June 2nd, 1939 – $2,500

Two thousand five hundred was the same amount he'd coaxed from his benefactress.

June second was the day before Amelia had taken her family on that studio tour.

"GOT IT!" Luddie held a reticule of aubergine velvet with a shiny black satin drawstring. "What a god-almighty relief. I might never have thought of it if you hadn't got me talking about Gil's freezing desert—" He caught sight of Amelia's astonishment before she'd had the chance to camouflage it.

"I wasn't snooping, honest. It was lying there, open, and I happened to . . ."

He joined her at the drawer. "If somebody had to see it, I'm glad it was you."

She drew an imaginary line under the withdrawal. "You're the benefactress."

He shoved the junk back into the drawer. "Where else was Polly going to get that kind of money?"

"But it was more than half your savings."

"She'll square the debt."

"Of course she will, but it's so much."

He bit down on his lower lip for a moment, then looked her straight in the eye. "Truth is, I've never had friends like you and Polly. The more I learned to cultivate my Mr. Man About Town image, the more I've needed to keep people at arm's length—from my past, from my family, from this place. I'm someone to make an entrance with. To be seen on the dance floor with. Make a husband jealous. Keep the dinner conversation light and witty. But you two. You and Polly . . ."

"What about us?"

"You don't need or want anything from me."

"Just your friendship."

"YES!" The word popped out of him, hot and raw. "And that means the world. More than I can say."

"So you said it with the benefactress loan."

He needed a moment to take in her observation. "And I'd do it again."

"Oh, Lud," Amelia said softly. "Right back at you."

They stared into each other's glistening eyes until Luddie broke the spell. "Anyway, these escort dates of mine, they pay well. *Very* well. And with the loan to Polly, I've needed to refill the coffers, so I've accepted every date I could find."

"Is that why we haven't seen much of you lately?"

"On top of *Dick Tracy*, I have to admit, painting the town red is exhausting."

"But Luddie, if you've got all this money, why do you live . . ." She traced an ancient water stain creeping down the wall.

"When you grow up not knowing if you'll have a roof over your head tonight, you'll do anything to ensure you never have to feel that fear again."

"You're saving to buy your own place, aren't you?"

"I am."

She pulled him into a hug and squeezed him as tight as she could.

"Promise you won't tell Polly about the loan," he whispered into her ear.

"That's a lot to ask."

He thrust her to arm's length, his hands clamped to her shoulders. "You're not leaving here until you give me your word."

"I could do that, or"—she stroked the velvet bag—"assuming Cedric Gibbons and Dolores del Río have that necklace insured—"

"Don't think it hasn't occurred to me." He laughed as he leapt up, snatching the bag. "I've got to get this back to Dolores, pronto. You want me to drop you off at Schwab's on the way past?"

As they headed west along Sunset, she filled him in on how Jerry Giesler had moved Bernice's trial out of Riverside. Meanwhile, Amelia and Irene had made peace over her exiting from *Sea Change*, but even though Selznick was less than thrilled, they hoped he wasn't opposed to a potential replacement.

"Assuming this Della girl can act," Luddie said.

"Right."

"And the best way to do that is through a screen test."

"But they're expensive."

Amelia watched Luddie's expression shift like a spotlight finding its mark. "What if you got Zara and Sibyl and Dorothy to do one on the sly?"

"What if I could?"

"I recently escorted Vivian Lubitsch to Baroness d'Erlinger's birthday party at Café Gala because Ernst was busy with reshoots on *Ninotchka*."

Only Luddie could make a statement like that and not resort to exaggeration. "Are the *Ninotchka* sets still standing?"

"They are. At MGM. Where Irene Selznick has significant pull."

"She's also good friends with the Lubitsches."

"Good enough to persuade him to fold the cost of Della's screen test into the *Ninotchka* company books?"

"Why, Mister Sinclair!" Amelia said, stifling a giggle, "who knew you were so wily?"

"Says the girl who wanted me to fence Dolores del Río's necklace."

"I was kidding. Sort of."

"So was I. Sort of." Luddie pulled to the curb outside Greenblatt's Deli. "Get the hell out before Cedric Gibbons calls the cops."

"You're the best." She kissed his cheek and slipped from his Pontiac onto the Sunset sidewalk, aware of a feather-light buoyancy lifting her chest. The feeling slowly dawned on her:

Hope.

40

Amelia sidled up to Irene as Sibyl and Zara made last-minute adjustments with the camera and boom mic. "You managed to pull this off!"

Irene kept her eyes on the ten pages of script Virginia had sent over. "My two young boys will be out of college by the time I've paid off my debt to the Lubitsches in dinner parties and bridge tournaments."

Amelia cringed inside. She had given little consideration to what this clandestine screen test might cost her. "Bad as all that?"

Irene indulged in a sly smile. "Honestly? They're marvelous company, so I would've invited them anyway."

A week ago, over Brown Derby coffee and pie, she had presented Luddie's idea for Della's test on the *Ninotchka* set. She should have known Irene would insist on meeting Della first. Better planning would have put Della at the counter, allowing Amelia to say, "She's right behind you."

"Irene Selznick's one savvy dame," Amelia had warned Della on the day of the meeting. "Be yourself—but the best version. She spots phonies at a hundred paces." At the same time, she had labored to convince Irene of Della's singular appeal. "Trust me on this," she'd pleaded. "You'll see what I mean soon as you meet her." Any hesitations Amelia might have harbored had evaporated the moment Della approached their table. In her dark green suit and carrying a burgundy patent leather bag, Della had struck the perfect note: charming and poised, relatable and earthy, but without a hint of the desperate starlet.

Amelia nodded at the pages in Irene's hands. "Della's scene?"

"If she can pull it off in front of the camera the way I see it in my head, I won't need to employ my powers of persuasion on David. But," she added with a sigh in her voice, "a soothing word or two to Dorothy might be time well spent."

Oh dear. What now? "Why is that?"

"This is not how screen tests are supposed to work."

"Her words or yours?"

"Could be mine; in this case, hers."

Zara had disappeared up a ladder to the rafters when Amelia had walked onto the set of a European café with wooden booths separated by foot-high curtains suspended from brass rods. Dorothy sat in a director's chair as she jotted down some notes.

Amelia sidled up beside her. "Ready to roll cameras?"

"I guess."

Her terse response landed like cold water on Amelia's scrappy let's-do-this enthusiasm. "What do you need?"

Dorothy slapped the clipboard onto her lap. "This is all so unprofessional. Irene convincing Mr. Lubitsch to fold the cost of this test into his budget. Sneaking onto a set to film—"

"It's not sneaking if we have Lubitsch's permission."

"It's ten o'clock at night, and we're in the middle of a deserted studio. I feel as though it's Prohibition and I'm rumrunning whiskey through Mexico like"—she waved a skeptical finger toward Polly, who was chatting with Luddie in one of the booths—"her father."

The empty MGM lot meant privacy—no chance of news about Della's screen test prematurely reaching Mr. Selznick. "It's not how I'd prefer to do this either, but no interruptions means getting this done in one or two takes—"

"If Miss Sloane can't nail this scene in less than three takes, she's not capable of playing the lead. Our budget is thin as cellophane. We can afford to do two takes per shot. If we need a third, the next setup must be captured in *one*. We need an actress who can deliver every single time."

"We wouldn't be testing Della if I didn't believe she had it in her."

What a shameless, bare-faced lie. Amelia had no idea if Della had what was required of her tonight. She had starred in more than a dozen stage plays, though, and theater performers lived without second takes, so perhaps it wasn't such a lie after all.

Dorothy fixed her with an exasperated frown. "Being the only woman director at my level means working twice as hard as the men. Can you imagine Capra putting up with a ruse like this? Or Ford? Wyler? DeMille? But yet here *I* am."

Amelia bit back her response: You haven't worked in two years. If this is your fresh start, then you stand here, ten p.m., after everyone's gone home, and do what those men can't, which is direct a woman through a woman's eyes. "I'll do everything in my power to ensure we're in and out as smoothly as humanly possible."

After Dorothy had acknowledged her with a curt nod, she hurried over to Polly and Luddie.

"You look like you copped an earful," Luddie said.

Amelia hadn't stopped thinking about the truth behind his polished facade—that shabby room, his disintegrating family—and had drawn strength from his example. When *Sea Change*'s obstacles loomed largest, she pictured him, rising each morning, somehow finding the will to press on.

Later that evening, she had spilled everything to Polly. Not the business about the mystery benefactress, but every detail of Luddie's circumstances down to the careful way he arranged his shoes. Over cold cream and toothpaste, they had wondered how they'd missed it all. Luddie was, they concluded, too skilled in the art of illusion to let any signs slip through.

"Have you prepared Della for Mr. Moss's matinee-idol looks?" Polly asked.

Poor Kenny had been so disappointed that day at Schwab's when she'd steered him away from any expectation of an on-set romance. "My heart belongs to another," she'd told him, even if Benji didn't know it.

According to Noah, Benji had finally done it—quit Paramount to drive the unbroken stretch of West Coast from Mexico to Canada. In the past, she had always dismissed his occasional mentions of the trip as idle daydreams. And now he was living it while she lay awake, steeped in regrets.

"Della can take care of herself," Amelia said. "She fought off Harry Cohn, didn't she?"

"But," Polly interjected, "have you thought about what you're going to do if it turns out Della can't act with a camera glaring at her? What if she's not Mr. Selznick's idea of Juniper?"

At first, Della had been nothing more than Amelia's hall pass out of the movie. But gradually, she had come to see Della as the ideal choice. Amelia stared at Polly, dismayed that the possibility Della might not be right for the part had never crossed her mind.

Hazel joined them. "Your leading lady needs a pep talk." Amelia had recruited her after Polly had reassured her that Hazel had tons of experience in professional makeup. Film differed vastly from burlesque, but Polly had insisted she was a whiz.

"Nerves?" Amelia asked.

"She's getting awful agitated. I've seen the same apprehension in new dancers at the Follies. You might want to stick your head in."

She scooted over to the temporary dressing room Lubitsch had built for Garbo. "You decent?"

Della had dressed in her own outfit: a tailored two-piece suit in cornflower blue with stripes along the cuffs and white palm trees embroidered on the lapels. She had tied her hair away from her face with a yellow grosgrain ribbon.

"Dorothy, Zara, and Sibyl are nearly ready," Amelia said, feigning light-hearted cheerfulness. "Everything okay?" Every line of Della's face screamed startled gazelle, telling her nothing was okay. Amelia stepped inside. "Isn't this what you've wanted all along?"

"I want it so damn much that I won't be able to live with myself if I screw it up. What if this is the one, single, and only chance I get?"

"Oh, sweetie, I doubt that very much."

Della's eyes had grown glassy. "I'm twenty-seven." Amelia fought to hide her surprise. She'd figured the girl was a year or two older than her own twenty-one years. "In this game, twenty-seven is unspeakably long in the tooth. All the more reason to be scared to death I'm going to—"

"HUSH!" Amelia ordered. "That kind of talk does no one no good no how."

"What about you? Weren't you nervous about your screen test?"

Looking back, what struck Amelia most about that day was her composure and how she'd faced the camera with nary a flutter. But, she wondered now, had she been so blasé because, deep down, she didn't want it as much as she thought she did?

"Here's what nobody mentions," she told Della. "The jitters only last a minute. Then you're in the swing. After that, it's goodbye Nervous Nellie." Della's eyes brightened. "Now, listen, I don't want to rush you, but we are racing the clock here."

Della assured her she only needed to give her makeup a final touch-up, and Amelia took that as her cue to skedaddle. Outside, she found Sibyl talking with Polly, Hazel, and Luddie. "One of the security fellows dropped by to let us know *At the Circus* is doing reshoots."

A Marx Brothers invasion was the last straw. "Time to roll," Amelia said.

Irene joined them, Virginia's pages in hand. "Is it true about those Marx lunatics?" She exhaled sharply. "David's already looking for reasons to ax *Sea Change*. We need to present him with the problem and solution together, or we're finished." She shook the script in frustration. "I'll be crushed if he pulls the plug."

"I suspect a part of you doesn't want any insider advantage."

Luddie paused to let his words have their intended effect on Irene. "You'd prefer to stand on your own two feet."

Her dumbstruck expression told Amelia he'd hit home—and not just with Irene. Though this nutty scheme had once deserved the title "Middle Child Gets Noticed," that dream had dimmed when she'd discovered her real joy came from working beside Irene, building *Sea Change* from the ground up.

When Amelia tuned back into their conversation, Luddie was quoting from an article in his *Examiner* about how, on hearing that Bernice's trial had been moved to Los Angeles, Wyatt Greene had asked, "Where are the girls who worked at the Sapphire Moon? Let's get *them* to testify against the Notorious Palm Springs Madam!" Luddie scanned down the page. "This buffoon's calling Bernice 'a strict tyrant who kept most of the girls' earnings for herself.'"

"I can answer his question," Hazel said. "Three of those girls are now at my folks' burlesque theater."

What a constant surprise this unassuming girl was proving to be. "Since when?" Amelia asked.

"A few weeks. None of them has ever performed on stage, but" —she shrugged—"it's not brain surgery."

Zara approached Luddie. "We're ready for you."

Virginia had concocted a story about an actress who escapes to Catalina for her first film role, fleeing an overly ardent admirer. The plot thickens when she—a former champion swimmer—rescues a tourist who proves to be her admirer's banker, who holidays on the island each summer. Della had the lion's share of the dialogue and Luddie was happy to help.

He handed the *Examiner* to Amelia and headed toward the set. The paper's two-inch banner headline read:

MORALS CRUSADER RENEWS
VOW TO KEEP SWEEPING

Under it was a photo of Wyatt Greene standing on the steps of LA City Hall, his fist raised in a histrionic performance for photographers. A chain of hangers-on had lined up behind him like posts in a picket fence. "Look at these sycophants."

"You have to wonder where the Wyatt Greenes of this world find people like that," Irene muttered.

"Holy cow!" Hazel showered Amelia, Polly, and Irene with a volley of hard-edged sniggers. "*This* skunk?" She tapped a face two thirds along the line-up.

The guy had thick, dark hair with a streak of gray running through it. "He'd fit in with those mad scientists Universal keeps casting," Amelia said. "What about him?"

"He sits in a limo parked near the Follies stage door with his window down and his right arm dangling out of the car."

Polly gripped her forearm. "Are you sure?"

"Positive. He's missing most of his pinkie finger. I noticed it because he wears this big, chunky ring, gaudy as hell, on the finger with the missing knuckles. It's a wonder the ugly thing doesn't fall off."

"He sits there?" Amelia asked. "Watching the girls go in and out?"

"Now and then he tries to lure them with promises of champagne and swanky night spots."

"Does it work?"

"With new girls who don't know any better. They get their street smarts real fast. Stage-door Johnnies I can handle, but this stinker? Yeesh. Kuh-ree-pee!"

Amelia ran a finger along the caption under the photo in which the *Examiner* had identified each picket-fence sycophant. When she arrived at the tenth name, her lip curled with scorn.

"Who is it?" Polly asked.

"The last person you'd expect, yet it won't surprise you in the least."

* * *

The next morning at seven, Mr. Schwab announced a full roster of waitresses—his first in weeks. Right when Amelia had found her rhythm, she was banished back to retail.

He'd also asked if she knew when her last day might be. If Della had dazzled as brightly on film as she had on set, she'd be a cinch for the lead in *Sea Change*. How had she failed to think this through?

Mr. Schwab, however, had taken the news she might not be leaving his pharmacy with seen-it-all-before equanimity. "That's showbiz, kiddo." If they'd had more time, she'd have explained that losing the role was a good thing, but there were breakfasts to be served, sedative prescriptions to be filled, and bottles of Vitalis to be put on charge accounts.

She had crawled home from MGM at one in the morning. How naïve she'd been to suppose a screen test would take an hour. When was anything in the movies simple? If one test had wrung her dry like this, what would an entire picture do to her? Yet if Selznick greenlighted *Sea Change*, she longed to be allowed to see it through to opening night.

As she wiped her counters and dusted her displays, she sorted through the distractions she hadn't had time to process: Della's jitters, Dorothy's fury, Sapphire Moon's girls, Bernice's trial, Cyrus's stumpy finger. Goodness, what a night! At least the Marx brothers hadn't invaded them. Once they had finished Della's test, Amelia had done a final sweep of the set—mostly to ensure they'd left behind no telltale evidence. And it was a good thing she had, because Luddie had forgotten his copy of the *Examiner*.

She laid out it out on her counter now to reexamine Cyrus Pattinson's grainy photo. Or more specifically, a garish ring on his maimed hand. Somehow, he had figured out how to ensure it caught the sunlight.

"Say, you're looking a bit pooped." Amelia had been scrutinizing Pattinson's finger too closely to notice Matilda approach. "Did that boyfriend keep you up all night?"

"If only." In a way, Benji had contributed to her tossing and turning. Benji had featured among the snapshots churning in the chaotic montage projected onto the screen in her mind. She wished she could have told him how Della had exceeded Amelia's expectations. "Do you need anything?"

"I was wondering if you've read Hedda Hopper yet."

"I try to avoid her on an empty stomach."

"She makes a big song-and-dance over how clever she's been to follow the trail from Lewis Selznick to *Pretty Pennies* to Bernice Hoag to the Notorious Palm Springs Madam to *Sea Change*."

Amelia slumped against the counter. How could they have thought no one else would connect all the clues? Of all people, it had to be Hollywood's most venomous gossip with a network of spies that reached across Los Angeles like a poison ivy rash. "What else does she say?"

"She calls it a tainted project and sneers that Selznick can't possibly think of going ahead with it."

Sea Change had stood a chance before anyone associated the Notorious Palm Springs Madam with Isadora Gibbs. Even worse, Hedda's column would only steepen Jerry Giesler's path to acquittal.

Matilda blew a raspberry. "I see my brother made the front page again. He never passes up an opportunity to hog a spotlight with his fire-and-brimstone act."

Amelia tapped Pattinson's face. "What about the guy behind him?"

Matilda peered more closely at the paper until her face soured. "Now do you see why I changed into the new me? Honestly, those two are peas in a pod. All but joined at the hip."

"Does Wyatt like to loiter at the front of burlesque houses, too?"

Matilda laughed out loud but stopped before it had run its natural course. "Was that a serious question?"

Amelia told her about Pattinson's penchant for leaning out the window of his limo. "What did you ever see in a guy like that?"

"He had an air about him," Matilda said. "Nothing you'd nail down, though. Back then, I read it as sophistication, if perhaps battered by hard living. Fat lot I knew. Reality slapped me across the face a little too late." She shrugged. "This business with the burlesque house, though? Ten-to-one Wyatt rides shotgun."

"And yet," Amelia added, "when the world is watching, he takes the high moral ground and pretends to be all for stamping out vice."

"That's some sweet irony, isn't it? Meanwhile, Bernice Hoag gets slugged in the breadbasket with a list of charges a hundred feet long."

As Matilda returned to her side of the pharmacy, Amelia mulled over Bernice's charges. "Selling alcohol to a habitual drunkard" was laughable, as was "Maintaining a public nuisance." But the rest could mean years behind bars. Even Jerry Giesler's courtroom magic mightn't be enough to beat this rap. Unless—she folded the *Examiner* with deliberate care—the charges disappeared.

41

The Hollywood Boulevard streetcar swerved to the right as it began its run into downtown. Bernice turned from the window. "As excited as I was about Juniper, I'm even prouder of your decision to walk away."

Amelia ran a finger along the strap of her handbag. "Hundreds of girls come to Hollywood every week, and here am I saying, 'No thanks.'"

"And I've dreamed of climbing Mt. Kilimanjaro, but if Hemingway himself volunteered to be my guide, I'd say the same thing. There's no shame in being realistic."

When Bernice had suggested a downtown trip for relief from the confines of the Hartleys' home, Amelia had hesitated—until Bernice had assured her she was a master at blending in. Her brown suit hovered between sepia and nutmeg, paired with a plain beige blouse and modest accessories down to a handbag straight from Woolworth's five-and-dime. No one on the Red Car gave them a second glance—or even a first.

"As long as you don't think I'm a loon."

"I don't," Bernice said with sudden solemnity. "Nor do your parents."

"I hope all this'll be worth it. Irene called to say how her husband won't risk the controversy if you're convicted."

"I'd feel dreadful if that were to happen."

"More dreadful than being in the clink?"

Bernice managed a smile, one part sweet, one part doleful. Their eyes locked for a moment before Bernice looked away. "It's bad enough I'm Hedda Hopper's latest hobbyhorse. Scarcely a day goes by that she doesn't mention me."

"I suspect you're the unfortunate scapegoat for her not forgiving Mr. Selznick for casting a British actress. All you can do is ignore her."

Bernice patted Amelia's knee as Echo Park Lake slid past them. "In my line of work, a girl learns mighty quick when to notice and when to turn a blind eye."

What a life she'd lived—from Hollywood's dusty paddock days to silent film stardom, then cross-country adventures with a candy salesman before running a theater, then becoming a madam. It was exactly the kind of life Amelia craved—minus the madam part, of course. And preferably without a sensational trial.

"You're staring at me," Bernice whispered, then waited until had looked away. "Now, tell me, where did you say we're meeting my girls?"

* * *

Lavinia, Rosalie, and Eileen were Amelia's first real-life hookers—and nothing like the Production Code's heart-of-gold fictions. Up close, they were small-town beauties who'd learned to trade on their charms. Amelia hung back while the trio mobbed Bernice at Manning's in Grand Central Market, their squeals echoing off the tile until they settled into a booth. Lunch for Amelia and Bernice, breakfast for the night-shift workers.

When Bernice had asked them about Cyrus Pattinson and his limo parked in front of the theater, it was Lavinia, a peroxide blonde with a wide smile and thick eyebrows, who laughed first. "Fifi warned us about him, so natch we had to get an eyeful. But we didn't need to bother. We already knew about his shenanigans. He used to pull the same stunt in Palm Springs."

"He did?" Bernice asked. "I don't remember him."

"Never at the Moon." Eileen played the Hollywood gypsy to perfection—waist-length black hair, ghost-pale skin, firecracker-red lips. "We'd see him outside the Cactus Blossom Café."

Bernice explained to Amelia that the Cactus was on the edge of town where, on the understanding that they didn't make a ruckus or wear indecent clothing, the Moon girls were welcome.

"Very few places accepted us." Rosalie was a chain-smoking titian redhead. "So we always followed the rules."

Eileen grunted. "Which is more than we can say for The Tent."

"The Tent?" Amelia asked.

"We called Pattinson that because, more often than not, he'd tent his pants, if you catch my drift."

"Would he approach you girls?" Bernice asked.

"First chance he got," Lavinia said. "I've heard every line from here to Nome, but I gotta admit his patter had panache. Didn't work with me, but on a greener girl? Different story."

Amelia had never thought of Matilda as the naïve farm girl type, but maybe this was how Pattinson's snake-oil charm had worked its magic on her. Some fellows pulled that trigger when an attractive girl wandered into his crosshairs. Benji wasn't like that, she thought wistfully. He'd been genuine to the core.

"I considered the Cactus your safe haven," Bernice said.

"It was," Lavinia replied. "Mostly. Oh, and one other thing. I guess there's no harm in telling you now. Two of the girls asked Doc Yar to perform his—ahem—specialty."

"They did?" Bernice clasped the cameo at her throat, twisting it like a worry stone. "Which ones?"

"It's all water under the bridge now."

"Oh, but to think any of you were going through that and kept me in the dark. I would've driven them to Beaumont myself, and looked after them afterwards."

"We knew that," Rosalie reassured her, "but Doc Yar came

around so often he was like an uncle—the kind you'd tell things to instead of worrying your lovely den mother."

"The two who saw Doc Yar," Amelia said, "did you hear where they landed after the Moon closed?"

"The coppers only gave us ten minutes to throw our stuff together."

While Rosalie lit a fresh cigarette from the butt of her dying one, Amelia clocked the man a few tables over. He'd been watching them, scratching in his notebook between drags on a Camel. Had he spotted the Notorious Palm Springs Madam? Her mind raced through the possibilities: newspaper man, Wyatt stooge, Hedda's snoop, DA's plainclothes dick—each alternative worse than the last.

Rosalie continued: "Before we knew it, we were standing on the sidewalk. One by one, we drifted away, most of us to the Greyhound terminal. Us three took the bus to LA, but we were the only ones."

"Anything you can tell us about Pattinson that might help them stop him in his tracks?" Bernice asked. "My trial starts soon. Girls, your den mother is getting desperate."

They all said they did their best to avoid Pattinson, so they had nothing incriminating. They'd think on it, they promised, but now they needed to get to the theater for the first of the five daily shows. After cracking wise about horizontal work being easier, they got to their feet and disappeared into the Central Market crowds.

Bernice finished the dregs of her coffee. "I wish I'd known what was going on under my nose."

Amelia chanced a furtive peek at Mr. Notebook. Still there, still smoking, still taking notes. She stood up. "Let's stretch our legs in Pershing Square. It'll lift our spirits."

"Thanks, but I haven't been alone in weeks." Bernice's voice had grown heavy with resignation. "I want to wander around some." She got to her feet, and Amelia did likewise.

Amelia lightly squeezed her shoulder. "I understand." She watched Bernice melt anonymously into the crowd, then turned to see Notebook standing from his own table. She tailed him as he headed for Hill Street and through the pedestrian crossing. The orange-and-black Angels Flight funicular waited at the Hill Street station, shrieking its departure bell. For a nickel, it would climb the hundred-foot slope to Olive Street. When Notebook rushed aboard, Amelia bolted forward and squeezed through the closing doors. He took a window seat, leaving the adjacent space vacant.

She slid in beside him. "You want to tell me what you were doing back there?"

He started slightly, but recovered quickly. "Not particularly."

She smelled the Murray's Pomade in his hair. "You were having coffee, smoking Camels, staring at our table, and taking notes because you are . . ." He kept quiet. "This is where you fill in the blank." More silence. "Reporter? Legman? Attorney?" He slow-blinked like it was his poker-game giveaway. "Attorney, huh?"

The bell rang again to announce they had reached the top of the hill. The exit door slid open, and passengers began to disembark onto the Olive Street platform.

"No, Miss Hartley, I'm no lawyer."

Her grip tightened on her handbag. "You know who I am."

He lifted his fedora and fanned his face. "I work for Jerry Giesler. He likes to watch over his clients. Not because he doesn't trust her. More like ensuring she's okay." He slow-blinked at her again.

"And?" she asked.

"I'm also doing it for Benji."

"BENJI!" She startled a flock of pigeons picking through bread-crumbs. "Keep talking."

He dropped his hat back onto his head and stuck out his hand. "My name's Lloyd. Benji and I got to be pals at Paramount."

"You an art director, too?"

"Nah. Lowly reader in the writing department. We met on the studio baseball team."

Amelia tuned out whenever Benji talked about sports. "I see."

"But my job doesn't pay much, so I do this on the side. The last time I saw Benji, he was about to take off on his road trip. When I told him about what Mr. Giesler assigned me, he asked me to keep an extra sharp eye out for you." The pigeons were back at their feast, wings blurring through the tears Amelia had to fight back. "I've been tailing you and Miss Hoag for days."

"You must be very good. I never noticed."

"I guess I got too cocky." He fanned himself with his hat. The weather wasn't especially hot, but a film of sweat had broken out across his forehead. "I'm possibly speaking out of turn, but someone needs to tell you that Benji regrets breaking up with you."

Amelia's white-gloved fingers straightened her hat's already-perfect angle. "He does?"

"To quote him: 'I made such a horrifying fool of myself that I don't deserve to darken her door again.'"

Oh, Benji, Benji, Benji. You did make a fool of yourself, but you're laying it on pretty thick. Don't be so hard on yourself. "Do you know when he's due back in town?"

"I'm telling you all this because he's back."

"He is? Can I call him?"

"Wouldn't you prefer to go see him?"

What Amelia preferred was for Benji to have spent the whole of his West Coast pilgrimage reflecting on what an over-zealous, over-jealous dope he'd been and to have come running straight to her the moment he drove inside the Los Angeles city limits. But that was too much to hope for. "Would he be at home right now?"

"This time of day, more likely hanging out at the Cherokee Pool Hall near Paramount."

"Thank you, Lloyd. I appreciate it so very much."

She tried to leave, but he stopped her. His face had calcified. "We suspect the prosecution is going to bring up the Avalon fire on Catalina."

"What does it have to do with Bernice and the Moon?"

"She was the star of the movie shooting there when the fire broke out. They'll paint a convincing picture that she was responsible. It'll go toward showing that Bernice has led a life of reckless hedonism with no regard for responsibilities or consequences."

Amelia's heart constricted. A month after their visit, not one paper had printed Yates's confession. To the outside world, the Avalon blaze's origin remained a mystery.

"Spend ten minutes with Bernice Hoag, and anyone would see she's hardly led a life of wild abandon."

"*Pretty Pennies* was made by Lewis Selznick, who is the father of David Selznick, who is filming the remake. They're going to construct a narrative stating that not only was Bernice responsible, but the Selznicks were complicit."

"Lewis was in New York when they were shooting, and David was a kid."

"It's not about facts; it's about character assassination."

"What a low-down, dirty—"

"Ever heard of the Agua Caliente Land Management Corporation?" he asked.

It was the dummy company Dudley Hartman had discovered, the one that owned nearly all the land surrounding the Palm Springs airstrip. "I have, yes."

"Do you know what they own?"

Amelia crossed her arms. "More to the point, what *don't* they own?"

"Tell me."

"The land beneath the Sapphire Moon."

A slow dawn of realization broke across Lloyd's face. "It's a land grab."

"All of it worthless scrub until they secure the last piece."

Amelia felt restlessness creeping over her. How much longer would Benji be at that pool hall? But this was more important. "All this is related to Selznick, how?"

"We're still trying to figure out that part. Does the name Jullo ring any bells?"

"Who's that?"

"A company—Jullo Inc."

"Sorry, no."

"What about a guy named Lorraine? First name Julian."

"Nope again. Who's he?"

"Julian Lorraine is listed as Jullo's owner of record."

"Jullo could be a contraction of Julian and Lorraine," Amelia observed.

"However, there's no such company registered in the city directories of LA, San Francisco, San Diego, Sacramento, Riverside, San Berdoo, Long Beach, or Palm Springs."

"Another dummy corporation like Agua Caliente?"

Lloyd nodded. "Which makes me wonder if Harry Cohn over at Columbia has his finger in that pie, too."

Cohn? Again? Ugh. "What makes you think he's got anything to do with this?"

Lloyd permitted himself a slight smirk. "Because he plays regular poker with Wyatt Greene and Cyrus Pattinson."

"Why am I not surprised?"

"In addition to which—"

"Oh, God. There's more?"

"Cohn is pushing the Breen Office to stop Selznick from using the word 'damn' in *Gone with the Wind*'s final scene."

"Frankly, my dear, why would he care?"

"Because powerful men take delight in screwing with one another's professional lives, personal lives, marital lives, and sex lives, but think nothing of it when they sit down to play poker in nightclub back rooms."

"The longer I live," Amelia said, "the less I understand men."

"At any rate, Wyatt Greene and Cyrus Pattinson—and for all I know, Harry Cohn, too—they're pushing hard for Bernice's prosecution. Especially now that Mr. Giesler wrangled for the trial to be moved."

Amelia checked her watch. It was a quarter of three. If she had all day to while away, she'd have marched him back to Manning's. "How can I contact you?"

"Benji's got my number."

"Might the Cherokee Pool Hall be on Melrose at Cherokee?"

Lloyd smiled, sly as a cat burglar. "It might."

Amelia told him, "Thanks for the tip," but the Angels Flight bell drowned her out.

* * *

Amelia slowed her pace as she approached the pool hall, still debating what she would do—if anything—when she got there. *He* was the one who'd behaved badly. Who'd not given her the benefit of the doubt. Who'd stalked off in a huff. Who'd decided they were through. And so, shouldn't *he* be the one to make the first move? Especially seeing as how *he* already knew he'd made a horrifying fool of himself.

But he also felt he didn't deserve to darken her doorstep. What did he think she was going to do? Slam the door in his face?

Windows dominated the pool hall's front, rising from sidewalk to roofline. If Benji was in there, he'd be too busy sinking balls into pockets to notice his ex-girlfriend pressing her nose against the glass. And if she spotted him, then she'd decide what to do.

She took a last step and cupped her hands to the glass. A haze of tobacco smoke hung above twenty-one pool tables, arranged like train cars in three rows. Pool sharks lounged around each one; Amelia could hear the sharp crack of balls all the way outside on the street. But Benji wasn't bent over any of the tables, thwacking his cue against shiny balls. He was sitting in the waiting area, smoking a cigarette and staring straight at her, open-mouthed and bug-eyed.

No point pretending she hadn't been caught snooping—she might as well go in.

He vaulted to his feet, a mix of shock and delight filling his face. "What are—?"

"Little bird told me I might find you here."

His eyes lost their focus as he ran down the list of likely birds. "Noah, huh?"

"Lloyd, actually."

"Ah." A silence, tentative as a ceasefire, followed until he said, "Sure am glad to see you."

"How long have you been back in town?"

"A few days."

"Couldn't find a phone booth?"

He smiled sheepishly. *Guilty as charged.* "I should've done better by you."

She wanted to tell him *Yeah, you should've,* but his acknowledgment was all she needed. For now, at least. "How about we agree we both could've done better?"

He crushed his lips to hers. How had she forgotten how full and soft they were? And the heat of his hand as it stroked the back of her neck?

They might have continued kissing, but one of the sharks called out, "Hey, lust birds. The Larchmont Motor Inn is a five-minute walk. Three if you run."

Benji raised his eyebrows. *Wanna get a room?*

She did—*Oh, sweet Jesus in heaven, she did!*—but she wouldn't relax until she had cleared her mind of the niggling questions Lloyd had brought up, so she guided him to a pair of empty seats. Jullo Inc. and Julian Lorraine drew blanks from Benji, but when she mentioned Cohn's murky connection to Bernice's troubles, he latched onto the same thought that had nagged her during the taxi ride from downtown: Could Noah know the dirt?

He winced. "Dammit, dammit, dammit."

"What is it?" she asked. "What's wrong?"

"I'm desperate to race you off to the Larchmont Motor Inn, but you'd be distracted." He heaved the sigh of a thwarted man. "Did Polly tell you where she and Noah planned on going tonight?"

"She said they were going dancing, but was short on particulars."

"He's taking her to the Palomar Ballroom on Vermont."

Amelia had been there once, but a rumba with a greeting card salesman whose breath could wilt flowers had left her in no hurry to return. "Are you aware how big their dance floor is?"

"We won't leave until we find them."

"And if we don't?"

He grinned. "We'll head over to the motel."

Amelia tapped his chin twice. "Can't we do both?"

* * *

Two rows of round tables with dark bentwood chairs and white tablecloths paralleled the vast, crowded dance floor. The band's lead clarinetist played "Moonlight Serenade" as countless couples rippled across the floor. Amelia and Benji orbited the ballroom, dodging satin-draped ladies and waiters with silver cocktail trays. They were halfway through their second lap when Benji located Polly and Noah near the center of the floor.

"How's your foxtrot?" he asked.

"Better'n yours, I'll wager."

He extended a gallant hand. "We'll see about that."

They glided across the floor, merging into the whirl of dancing couples. The muscles along his shoulder twisted and flexed beneath Amelia's palm as he steered them closer. She had danced with him before, but only in a slow sway to a romantic ballad. "Say, you're not half-bad."

"If that's your best compliment, I'll take it."

She stared back, the clever response she had planned evaporating in the moment. The lush music and their sudden reunion had created a spell too delicate to shatter with ill-chosen words.

"Man the battle stations," he whispered in her ear. "Target approaching on the starboard side."

Noah stumbled over Polly's feet when he looked to see who had tapped him on the shoulder. "It's you two. Together."

Polly looked equally amazed. "Together in the same place by chance?" she asked. "Or *together* together?"

Amelia tilted her face toward Benji's, warmth spreading through her at the optimism filling his eyes. "The latter."

"What miracle has transpired while we've been out here battling for elbow space?"

The band chose that moment to segue into a peppy rendition of "Ain't She Sweet."

Amelia half-shouted over the energetic saxophone. "Could we go back to your table?"

They zigzagged off the dance floor and followed Polly and Noah to a table tucked away in a quiet corner, where they enlisted a nearby waiter for a round of drinks. While they waited, Amelia recounted the coffee date with Bernice's girls and her later conversation with Lloyd. Noah flinched with a lightning-fast blink when he heard her say "Jullo," but made no comment.

"I gather you've come across that name before?" she asked.

When he nodded curtly, Amelia caught a hint of reluctance. "It's a dummy corporation Mr. Cohn instructed me to set up earlier this year." Noah was a precise and circumspect speaker at the best of times, but now he was choosing his words with palpable care. "He's ordered me to do that plenty of times."

"So this wasn't unusual?"

"Hardly. But then he told me to list the head of the company as Julian Lorraine. When I asked who that was, he gave me one of his villainous chuckles."

"Did he tell you Julian Lorraine is?"

"Get this: It was the lead character in a movie called *More to Be Pitied Than Scorned*. Nobody remembers it now, but it was the first feature the studio ever produced. And a huge success, so Mr. Cohn is very sentimental about it."

"Harry Cohn? Sentimental?" Polly scoffed. "I'll believe that when I see it."

"I saw it and I still don't."

"But isn't this another smokescreen in his maze of companies hiding Columbia's cash flow?" Benji asked.

"Sorry, folks," Noah studied his cufflink with sudden fascination, "but I can neither confirm nor deny—"

"You can't be serious," Polly jeered. "You're stonewalling us *now*?"

"I file it with the relevant government department. After that, I rarely have anything to do with it unless I'm asked to transfer money."

"And have you?"

"Only for the other Palm Springs company I set up."

"There's *another* one?" Amelia asked.

"It's called the Agua Caliente Land Management Corporation."

Amelia gaped at Polly. "Everything is connected to everything else."

"And everyone is connected to everyone else," Polly finished for her before turning to Noah. "Does this pretend-legitimate company have an owner who exists in real life?"

"It does. His name is Cyrus—"

"Pattinson?" Comprehension flickered across Noah's pale face. "Is this the guy you've been talking about lately? I wish now I'd put that together."

"You said Agua Caliente pretends to be a legitimate company," Benji said. "Does this mean you've deposited money into it?"

"Uh-huh."

"Do you know how much, give or take?"

"I know precisely." He paused as the waiter delivered four Gin Rickeys to the table. "Forty-three thousand, seven hundred dollars in four equal sums."

"How much is that per deposit?"

"Ten thousand, nine hundred and twenty-five."

Polly's pocketbook slipped from her lap as she sagged against the velvet bench. "Does that amount sound familiar?" she asked Amelia.

It did, but only vaguely. She had no head for numbers and had long ago given up trying to balance her checkbook. "Remind me?"

"Remember when we were on Catalina and Irene showed up furious with her husband because of a poker game?"

"Yes."

"Do you recall how much Mr. Selznick had lost?"

Amelia wouldn't have recalled the figure on her own, but with Polly nudging her along, the jaw-dropping amount crystallized. "Ten thousand, nine hundred and twenty-five."

"And," Polly addressed Noah, "you're saying the bank account for this Agua Caliente company has four times that?"

"To the penny."

"He only admitted to a quarter of it?" Amelia asked nobody in particular. "Because he couldn't fork over his actual loss in one payment?"

"Are you suggesting the producer of *Gone with the Goddamned Wind* pays off his gambling debts on an installment plan like it's a Frigidaire?" Benji ran his fingers through his sandy hair. "I swear, this town gets nuttier and nuttier."

"The question is," Amelia said, "who did he lose to? Noah, can you tell us?"

He shook his head. "Each of those payments was in cash."

"Who dropped it off?" Polly asked.

"He never introduced himself."

"Can you describe him?"

"Five foot ten. Ordinary brown hair, cut short, military style. Snaggle-toothed smile. Breath reeking of licorice—"

Amelia's head snapped backward. "Farley Winchester."

"The Case of the Disappearing Agent?" Polly asked.

"He always smelled of Sen-Sen. Now, let me get this straight —" Amelia ticked off points, finger by finger. "Cohn's Agua Caliente is gobbling up land around the Palm Springs airstrip. He's funneling Selznick's poker losses into Jullo. Winchester's playing bagman for Pattinson, who's bankrolling Wyatt's crusade against the Sapphire Moon—the only piece of land Agua Caliente hasn't snatched up yet. Am I crazy to think Cohn is bleeding Selznick at poker to fund his Palm Springs land grab—*and* to settle a bitter score into the bargain?"

She expected someone to call it a Dashiell Hammett plot run amok. Instead, their solemn faces confirmed every word.

"Irene visited the office recently," Polly said, twisting her pearl ring, "wearing this dream of a dress. When I mentioned it, she admitted to me that she and Mr. Selznick squabbled at the Cocoanut Grove. He ditched her for some mystery table, and when she asked who they were, he snapped, 'Poker buddies.' A few days later, she wore that knockout outfit to the Retake Room for what she calls 'Reconciliation Refreshments.' Seems they need quite a few of those."

Amelia thought of the grainy front-page photograph on the *Examiner*. Cyrus Pattinson had been recognizable. Maybe Irene could identify him. "I have an idea," she said. "But I'd rather not do it alone."

* * *

Amelia was relieved when the maid told them Mr. Selznick wasn't at home, but Mrs. Selznick was putting the children to bed and would be down shortly. On the drive over, Amelia had fought to quash a growing feeling of dread. "Tell me there's going to be a perfectly reasonable explanation for all this," she ordered the other three. But they couldn't. And now they were standing in Irene's tasteful living room with the matching cabbage-rose drapes and Toby mugs lined up along the mantel. Amelia had a copy of the *Examiner* in hand.

Irene appeared in the doorway. Even with no shoes, no makeup, and plain gray slacks, she still radiated elegance. "You lot look like a delegation to the League of Nations." Her eyes dropped to the folded newspaper. "Whatever that's for, will I like it?"

Amelia held up the paper for Irene to see. "Do you recognize anyone standing behind Wyatt Greene?"

Irene's finger shot straight to Pattinson. "Him, for starters." She ran her eye across the gallery of faces and stopped almost halfway along. "And this one." Her finger landed on a man with a military crew cut. "And him." Irene indicated a third figure on the far right. "Why? What's all this about?"

Polly stepped forward. "Remember the night you and Mr. Selznick fought at the Cocoanut Grove?"

"Could you be more specific?"

"The *Goodbye, Mr. Chips* premiere."

"Ah." Irene responded drily. "The multi-part humdinger. What about it?"

"Were those three at the table Mr. Selznick visited after he stormed off?"

Irene snatched the newspaper from Amelia. "That's them, all right."

"Was Harry Cohn with them?" Noah asked.

"No, but his table wasn't far away. When I went table-hopping, I avoided it like they were busily dipping smallpox into malaria. May I know why you're asking?"

"They're your husband's poker buddies."

"He took malicious pleasure in telling me."

"Is that where he is right now? Playing poker with them?"

"No. He called me around six, saying he had to stay late to give the *Intermezzo* edit a final pass."

"That can't be right," Polly said. "He locked the film yesterday, and this morning I called the duplication department to tell them to pick up the negative."

"That goddamn lying son of a bitch!" Irene exploded. "He's going to lose again because why stop at ten grand? Why not make it twenty?"

"Or forty-three thousand, seven hundred."

Irene fixed Noah with a furious glare. "Explain yourself, young man."

"Ma'am," he said, "we believe your husband has lost a good deal more than ten grand."

Irene gestured to the sofas facing each other over the coffee table. "I think we all need to take a seat while someone starts at the beginning."

Irene held herself still as a portrait while they took turns spilling out the tale that had brought them to her doorstep.

It wasn't until they had reached Noah's part in Jullo Inc. and Agua Caliente that Polly jolted upright. "Jullo! JULLO! I'm such a numbskull."

"Polly, dear," Irene said, "nobody thinks you're a numbskull."

"I never heard it spoken out loud—only saw it scrawled upside down." She breathed deeply to calm herself. "I was taking notes on *Wind*'s Atlanta premiere in Mr. Selznick's office. During his thinking pauses, my eyes wandered to his legal pad—just a mess of numbers and words with arrows everywhere. His chicken scratch is hard enough to decipher right-side up, let alone when you're sneaking glances. Still, I got the gist."

"Such as?"

"The words 'ten percent' and 'share' and the name 'Jullo.' I had only caught sight of them when Mr. Selznick started dictating again."

The racket of two obstreperous boys fighting over the Lone Ranger reached them from upstairs.

Irene drew in a long, deep breath. "I'll kill him. That's what I'll do. I'll take my carving knife and I'll slice him up into forty-three thousand, seven hundred pieces. Then I'll get Jerry Giesler to defend me, and he'll get me off with Justifiable Husbandcide."

"Irene," Amelia said, as placatingly as she could, "I understand you're—"

"Learning he'd lost *only* ten thousand cost me untold sleepless nights. We used to manage when he had that MGM salary." She rose, stalking the length of the Steinway. "All this—it's smoke and mirrors. The Selznicks aren't cash poor, we're cash *destitute*. And now I learn he's lost forty thou—?" Her fingers traced the piano's gleaming curves. "God only knows how he settled the rest."

"Wasn't Jock Whitney a key financier who helped get Selznick International up and running?" Noah asked. "He's one of the richest men in America."

"I'm afraid David dipped into the Whitney money well once too often; Jock cut him off."

"Do you own stocks and shares?" Amelia asked.

"We do, yes, but that's more David's domain."

"If you were to estimate their total value?"

"Gosh. If I had to guess?" Irene slapped her sides. "Thirty-five, maybe forty—" Her hands flew to her cheeks. "The *louse*."

Noah cleared his throat. "If your husband has cleaned out your stock portfolio, and possesses no other options, he does have one asset he can sell off."

"Please, Noah, tell me you don't mean the house."

"I don't."

"What, then?"

"Polly saw the words 'ten percent' on that legal pad. I suspect he might sell off ten percent of his stake in *Gone with the Wind*."

"OVER MY DEAD BODY!" Irene slapped the Steinway. "They all sneered at 'Selznick's Folly' until the Riverside preview changed everything. And now the whole town's scrambling for a slice." She pinned Polly with a look that could freeze gin. "Any idea where he might be? Did he let any clue slip? The smallest hint?"

"You know what our office is like—telephones, typewriters, people coming and going all day long. It's hard to overhear anything."

"I can't sit around knowing he's off somewhere losing ten percent of the most valuable asset we'll ever own. Marcella's our only hope." Irene headed to the telephone sitting on a small wooden table. She stopped midway across the room when Amelia pointed out, "You're the boss's wife. And, if I may say, you can also be intimidating. So maybe Polly should make the call?"

Hesitation clouded Irene's eyes as she chewed on Amelia's suggestion. "You're right," she conceded. "I'll be listening on the office extension."

Polly knew Marcella's home number by heart and dialed it as Amelia listened in, their ears almost touching as they huddled over the receiver. Polly dispensed with the usual niceties. "I'm looking for Mr. Selznick."

"He's not here, if that's what you're hoping."

"Any notion of his current whereabouts?"

"He devours enough of my waking hours without having to worry about him after dark, too." Her timbre had switched from irritated to defensive. "My husband's nose is already out of joint over my schedule."

"I didn't mean you were hiding him in your attic. Just that you might know his movements."

"I'd have thought Mrs. Selznick would be the better person to ask—"

"Marcella! Marcella!" Irene called down the line. "It's me here on the extension."

"Whatever's going on, I'm in the dark." Marcella's indignant voice wobbled. Amelia cupped her hand against the receiver and mouthed at Polly, "She knows something!"

"I'll take full responsibility," Irene assured her. "But I need to know where David is. Time might be of the essence."

"I wish I could help you, Irene."

"Marcella," Polly said, "did you type up an agreement to sell ten percent of Mr. Selznick's stake in *Gone with the Wind*."

Marcella's gasp was soft but audible.

"I saw his handwritten notes," Polly persisted. "Tell us, was the agreement made out to a company called Jullo Inc.?" The silence on Marcella's end hummed with unspoken admissions. "It's to pay off his gambling debts, isn't it?" When Marcella still refused to speak, Polly pushed harder. "Did you know that Jullo Inc. is one of Harry Cohn's companies?"

"WHAT?"

"Giving ten percent of *Wind* to Jullo is handing over ten percent to Cohn."

"I wasn't aware," Marcella said quietly.

"Do you think my husband is?" Irene asked.

"He told me to type it up, no questions asked, but on SIP letterhead because it 'has to be official.' I got this sickening feeling of dread and asked him if he was sure. He was very secretive, very defensive. Snapped at me, 'Just damned well do it!'"

"Did it look legally binding?" A tremor ran through Irene's voice.

"As legal as anything I've ever typed. Party of the first part, et cetera, et cetera."

"So where is he?" Irene demanded. "He sure isn't finishing up on *Intermezzo*."

"No idea," Marcella said. "Truly, Irene, I don't know."

Polly picked up a matchbook lying next to the glass ashtray. "I think I might."

They thanked Marcella and reconvened in the living room. "You know that triangular building across Washington Boulevard from the studio?" Polly asked.

"The one with the oil field behind it?" Irene asked.

"For the past few months your husband has been lighting his Cabañas with matches from—" She turned over the matchbook to reveal the logo.

90-90 Club
9090 W. Washington Blvd
Culver City
Where the number and the name
are both the same.

Amelia spoke first.

"Who's driving?"

42

Irene eased to a halt where Washington crossed Ince. Benji rapped a knuckle against a window. "There's a decent-sized parking lot out back."

"If we get him outside," Amelia said, "we run the risk of someone following him, yelling blue bloody murder, so maybe we should park someplace else in case we need a quick getaway."

"Good point." Irene pulled away from the curb.

Single-story offices gave way to a field of derricks, towering over oil pumps bobbing at the ground like mechanical cranes pecking at the earth's crust. Stepping from the LaSalle, Amelia recoiled from the stink of crude oil and rusting metal burning her nostrils. The pumps' endless rhythm vibrated through her shoes, their iron bones backlit by streetlights.

Irene locked her door. "Let's check for David's car."

"Wouldn't he simply walk across Ince Boulevard?" Noah asked.

Irene shot him a withering look. "My husband wouldn't walk to the corner store if he could drive. Not that he's been in a corner store since the Roosevelt administration—and I mean Teddy's."

The 90-90 Club's parking lot had a single streetlight shining over it—dim, but enough for Irene to spot her husband's Chrysler Imperial. "I should've known."

Amelia gifted Irene with five seconds of self-indulgence before she tugged at her elbow. She wasn't looking forward to whatever was about to happen, but anything was better than standing around in this god-awful oily air. With Bernice's trial starting in three days, they didn't have an hour to lose.

The vestibule past the stage door was deserted. They slipped down a corridor into a shabby anteroom, its walls flaking paint and wearing scuff marks like battle scars. Six men lounged about, trailing cigarette smoke and leafing through *The Saturday Evening Post*. Their off-the-rack Harris & Frank suits stretched across prize-fighter shoulders. Amelia guessed they alternated between chauffeur and muscle.

Mismatched chairs hugged three walls, sharing space with battered coffee tables. An expensive attaché case gleamed on the nearest table. The fourth wall stood bare except for a door.

The man closest to the case addressed Benji. "You got the wrong place." He pointed behind them. "Showroom's thataway."

Irene stepped forward. "I am Mrs. David Selznick, and this is his secretary. We have come with very urgent news concerning *Gone with the Wind*. I know my husband is in there, so if you don't mind . . ."

The palooka held his ground. "I do mind."

"My father is Louis B. Mayer. He fricassees twerps like you for breakfast, so don't think for a minute you intimidate me." She almost reached the closed door, but he blocked her again.

"I don't care if you're Queen of the Rose Parade; my orders are specific. While the game is on, nobody—but *nobody*—is allowed in."

"And if the elaborate plans for the Atlanta premiere blow up in Mr. Selznick's face, *you* shall take the fall."

"I'll risk it." His mouth curved without warmth, accentuating a scar that slashed from nostril to lip.

Polly rummaged around in her purse for a pen and paper. "At least pass on a message?"

"Leave. Now."

Out in the corridor, Amelia whispered, "No interruptions under any circumstances means this game is probably the big one. Maybe there's another way in?"

"Chasen's also has a back room," Benji said. "It's got a second door to deliver booze and food. If we find the kitchen—"

A trio of showgirls clad in little more than purple ostrich feathers giggled at the end of the corridor. The tallest of them looked familiar.

Amelia stepped forward. "Fifi Champagne!"

The girl spun around. "Friend of Hazel's, yeah?

"No longer at the Follies?"

"Nope." She adjusted a bracelet of pink rhinestones. "The Brewsters, well, you know, they pay well enough and they're decent, respectable people, but burlesque is going the way of vaudeville, so I jumped ship." She took in the group behind Amelia. "What gives, honey?"

Amelia lowered her voice. "Can I ask you about The Tent?"

Fifi fluttered her false eyelashes and told her fellow showgirls she'd meet them in the dressing room. They reminded her that they had only eight minutes for their costume change and disappeared.

"The Tent and his lingering limo." She yanked a plume from her hair. "He's part of the reason why I quit the Follies." Her eyes darted to the door. "One of those gals was dumb enough to say yes. Wound up in some clip joint past Warners. She got wise watching him work over some poor sap who owed him money. But then she was stranded out in Burbank without a taxi in sight, so she hadda hoof it clear to the Cahuenga Pass streetcar—in heels. That guy is bad news."

"Brace yourself," Polly said. "We suspect he's in the back room."

"The Tent? *Here*?" She landed a palm against the wall as though to say, *If that don't beat all.*

"We think he and his cronies are trying to hoodwink my husband." Irene's voice was two notches below a squeal.

"And who's that?" Fifi asked.

"David Selznick."

"Oh, *honey*!"

One of the showgirls thrust her head into the corridor and yelled, "Five minutes, Feef!"

Fifi acknowledged her with a wave. "I suppose that wall of muscle with the IQ of a brick won't let you through?"

"Any other options?" Amelia asked.

"Some of the other girls get paid to pour drinks and make sandwiches for all-nighters. Listen, I have to prepare for the next show, but I'll send Lorelei out."

Fifi vanished into the dressing room. Moments later, a girl emerged. Eighteen at most, she'd been poured into black-and-white striped satin and was wrestling with ruby opera gloves. "Feef says you're asking about another entrance into the back room. There ain't one. That door's it."

"Any windows?" Noah asked.

"A couple, but they're high and narrow. You'd need a ladder on both sides."

Amelia looked at Irene. *What now?*

"There is a dumbwaiter, though. It's how they get in booze and grub without interrupting the game."

"The kitchen's upstairs?" Benji asked.

"Just the ice machine. Holdover from Prohibition. It opens into a little serving area downstairs."

"Can you show us?" Irene asked.

"I'm on in two minutes," Lorelei said. "Take the outside stairs to the second floor. Nobody watches those."

The space was no bigger than Amelia's bedroom, with a counter and sink. Stale beer and dust hung in the air. The dumbwaiter's hatch gaped open, and they crowded around it in a half-circle.

"I thought they were roomier," Noah said.

Amelia did too. There was no way on God's green earth Irene could fit in there. Let alone either of the boys. Amelia pushed past them. "I'll go." Irene demurred with tepid resistance that fooled nobody. "Your husband might be gambling away *Wind* right now. I'd never forgive myself if I didn't at least try to stop it."

While Amelia pretzeled herself into the dumbwaiter, they settled on three minutes—enough time for the others to make it back downstairs before Polly worked the pulleys. Then Irene would stand in the anteroom and pitch a fit too ferocious for David to brush off.

Polly waited until their footsteps receded. "It's okay if you've reconsidered."

"I'm not afraid of those sharks."

"Even Cyrus?"

Pattinson's name gave her pause. "As long as he isn't armed—"

"Don't joke about that!"

"Lookit," Amelia said, "if you can tackle Harry Cohn on top of a rickety old movie set, I can do this." Assuming, of course, she didn't become stuck halfway down.

"Oh, yeah?" Polly said. "Tell that to my busted leg."

Gadzooks. She hadn't thought of that. "It healed, didn't it?" Before Polly could protest, Amelia pressed on. "Those cretins are bleeding Selznick dry, so lower me down there before I lose my nerve."

Darkness swallowed her as Polly lowered the cover. Amelia had braced for cramped quarters, but the musty air stole her breath. The pulley squealed as the rope threaded through its wheel. Halfway down, Benji's baritone filtered up from below, distant but unmistakable, lifting her heart. The dumbwaiter hit the bottom with a jolt. A splinter of light showed at the base. If she could contort around her knee, wedge her nails into the gap, and leverage . . .

The light grew to a half-inch. Then an inch. Then a few inches until the hatch jammed two-thirds open. Amelia shook the damned landing door, but it wouldn't budge.

"Hold on!"

Amelia might have identified the voice had mild panic not started to inch its way up her chest.

A loud click.

"There we go." The cover shot up and a male hand, thick-wristed with hairy knuckles, reached in. "Come on out, my little stowaway."

She freed one leg, then the other, ignoring his offered assistance as she gripped the sides of the dumbwaiter hatch. Sliding to the counter's edge, she faced her unwanted rescuer.

Farley Winchester rocked back on his heels. "What the—?"

She stumbled into a landing a three-legged cat would mock. "Thought you'd vanish, did you? Up and out? No word to anyone?"

His cufflinks winked in the light as he took his sweet time pulling out his cigarette case. "Since when was I under legal obligation to inform anybody if I decide to relocate?"

"When it's the decent thing to do. But considering whose campaign you're running, I guess all things decent are out the window." A metal tray sat on the counter; she picked it up. "Who cares? I'm not here to see you." She side-swiped his cigarette, hitting a knuckle with a loud crack. It did the trick; he left her alone with a half-assed "Screw you!" to join the poker players crowding around the open door that led to the anteroom, where she could hear Irene's hollering more clearly.

Only one gambler had remained seated. Jacket abandoned, tie at half-mast, Selznick watched his last chips disappear while the other stacks swelled.

"Sir?"

He peered up at her through his wire-rimmed spectacles. "Amelia?"

She bent down to whisper in his ear. "They're cheating you."

He waved a limp hand over his chips. "I've had a bad run tonight."

"No. Those guys." She pointed to Cyrus Pattinson, Wyatt Greene, and some other fellow she didn't know. "It's been their plan all along to bilk you out of thousands as part of a shifty land grab in Palm Springs to cheat Bernice out of the Sapphire Moon."

"They what?"

"Until they came up with a better idea: swindle you out of a percentage of *Gone with the Wind*."

"How could you possibly—"

"Ten percent will be worth far more than the thirty grand you owe them." She gestured at his puny stack of chips. "How much are you down?"

He looked away. "Nearly eleven grand."

Where do these men find the chutzpah to jeopardize money they don't even have? She fixed him with a steady eye. "Don't hand over the IOU that Marcella typed up."

He picked up a cigar burning in a glazed black 90-90 Club ashtray and savored a brief pull. "You even know about that."

"Where is it now?"

"Cyrus put it into his briefcase."

"The one in the outer room?"

Selznick shrugged. "My attention's been on my cards."

Irene's strident voice pierced the room. "UNHAND ME!"

Selznick sprang up. "Is that my wife?"

"She's out for blood," Amelia told him.

"Yeah. Mine."

Amelia steadied him with a gentle touch to his shoulder. "Only if you sign away ten percent of *Wind*."

"I already have." He ran a trembling palm over his scalp. "I'm so deep in debt they wouldn't start the game unless I did."

"It's in Pattinson's briefcase, yes?"

"Uh-huh."

"So if the only copy disappears . . .?"

Selznick stared at her, needing a moment to read her mind. "You'd do that for me?"

"For you, for Irene, for Juniper."

A switch flipped behind his eyes. They flitted to life, luminous and alert, fireflies in a mason jar. "I'll throw myself into that raucous scuffle out there. You grab the bag, using me as a shield."

He threw himself through the open door, yelling, "WHAT THE SAM HILL IS GOING ON?!"

Amelia shadowed Selznick into the bedlam and snatched the

attaché. The corridor churned with flying fists—Benji and Noah flailing like newsboys against prizefighters. Above it all, Irene kept up her full-throated tirade.

Amelia sprinted past the club's stage manager impotently begging for quiet, out the exit, and into the shadowy parking lot. The closest car was a beat-up Plymouth. She sat the case on its trunk, popped open the buckle and rifled through its contents.

"HEY, YOU!" Cyrus Pattinson stood at the stage door. "DON'T YOU FUCKING DARE."

She snapped shut the case and tore away from him, searching for an escape route.

"I was the state champion marathon runner in college," he called out. "I can out-run you and out-last you. Save yourself the bother."

The briefcase dragged her down like an anchor. One quick search for that IOU, then she could lose the dead weight.

A fence materialized—chest-high, unexpected. Beyond it, pumps bobbed and groaned, their sulfurous stench curdling the air. Amelia hurled the case over, then threaded her Mary Janes through the links. Up and over, landing on damp, unstable earth. She staggered, toppling to her knees beside the case.

Behind her, the near-full moon painted silver walking paths through the darkness. Heart pounding, she knelt next to the bag and tilted it toward the moonlight. Typewritten memos, store receipts, reminders scrawled on legal paper. *Jesus, what a bore.* But then she hit pay dirt.

The IOU on Selznick International letterhead, typed, signed and witnessed, legitimate and lawful.

"I'll have you arrested for theft!"

She stuffed the IOU down her summer-light sweater and turned around. Pattinson gripped the wire, not the slightest bit out of breath. She smiled at him, sweet as marzipan. "Most men your age would've run out of oomph before they got halfway. Impressive—especially seeing as how you're not quite healed from Yarborough's treatments."

Outrage flared in his eyes. He rattled the fence like a caged gorilla. "There's nothing in there to interest a girl like you."

A gust of oily air whipped across the field, its cocktail of sand and crude stinging her cheeks. She returned the papers to the case. "I know about your plan to scam David Selznick out of ten percent of the fortune he's about to earn from *Gone with the Wind*. You're going to have to make do with the forty grand he's already forked over, plus another ten from tonight's chicanery."

"It isn't chicanery when the guy can't play cards any better than a one-eyed dodo bird. Gamblers like Selznick, they're always desperate to believe they're on a roll that'll last all night or their luck'll change with the next hand. Selznick is too much of a gentleman to renege on his gambling debts. They all are: Zanuck, Warner, Wilkerson, Gable, Schenck, DeMille, Wanger. The list is longer than Route 66."

He didn't look like he was about to jump the fence any time soon, so she ventured a couple of steps closer. The moonlight picked up the gray streak in his hair; it shone like a trail of frost. "Before we drove over here, me and Irene Selznick and Bernice Hoag called Aggie Underwood at the *Herald-Express* to spill the whole story."

"What whole story?"

"HEY! BOSS! YOU OKAY?"

One of his bruisers stood at the edge of the parking lot. Pattinson kept his eyes glued to Amelia as he swiveled to the left. "Tell the others we'll pick things up again in a minute." He waited until the sound of the bruiser's footsteps faded away again. "You were saying?"

Amelia should have known he wouldn't believe her. It was a little far-fetched—but she couldn't backpedal now. "Aggie was very interested. Took tons of notes. Asked loads of questions."

He withdrew a cigarette out of a brushed platinum holder and struck a match from a 90-90 Club matchbook. The match burned bright orange as he lit up, then tossed it away. "You seem to be an expert about what we've been doing."

Crude oil coated Amelia's tongue, leaving a soapy, bitter

residue. She doubted that lighting a cigarette near a forest of restless giants was a smart move, but what would an interfering little so-and-so like her know? "You've acquired almost all the land surrounding the Palm Springs airstrip."

"Have I?"

"You're behind Agua Caliente."

"Agua what?"

"You and Wyatt Greene and Harry Cohn." His cigarette froze midway to his mouth. "Except for the plot that the Sapphire Moon sits on, which is why you orchestrated the raid. Once you've snatched up the Sapphire Moon for cheap, the government will be forced to purchase your land at whatever exorbitant price you charge if they want to turn the airstrip into air force training grounds or a commercial airport—or both. I'd have thought the forty grand you lot have bamboozled out of Mr. Selznick would be more than enough to buy the Moon."

A sharp crease in the IOU scraped down Amelia's stomach as it wormed south. Pretty soon, it'd start peeking out of the bottom of her sweater. She picked up the attaché case from the spongy earth and held it in front of her. "What I can't figure out is why you need ten percent of *Gone with the Wind* as well. Ever heard of quitting while you're ahead?"

"You're wasting my time." He was spitting words at her now.

"You figured why nickel-and-dime him for ten grand at a time when you can scoop up all the money you need with a legal IOU."

"Give me back my briefcase, then turn around and go to hell."

"I can prove it," she told him.

"Prove what? That Farley, Wyatt, and I have been cheating at cards to bilk Selznick out of his dough? Good luck with that."

"Don't forget Harry Cohn."

"Cohn? You don't think he's here, do you?"

"Jullo Inc." Amelia said the name succinctly over the metallic scraping from the nodding donkeys behind her. "And what about Julian Lorraine? Can you prove he exists? Oh, wait. He doesn't. Because Julian Lorraine is a character from a movie."

"Okay. That's it." He ran to the fence. Landing his hands along the top, he propelled his feet into an overhead arc and landed neatly on the soft earth. Amelia had only just started backing away when he lunged at her.

She flung his bag at his head but caught his shoulder instead. He watched it thump to the ground. "You've got it, haven't you?" The oil-soaked terrain sucked at her heels as she edged back, not daring to break his gaze. "Hand it over now; otherwise, so help me—"

His eyes dropped to the waistband of her tartan skirt. She looked down and spotted the corner of the paper sticking out from beneath her sweater. He sprang forward, arms extended. He missed, but only by inches. She shuffled backward a few steps, pivoted, and ran full pelt toward the checkerboard of bobbing pumpjacks.

The dark closed in. Her feet ached from the effort of running on pulpy earth. The *chunk-shhh-chunk-shhh* swelled in her ears as she rounded the first pumpjack. "I might not have pursued any of this," she yelled over her shoulder, "if you hadn't forced Wyatt's sister to go see Doc Yar."

His footsteps died away—and thank God, too. Her legs couldn't take much more of this lumpy, slimy terrain. No fence stood between them now, just a bobbing grasshopper. "Y'know? The one you knocked up? Lucky you knew that small-town doctor. He had to be discreet because you'd hate anyone to know you landed yourself a dose of syphilis." She carved the word into three jagged shards—SIH! FUH! LUSS!

"You're that girl."

"I'm *a* girl." She turned toward him, then shuffled backward, toes testing each inch of ground.

"At Schwab's. The one who works with Tillie." He rounded the derrick and closed the space between them to a couple of feet. "The Greenes are Catholic. So am I." Withdrawing his cigarette case again, he flipped it open, and surprised Amelia by offering her one. She shook her head. He lit up. "I would've gone along with whatever Tillie chose. I got her into that jam, so when she decided to get rid of the problem, I drove her to Beaumont."

Oh, he's good—pouring it on thick as greasepaint. And get a load of those puppy-dog eyes—they must've taken hours to perfect. With a poker face that slick, he must be murder at the card table.

"What hypocrites you all are," she said.

"Whoa!" He held his hand up as though in surrender. "I was being honest with you."

"Baloney! Matilda hadn't made up her mind about the kid. You and Wyatt took that decision away from her the moment you ordered her into the car. Being Catholic never entered into it. Nor was it a factor when you rented out the Sapphire Moon." She watched his face as the words landed. "Back when MGM opened the Plaza Theater? *Camille* premiere?"

Pattinson's puppy-dog eyes gave way to a predatory glint. His lips were now a long, thin line. "You got nothing on me."

"Oh, yeah?"

"I signed no contracts, no checks, no paperwork."

"You didn't?"

"There's nothing to pin me to that weekend."

"Just because Bernice Hoag was running a house of ill repute doesn't mean she lacked the sense to run a business and protect herself. I saw it all when we were handing everything over to Aggie—along with the instructions to sit on it in case you were resistant to our suggestion that you convince the authorities to drop all the charges against Miss Hoag."

"I can't—"

"You'll be responsible for Wyatt's campaign disappearing into the crapper. And your plan to buy up all the land around the Palm Springs airstrip for cheap will disappear right along with it. So here it is: Take that thirty grand you gypped from Selznick and use it to make an offer for the Sapphire Moon."

"Thirty grand for scrub in the middle of the desert?" Pattinson scoffed. "She'd be lucky to get three."

"Which is why she'll say yes."

Pattinson blew a fog of cigarette smoke into Amelia's face. "And if I don't?"

"I'll tell Aggie to go ahead and publish her story."

It was all a load of bull, of course, but questions spun in his eyes like reels in a slot machine. Had he overlooked a tiny, telling detail? What did she have? A photograph? A sample of his writing? Had he unwittingly disregarded a letter or receipt that might prove to be his undoing?

"HA!" she threw at him. "Aggie'll have a field day."

But she shouldn't have. Her contemptuous jeer jostled the sheet of paper out from under her sweater. The bottom half now dangled at her waist.

He lunged. She twisted, her heel sinking into thick muck just as the derrick's spinning drum plunged earthward, catching her with brutal force. She ricocheted off its surface, then tumbled to the ground. Her hands skated through oil-slick earth until she landed face down in crude. She looked up, expecting to see Pattinson standing over her, the IOU gripped triumphantly in his hand. Instead, he crawled nearby, cursing as he searched. The paper crinkled against her belly as she braced to rise. The IOU was safe—if she stayed put.

He sucked on the cigarette still wedged between his lips. "It's under you, isn't it?" He took a final drag and spat out the butt. It bounced off the pump's counter-weight and onto the ground. He scuttled over to her like a crab and then, gripping her shoulders, he flipped her over as though she were made of chiffon. The sheet of paper was slick with oil. Were contracts legal if they were coated in crude? He lifted it off her stomach and rose to his knees, peering at the soggy paper triumphantly. She scrambled to her feet and tried to seize it, but a whooshing sound behind him made him turn. A glimmer of orange-yellow flame erupted from the ground.

"Your cigarette," she rasped.

He was still on his knees, but had spread them wide apart for balance, leaving his tenderloin open and defenseless.

She kicked. Hard.

He reeled backward, gasping in pain, and landed with his head near the puddle of oil. The flames were now reaching higher and higher; she could feel their heat from where she stood.

Groaning, he hobbled clear, paper held high. Amelia saw her

chance. She balled up her fist and swung, catching his wrist dead-on. He clutched the paper tighter. She followed with a right hook to his chest. His chuckle dripped with mockery. "Points for effort, kid."

Behind him, flames licked toward a second, wider pool of fuel. If that caught fire, they'd have themselves a real inferno.

She reached for the IOU again, deliberately slow enough for him to jerk it out of reach. He whipped it away as she flattened her palms against his chest and shoved with everything she had in her. He fell to the dirt, stiffening his arm above his head as the oil-fueled flames gnawed at the edge of the puddle of fuel, filling the air with hot, peppery smoke.

Amelia hurled herself backward as the flames leaped into the puddle and exploded into a blinding inferno.

43

Polly stepped onto the Selznick front porch. "You're sure you have those papers in your purse?"

Amelia reached past her and pressed the buzzer. "You mean the ones I checked, double-checked, and triple-checked on the drive over?"

The door swung open. Irene opened her arms for a hug. "After all you've been through!"

Amelia thrust out her hand. "I still reek of oil."

"'Reek' is an exaggeration," Polly commented.

"I've tried everything: baking soda, lemons, vinegar, tomato juice, coffee grounds—"

"Coffee?" Irene asked. "Does that work?"

"Only if you prefer smelling like a bucket of Folgers."

"A girl could reek of worse." Irene hugged her anyway, although she didn't shy away from giving Amelia's hair a vigorous sniff. "Cinnamon?"

"She tried that too," Polly said.

Irene guided them toward the living room and called up the stairs. "David! The girls are here."

Amelia gingerly lowered herself among the cabbage roses. It had nearly been two days since that ugly scene at the oil field.

Bruises had bloomed all over, and she was still aching in places she didn't know she had places.

"I found some new Ceylonese tea at Premier Market," Irene said. "Or would you prefer stronger refreshment?"

"The time for a double bourbon was when I got home," Amelia said. "And wouldn't you know it? We hadn't a drop of Mad Ox in the house."

"The first bottles are due off the assembly line *next* week," Polly said. "Otherwise, Helga the Hero could've bathed in it if she wanted."

"'Hero' is an exaggeration."

Most of what Amelia had weathered that night in Culver City had sprung from a concoction of nerves, panic, fear, and adrenaline—and okay, maybe a dash of chutzpah. The more time passed, the more that scrappy confrontation played in her head like a scene from a crime melodrama, with a plucky would-be Ann Sothern facing down a second-rate Jimmy Cagney.

"No, it isn't." David Selznick stood in the living room doorway, shoeless, beltless, shirt untucked, hair ruffled.

Irene tsked. "Look at the state of you."

"I've been roughhousing with my sons. It's what fathers do. And besides"—he stepped into the room—"I bet I don't look half as bad as Cyrus Pattinson." He joined his wife on the sofa, a broad smile plastered across his face. "Please tell me he was in horrendous pain by the time the ambulance pulled up."

Amelia still heard the anguish in Pattinson's screams. "That puddle of oil was no bigger than a breadbox, but those flames! It was like looking into the sun."

"And then the fool stuck his hand in," Selznick said. "And for what? A piece of paper."

"Yes, well," Irene said, her face pinching slightly. "It wasn't just any old piece of paper, was it?"

Selznick kept his eyes on Amelia, but addressed his wife. "We agreed not to use that damned IOU as artillery."

"No-o-o-o." Irene stretched the word over several syllables.

"*You* agreed with *my* proposal." She winked at Amelia. "I'm free to do as I please."

Amelia pictured their shouting match, barbed words flying back and forth. They must have patched things up; she detected no hint of tension between them now. "Pattinson has nobody to blame but himself. What kind of chowderhead lights up in an oil field?"

"It was *his* cigarette?" Selznick rocked with laughter. "Even better."

"Yes, yes," Irene said, "we're all aware that Cyrus Pattinson caused his own third-degree burns, but does it help Bernice? Jerry Giesler hasn't been able to get a continuance, so her trial will be starting in a couple of days. Unless fresh evidence—"

"Funny you should say that." Amelia pulled a stack of six sheets from her purse and rattled them like maracas. "Guess who was so distracted by his burning hand that he forgot all about his attaché case. Everybody was running around in hysterics; nobody was thinking about some filthy bag."

One of Amelia's clear memories was kicking that bastard's bag behind a pumpjack. As sirens had wailed—ambulance, police, fire trucks—Irene had sped off with her husband. With pandemonium reigning and Pattinson howling, none of his goons noticed the mud-stained, oil-soaked woman in the shadows waiting for the Culver City firemen to rewind their hoses and drive away.

"One thing I'll say for Hot Fingers Pattinson, he's meticulous. However, retaining everything in his head is not his forté."

"Define 'everything,'" Selznick said.

"The next morning, I rummaged through his briefcase."

Irene flicked cigarette ash over a crystal ashtray. "Tell me you've uncovered enough dirt to bury him."

"The whole time we were tussling, I assumed he thought it was the ten percent IOU I'd stuffed up my sweater."

Amelia rotated Pattinson's papers toward the Selznicks. His own handwriting laid bare the entire scheme: Wyatt's Broom of Purity campaign, the Sapphire Moon raid, Jullo Inc., Harry Cohn. He'd even calculated the cash needed for each land grab, along with a list titled "Easy Targets" to squeeze when the coffers ran dry.

"Eleven easy targets," Selznick moaned, "and mine's the only name he underlined twice."

"Three cheers for Amelia!" Irene said. "But why is there an arrow running from 'Moon raid' to"—she squinted—"what does it say?"

Amelia turned the sheet back to her. "'Call sheriff now. Raid immed.' My guess is that his goons were keeping an eye on the place. So when we showed up, a bunch of women, they figured they'd better get the ball rolling."

"I'm still marveling that he'd be stupid enough to write all this down," Polly said.

Selznick told her, "That's because few of us walk around believing we're so smart that we can retain everything in our heads, and so invincible that nobody would dare to touch our belongings."

Irene shook her head slowly. "But is it enough to secure a dismissal or acquittal?"

"We ought to get this to Giesler," Selznick said. "Preferably today."

"Polly and I are going to see my parents later. We can drop it off."

"Let's hold off on the champagne. Myron tells me Jerry thinks those charges against Bernice are all open to interpretation and negotiation. Amelia's discovery might not sway the verdict—let's not forget how Bernice did run the Sapphire Moon—but worst case? Either a suspended sentence or a brief stay at Tehachapi. And that prison is so far out in the desert, they barely need to lock their doors. But on to happier matters." He swung one leg over the other. "Della Sloane's screen test."

Amelia slipped Pattinson's papers into her purse. In all the madness, she'd clean forgotten about Della. "And?"

"I have to admit, she's a natural. She might make an excellent lead in *Sea Change*."

"Might or will?"

"You need to appreciate how boiling mad I was when you said you wanted to quit."

"Can't say as I blame you." Amelia ducked her head. "But now that you've seen what Della is capable of?"

"What's more important, Amelia, is that I realize what *you're* capable of."

The last guy who'd discovered what she could do had ended up in the hospital screaming like a little girl and smoking like a Sunday roast. "Oh yeah?"

"I've been watching you, seeing how you operate."

Amelia looked at Irene, who was slowly, almost imperceptibly nodding as she wiped away tears collecting in the corners of her dark brown eyes. "Operate?"

"You and Irene found a project you believed in and you went after it, despite all obstacles. That's what separates the men from the boys."

"Or the girls from the women," Irene corrected him.

"Yes, yes, of course." He lit his pipe with deliberate care. "I'd like to give you a screen credit."

Amelia turned to Polly, wide-eyed. "Did you know about this?"

"I refuse to answer on the grounds it may incriminate me." Polly fought to suppress her smile. "Tell her what we came up with."

"Supervising Producer," Selznick said.

Amelia sank deeper into her chair, as if gravity had doubled. She swiveled toward Irene. "Our names would appear together on the screen."

"As a matter of fact, no," she said. "It wouldn't do for my name to appear on a Selznick International picture."

"But you've worked so hard," Amelia protested. "You deserve a screen credit more than I do."

"Thank you, sweetie, but it took me an embarrassingly long time to realize I'd be laughed out of town for what everyone would call a vanity credit. I can do without sneering backstabbery. Credit where credit is due, and it's all yours."

Still stunned by this development, Amelia turned slowly back to Selznick. "I don't know what to say."

Polly snickered. "Say yes, you big dummy."

* * *

Amelia's thoughts were still pinwheeling when Polly parked at the Hartley house. "This screen credit."

"Never saw it coming, huh?"

Amelia gave Polly's arm a playful punch. "No thanks to you."

"My boss ordered me to keep my trap shut."

"Supervising Producer. Sounds so important."

"*Sea Change* wouldn't be going into production without you." Polly slid her key from the ignition. "For the record, the title credit was Irene's idea. She and Mr. Selznick, Marcella and I all batted around ideas. He suggested 'Co-Executive Producer,' but Irene shot that down real quick. Said she grew up surrounded by people who have their name up in lights, so for her it's no big deal. Then she landed on 'Supervising Producer'—and we decided that did the trick nicely. Now, come on, let's share your news before Samuel and Sebastian get back from Scouts."

Cookie and Jewel greeted them as though they hadn't seen a living soul since Thanksgiving. "They've been particularly rambunctious this week." Lois scraped back a loosened lock of hair. "Is it a full moon?"

"I'll take them outside." Polly beckoned the hounds to follow her into the backyard.

Through the rumpus room window, Lois lit a cigarette as she and Amelia watched Polly throw their favorite drool-drenched tennis balls in opposite directions. "Is Bernice around?"

"We decided she needed a trip to the beauty parlor. I told her not to come back until she looked like the town librarian from an Andy Hardy picture."

"Where's Dad?"

"Your father volunteered to drive her. I suspect he rather likes to play the bodyguard. I can't tell you the relief it's been to see the two of them get along so well. She's an excellent cribbage player, so that helps. And her darling kitty-cat, Charley, won't leave him alone. Bern's going to miss her when she—if she—"

"Some new evidence has come to light," Amelia said. "Pol and I dropped it off at Giesler's office on the way here."

"What's happened?" The ash of Lois's cigarette had grown long, but she didn't seem to notice. "Between Bernice's trial and Faith's woes, we'd appreciate some good news around here." She hovered over Amelia's cautious descent onto the sofa, then took a seat beside her, setting her cigarette in the ashtray. "Why are you moving like that? I don't know how much more bad news I can take."

Amelia pressed her hands on top of her mother's. "Good news, I swear."

Lois squared her shoulders. "Okay. Ready."

"Mr. Selznick is fine with me backing out of *Sea Change*."

"He is?" Lois stared back at her, eyebrows pinched. "I'd have thought he'd be mad as heck."

"He was. Until he wasn't."

"So . . . what are you saying?"

"Mr. Selznick has *promoted* me."

"To what?"

"Supervising Producer."

"Oh darling! I don't know what that means, but it sounds important."

Come to think of it, Amelia had no idea what a Supervising Producer did, either. "Kinda does, doesn't it?"

"How thrilling. Well done. I'm so very proud."

Tears stung the backs of Amelia's eyeballs. "Are you?"

"Of course! What a question to ask."

"It's just that—never mind."

Amelia looked away, but Lois cupped her chin to guide her face around. "It's just that what?"

The moment had arrived to speak the words out loud that she had yearned to confess to her mother for as long as she could remember. Why, then, was it so hard? Because, she told herself, you're afraid of what you'll hear in reply.

To hell with caution. She perched herself on the cushion's edge. "I'm relieved to finally impress you." She glanced away from her mother's puzzled expression, but immediately regretted it. She needed to say it to Lois's face. "I've always felt invisible. Faith was Miss Perfect—straight A's, Girl Most Likely To, Valedictorian, Wellesley, marriage, baby, bestseller. How am I supposed to compete with that?" Lois drew a breath to respond, but the pent-up words were gushing out of Amelia now. "And then the twins came along. I know they're double the work—especially when you weren't planning on more kids. But let's not pretend, Mom. They're hurricanes who suck the air from every room they barrel into. And there I am in the corner, the forgotten middle child."

Lois fell silent, the color draining from her cheeks.

Aw, jeez, Amelia thought. I've gone too far. Said too much. "Mom, let's—"

"My sweet girl . . . I never saw you needing guidance or attention. You've blazed your own trail, so forthright and confident. From your very first steps, you've marched through life. Out of all my children, *you* were the one I knew would be all right. No question about it."

Amelia's mind emptied; her hands suddenly felt like foreign objects.

"Your sister wanted reassurance before every exam, every recital, every race, every milestone," Lois continued. "No belief in herself—ironic, considering the name we gave her. Meanwhile, the twins require constant corralling. But you? Nope. You walked your own path without anyone's help. Truth be told, I admired that. Wished I had your confidence."

For once in her life, Amelia's habitual torrent of words dried up. If only she had summoned the courage to voice her deepest fear before now. How different her life might have been.

Or would it? *You've always been your own person.* Her mother's words had a ring of truth. Okay, so she'd never graduated top of any class, never gone to college, let alone written a book that topped the *New York Times* bestseller list. But look at what you *do* have: Polly and Luddie and Benji, a job you like, and a screen credit on a major motion picture. Not to mention a mane of bold, copper curls that most girls would kill for.

A soggy tennis ball hit the rumpus room window with a dull splat. Cookie had wedged herself between Polly's knees and Jewel had leaped up to plant her paws on Polly's shoulders. Polly mouthed the words, "MAYDAY!"

"She needs me," Amelia said to her mother.

"Darling, we all need you," Lois said, her voice husky with unexpressed regret. Following Amelia's gaze out the window, a small smile bloomed on her mouth. "But right now, your friend *really* needs you."

Amelia hugged her mother and whispered a gravelly "Thank you," before bounding up from the sofa. She burst from the screen door and landed on the grass. "Hell's bells, you hellacious hounds, if you want to drown someone in drool, how about you leave Aunty Pol-Pol alone and try me on for size?"

She threw open her arms and, like a backyard Scarlett O'Hara, beckoned whatever glorious mayhem awaited.

THE END

Did you enjoy this book?

***You* can make a big difference.**

As an independent author, I don't have the financial muscle of a New York publisher supporting me. But I do have something much more powerful and effective, and it's something those publishers would kill to get their hands on: a committed and loyal bunch of readers. Honest reviews of my books help bring them to the notice of other readers. If you've enjoyed this book, I would be so grateful if you could spend just a couple of minutes leaving a review.

Thank you very much,

Martin Turnbull

AUTHOR NOTE

As with most historical fiction, *Selznick's Spotlight* is a blend of fact and fiction. To help you sort out which parts were real and which I invented, here are some clarifications and links for further reading.

The scene in which David Selznick brings Vivien Leigh home because she suspects she is pregnant was based on a real-life event that took place during the filming of *Gone with the Wind*. On April 17, 1939, Leigh went to Selznick and declared she was pregnant. He was terrified in case the news reached the press and made plans to give her five days off for an abortion. She later reported a false alarm and the crisis resolved itself. That same week, her lover, Laurence Olivier, opened in New York on Broadway in *No Time for Comedy* opposite Katharine Cornell.

In May 1939, Ingrid Bergman arrived in Los Angeles ahead of filming *Intermezzo*. Until a house could be leased for her, she stayed at Selznick's home for a few days. Selznick's New York agent, Kay Brown (who, in 1936, had talked Selznick into securing the screen rights for *Gone with the Wind*), sailed to Stockholm to escort Bergman to Hollywood. The evening of Bergman's arrival, Irene took her to a party at the home of Mariam Hopkins, which is where Bergman met Selznick for the first time—at one o'clock in the morning, when he was in the kitchen shoveling food into his mouth because he'd been working all evening.

Bergman's fascination with ice cream sundaes was a real thing. Apparently, they weren't available in Sweden back in the 1930s, and she thought of them as a quintessentially American dish. One account I read described that she consumed them without regard for the fact that she was about to face the cameras for *Intermezzo*.

For the scene where Irene Selznick talks about adopting a "for the duration" mentality during the production of *Gone with the Wind*, I took inspiration from Irene herself. In her wonderful autobiography, *A Private View*, she wrote: "After shooting began, it was like being under siege. We were in a war and we were in it together. I had the house organized 'for the duration.' Breakfast was earlier, dinner was later, and the children were neglected. So were the amenities. His burden was formidable. He had to lay it off on someone; it would have been intolerable to carry it alone. I didn't know what a beating I was taking until David told me what guilt he felt when he looked at me."

I took inspiration for the idea of Irene Selznick becoming a producer in her own right from Irene's actual life. After David O. Selznick left her for actress Jennifer Jones, Irene moved to New York in 1945, where she became a theatrical producer. She produced five Broadway plays, including *A Streetcar Named Desire*, *The Chalk Garden*, and *Bell, Book, and Candle*.

Virginia Van Upp was a real person, whose first screenwriting credit was for Paramount's *The Pursuit of Happiness* (1934). She was a prolific writer and re-writer of screenplays for Paramount until 1943, when she wrote the screenplay for *Cover Girl* (1944) at Columbia starring Rita Hayworth. She later impressed Harry Cohn so much that he promoted her to Associate Producer and then Executive

Producer, making her only one of three female producers working in studio-system Hollywood at the time. The other two were Joan Harrison, who worked with Alfred Hitchcock, and Harriet Parsons, daughter of gossip columnist Louella Parsons. It was this trio of female movie producers that gave me the idea to finish this novel with Amelia being a credited producer on *Sea Change*.

Much of the action of this novel takes place at the real-life Schwab's Pharmacy, which stood at 8024 Sunset Blvd, half a block east of the Garden of Allah Hotel. You can see a collection of photos on my website (martinturnbull.com)

The plot point about Selznick losing $10,925 in gambling was based on a real event. Sometime in August 1939, while he was editing *Intermezzo,* he lost $10,925 during a single night of gambling. That's the rough equivalent of nearly a quarter of a million in mid-2020s dollars.

The screenwriter whom Irene pursues at the RKO ranch was a real person. In the late 1930s and early 40s, Sonya Levien wrote or co-wrote a string of high-profile movies including *In Old Chicago* (1937), *Kidnapped* (1938), *Drums Along the Mohawk* (1939), *The Hunchback of Notre Dame* (1939), and *Ziegfeld Girl* (1941). She moved to MGM during the making of that last movie, but in real life, it wasn't because Louis B. Mayer sent his daughter, Irene, to woo her.

Jerry Giesler was a real-life defense attorney, the most prominent of his era. In the course of his long career, he represented Clarence Darrow, Errol Flynn, Busby Berkeley, Bugsy Siegel, Charlie Chaplin, Lily St. Cyr, Marilyn Monroe, and Cheryl Crane, Lana Turner's 14-year-old daughter, who was accused of fatally stabbing Johnny Stompanato. One account I came across said, "His reputation for winning cases that appeared unwinnable was such that 'Get me Giesler!' became a media epithet attached to any celebrity or prominent public figure facing serious criminal charges or an onerous civil dispute."

In Chapter 7, I mention the name of an MGM security guard, Ken Hollywood. Yes, that really was his name.

Club Bali, where Amelia, Polly, and Luddie go to pitch the *Pretty Pennies* remake to Dorothy Arzner, was a real place. It stood at 8804 Sunset Blvd, where Sunset meets Holloway Dr. and Horn Ave. Bruz Fletcher was a real person, and a popular entertainer who played at Club Bali for four years, including during the time this novel is set. You can read more about Club Bali **here**.

The bookstore in which Luddie buys *Rebecca* and Polly buys *The Postman Always Rings Twice* was a real place. The Satyr Book Shop stood at the southern end of the building that housed the Vine Street Brown Derby.

The Cherokee Pool Hall, where Amelia reunites with Benji, was not a real place. There is, however, a street called Cherokee Ave., and it intersects with Melrose Ave. around a dozen blocks west of Paramount. Also mentioned in this novel is the Retake Room, which was a real-life bar not far from MGM.

Fans of my *Hollywood's Garden of Allah* novels might have recognized the reappearance of the private eye, Dudley Hartman. Marcus Adler hired him in Book 6 of that series — *Twisted Boulevard* — to track down Oliver Trenton. In Book 8 — *City of Myths* — Kathryn Massey hired him to find Sheldon Voss.

The incident mentioned around halfway through this novel in which a tractor almost killed Clark Gable was based on real life. On June 17, 1939, *Los Angeles Herald-Express* columnist Harrison Carroll reported Gable was showing off his new tractor to his neighbor, actor Andy Devine. While he was trying to uproot a stump, the tractor toppled over, forcing Gable to jump clear to avoid being crushed. At the time, *Gone with the Wind* was in its fifth month of principal photography. Had Gable died, David Selznick would have been left without his male lead—and the only actor the American movie-going public would accept as Rhett Butler.

In a tragic coincidence, two months later, on August 23, 1939, *Gone with the Wind*'s main screenwriter, Sidney Howard, was killed by a tractor on his farm in Massachusetts. He was only 48 years old.

Vivien Leigh's stunt double on *Gone with the Wind* was a woman named Hazel Warp. I read somewhere that everybody called her Miss Warp as a way to show respect for the woman's skills, bravery, and commitment.

You can see the scene where Scarlett falls down the stairs on YouTube: "Gone with the Wind - Scarlett's Fall".

On June 27, 1939, Vivien Leigh went from filming her last scene in *Gone with the Wind* straight into her screen test for *Rebecca*, and then from that to the wrap party for *Gone with the Wind*. I have only seen one photo taken that day. It did not show any cake, but I assumed there was one. I invented David Selznick's speech and the inscription on the cake. I also presume Irene Selznick would have been there.

On December 12, 1936, the Plaza Theatre opened on Palm Canyon Drive in Palm Springs with the world premiere of MGM's *Camille*, starring Greta Garbo. One report I read said that seats for the gala cost $10 each, which is around $250 today.

In one scene, Amelia and her co-worker talk about new beauty products from Westmore Brothers. They were a real-life family of makeup maestros, who all worked at the studios. Monte primarily worked at Selznick, Perc at Warner, Ern at RKO and then 20th Century-Fox, Wally at Paramount, Bud at Universal (well-known for his monster makeup), and the sixth brother, Frank, worked freelance. Like their rival, Max Factor, they also had a store and a line of products. It stood at 6638 Sunset Blvd. The Westmore brand is still around today.

Gemey, the eau de toilette in the bottle that Amelia accidentally shatters while working at Schwab's, was a real fragrance. It was made by the then-popular cosmetics company, Hudnut. The head of the company, Richard Hudnut, had a stepdaughter, whose name was Winifred Kimball Shaughnessy. Later in life, she changed her name to Natacha Rambova, and in 1923 she married heartthrob actor Rudolph Valentino.

Polly's co-worker, Hazel Brewster, was a character of my own invention; however, the burlesque theater her parents ran was real. The Follies Theatre stood on Main St between 3rd and 4th Streets in downtown Los Angeles. It closed in 1968, but not before it had undergone many transformations. You can read more about it on the Los Angeles Theatres blogspot website.

In real life there was no cast-and-crew preview for *Beau Geste*. However, the Paramount Theater was a real cinema, and you can read more about it on the Los Angeles Theatres blogspot website.

The pact that Irene Selznick talks about when she arrives unannounced on Santa Catalina Island took place on August 23, 1939, when Hitler and Stalin signed the Molotov-Ribbentrop Pact. Their agreement was to divide Europe between themselves (Finland, Estonia, Latvia and eastern Poland to the USSR; Lithuania and western Poland to Germany) so they would not have to fight on two fronts. The news was made known the next day, on August 24. In Hollywood, this shattered the informal coalition between Communist Party members and progressive-minded, liberal writers, actors and directors. The Hollywood Anti-Nazi League lost most of its important members and was forced to change its name to the Hollywood League for Democratic Action.

On Santa Catalina Island, the real-life Rose Hotel was where the real-life Avalon fire started in 1915. A resident of the hotel wanted to dispose of his mother-in-law, so he first started a fire at 200 Eucalyptus St. in order to distract the fire department. As they were attending to that fire, he snuck back to the Rose Hotel, where he had locked his luckless mother-in-law in the attic, and set fire to that building as well. This scenario became the inspiration for the scene where Polly and Amelia return to Catalina. The Wrigley Memorial that Amelia and Polly visit with Irene and James Tate is a real monument you can visit when on Catalina. The Avalon amphitheater also existed in real life.

Deep in this novel, Amelia, Polly, Lois, and Bernice visit Irene and find the Selznicks are about to head off to Riverside for the first sneak preview of *Gone with the Wind*. I cover that preview in Book 3 of my Hollywood's Garden of Allah series—*Citizen Hollywood*—so I didn't take the action in this book there. However, I did find a description of what happened the night of September 9, 1939:

"At around 5 o'clock at the gates of 1050 Summit Dr., David Selznick, Jock Whitney, and Irene Selznick got into one car while Hal Kern, David's chief editor, and Bobbie Keon, David's script assistant, traveled with more than 50 cans of motion picture and sound track to Riverside in 104-degree temperatures for the sneak preview of *Gone with the Wind*."

And this from Hal Kern: "When Margaret Mitchell's name came on the screen, you never heard such a sound in your life. They just yelled, they stood up on the seats. Mrs. Selznick was crying like a baby, and so was David, and so was I. Oh, what a thrill! And when 'Gone with the Wind' came on the screen, it was thunderous. The film ran on past midnight. There was enormous applause when it was over. The preview cards were astonishing. They were 2/3 excellent; people begged that the movie not be cut; some said everyone everywhere should see it; they were those who fell in love with Vivien Leigh that night; everyone found it true to the book."

The Parisian Florist on Sunset Blvd. mentioned late in this novel was a real place. It opened on the corner of Sunset and N. Sierra Bonita Ave. in 1924, and for 20 years was the florist Joe DiMaggio used to send roses to Marilyn Monroe's grave.

Dolores del Río's necklace was my own invention, but the book where Luddie first hid it, *The Amateur Gentleman* by Jeffrey Farnol, is real. It was first published in 1913 and became a bestseller. It was made into a silent film in 1920 and again in 1926, and then a talkie in 1936 starring Douglas Fairbanks, Jr.

The premiere for *The Women* took place on August 31, 1939, at Grauman's Chinese Theatre in Hollywood. According to one account I read, over 15,000 people lined Hollywood Boulevard, hoping to catch a glimpse of the stars lucky enough to attend. I concluded, then, that it must have been a tumultuous evening.

In the course of my research, I did come across an anecdote that talked about how Harry Cohn approached the Hays Office about stopping Selznick from using the word "damn" in *Gone with the Wind*.

The Columbia movie mentioned in this narrative, *More to Be Pitied Than Scorned,* was the first feature the studio ever produced. It was such a huge success that it set up Columbia for all its future successes.

The Palomar Ballroom, where Amelia and Benji track down Polly and Noah, was a real place.

The 90-90 Club was a real establishment located at 9090 W. Washington Boulevard, Culver City, which put it across the street from the Selznick studios. At time of this writing in 2025, it is known as the Culver Studios and is also home to Amazon Studios. While I could find no evidence of oil wells near the 90-90 Club, its location was at the northwestern tip of the Inglewood Oil Field which is the second-most productive in the Los Angeles Basin. It has been in continuous production since its discovery in 1924. The 90-90 Club probably opened in 1940 and had a fire in 1943, after which it was sold to new owners. They renamed it the Jack London Inn, and it burned to the ground in 1948.

~oOo~

ALSO BY MARTIN TURNBULL

The Hollywood's Garden of Allah novels

Book 1 – *The Garden on Sunset*

Book 2 – *The Trouble with Scarlett*

Book 3 – *Citizen Hollywood*

Book 4 – *Searchlights and Shadows*

Book 5 – *Reds in the Beds*

Book 6 – *Twisted Boulevard*

Book 7 – *Tinseltown Confidential*

Book 8 – *City of Myths*

Book 9 – *Closing Credits*

Chasing Salomé: a novel of 1920s Hollywood

The Heart of the Lion: a novel of Irving Thalberg's Hollywood

The Hollywood Home Front trilogy

A trilogy of novels set in World War II Hollywood

Book 1 - *All the Gin Joints*

Book 2 - *Thank Your Lucky Stars*

Book 3 - *You Must Remember This*

The Hollywood Home Front trilogy

A trilogy of novels set in 1939 Hollywood

Book 1 - *Selznick's Girl Friday*

Book 2 - *Selznick's Spotlight*

ACKNOWLEDGMENTS

Heartfelt thanks to the following, who helped shaped this book:

My editor: Jennifer McIntyre for her keen eye, unfailing humor, and the willingness to debate every last letter and comma placement.

My cover designer: Damonza

My beta readers: Steven Adkins and Gene Strange for their invaluable time, insight, feedback and advice in shaping this novel.

I'd like to thank John Luder for his time and efforts assisting my in research of the history and layout of Santa Catalina Island, which does, indeed, as the song says, lay 26 miles from Los Angeles.

My extraordinarily eagle-eyed proofreaders: Bob Molinari, Susan Perkins, and Leigh Carter, whose final polish raised this manuscript to gleaming perfection.

ABOUT THE AUTHOR

A lifelong love of travel, history, and sharing his knowledge with others has led Martin Turnbull down a long path to authorship. Having made the move to the United States from Melbourne, Australia in the mid-90s, Martin staked his claim in the heart of Los Angeles. His background in travel allowed him to work as a private tour guide--showing off the alluring vistas, mansions, boulevards, and backlots of the Hollywood scene. With stints in local historical guiding with the Los Angeles Conservancy as well as time on the Warner Bros. movie lot, Martin found himself armed with the kind of knowledge that would fly off the very pages of his future works. As a longtime fan of Hollywood's golden era and old films, Martin decided it was time to marry his knowledge with his passions and breathe life back into this bygone world.

The product of his passions burst forth in the form of Hollywood's Garden of Allah novels, a series of historical fiction books set during the golden age of Hollywood: 1927-1959. Exploring the evolution of Hollywood's most famous and glamorous era through the lives of its residents, these stories take place both in and around the real-life Garden of Allah Hotel on iconic Sunset Boulevard. Although Martin's heart belongs to history, his energy remains in the present, continuing to put his passions on paper and beyond.

CONNECT WITH MARTIN TURNBULL

MartinTurnbull.com

Facebook: facebook.com/gardenofallahnovels

Blog: martinturnbull.wordpress.com/

Goodreads: http://bit.ly/martingoodreads

Amazon author page: http://bit.ly/martinturnbull

Be sure to check out the **Photo Blog** for vintage photos of Los Angeles and Hollywood on Martin's website: martinturnbull.com/photo-blog/

To hear about new books first, sign up to my mailing list:

http://bit.ly/turnbullsignup

I won't fill your inbox with useless drivel or I email you too often or never share your information with anyone. Ever. (And you can unsubscribe at any time. No hard feelings.)

* * *

Printed in Dunstable, United Kingdom

68103418R00231